The Chronograph

To Paul,

Happy reading!

Harriet

HARRIET INNES

The Chronograph

HARRIET INNES

Daisa
PUBLISHING

The Chronograph
First published in Great Britain in 2022 by
DAISA PUBLISHING
An imprint of PARTNERSHIP PUBLISHING

Written by Harriet Innes
Copyright © Harriet Innes 2022

A CIP catalogue record for this book is available from the British Library.
ISBN 978-1-915200-08-2

Book cover design by: Partnership Publishing
Book Cover Image © Shutterstock 1121133503

Book typeset by:
PARTNERSHIP PUBLISHING
North Lincolnshire, United Kingdom

www.partnershippublishing.co.uk
Printed in England

Partnership Publishing is committed to a sustainable future for our business, our readers, and our planet; an organisation dedicated to promoting responsible management of forest resources. This book is made from paper certified by the Forestry Stewardship Council (FSC) an organisation dedicated to promoting responsible management of forest resources.

We operate a distinctive and ethical publishing philosophy in all areas of our business, from our global network of Authors to production and worldwide distribution.

DEDICATION

For
Mum and Dad
Ilana and Meta M
Brenda and Richard
and Emma
who all played their part.
With love and deepest affection. Thank you.

CONTENTS

PART II

THE MISTS OF THE PRESENT

PART III

THE STARLIGHT OF THE FUTURE

PROLOGUE

The Court of Time

Glenelven stood in the shadows and waited. His arrival a half hour ago had been greeted with a mere grunt from his Lord who resumed pacing up and down the chamber. When a series of screams and a great bustle issued from above, the man's face turned white and he flung a look of panic at Glenelven, his Guardian of the Present Age and the most trusted of his Inner Circle.

"It will soon be over, I think." Glenelven helped himself to mulled wine from the table, then returned to his place in the darkest corner of the room. From here he could watch the night unfold, a comforting yet unobtrusive presence for the Lord, ready to give his counsel as needed. And it would be needed. The Guardian sighed. This could have been avoided if only the man before him, the Great Lord of the Court of Time, had listened to him. The Lord had no business promoting an Apprentice with a history of misdemeanours, even if it was only to be Keeper of the Hours. Now they were in crisis, and it was up to Glenelven to find a solution, a grand exercise in saving face for a man who would never appreciate it anyway... Glenelven slugged back the remains of his wine impatiently. He had no time for fools.

A soft footfall on the stairs made him look up and a dark-haired young woman of about nineteen entered. The Lord's daughter. Not noticing Glenelven, she hesitated slightly before holding out a bundle in her arms towards her father. A dark shadow flitted across the man's face, and he turned away. "I told you. I don't wish to see."

The young woman spoke coldly. "You don't want to see your grandchildren?"

"Children? You mean there's more than one?" He looked stunned.

She gave a wry smile. "Twins. Aren't you pleased?"

"Put them over there." He indicated the table by the fireplace. The girl did as she was commanded and turned to face him, glowering under dark brows in mirror image of her father.

"You haven't even asked about my sister," she hissed. "Shut away for nine months and only me to help her when the time came, not even a proper midwife. How can you be so heartless?"

"She brought this on herself, as did you. What your mother would think if she were still alive…" The Lord's voice grew hard. "Your treachery shall not go unpunished. You will both leave. I do not care where you go. From now on you are nothing to me."

"Father!" The girl's face crumpled and Glenelven felt his anger rise. The Lord was about to make another huge mistake. It was time for him to speak. He stepped forward from the shadows.

"If I might make a suggestion, my Lord?"

The girl gasped in surprise at seeing him and Glenelven smiled at her reassuringly. He turned to the Lord, who regarded him suspiciously from under half-closed lids.

Without waiting for a response, the Guardian ploughed on.

"We all agree you've been wronged," he said, "but only the Inner Circle knows of this…delicate situation. To banish your daughters to wander destitute, without reason, would take some explaining to the rest of your people."

"They deserve to be punished!" the Lord spat angrily. "Fraternizing with a traitor and creating this mess!" He pointed at the sleeping bundle on the table. "You've forbidden me to send the Armies after him, and now you think you can tell me what to do with my own daughters? You go too far!"

Glenelven took a deep breath. "The Armies are needed for a Time of greater danger. If the prophecy in the Book of Infinity is correct…"

"The Book?" The Lord snorted. "Now disappeared with the Keeper, much good it will do him. A useful record of the past, I'll grant you, but other than that, mere myths and fairy tales. You and our traitor friend are the only ones who believe in it these days, Glenelven."

"I do hope you're not placing me in the same category as the one you appointed Keeper." Glenelven's voice was steely. "As for your daughters, yes one is guilty of falling in love, and yes, the other covered up her sister's affair, but face it, the man even had you under his spell – for a while, at least. Have some mercy."

The Lord's eyes narrowed and Glenelven knew he'd hit home. His master had allowed a power-crazed individual to flatter his ego and by the time he'd realised the danger, it was too late. The traitor had disappeared, taking two precious instruments of Time and leaving one pregnant lover. Now the Lord seemed determined to sacrifice his daughters in an attempt to reassert his authority.

"They defied me," he said obstinately, "and now their disobedience has landed us with not one but two of a traitor's offspring. This cannot be allowed to get out, the Court of Time will be a laughing stock, let alone the personal embarrassment it will cause me. You say you have a suggestion, so let's hear it."

Glenelven nodded. "Two of our key posts need filling. The holders should have retired by now, but we have yet to appoint replacements. Maybe if…"

"They are senior positions. How would it look if I gave them to my own family?"

"We can say it is a temporary solution until others are found. Your daughters are well-liked by your people, my Lord. None know of this…problem…so they may even view this as a great act of charity, sending two of your own Outside Time to allow those who have been there so long to return home."

The Lord thought for a moment. Glenelven held his breath. No doubt his master knew he was being manipulated, but at the same time Glenelven was offering him a way to save face. Finally, the Lord nodded. "Very well. But they leave tonight."

Glenelven breathed a quiet sigh of relief. Thank goodness. The young women would be in place for when they were most needed. This was far from over.

The dark-haired girl looked at Glenelven gratefully. "I know my way," she said. "My sister is weak, but I'll go pack things for all of us for the journey." She moved to collect the bundle from the table, but the Lord barred her way.

"Leave them," he said. "They stay."

"But they're my sister's children…"

"…which, in her new position of responsibility, she will have no time to rear. You will reside in two different places and she will have to manage alone - without your support."

The young woman blinked hard as the reality of separation from her sister set in. Then she looked from the babies to her father and fear crept over her face.

"What will you do with them?" she whispered.

"That is none of your concern. You will both remember that I am showing leniency in the face of treason. You are being granted positions of privilege when casting you into oblivion would be a more just punishment. Now go, before I change my mind!"

The girl cast a final, imploring look at Glenelven, who shook his head slightly. He knew his boundaries and had pushed them enough already. Besides, he had his own reasons for wanting the children apart from their mother. The Lord's daughter drew herself up to her full height, cast a look of pure hatred at her father and left. Glenelven crossed to the table by the fire.

"She asks a good question, my Lord. What will you do with them?"

"I rather hoped you would tell me." The Lord joined him and looked down on the babies, one light-haired, one dark, who were turned towards each other in slumber, foreheads gently touching. One of them gave a small sigh and his little hand reached out to rest on his brother's shoulder. The Guardian felt a pang in his heart.

"It's a tragedy to separate them from their mother," he said. "But you are doing the right thing. The Keeper of the Hours must never learn of their existence. Imagine the power he would attempt to wield…"

The Lord wiped his hand over his eyes. His face was gaunt, the cheekbones almost poking their way through a tightly stretched skin, grey with worry. "My niece has just returned after several months away. I will ask her to take one as her son. Only the Inner Circle will ever know the truth."

Glenelven nodded approval. "She's a sensible woman and will be a very loving mother. But there are two children, my Lord."

The Lord turned away. "Get rid of it. The darker one, he will remind me too much of his father. I don't care what you do."

"Very well." Glenelven smiled to himself as the plan he'd already formed in his mind began to unfold. "I will follow a complex path to make sure he is well hidden. But I need your permission to cross between Ages." The Lord looked at him sharply, but Glenelven was saying no more. His master had summoned him to control the crisis and that's what he was doing. What Glenelven did with the child was no longer any of his business.

"Very well," the Lord said. "Just this once."

"Of course." Glenelven gently scooped up the designated child. The other woke and gave a small wail as he was separated from his brother.

"For God's sake, hurry, man!" The Lord looked nervously about him.

Glenelven held his tongue. When this was done, he'd be all too glad to get back to his duties in the Present Age. He gathered his cloak around the child and had just settled him when the door burst open. A young man in his early twenties barged past the Guardian, his face flushed with excitement. The newcomer's blond hair was sticking up on all sides and his clothes were so dishevelled that it took a moment before Glenelven realised that it was the Lord's son. The young man strode towards his father, brandishing a scroll.

"I have it!" He slapped the scroll down on the table and began to unfurl it. "I have it, Father, at last. I've been in the Tower these past three nights, I've hardly eaten or slept, and finally...Eureka! The breakthrough I've been looking for!"

Glenelven groaned inwardly as the Lord lost his temper. "More plans! Are you so...so oblivious to what's been going on, to what I've been dealing with, while you've been indulging in fantasy? Are all my children determined to frustrate me?" He grabbed the scroll, which closed with a snap and the young man watched helplessly as his father tossed his precious documents into the fire.

"Now," the Lord said grimly. "We understand one another."

"That's the last time I show you anything. You think I haven't kept copies?" the son muttered, but only Glenelven heard him. The Lord was gathering his energy for another tirade.

"Your sisters are leaving in disgrace and our reputation is hanging by a thread! It's bad enough that I'm already having to cover for a harlot and a traitor – do I now have to cover for a lunatic so-called scientist as well?"

The young man scowled. "I'm sorry I vexed you, father."

The Lord spoke more calmly. "You will remember that you are a Son of Time and my heir. You would do better to spend your hours considering what that means, instead of tinkering with foolish inventions."

Glenelven clasped his precious bundle close to his chest and closed the door behind him. After their mother's death, the Lord had raised his children not with tenderness, but an iron fist, and look at the result. Glenelven knew that the trouble caused by the daughters would be nothing next to that brought by the son. What he'd gleaned from the Book of Infinity was fast becoming reality. And the worst was yet to come.

PART I

THE FALLS OF THE PAST

CHAPTER 1

Lorna ~ The Present Age

Lorna swung back on her chair and yawned loudly. The Middlebridge town clock had already struck four, but the one on the classroom wall still said ten minutes to go. She looked at the paper on the desk in front of her. Lorna Lomax, she read. 1st July 2015. Why it's wrong to fight in school.

It wasn't her fault. Today was always going to be difficult, what with it being her dad's anniversary, and it only got progressively worse. First there was her stepfather, slopping all over her mother at breakfast, making Lorna want to gag, and then the Populars followed her all over school, teasing her about her hair dye job. Lorna touched the top of her head self-consciously. Clearly you couldn't go from black to blonde in one go. Good thing she'd had sense to test a section first, otherwise the whole lot would be that grungy orange instead of only that streak. Simon had laughed himself senseless when he saw her that morning, which had really pissed her off. The blonde thing was his idea in the first place. And then one of the Populars, all fashion clothes and expensively highlighted hair, said Simon was going to dump her for being such a freak. She'd lashed out and that was it. Instant detention. Still, at least the other girl had a black eye to wear to the school dance tomorrow.

Lorna grinned, then twizzled her nose stud nervously. What if Simon did dump her? She'd only agreed to go out with him to spite the Populars, who all fancied him rotten, but it gave Lorna a smug sense of satisfaction that Simon Shawcross, the heartthrob in the year above, should ask her. The girl with no friends was now dating the coolest guy in school. It made people look at her differently somehow, and she liked that.

The hands on the clock had barely reached four when the classroom door opened and a woman in sports gear stuck her head round with a questioning look.

Mr Parsons, who was supervising detention, looked nervously at Lorna, and coughed. "Give me five minutes, Miss Peterson." The woman withdrew and Parsons started stuffing exercise books in his briefcase. Lorna smirked. The chemistry teacher and the gym teacher were the school's worst kept dating secret.

"Sure you don't want me to stay longer, Sir?"

Parsons gave her a dirty look. "You've wasted enough of my time. The pity of it is, I doubt it's taught you anything. Hand in your essay on the way out." Lorna tossed her paper on the desk and, waggling her tongue at Parsons, sloped out of the classroom. Parsons sighed and picked up the essay on Why it's wrong to fight in school. The Lomax girl had written only four words.

You try being me.

~

Simon was waiting to walk her home.

"What did old Parsons make you do then?" They turned into the alley that led from school to the road of detached 1930's properties where Lorna lived. A light mist was curling along the ground.

"Just some dumb old essay. Hey, guess who showed up at four to get him. Peterson!"

"He still seeing that old slag?" Simon stopped to light up one of the joints his older brother had left behind when he went on his gap year. He offered her a drag, but Lorna shook her head, wondering what her dad would think of her weed-smoking older boyfriend. Not much probably. That was the trouble. The devil on one shoulder pushed her in the direction of hard-core rebel, but her dad was the angel on the other, stopping her from going too far. It made life complicated.

"You should try it," Simon was saying. He inhaled deeply. "Might make you loosen up a bit."

"Nah. That crap rots your brain. Can't see the point…" The angel won as she knew it would. Simon reddened and tossed the butt into the bushes.

"Whatever. I can take it or leave it. And if you don't want to…"

Lorna stared ahead, saying nothing. The mist in the alley was starting to curl bizarrely round their feet, although Simon seemed not to notice. No doubt his mind was focused on the usual. She wanted to go home.

Simon grinned and pulled her towards him, touching the streak in her hair. "You look like a skunk. A beautiful, orange, skunk." He leaned her against a tree and began kissing her, his breathing growing heavy. Lorna sighed inwardly. She didn't know why she let him suck half her face off like this.

She'd always expected to feel…something. But she didn't. It was like kissing a damp dishcloth. If she was honest, she was bored of him and his weed smoking and groping. She turned her face away.

"That's enough."

"Not yet," his voice was husky in her ear, then he began kissing her harder, his hands beginning to roam.

"I said enough!" She gave him a violent shove. "What's wrong with you?"

Simon glared. "What's wrong with me? You're the one who acts like she's this tough bitch who's up for anything." He looked down his nose at her, suddenly full of superiority. "You know what, forget it. I can get better elsewhere."

Lorna felt like she'd been slapped. Heat rose in her cheeks. "Go ahead then. Like I care. You can't kiss for crap anyway." She started to walk up the alley towards home.

"Frigid cow!" Simon yelled after her. "Don't be hanging round me no more, y'hear me? You're bad for my image."

"Yeah well, just remember it was me broke up with you!" she shouted, but he was already walking away, laughing. She yelled again. "It was me that broke up with you."

Lorna turned and ran home as fast as she could. She wanted to curl up in a ball in her room and die. Pausing at the gate, she noticed that the mist appeared to have followed her part way down the road and was now hanging around the corner as if waiting for something. Wiping an angry tear from her eye, she told herself not to be so daft and opened the back door. Her mother was there, reading at the kitchen table, while her ten-year-old brother, David, sat "repairing" the vacuum cleaner in the corner.

"You're late," her mother said, not even lifting her eyes from the newspaper. Lorna ignored her and stormed across the room, desperate to get upstairs.

"You're babysitting tonight," her mother called after her. "Stephen and I are out for dinner."

Lorna stopped stock still. "You can't," she exclaimed. "Not tonight. It's Dad's…"

"…anniversary," her mother finished for her. "Yes, and it will be every year. I suppose you'll be ignoring your birthday tomorrow as usual." She got up to put the kettle on. "It's been ten years now, Lorna. Time to stop wallowing in the past. Start looking forward."

"Is that what you were doing when you met Stephen?" Lorna asked. "Looking forward?" For a moment, she thought her mother would slap her and she jutted out her chin, almost daring her to strike, but the moment passed. Her mother glared and went back to the newspaper. David grinned malevolently.

Lorna slammed out of the room, eyes smarting. Just when she thought the day couldn't get any worse, she was stuck with David for the evening. He was tall and strong for his age, a real bully who could pick a fight with an empty room when it suited him. Lorna invariably got the blame.

Her dad wouldn't have let him get away with it, for sure. When he'd been around, everything had been fun, he even made her mother laugh. Her heart sank all over again as she remembered that dreadful day before her sixth birthday when he was killed in a car crash. The other vehicle had never been found.

Her mother, attractive and eight months pregnant at the time, was determined not to raise two children on her own. It took very little for Stephen Latimer, a businessman new

14

to the area, to sweep her off her feet. Everything happened confusingly fast for little Lorna, who hated her new stepfather and wanted her dad back more than anything. There was soon a wide gulf between Lorna, who wanted to remember, and her mother who was moving on with Latimer. David, her brother, had never known his real father so it made little difference to him. Lorna was left on her own with her memories and an aching hole in her life that never seemed to get any better. All that was left was rebellion in the form of bad grades and boyfriends like Simon.

She slammed into her room, tore off her school uniform and pulled on her black jeans and a black blouse. What a bloody awful day! She plonked herself at her dressing table and looked in the mirror. Her father's green eyes stared back at her, the only thing about her face that she really liked. Her dad had such kind eyes. Latimer's were cold, steely grey. She hated him looking at her, he gave her the shivers. He had that creepy black beard too. She began to daub thick liquid liner and black mascara round her best feature, knowing how much her stepfather hated it. Then she sat on the stool, wondering what to do next.

On the fateful morning of his accident, her dad had secretly given Lorna a special gift, which she kept carefully hidden in a tin under the floorboard in the corner of her room. She hadn't looked at it in ages, but today felt appropriate, with it being the anniversary and her birthday the next day. She decided to light some incense and have a little ceremony, there was just enough time before the evening of hell started with "babysitting" David.

She heaved aside the old chest of drawers covering the floorboard, retrieved the tin and took it back to her dressing table to open it.

Inside was an old-fashioned pocket watch on a chain. Lorna took it out and looked at it closely, warming the metal in the palm of her hand. The face of the watch was discoloured enamel, studded with a few coloured stones. The hands were black and the numbers gold. There was some faded engraved writing on the back of the case, in beautiful, scrolled letters that she couldn't decipher, along with a faded image of what looked like a dragon.

The watch had never worked, but she still thought it was the most beautiful thing she'd ever owned. Her father told her it was called a chronograph and had made a great game out of telling her it had been given to his grandfather during the war and she must keep it safe.

As a little girl, Lorna had thought it must have some sort of magical powers, although of course she thought that was crap now. The only real reason to keep it hidden was to stop Latimer getting his hands on it, especially after she came home one day to find him in the attic going through boxes of her father's things. The chronograph wasn't worth anything, but the thought of her stepfather handling something that belonged to those precious final moments with her dad made her feel physically sick.

"Lorna, get down here!" a voice bellowed from below, making her jump. Latimer was home. "What d'you want?" she shouted, scrambling to stuff the chronograph back in its tin. She fumbled in her panic, and in her attempt to stop the tin crashing to the ground, dropped the chronograph instead. There was a loud cracking sound. Lorna groaned and picked it up. The glass face now had one single crack running across it, side to side. The one thing she had of her dad's that she treasured, and she'd ruined it. It was all Latimer's fault.

The room suddenly grew dark. She thought a storm must be gathering to block the sun, but when she looked out the window, bright light still glared outside. Then she noticed wisps of black smoke making their way under the door. At first, she thought the house must be on fire, but she could hear her mother clattering pans below and asking David what he wanted for tea. Her stepfather's heavy footsteps sounded on the stairs, then began to cross the long landing to her door. The smoke hesitated, then as it began to crawl towards her, the chronograph jumped in her hand.

As Lorna looked at it, the hands jerked forward five minutes, then suddenly swept round the face backwards as a strong wind began to blow from nowhere. The walls of her room seemed to close in around her, then dissolve as she was caught up in some kind of spinning mist. At the last moment she caught sight of her own terrified face in the mirror, suddenly flanked by two others - the first of a proud young man with white-blond hair, looking wildly for something and then the round, dirty face of a small boy with sandy brown hair, staring out at something unknown. They were gone in an instant as the white mist spun faster, lifting her out of her room and away from the mirror and the dark smoke rising below.

Lorna thought she heard her stepfather shouting something, but the wind was now rushing and the mist spinning so fast that she couldn't be sure. She blacked out, and was carried away, the chronograph still clutched in her hand.

CHAPTER 2

Sebastian ~ The Age of the Past

"Thank the Lord that's over!" The old clockmaker smiled at his apprentice. The boy was starting to look haunted again, he thought, much as he did when he first came to him. Something about these past few weeks had really got to the lad. Not that the old man could blame him. The stranger had been an unsettling presence in their lives. It would be good to get back to normal business.

"Why don't you go make supper?" he said kindly. "While I make the entry in the ledger." The apprentice watched while his master wrote the date in his neat, sloping hand. 1st July 1785.

"I'm glad he's gone," the boy said. "Now things can be like they was before."

"Quite." The clockmaker looked at him through the half-moon spectacles on the end of his nose. "You've done well, Sebastian," he said. "I could not have completed this commission without you."

The boy smiled his thanks and left. The clockmaker looked after him thoughtfully. Six months had passed since he'd found the lad collapsed on his doorstep. Ignoring the advice of his customers, that the boy should be left for the workhouse to deal with, he took him in. He shuddered as he remembered the bruises he'd found on the boy's back while helping him bathe that first evening. Some fathers did not deserve the children they'd been blessed with. The clockmaker was glad he'd given the lad a home. He'd turned out to be a damn good apprentice. With hard work under his tutelage, and a little luck, the boy need never be destitute again.

There was a clap of thunder overhead and the man frowned. Another summer storm seemed to be rolling in from nowhere. Hoping the roof didn't leak in the workshop this time, he closed the ledger and put it in a drawer. Time for supper, then bed, and a fresh start tomorrow.

~

Back in the kitchen, Sebastian poked the soup pot gloomily while he waited for his master. He hoped that now the stranger had gone, it really was the end of it. If not, he didn't know where he would go. There was no chance of going home. He poked at the pot again, thinking about the night he'd run and all that had happened since.

His father was a drunk. When he fell through the doorway that last night at home and reached for the strap on the wall, Sebastian's only thought was that another beating for him was one less for his mother. Her crime, according to his father, was "going with another behind his back." Sebastian didn't understand. All he knew was that he looked nothing like either of them and for some reason that made his father angry.

"C'mere," the man snarled, advancing towards him. "Don't you be lookin' at me with them nasty green eyes." Sebastian felt a rough hand on the scruff of his neck, then the burning sting of the belt as it slammed down across his back. "Stop it!" his mother pleaded, but the man ignored her, spitting out words with each strike of the belt. "Little...green-eyed...bastard!"

Sebastian could feel the vomit rising in his throat. His father would kill him this time, for sure. Sebastian squirmed, but the rough hand pressed his face into the man's thigh, almost smothering him. There was only one thing for it. Sebastian opened his mouth and chomped down. When the man fell back in pain, he ran.

He only looked over his shoulder once, expecting to see his father raging after him, belt in hand. But only his mother stood on the doorstep looking after him. Sebastian hesitated, but when she made no move towards him, he turned and ran on. He couldn't see her tears or know that she was weeping for the double loss she'd suffered. Once for the stillborn child she'd had in her husband's absence ten years ago, buried secretly in the churchyard. And once for the boy presented to her that same night by a mysterious cloaked stranger. The boy she had hoped would pass for her own, so her husband would never know the truth, had now run out of her life for good.

Sebastian pelted down the dark road till his burning chest forced him to stop. He slid into a ditch where he hid until morning, then stowed away among the sacks of vegetables on a farmer's cart as it trundled past on its way to St Mark's Bar. As soon as the cart entered the old city gate, the "bar" that gave St Mark's Bar its name, he jumped off and looked around him. The colours and sounds of the market seemed to be crowding in, almost suffocating him. Sebastian staggered up a side street and collapsed in the doorway of the clockmaker's shop, where Hanson, the shop keeper, found him.

"You'll have to earn your keep," the old man told him as they sat eating in the little kitchen that first evening.

Sebastian shovelled stew in his mouth and thought for a moment. It couldn't be much worse here than home. And if it was, he could always run away again. "All right then," he said.

Over the next few months, Sebastian began to relax. He enjoyed being trusted with the many important errands he had to run around town and being told when he'd done well. It made a change from dancing on eggshells waiting for the next strike of the belt. When Hanson made him responsible for winding the precious clocks in his workshop, he almost burst with pride. He learned to tell the time and soon he knew his letters and could do basic sums too.

"I love it here!" he shouted as Hanson laughed. "I want to live here forever!"

One day, Sebastian was standing on a box at the workbench as he usually did, watching his master clean a small pocket fob. Suddenly the door opened, letting in a gust of warm spring breeze from outside and spoiling his concentration. A young blond man stepped over the threshold. He wore a strange travelling cape of midnight blue, tan leather boots and trousers made of some shimmering dark fabric. Sebastian scowled. This was not one of their regular customers, and he didn't like strangers. From his dress, the man had to be wealthy, but he wasn't from round these parts.

"Good day," the young man smiled, showing perfect white teeth. Sebastian glowered and shrank beneath the table.

"Good day, Sir," said Hanson politely. "How may I be of assistance?"

"You make clocks," said the man. Sebastian snorted into his sleeve. The workshop was full of the things, talk about obvious. Hanson gave him a look. "You make pocket watches too." The man nodded to the repair on the bench.

"Clean and repair usually," Hanson replied. "What is it you want?"

"Ah, yes," the man gave a nervous laugh. "Could you make one from scratch? A pocket watch I mean."

"I daresay I could try," Hanson didn't sound keen, Sebastian thought. Maybe he didn't like strangers either.

The man seemed to be trying to decide something. "Good," he said, then turned and walked out of the shop.

"Odd," said Sebastian. A prickle ran down his back, like it used to when he knew his father was due home.

"Hmmm" said Hanson, "Well, put it from your mind, Sebastian. I doubt he'll be back." But Hanson was wrong. The next day, around the same time, the man appeared again, accompanied by a large black dog.

"I thought your boy might like this," he said by way of greeting.

"What need have I for a dog?" Hanson raised his voice, something Sebastian had never heard him do. "I can barely afford to feed the boy and myself, let alone a great hound like that! Now I don't know who you are, or what you think you're doing, but..."

"Please!" the young man interrupted. "Forgive me. I'm not good at this sort of thing. Asking for help I mean. Look, I need you to make this."

He removed a piece of parchment from a pocket somewhere inside his cape, unfolded it carefully and placed it on the workbench. Hanson bent over it, adjusting his glasses. Sebastian clambered onto his box. On the parchment was a fine ink drawing, with a mass of inner workings for a clock-like instrument, more complicated than anything he had ever seen.

Eventually, Hanson spoke. "It's very small and delicate work. I'm not sure my eyes can handle it."

"But you must!" the man exclaimed. "This piece must be made, and it must be by someone I know I can trust."

"There is no must about it," said Hanson sharply. "I hardly know you, and you talk about trusting me? What nonsense is this?"

The man took a deep breath. "Can we talk? Privately?"

Before Hanson could reply, the shop bell rang and a tall man in riding clothes entered. The clockmaker didn't bother disguising his relief. "I think our conversation is at an end, Sir," he said, and turned to his customer. The stranger withdrew, scowling, to the corner.

"Hanson," the newcomer nodded his greeting.

"Good day, Sir William. Here for your clock?"

"Indeed. I will settle the account and my man will collect it later. I'm sure you have given me your best work, as I have come to expect."

"Of course, Sir William. We value your custom too much to do otherwise."

"I've had enough of this," the stranger said suddenly and raised his hand, fingers splayed, towards Sir William. Without a word, the man suddenly froze, mouth open as if about to reply to the clockmaker.

"What in the name of heaven?" exclaimed Hanson, crossing himself vigorously. Sebastian dived under the bench to find himself eye to eye with the black dog. The hound stared at him one moment, then yawned and turned its head away, not seeming at all bothered by the turn of events.

"He is in stasis," said the young man, as if this were the most natural thing in the world. "And will remain so until you listen to me."

"You can't threaten me," said Hanson defiantly.

"I don't intend to, but please hear me out. Then turn me down if you wish, but at least listen before you decide."

The stranger turned to Sebastian. "Take the dog into the kitchen and wait there. This isn't a conversation for the ears of small boys."

Sebastian felt slighted. "I am the apprentice," he began to protest.

"Quiet, Sebastian," Hanson said sternly. "And you, Sir, unfreeze my customer, or whatever you've done to him. Then maybe we'll talk."

"Naturally." The stranger lifted his hand, palm out this time, and stepped back.

Sir William came to abruptly. "Now, I believe this is what we agreed," he said, handing over a few coins as if nothing had happened. "My man will collect the clock tomorrow." He bade Hanson good day and departed.

"Good," said the stranger. "Now lock the door. And can we please speak privately?"

"You still here, Sebastian?" Hanson asked. "You were told to leave. You can start preparing our supper." Sebastian would rather have stayed, but he didn't like the sharp edge Hanson had to his voice. He hoped the stranger would soon leave, but an hour later Hanson still had not emerged from the shop. Sebastian slunk back down the passageway, the dog behind him, bumping its wet nose on the back of his knees.

"Shh!" Sebastian motioned to the dog. From the shadows of the doorway, he could see the two men still bent over the parchment, deep in conversation. "Very well," he heard Hanson say. "I confess, I'm more intrigued than anything – and I hope I don't live to regret it. But if this is as important as you say – I'll do it."

~

Next day they started work on their new commission.

"Never seen anything like it," Hanson said. "Look here. It seems to run backwards as well as forwards."

Sebastian examined the diagram, wishing he knew what this was about. They hadn't discussed the stranger's visit, or the way he'd mysteriously frozen Sir William. Nor was Hanson inclined to say anything about their conversation. "Better you don't know," he said, which didn't make Sebastian feel any better. He had the looming sense of a dark shadow closing in on them. He hoped it would pass once they'd finished this commission.

"Three hundred and sixty-five teeth round this outer wheel," Hanson pointed. "And this notch seems to operate on every fourth turn. I shall rely on you to help me, Sebastian. My old eyes aren't as good for this kind of work as they used to be."

This was nothing like any pocket watch they'd ever worked on. The mechanism was a maze of intricate cogs, built in three layers and connected by tiny levers and pins, all of which sat inside one tooth-edged circle. Sebastian could see that when the cogs moved, so did the outer circle – but this circle went the depth of the three layers and could be turned by any one of those layers of cogs as it operated. He and his master now worked painstakingly to form these tiny parts in the bronze, silver and gold that magically materialized, as if ordered by telepathy, at regular intervals on the doorstep.

After three weeks, their client whirled into the shop, not even bothering to say good morning. "You have to work faster!" he said.

"This is a very delicate and intricate timepiece, Sir," Hanson said mildly.

"I'm aware of that!" the stranger snapped. "I'm the one who designed it!"

Hanson took a deep breath. "I'm doing the best I can, Sir, but I have other customers to satisfy."

"They don't matter." The stranger gave an arrogant wave of the hand.

"Not to you maybe," Hanson said. "But if I ignore them all, I won't have any business left by the time your commission is complete."

"But I must have it soon!" the stranger cried, clearly upset. "Or it will be too late."

"Too late for what?" Hanson asked, suspicious.

The young man looked at him. "Just have it ready within the week."

"Two," Hanson said firmly. The stranger paused a moment, then nodded curtly and swept out of the shop.

They worked even longer days, often finishing by the light of three large oil lamps placed on the workbench. Finally, at four o'clock one afternoon, two weeks after the stranger's last visit, Hanson slipped the final pin in place and closed the back of the instrument. He looked at Sebastian. "Well?"

"It's…beautiful," Sebastian whispered in awe. "Beautiful and odd."

He couldn't quite believe he had helped build this gorgeous object, set in a large fob of very pale gold, so pale it was almost white. The ivory dial was encased in glass and contrasted with its three ebony hands, two large, one small, their tips dipped in yellow gold. The Roman numerals on the dial were surrounded by a ring of pictures representing the four seasons. Each miniature design was a thing of beauty. A tiny emerald leaf bud for spring was followed by a ruby rose for summer. A tiny wheat sheaf of gold depicted autumn, while winter had a tiny silver wire snowflake with a diamond at its centre. The back of the case was equally beautiful, etched with strange scrolling letters with a dragon in the middle of them.

Sebastian looked at Hanson in admiration. His master wasn't just any old clockmaker. He was a true artist. The stranger must have guessed that too.

Less than an hour after they'd finished, the stranger returned. Sebastian hardly recognised him.

The man's swagger had gone, and he looked hunted. There was also a fresh scar on his cheek. "Is it done?" he said to Hanson.

Hanson nodded. "It's done."

"Thank God!"

The young man paced up and down anxiously while Sebastian fetched the precious commission from the workshop. "Let me see!" He snatched the timepiece from the boy's hand, then stood for several moments, inspecting the case and dial before flipping open the back to examine the intricate workings inside. "You've done well," he said, seeming to relax a little. "Here's your payment." He threw two heavy pouches onto the counter.

"Won't you stay and take some refreshment?" Hanson asked. "You'll excuse me for saying, but Sir does not look at all well."

"No, thank you kindly," the younger man smiled wanly. "I must be on my way. Thank you again." With a final nod to Hanson and a wink at Sebastian, he left the shop. The dog, which had greeted him enthusiastically, now sloped back to the kitchen with his tail between his legs and lay in his basket whimpering.

"D'you think he's in trouble?" asked Sebastian.

"Maybe," Hanson said, "but it's no business of ours. We've done as we were asked and been paid handsomely for it." He began to write in the ledger. 1st July 1785. "Why don't you go make supper?"

~

Sebastian poked at the soup pot again, still deep in thought as speckles of rain started to pitter patter on the window. The stranger was gone and the timepiece with him, but the sense of creeping darkness remained. A sudden flash of light across the sky made him look up and he dropped the spoon in the pot in shock. There was a face at the window. He rushed over and looked out but could see no-one.

But there was, he told himself. There was a girl with dark hair. Looking in at me. Prickles were now going mad up and down his back, the old, advanced warning that something bad was about to happen. He closed his eyes and prayed that it was just his imagination. During supper, the storm came.

CHAPTER 3

Flight

A strong wind swept the grey clouds across the sky to gather over St Mark's Bar, where they rapidly blackened as though soaked in ink. The light of the summer evening was snuffed out suddenly, replaced by smoky mist and teeming rain.

"Filthy!" muttered Hanson. "I'm glad we're indoors." Sebastian said nothing but slopped hot stew into two bowls.

"Mr. Hanson," he said suddenly, "look at Blackie."
The dog was standing in his basket, head cocked on one side and ears alert. A low growl rumbled in the dog's throat.

"Now, Blackie," Hanson said. "Easy lad, it's only a storm." At that moment, there was a thundering knock on the front door. The dog went berserk.

"Blackie, quiet!" Sebastian commanded him. Someone pounded on the door again.

"Now who in the Lord's name can that be?" Hanson said, rising from his chair.

"Don't go!" Sebastian cried. The sense of approaching darkness was now fully upon him.

"What? Don't be daft, lad, of course I'm going. It's a terrible night and I'm not leaving someone standing out there on my doorstep!"

"Look at Blackie! He doesn't want you to go!" The dog was now running back and forth across the kitchen door, growling fiercely.

"It's just the storm, lad. Does all kinds of things to animals, this weather. I'll be back in a moment."

"Don't go, please!"

"Sebastian!" Hanson was severe. "Our caller may need help. He could be lost and need shelter."

Sebastian shivered. "Then let 'im go somewhere else."

"And what if I'd said that when I found you?"

The knocking came again, more urgently this time. Hanson squeezed past Blackie. "You stay here," he said, and closed the door behind him.

Sebastian tried to calm his fears. Maybe it was that girl. She couldn't do much harm, could she? But something told him it wasn't her. The knock for a start. Great big blows, raining on the door like that. The hairs stood up on the back of his neck, like Blackie's. The dog stayed by his side, now pawing at the door. Sebastian opened it a crack. He could hear voices coming from the front of the shop. He tiptoed down the passageway, Blackie behind him, still growling low in his throat.

Another stranger stood in the shop. Sebastian could not make out much in the lamp light, but he could tell this was not their fair-haired visitor of before. This man was dark, both in dress and appearance. Sebastian shivered. The man was well-spoken enough but turned the air cold with a genteel menace.

"So, you say you do commissions?" the dark stranger was saying.

"Sometimes," Hanson answered cautiously.

"And have you had any lately?"

"One or two. Why do you ask?"

The dark man sighed. "I'll be frank," he said. "Something was stolen from me. A design. And a special one at that. I had hoped to make the piece and sell it."

"Really?" Hanson sounded unconvinced.

"Look." The man leaned against the counter and lowered his voice conspiratorially. "I have a family to support. Business has been bad. I'm relying on that piece to salvage things. Come on man! You know how it is in our business!"

"Do I?"

"I know he's been here," the stranger snarled, pushing his face into Hanson's. "He's been here, and he's had you making it for him. Now hand it over!"

"I don't know what you're talking about." Hanson held his ground.

"Yes...you...do!" The stranger was over the counter, his hand round Hanson's throat, pressing him against the wall. Sebastian stifled a gasp and shrank against the door frame.

"I...don't...have...any...design," the old man choked.

"Did you make a timepiece?"

"I make lots of timepieces."

"Last chance." The stranger squeezed harder. "Have you made a timepiece for a fair-headed young man over the past few days? Tell me the truth and you shall live!"

"Yes!" Hanson finally cracked. The man released his grip and let him down from the wall.

"Good, now you see how easy that was? Now bring it to me."

"I don't have it."

31

"Don't lie!" the man snarled. "Bring me the Chronograph!"

"I can't," Hanson said. "It's gone."

"Gone? But you've finished making it already?"

"Yes," Hanson said, feeling his tender throat. "Finished and gone. Your friend collected it this afternoon. If you want it, you'll have to go after him."

"How did he get through?" the stranger said to thin air. "I had this whole area under a time seal. I should have felt it..."

"I don't know about any time seal," Hanson said sharply, "but the customer collected his order and I was glad to see the back of him. Now, I'm sorry it's a bad night, but will you please leave my shop."

The stranger gave a cruel smile. "Oh yes" he said. "I'll leave. And you will regret having tried to deceive the Keeper!"

With one great gesture, he splayed out his fingers in the way the fair-haired man had done a few weeks earlier. But the effect was different. Sebastian remembered the young man using the word "stasis", but this was not the same thing at all. Hanson froze, but his eyes continued to blink furiously, still very much aware of what was going on. With another gesture, the stranger flung the old man's body up against the ceiling, then across the room, before letting him drop several feet onto the cold, hard floor. Hanson moaned slightly, moved his head for an instant, then moved no more.

"No!" Sebastian shrieked.

"What?!" The dark stranger turned, then burst out laughing. "So! A small witness. We can soon deal with you!" He raised his hand. Blackie growled in Sebastian's grasp and the man seemed to change his mind.

"Perhaps not. Two bodies will arouse suspicion. Far better for the authorities to think the young apprentice murdered his master. And then you'll hang, for who will believe a story of some stranger out on such a wild night, seeking an old pocket watch?" Sebastian cowered in the doorway as the man stepped towards him. "I'll place you in temporary stasis till they find you."

It was Blackie who came to the rescue. Tearing free from Sebastian's grasp, the dog leapt at the dark stranger. The man shouted out and fell back, the dog on top of him, snapping and growling. He finally tore his arm free and pointed at Blackie, felling the dog instantly. Then he turned to where the boy had been standing.

Sebastian had already taken his cue. One thing he knew, was how to dodge trouble, so when Blackie sprang, he bolted through the kitchen and out into the maze of alleyways behind. He doubled back several times, hoping to confuse the stranger, then skidded to a halt by the inn on the opposite side of the marketplace. A black figure emerged from the alley where Hanson's shop stood, paused for a moment, then began to stride purposefully across the square. Sebastian felt panic rising. What on earth was he going to do? Nobody would believe him.

The sound of hooves and wheels clattered across the cobbles of the inn's courtyard behind him. The stage was leaving, undeterred by the bad weather. Sebastian seized his chance and leapt onto the back of the coach and held on, praying they would not leave through the square. The stage turned out of the yard and then onto the main road out of town. Nobody tried to stop them. After several miles, when he was sure no-one was following, Sebastian dropped onto the road and rolled into a ditch where he lay, breathing hard.

The dark stranger had killed Hanson and Blackie too. He was now worse off than ever. People would believe he'd murdered the old clockmaker, and he'd have a price on his head for certain.

He was back where he'd started six months ago – hiding in a ditch by the roadside. Sebastian felt a sudden rage towards both strangers, especially the fair-haired one who had brought the design that had caused so much trouble. Wiping a grubby hand across his tearful eyes, he fell into an uneasy sleep.

When he awoke, the sun was high, and his stomach was rumbling. All was quiet. Sebastian poked his head out of the ditch and looked around. The road was on one side and on the other was a meadow edged by a thick wood. A cart clattered round a bend in the road, and he dropped back out of sight. He couldn't stay in the ditch all day, but the road was too risky. He'd best make a run for the woods. They'd be a good hiding place while he decided what to do next.

Feeling pleased with this plan, he started to haul himself out of the ditch when suddenly there was a great rush of wind and a large object fell out of the sky, landing not ten feet in front of him. It was a body. Sebastian watched, breathing hard, as the body, a girl, stood up and looked about her. He crouched down low in the ditch and swore. What the hell was going on?

CHAPTER 4

The Two

Lorna picked herself up, rubbing her backside where it had hit the ground. Everything had happened so fast. Latimer would find it pretty weird she wasn't in her room, but then given previous history, he'd probably think she'd climbed out of the window. She looked around. The weird smoke and the spinning mist had disappeared, and she was in a large meadow bounded on one side by a dark, murky-looking wood, and by a wide dirt road on the other. A bird chirped somewhere nearby, but other than that it was strangely quiet. There was no sound of traffic or farm machinery, not even the distant rumble of an aeroplane climbing in the sky.

The Chronograph was still in her hand. Lorna looked at it. The second hand was still working its way steadily round the dial. It seemed the shock of dropping it on the floor had done it good, although why this had triggered some sort of teleport effect was anybody's guess. As she stood wondering what to do next, Lorna had the feeling she was being watched. She looked round slowly, then glimpsed a movement out of the corner of her eye, from the ditch alongside the road. Maybe it was an animal of some sort. As she looked at the ditch, she saw it again. It wasn't an animal; it was a person. Why would anyone be hiding in a ditch? Hiding or not, they might at least tell her where she was. She started walking towards the movement.

~

Sebastian recoiled inside the ditch, heart thumping. The girl had seen him and was coming over. She looked pretty fierce, and her clothes were odd, more like a man's clothes, and all black. How could someone drop out of the sky like that and not even be hurt? Maybe she was a witch! Sebastian began to whimper. But this was daytime, not night, and this was quite a pretty girl just a bit older than him, not an ugly old crone with a wart on her nose. Maybe they had apprentice witches like he was an apprentice clockmaker. And this one had fallen off her broomstick and it was still whizzing about up there without her. He stole another look. She was nearer now, and he nearly wet himself in terror. Her face. It was the one he'd seen at the window last night. In blind panic, Sebastian scrambled frantically out of the ditch, got tangled up in his own feet, and fell face down on the road.

"You okay?" the girl called.

Sebastian got to his feet, and looked wildly up and down the road, hoping that by some miracle a cart or stage might appear. He'd forgotten his fear of being arrested and hanged for murder now this new threat was looming. Witches could do unspeakable things. The girl called to him again. "Here! Are you all right?"

No sign of rescue appeared. Trembling, Sebastian looked at the girl who now stood just one jump away from him on the other side of the ditch.

~

Lorna looked the boy up and down. He was a bit jumpy – not to mention filthy. "You okay? What's your name?"

"Sebastian." The boy's voice came out strangely high, like a scared mouse.

"All right, Sebastian. I'm Lorna. D'you know where we are? I'm a bit lost, see."

Sebastian shrugged. "Dunno. Ten-mile marker for St Mark's be somewhere back there." He pointed.

"St Mark's?" Lorna thought for a moment. He must mean St Mark's Bar. That was way over the other side of town. "Which way is Middlebridge then?"

"That where you be from?" The boy eyed her suspiciously. "They got all strange folks there, don't they? Witches an' all I heard."

"That what you think I am?" Lorna laughed. The boy nodded. "Well, my stepfather calls me a right little witch, so ... Grrraaargh!" She lurched playfully towards him. The boy shrieked and fell to his knees, crossing himself.

"Bloody hell, you're serious, aren't you?" She couldn't believe the boy was so terrified. Now he was reciting the Lord's Prayer. "Look, if I was a witch, I wouldn't be asking for directions, would I? I'd just magic myself out of here!"

"Well, you magicked yourself over here, didn't you?" Sebastian looked up. "So how d'you do that?"

"Dunno," she twizzled her nose stud thoughtfully. "Look, Sebastian, we can't keep talking across a ditch. Why don't you jump over here so we can talk properly?"

The boy stood for a few moments making up his mind. Finally, he jumped over, then stood looking at her mistrustfully from under his matted, dirty hair. Something twisted in Lorna's heart. He was such a scrawny little soul.

There was something about his face too, but she couldn't be sure under all that dirt.

"Here, Sebastian." She beckoned him forward. "I dropped this thing in my bedroom, and it started ticking, next thing I know, I'm here."

Sebastian looked at what she held in her hand, then frowned and took it from her. He turned it over, inspecting it closely.

"Where d' you get this?" He suddenly sounded older and more serious.

"I've had it for years," Lorna said. "My Dad gave it to me. Before he died."

"My master made it," Sebastian said.

"Your what?"

"Master. I helped him. We made it for this gent what come to the shop."

"I don't see how you could've made it," Lorna said. "I mean, it's a few hundred years old."

The boy paled. "That ain't possible. I know it looks older, but he only finished making it yesterday. I know it's the same piece, there's the dragon on the back and everything."

"Maybe we can ask him," Lorna suggested.

"He's dead," Sebastian said shortly. "The man killed him. Not the man we made this for. A different one. He wanted this chrono…chrono…watch-thing, but we didn't have it, so he killed my master and then he killed my dog. And everyone will think it was me!"

"Well running away wasn't very smart then," said Lorna. "We should go back and explain to the police."

"No!" the boy exploded. "I don't know about no police, whatever that is, but I ain't going back. They'll hang me!"

"Don't be daft," Lorna snorted. "They don't hang people anymore. 'Specially not small boys."

"Course they do!" Sebastian said. "Don't you know anything?"

Lorna looked at him, an uncomfortable thought forming in her mind. "Sebastian," she said slowly. "This may sound stupid – but what year are we in?"

"What year?" The boy looked at her uncomfortably. "It's 1785."

Lorna stood stock still. "Yeah right," she said finally, tossing her head. "So…where d'you live then?"

"You deaf? I told you. St Mark's Bar, with my master, Mr Hanson. But I can't live there now."

"What about your Mum and Dad? Don't they live there?"

The boy shook his head. "Nah. Ma and Pa live a long way from here. Little Stonebrook."

"But Little Stonebrook…" Lorna stopped herself. Little Stonebrook was an abandoned village about five miles outside Middlebridge.

"You sure?" she said. "You haven't hit your head or something? Nobody lives in Little Stonebrook anymore."

"I'm not mad y'know!" the boy shouted, catching her drift. "It's not me wot fell out of the sky and don't know where they are!"

The two stood glaring at each other. Their standoff was suddenly interrupted by the sound of horses in the distance and a coach rumbled into view. Sebastian made to jump back into the ditch, but Lorna held him fast.

"They have coaches at the museum," she said. "Probably been out for an event somewhere. We can scrounge a lift back." She manhandled the boy onto the road.

"I can't go back!" the boy protested, squirming in her grip. "They'll hang me I tell you!" Lorna ignored him and flagged down the coach, which slowed and came to a stop.

"What d'you want?" snarled the driver. "I ain't got room for scruffy kids."

"Please," Lorna begged. "This boy's ill and we need to get him back home."

There was a clatter as an elegant man wearing a top hat stuck his head out of the window. "Ho there! Why have we stopped?"

"Beggars," said the coach driver. "Something about being sick and needing a ride. More like they want to nick your pocket watch and give you whatever nasty disease they're carrying."

"The road is no place for children all the same," the elegant man said. "Where do you live?"

"Middlebridge," said Sebastian, before Lorna could say anything.

"Middlebridge? Well, that's the other way. We're for St Mark's Bar." The man sounded relieved. "Good luck now! Make sure you're off the road before dark. I hear some boy's on the run for murdering his master. Nice old clockmaker. You don't want to run into him!" He withdrew, banging on the ceiling of the coach with his stick. "Move on!"

The driver leered at them and flicked his whip, making them jump out of his path. The coach sped away, leaving a cloud of dust in its wake. As it settled, the sun went in and there was a distant rumble of thunder. A fat raindrop hit Lorna on the nose. She looked at Sebastian who seemed to be waiting for her to say something.

"Just tell me one thing, Sebastian," she said. "Did you kill your master?"

"No," Sebastian looked at her levelly. "It all happened just as I told you."

"And he really only made this yesterday?"

"Yes. Well, it took a few weeks. Looked the same as yours anyways, except yours is older. Now d' you believe me?"

Lorna looked away for a moment. "I saw you," she said. "This afternoon. In my bedroom mirror just before...well just before I got here. I'm sorry, I just didn't want to believe any of this. It's all so weird."

Sebastian shrugged. "Don't matter. Saw you too. In the window, last night."

"Did you? Nothing would surprise me. Not anymore. Seems this thing didn't just boot me out of my room, it kicked me back a couple of hundred years as well."

"What year is it where you come from?"

"Twenty fifteen."

Sebastian's eyes grew round. "Blimey! No wonder you didn't believe me."

"You believe me though." Lorna looked at the boy thoughtfully. There was something about his eyes. Looking into them made her feel like she was looking into her own soul. She was sure he'd known many unhappy times, and not just the past couple of days either. "I think we'd better stick together," she said. "At least till we figure things out." Sebastian nodded agreement. There was a massive crash from overhead and the skies opened.

"The wood!" Sebastian pointed. "We can hide there. Get out of the storm too."

There was another crash from above and the two of them pelted for the shelter of the wood, barely seeing their way through the torrential rain.

"Crap," Lorna said. She was soaked, her jeans clinging uncomfortably to her legs. Sebastian was drenched too but seemed not to notice. Maybe it was because he'd already spent the previous night in a ditch.

"We should go further in," he said. "Trees'll be thicker. More shelter. Come on."

After a while, the trees broke into a tiny clearing, their branches growing so close over the top they made a knitted canopy that cast a strange green light, darkened by the storm. At one end of the clearing was a dilapidated stone cottage. Smoke was curling from the chimney.

"Come on," Lorna said. "We can't stay out here all night."

"Don't!" Sebastian pleaded. "They might've heard things...about Mr. Hanson...about me!"

"I doubt it. We're nowhere near the road. News probably hasn't reached here yet."

Sebastian looked doubtful. "Look," Lorna said. "We can't stay out here, can we? If they have heard something, we'll be out of there before they can raise the alarm, I promise you."

They walked through the long grass, stepping over a large protruding tree root to reach the door. Lorna knocked. There was no answer. Hesitating, she pressed the latch. The door groaned on its hinges and opened slightly, scraping on the floor. She pushed it again, harder, and entered a small, dimly lit room, Sebastian close on her heels.

The room was dusty as if it had not been lived in for some years. Yet there was a fire crackling in the grate and the smell of something cooking mingled with the lingering staleness of the air. "Come on," Lorna whispered. "I don't think there's anyone here."

No sooner had she said this, than a figure rose out of the darkness from a high-backed chair in front of the fire. The door, which had been so hard to open, flew shut behind them with a bang. Lorna gave a little scream and reached for Sebastian.

A young man advanced towards them, fully grown in height and of lean athletic build. Lorna guessed that he was probably about seventeen or so. She was suddenly conscious of her lank hair and sopping wet jeans. This guy beat Simon Shawcross hands down. He was dressed a lot better for a start, in a dark suit with silver buttons that shifted like mercury. His hair was white-blond, his eyes an icy blue and his handsome face held an air of superiority. It was the second face from her mirror.

"So here you are at last," he drawled. "The boy who observed the making of the Chronograph, and the girl who now carries it."

Lorna heard Sebastian gasp, and looked at him in shock, not knowing what to say. They dripped in silent misery on the cold stone floor.

"Oh yes, I know who you are." The youth smiled, not very reassuringly. "Well come on in then. I'm Patrick."

CHAPTER 5

Patrick ~ The Future

As an Apprentice of the Court of Time, Patrick had known he was out of bounds the previous evening. He pressed himself against the wall of the Court's main Tower and hoped he wouldn't be seen by the two cloaked figures who had chosen to hold their conversation in the shadows nearby, blocking his path home. He stood, barely daring to breathe, wishing they would leave. He needed to get back to his rooms and think.

The twenty-fifth century sat in the valley below, stuck, and unable to take its rightful place in the sequence of the Ages. Damn shame, Patrick reflected. This amazing creation for the Future was once full of hope. Shimmering buildings rose among trees permanently laden with ripe fruit, while silvery transport pods skimmed silently, almost magically, along the skyway above. At the far end of the valley stood the water mill, a feature kept by the Guardians in every century's creation, although to Patrick it didn't seem to serve much purpose. This new century was lush and peaceful and should have been birthed to become the Present. Now, its sense of hope was beginning to fade, replaced by a strange sense of fragility.

The whole situation made him angry. He'd been raised among the people of this new Age until he'd been brought to Court aged ten to start his training. He felt the people's worry and their sense of abandonment by the Court of Time, whose great glacial portals now stood firmly shut against them. Apart from the Guards who sometimes descended below to check on the Age's stability, there was no further traffic between the two. The people below waited in panic, while the Court of Time flailed uselessly to deal with the Chaos.

The ground gave a sudden lurch beneath his feet, a regular happening these days. Patrick recovered himself and gathered his cloak about him, mind racing. He'd spent the past several weeks ensconced among the ancient journals in the Tower, searching for something that would help him recover what he'd lost so cruelly as a ten-year-old boy. Now he just needed a way to act upon what he'd discovered. Not that it would be easy. None of the senior officials were likely to help.

The two men in the shadows showed no signs of leaving.

"It's no good I tell you," one of them was saying. "The situation is escalating, and we have so many people working on damage control that it's taking too long to resolve the other matter."

"The Salvation of Time," his companion said. "The Chaos is deepening, Faramore. Another great rent appeared this morning. Hitler nearly fell into the twenty-third century and just think what that would have meant with all that technology at his disposal."

Patrick grinned. Faramore was the Great Lord's right-hand man. What would the Lord say if he knew about this clandestine conversation? The face of his taller companion was obscured by the cowl of a heavy travelling cloak and his voice was unfamiliar.

"This matter will not be resolved here at Court," the man continued. "All this work I hear about is wasted effort."

Faramore spoke nervously. "Is it him? Do you think he has it?"

"Most certainly, a lot of the Chaos is him. He knows many of the secrets of the Book of Infinity and he now has the Dark Glass as well... But no, he does not have the final instrument. He can make some moves, but he can't do it accurately. That's why so many rips are appearing.

We can be sure if he had...It... then he would have reset, and the Past and Present Ages would already be looking very different. We are safe for now, but who knows for how much longer."

Patrick frowned. Reset what? And what was "It" and who was "he"? He edged forward, straining to hear more.

"We're safe while It lies dormant, but we need to take action," Faramore was saying. "You've been away from Court for many years, my friend, and the Great Lord has grown afraid of his own shadow. His Councillors fight among themselves while he sits and does nothing."

"Careful, Faramore," the other warned. "The Great Lord became jittery after the Keeper's betrayal. Such talk would be enough for him to cast you into permanent suspension."

Faramore shuddered. "Look what he did to his own daughters – Guardians of the Places Outside Time."

"Those are privileged positions," the other said shortly, "and better than the alternative that would otherwise have faced them. However, I agree with you. Something must be done, if only because I sense that the greatest of all the Instruments is about to reawaken."

"You don't mean that! How do you know?" Faramore sounded shocked.

"Unlike most of the Court, I bothered to study the Book of Infinity for many years," the other man said with a touch of pride. "And of course, I know where the Instrument is..."

"You know? But this is incredible! We must tell the Great Lord! The Court must act..."

"Are you insane?" his companion hissed. "The Great Lord does not even know I am here, and that, Faramore, is how it will stay. I have not spent all these years searching and then watching over the thing for it all to be jeopardized by the rash actions of a desperate man and a Court full of well-meaning blabbermouths!"

There was a long silence, then the man gave a deep sigh. "I am sorry, Faramore. I repay your loyalty to me poorly. These are dangerous times, so in case anything happens to me, I will tell you – but this goes no further."

He leaned forward and whispered in his friend's ear. Faramore threw his head back and laughed. "Oh, very clever! And the Keeper has not discovered It in all these years?"

"No," said his companion. "But that is about to change. For once it reawakens, it will be more difficult to hide."

"Then it is time for the Three," Faramore said. "Don't look so surprised, my friend. I too studied the Book of Infinity – I am not as learned as you, it's true, but I still know that the Three are part of the Great Prophecy it contains."

"You must tell no-one of your understanding," urged the other. "Even the little you know could spell disaster in the wrong hands – and we already know how even well-meaning hands can cause harm."

"I agree," said Faramore. "If only the Great Lord's son hadn't built the wretched thing…. but no matter. What of the Three?"

"The Maker and the Bearer are in place. When It reawakens, they will be brought together."

"And the Third?"

"The Third," his friend said, "the Protector, is here. Come out boy, you've been listening in the shadows long enough!" Patrick froze. For a moment, he thought about running, then realising there was no escape, he stepped forward.

"Well now, my young friend," the man advanced, his face still in darkness. "You're going on a journey."

"And who are you to send me?" Patrick jutted out his chin. He might fear the man but wasn't going to show it.

"Mind your tone," said Faramore sharply. "Glenelven is one of the Great Guardians, and you have been eavesdropping on a private conversation. You will do as he says."

Patrick swallowed hard. Guardians were powerful people, yet could this particular Guardian and his friend Faramore be trusted? They seemed to have little respect for the Great Lord, or even the Court itself.

"You will travel with two others," Glenelven continued. "A boy, much younger than yourself, and a girl. You will have two tasks. First you will traverse Past and Present Ages and their Guardians will give you directions which can only be given in their Time. From the Present Age, you will go to a place Outside Time where you will bring round the Future Age, the twenty-fifth century. The normal methods are impossible for now, so you will be shown the Old Way. Second, the girl is carrying a powerful Instrument of Time. When you have completed the first task, you will bring the young boy, the girl, and what she carries, back to the Court."

"And how exactly will I do that?" Patrick asked.

"If you complete the first task successfully, the Present will move to the Past. The Future Age, which will still at that point have its pathway to the Court intact, will become the Present. Therefore, when you return to the Present Age from the place Outside Time, it will be the new Present. Understand?"

"I think so." Patrick stood thoughtfully, his mind on his discovery in the Tower, the clues to the disappearance of the one person he wanted to find. The journals were difficult for someone at his level to understand, but he'd gleaned that the answer would not be found here, but in a previous Age. This journey was the solution he'd been looking for. They needn't know that he had his own quest and if he could find who he hoped to find, it would save the day and he'd return a hero. He mustn't seem too keen though, or Faramore and the strange, cloaked Glenelven might suspect his motives.

"I still don't see why I should go," he said. "I'm a mere Apprentice; why not send one of the Keepers? Or another Guardian?"

"Because two senior members of the Inner Circle have caught the mere Apprentice loitering at the bottom of the High Tower outside of permitted hours, listening to their conversation!" Glenelven spoke harshly. "By rights we should turn you over to the Council, with the likely outcome that you will be booted down the ranks to clean Hour Glasses for the Junior Guardians until such Time as pleases the Great Lord!"

Patrick swallowed hard. "I'll go," he said. "But what if I fail?"

"Then the Great Prophecy as seen by him who holds the Dark Glass will come true, with blood, death and vengeance that will last until Time unfolds and then caves in on itself, and we are all destroyed."

"Well, if you put it like that...," Patrick laughed nervously. "Where do we start?"

"In the Age of the Past," said Glenelven. "That is where the Two will be united, and that is where you will meet them. You will not tell them anything that has been said here tonight."

"How are you to get there?" Faramore asked. "It's all very well for you – as a Guardian you can travel back and forth unnoticed, but the sentries will awaken if an Apprentice tries to go. Even your own transference into the Past could draw attention when you should only..."

"Enough!" Glenelven interrupted him. "We will ride the next shockwave out of here. People are so focused on the Chaos, no-one will notice."

"Then we must hurry," said Faramore. "They say another one is imminent."

"Very well." Glenelven turned Patrick. "We're leaving. Now."

The young man reluctantly followed the two men as they hurried past the fountain in the centre of the courtyard and towards the East Cloister. What on earth was he getting himself into? They were collecting supplies from Faramore's rooms when the ground gave another heave and began to shudder. "It's happening!" Faramore cried. "Go! And good luck!"

Patrick ran after his new-found master, down the cloister and out of the East Door into a smaller courtyard, at the far end of which stood a large oak tree. "Faster!"

the older man urged. "We must not miss this, or things will be harder!"

They sprinted towards the tree. As they reached it, there was another rumble and a great cracking sound. A flash of black lightening crossed the sky, but instead of disappearing it remained, a great black fissure stretching from heaven to earth.

"Don't let go!" Glenelven cried and he leapt into the crack, pulling Patrick after him. The young man felt a great rush of wind in his face and then blacked out. When he came round, he was lying on his back in the middle of a dense wood. The wind was still blowing.

"How long have I been out?" he asked, feeling groggy.

"Only a moment or two," the older man said, sounding relieved. "Now, let's go into this cottage here. We can get some rest and I can tell you more..." He stopped abruptly.

"What is it?" Patrick asked.

"The wind. It's getting much stronger." There was a clap of thunder, and another fork of lightning, white this time, lit up the sky. The wind tugged hard at the man's cloak, and he was struggling to stay on the ground.

"Damn it all!" he exclaimed in anger. "Now listen, before the Age tears me away. The Two will come to you. The boy is Sebastian, the girl is Lorna. It is she who carries the Chronograph, the greatest Instrument of Time. On no account must it fall into the hands of the Keeper of the Hours."

"Who?" Patrick felt his anxiety rising as he realised he was about to be left alone. The wind was blowing harder, nearly lifting Glenelven into the air.

"The enemy." Glenelven had to shout as the gale whipped his words away. "He has overstepped his bounds in his thirst for power. The Book of Infinity and the Dark

Glass are already in his hands and have given him enough insight to move between the Ages, but he is a novice and careless. Every time he moves, he causes great rips in the fabric of Time, and Chaos ensues. But the Dark Glass enables him to see the darkest of possible outcomes across all Ages in the Book and I dread to think what he intends to do if he has the Chronograph."

"Can't the Court stop him?"

"The Court?" The man was scornful. "The Salvation of Time is in your hands now, Patrick. The Book has decreed this, and he knows it too." The wind lifted him several feet in the air. "Find the Maid," Glenelven yelled. "She guards this Age and the Falls Outside Time. She will give you instructions!"

"You're making no sense!" Patrick cried.

"Find the Falls," Glenelven bellowed again, and the wind whisked both the man and his words further into the air before carrying him off into the distance and out of sight.

Patrick stood at a loss. The wind had dropped, and a steady rain was beginning to fall. If only he'd gone back into the Tower to hide instead of listening, he wouldn't be in this mess. What they were doing was clearly without the knowledge of the Great Lord, probably illegal. And what if Glenelven and Faramore only wanted this Chronograph object for their own ends?

"It was probably his plan all along," the young man grumbled as he entered the cottage. "Dump me here, leave me to do the dirty work, and then take this thing for themselves. And another thing. This Glenelven's supposedly been away from Court for years, and I've never met him... and there's a couple of hundred

Apprentices. So why me? And how did he know my name?"

He'd just lit the fire and sat down to think when the door scraped open behind him. He rose to meet the young girl and small boy who stepped nervously inside.

CHAPTER 6

The Three

Lorna felt her face grow red as Patrick looked her up and down. Typical. The guy was fitter than any she'd seen in the whole of Middlebridge and here she was looking like a drowned rat. Or skunk. She cursed Simon and the streak in her hair. Patrick seemed amused by her appearance and she looked away, embarrassed and a little scared. They should get out of here. She looked at Sebastian.

"It's raining," he said, drawing himself up to his full height. "We didn't think no-one was here, we don't want no trouble. We'll be on our way."

"Yeah," Lorna said, following his lead, "forget we were here."

Her hand was on the latch, but Patrick stepped neatly round Sebastian and stopped her. She felt heat rise again in her face as he removed her hand from the door and slid the bolt into place. "You are Lorna," he said. "And Sebastian. No use denying it, there can't be too many kids walking around here lost."

Lorna flushed. She hated being called a kid. "You're not that much older than me," she said, and sneezed. The young man laughed.

"Touchy!" he said and looked at Sebastian. "You're wet through, and I'll bet you're hungry, right?" Sebastian gave a small nod.

"Come in then and sit by the fire. Or would you rather stand by the door all night?"

Sebastian looked at Lorna, then shrugged. "Might as well. And I am hungry."

Their host took charge, sorting out blankets and pointing out where Lorna could change, then he rigged up a rope like a clothesline to dry their clothes by the fire. It looked like he'd cooked something too. Lorna grudgingly allowed herself to be impressed. Sebastian sat on a stool by the hearth, wrapped in his blanket. He accepted a bowl of whatever-it-was with a grunt and started shovelling it into his mouth, saying nothing.

"How d'you get here then?" Patrick asked.

"We walked," Sebastian said.

"No, I mean how do you both come to be here."

"I know what you mean," the small boy said rudely. "But we don't know nothing about you. Just 'cos you're feedin' us don't mean I'm talking."

"What about you?" Patrick looked at Lorna with a grin. She jutted out her chin in defiance. "Me neither."

"Oh, for heaven's sake!" He threw some remnants of bread on the fire. "Have it your own way. Look, I landed here from the twenty-fifth century. I know that sounds mad, but my guess is it's no stranger than what's happened to you." He looked up expectantly, but Lorna and Sebastian remained silent. He gave a sigh and continued.

"I came here with a Guardian from my time. He told me to look after you. I've got to make sure you and what you're carrying get safely to the Future Age."

"We don't need no lookin' after," Sebastian said coldly. "We're fine on our own."

"Sure you are! What are your plans? Where are you going next? I'll bet you haven't a clue as to your next move!"

"And you do?" Sebastian glared. "I'm off. You comin' Lorna, or what? I don't trust 'im. He's like them other gents what come to the shop and they was nothin' but trouble." He got up to retrieve his wet clothes.

"What other gents?" Patrick seized the boy's arm. "Look, this is important, you need to trust me. What other choice do you have?"

"He's right," said Lorna, breaking her silence. "What else are we going to do Sebastian? We can't just run around hiding in cottages and hoping." She reached under the blanket.

"Lorna, no!" Sebastian cried.

"He already knows we have it. Maybe he can use it to help us." She opened her palm to reveal the Chronograph, ticking away in her hand.

Patrick gave a low whistle. "May I?" She nodded and he took it from her, turning it over and examining it closely. "It's beautiful," he said finally, and returned it to her.

"I helped make it." Sebastian seemed to have forgotten about not telling Patrick anything. "I did some of them small cogs and put 'em in. Then this gent come looking for it and killed my master."

"It made me fall out of my bedroom," Lorna added. "I saw both of you in my mirror before it happened. Then I found Sebastian hiding in a ditch. Oh – and he's wanted for murder by the way, so we can't let him get caught. He forgot to tell you that bit."

Patrick looked stunned. He opened his mouth, then shut it again without saying anything.

"Well?" Lorna said. "Do you know what any of this is about?"

"I think the sooner we can get you out of here the better," Patrick replied, getting up.

"So, you don't know. Either that or you're not telling." Lorna was disappointed in him. "Look, you said this Guardian, whoever he is, told you to take us to the Future Age. How do we get there? You can tell us that, can't you?"

"And can I stay there, wherever it is?" added Sebastian. "Cos things ain't lookin' too rosy for me here."

"I don't know about staying," Patrick said. "But to get there, we must find the Falls. They're round here somewhere, and once we've found them the Maid will help us."

"What Maid?" Lorna was fed up. This Patrick made about as much sense as Simon after a weed session. Which was no sense at all. "Look, how do we know you're not just having a laugh? Or leading us into a trap? First there was some Guardian, whatever he is, and now we've got a Maid. And I've never even heard of a waterfall round here, have you Sebastian?"

The younger boy shook his head. "Nah. But then I've only lived in Little Stonebrook and St Mark's."

"Whatever. Neither of us knows about this mysterious waterfall." Lorna glared at Patrick. "Well? You can't just keep saying stuff and expecting we'll follow along."

Patrick glared back. "Look, I'm in the dark almost as much as you. This Guardian, Glenelven, he gave me my orders and that's all I know. I'm not even sure what he looks like, he was wearing this hooded cloak thing all the time. The other bloke that was with him, Faramore, well he's a big deal where I come from and... well, if Faramore trusts Glenelven, then I guess we all have to."

"Yeah right," Lorna sneered. "Like we should trust you just because you trust some Faramore person we've never met and a faceless so-called Guardian. Sounds like a load of crap to me."

"Like your story's so much better!" Patrick said hotly. "You fell out of your bedroom, and he killed someone!"

"I didn't kill nobody!" Sebastian protested. "It's all lies. It was that creepy gent, I'm telling you!"

"Okay, okay, so you didn't kill anyone. Dear Lord!" Patrick exclaimed. "Look, we're stuck with each other so we might as well get on with it. Right?"

Lorna looked at Sebastian. He was dead on his feet, and she didn't feel much better. "All right," she said. "We'll go along with you, but only because we don't have much choice. But let's avoid St Mark's and Little Stonebrook. We don't want anyone recognising Sebastian."

"Fine. Whatever. No point, seeing as Sebastian's never heard of any Falls over there anyway. We'll head in the opposite direction. Okay?"

"So long as we keep Sebastian away from trouble, that's all I care about."

There was a small snore. Sebastian had fallen off his stool and was sprawled on the remaining blankets by the fireplace.

"You take the chair," Patrick said. "You're surely not going to argue with me about that, Lorna? Whatever you think of me, I do have some manners, you know."

Lorna flung herself sulkily into the chair, pulling her blanket around her. Patrick gave her an exasperated look, then stacked his travel bags in the corner and settled himself against them. "Night," he said.

Lorna gave a little snore and peeked at him from under her eyelids. Pity she'd argued with him, he really was quite fit. She felt a strange warmth rising in her stomach and mentally pushed it down. It wouldn't do to feel too close to him, people you felt close to usually rejected you or died. She felt Patrick looking at her and closed her lids tight shut.

"Damn you, Glenelven," she heard him whisper. "As if all the lies you Guardians have told me for years weren't bad enough - you go and dump me here with two kids and a half-baked story. Well, you're not the only one who needs something brought back. I know the truth's here somewhere, but how am I supposed to find it when I'm stuck here babysitting?"

She heard him thump the bags and then, before too long, the deep regular breathing of someone asleep. So, he thought they were kids that needed babysitting, did he? Just as well she'd decided not to feel too much for him. Boys really were idiots.

CHAPTER 7

Darkness on the Track

Patrick woke early after a fitful night against the wall as a cold dawn light filtered through the shutters. He could make out the form of Sebastian splayed out on the floor. Lorna was still hunched in the chair. The bizarre orange streak in her hair had fallen forward to cover half her face. Patrick grinned. The girl was a case, what with her hair and that freaky nose stud. Pretty though. For a moment, he felt like gently pushing the streak back so he could see more of her sleeping face. Then he came to his senses and let himself quietly out of the cottage. He needed a wash.

Down the side of the building was a trough filled with water from last night's storm. Ignoring the brown silt and dead leaves floating in one corner, Patrick stripped to his waist and was just splashing himself under the arms when the sound of voices interrupted him. He pressed himself against the wall, thinly disguised by a young sapling sprouting on the corner, as two men came into view.

"'Twere a foul night," one was saying. "All that wind bellowing and rain slashing against the shutters. Fair made me hair stand on end!"

"That it were, Walt," his companion agreed. "Our Tom came in soaked to the skin. Said he'd nearly stopped here for the night. Sez he saw smoke coming from the chimney so's at least there'd be a warm fire."

Patrick felt himself go hot and cold. The thought that someone could have discovered them last night, despite the storm, was too close for comfort. He listened anxiously as the men continued.

"Don't like the sound of that, Arthur," the one called Walt was saying. "Place has stood empty since old Duggan died, and that's bin five year now. Catch me goin' in there, rain or no rain – folks say it's haunted!"

"Poppycock!" Arthur sneered. "That young Cathy Cooper was always here meeting that soldier fella till she ended up... anyway, Tom thought it best to get along home."

"Best not get caught with them pheasants he bin poachin' you mean!"

"Can't say I know what you're talkin' about – but we did 'ave ourselves a very tasty supper last night!" The two men roared with laughter.

Patrick came to a decision. Poachers weren't likely to fetch the law, and they might know about the Falls. He'd say he was travelling and got lost in the storm. It was pretty much the truth anyway, and it was Sebastian that people were looking for, not him.

He was about to step out of hiding when there was the sound of something large approaching through the bracken and a new voice called to the men.

"Ho there!" The voice was deep and dark. Patrick shrank back again, shivering as a sudden chill ran down his spine.

"Have you seen a small boy?" the voice enquired.

"I seen lots of small boys," Arthur replied. His companion laughed nervously.

"This one is about so high," the dark voice said. "Sandy hair. Dirty looking."

"Plenty of us dirty looking!" Arthur sounded indignant. "T'ain't no sin. That's what hard work does for you."

"Indeed. But have you seen the child? It was a dreadful storm last night; he must have sheltered somewhere. With you here in your cottage perhaps?"

Patrick felt himself blanch. He knew the search was on for Sebastian, but for him to have been tracked here already was bad news. It only needed these two men to say the cottage was nothing to do with them, but they'd seen smoke, and the stranger would be through the door in a flash. He held his breath as Arthur spoke again.

"Can't say I seen anyone. What about you, Walt?"

Walter said nothing, but Patrick surmised he must have shaken his head. "Sorry then, can't help you," Arthur said. "What's your interest anyway?"

"The boy has stolen something valuable," the dark voice said. "And I need – we need – to get it back most urgently."

"Valuable you say?" Walt sounded interested. "There a reward then?"

"Naturally," the dark voice replied, "if that makes a difference. Now, have you seen anything, anything at all that might tell me where he is?"

"Well..." Walt began, but his friend interrupted.

"Reward makes no difference," Arthur said curtly. "We ain't seen nobody. Right Walt?"

"Very well," the dark voice said. "But I must warn you to be careful. The boy murdered his master, and he may not have acted alone. Others may be with him."

"We'll have to watch our backs then," Arthur replied. "Thank you for the warning."

There was a sound of cracking twigs as the dark voice turned his mount on the path. "Red Lion, St Mark's Bar," he called, "in case you remember anything!"

"Why didn't you tell him about the smoke?" Walt said after the stranger had gone. "And let him think this was our place? My Missus wouldn't be happy with that. Takes pride in our home she do."

"Twasn't me what saw the smoke," Arthur replied. "Besides, I wasn't tellin' nothin' to the likes of him."

"But the reward!" Walt said. "You heard. The boy killed his master. Hangin' offence that is, likely be a good fat purse for the right information."

"Then you should have spoken. But I say we let well alone. If it was the boy in the cottage last night, then good luck to him. Master probably beat 'im half to death and likely deserved what was coming to 'im. Besides, we don't want the law sniffing around, do we?"

"Nah, you're right. I didn't like him neither, all tall and dark on that ruddy great horse. Funny eyes too. Like as not he'd find some way not to pay anyway. Can't trust his sort!"

"Then we forget it," said Arthur. "Now I'm getting home with these fish. Nice lot of trout in the river t'other side of Moorlands. You should take a look."

"Squire, being generous again, is he?" Walt scoffed.

"You might say that. Although I doubt he knows just how generous he's being!"

The two men roared with laughter again and Patrick heard them move off. It was urgent to wake the others now and leave.

~

Back in the cottage, Lorna was awake and examining the Chronograph by the now dead fire and wondering what to do next. It was all very well this Patrick showing up with his story about Guardians and helpful Maids at waterfalls, but just because the guy made her stomach flip didn't mean they could trust him. From what she'd overheard last night when she was supposed to be asleep, he clearly had his own agenda. They would have to be careful.

The door scraped open, and she looked up, then away again quickly as Patrick came in, pulling his shirt over his head. Her face flamed and she pretended to be busy, poking at the ash in the grate with a stick. "Everything okay?" Patrick asked.

She nodded, still averting her eyes. "Chronograph seems fine. Not doing much. Just normal."

"Wish I could say the same for out there. We need to leave. People are out looking for us." He quickly recounted the conversation he'd overheard outside.

"Sounds like him what come looking for the Chronograph," Sebastian said.

"Oh, you're awake, are you?" Patrick replied. "I thought so too, Sebastian. We need to move. That Walt fellow might change his mind about the reward. Here, we'll eat last night's soup. Have to have it cold – there's no time for another fire and we can't risk the smoke anyway."

Lorna swallowed a couple of spoonfuls of soup and ran her fingers through her hair. If she looked anything like Sebastian, she was filthy. At least her clothes were dry.

"Which way then?" she asked as they left the cottage.

"Have you heard of Moorlands?" Patrick asked. "One of the men said something about a river near there. On someone's land, it sounded like. If there's a river, then maybe there's some Falls further upstream."

"Not as daft as you look, are you?" Lorna said grudgingly. "I haven't a clue. So many places don't exist anymore in my time."

"I heard about Moorlands once," said Sebastian. "Big estate down the valley. I ain't been there, but Pa said the Stony Brook's a big river thereabouts. So, it'd be...somewhere over there." He waved his hand vaguely.

They traipsed for what seemed like hours before reaching a bank where the trees abruptly ended. Lorna slid down after the others, landing on the narrow dirt track below. After a short debate about which direction to head, they set off again. All was quiet, except for birds chirruping from time to time in the hedgerows.

"It's my birthday," Lorna said suddenly. Then she bit her lip and stopped in her tracks, berating herself for being so stupid. She never talked about her birthday. Yet for some reason, she especially wanted Patrick to know she was closer to his age than maybe he thought she was. Damn him and his shirt – or rather lack of it - that morning. She felt flustered.

The only one to show any interest though, was Sebastian. "It's your birthday today? What do you do where you come from?" The questions came thick and fast, and she answered them in a monotone till Patrick finally asked the one that mattered.

"How old are you then?"

"Sixteen." She tossed her hair and for a moment she thought he looked at her a little differently.

"Sorry you've got to spend it with us," he said brusquely, and strode on.

"Doesn't matter. Don't much celebrate it anyway."

"Why not?" Sebastian asked.

"Cos of my dad...He died."

"We've all lost someone," Patrick said.

"Is that what you're looking for?" Lorna asked. "Someone you've lost?"

He stopped dead in his tracks and stared at her. "What's that supposed to mean?"

He had a strange look in his eye and Lorna wished she hadn't asked. "It's just...well, it sounded like there was something else. Something else besides us and the Chronograph."

"I don't think so."

"Yes, there was. You said something about the Guardian not being the only one who wanted something brought back. You were talking to yourself last night. When you thought we were asleep."

"Then whatever I said isn't any of your damn business, is it?"

"I think you should tell us," Sebastian chimed in. He'd been trailing behind them, dragging a stick he'd found in the dust.

"Listen, you little runt!" Patrick exploded and grabbed the boy by the collar. "I don't have to tell you anything. I've got my orders, see, to get you and her and that damn Chronograph back to the Future Age. Whatever else I do while I'm here is my own business. Got it?" He released Sebastian with a small shove.

"Stop it!" Lorna felt Sebastian shaking as she put her arm round his thin shoulders. She glared at Patrick. "Go on then. Just piss off and find whatever it is you can't tell us about. If the Guardian doesn't know about it, I don't want to either. I'll bet it only means more trouble."

"I'm not going anywhere. I'm supposed to look after you."

66

"Give me a break," she curled her lip. "You've told us all we need to know. Me and Sebastian can find the Falls and the Maid and do whatever she asks us to do. We can return the Chronograph to wherever it's supposed to be. We don't need you."

Patrick's pale face reddened. "Think you know it all, don't you? Fine then..." He broke off suddenly. A chill was descending rapidly, and the air had become heavy and still. The birds chirruping in the hedgerow had fallen silent. A dark, smoke-like mist was creeping up the track towards them.

"Quick," Patrick urged. "Get off the road."

Lorna didn't argue. She shoved Sebastian ahead of her as the three of them scrambled back up the bank and took cover in the long grass in the shadow of the trees. She lay there, looking down onto the track, feeling the small boy pressed against her one side and Patrick the other. The black mist hesitated, then turned and rolled back up the track away from them. "What the hell is it?"

"Dunno," Patrick replied. "Doesn't feel good though."

"I can hear a horse," Sebastian whispered.

A chestnut stallion came into view, snorting and tossing its mane, clearly not liking the rider on its back.

"Behave," the rider commanded, pulling hard on the reins. It was a tall, dark man, dressed in black, with a lean face and small, neat beard upon his chin. Horse and rider paused for a moment, as if sensing something. Lorna stared open-mouthed as the man took something small and dark out of his pocket, gave it a shake and looked at it, perplexed.

"Damn this thing. Just when I think I've got it to work...Will you come out of there?" he yelled. "What use are you to me otherwise?"

Lorna froze. She could feel Sebastian's heart beating hard beside her. Then she realised the man was yelling not at them, but at the object in his hand. She held her breath, willing him to ride on. There was a rustle in the branches above them, then the horse turned its head, gave a great sniff, and took a step towards the bank. Its rider sat up, lips curved in a cruel smile. "What have you found then? That's it, slowly now."

The horse hesitated, then advanced another step, tossing its head. "Come out, come out," crooned the rider. Black wisps began to emerge from the object in his hand.

Lorna buried her face in her hands, as if she could somehow shrink herself into the ground.

Sebastian pressed even closer, while Patrick's arm crept over the two of them. All three held their breath, waiting. Something suddenly flew out of the branches above them, squawking, and the horse reared, startled.

"A bird!" the man cried in disgust. "A bird, you stupid nag! And as for this thing…" He stuffed the dark object angrily in his waistcoat and the black wisps were sucked suddenly up into the air and disappeared. The rider gave the horse a brutal kick and galloped up the track, pausing momentarily at the crossroads before turning right and heading off again in a cloud of dust.

Patrick crawled forward cautiously, then stood up and beckoned to the others.

"That was close," he said. "He was outside the cottage this morning, asking questions. I didn't like the sound of him."

"That w…was him," Sebastian stuttered, his knees shaking. "The dark stranger. He killed my master. He was after the Chronograph."

Lorna felt a sick feeling rising in her stomach.

"That's your stranger?" she asked Sebastian. He nodded.

"I…I don't get it," she was shaking violently. "That's my stepfather, Stephen Latimer. How on earth did *he* get here?"

CHAPTER 8

The Keeper

"Your stepfather!" Patrick exclaimed.

"He's bad," Sebastian said. "Why'd he want the Chronograph?"

"I don't know," Lorna said. Her head was in a whirl. Sebastian was looking at her warily. "What?" she said. "Oh ... you don't think *I've* got anything to do with all this? For God's sake, Sebastian, don't be such an idiot!"

The small boy scowled. "Well, how do I know? He could've used bad magic to drop you out of the sky to find me and pretend to be my friend."

"I think your imagination's running away with you," Patrick said.

"Oh yes?" The boy turned on him. "And who are you, Mr Twenty-fifth Century, talkin' about Guardians and stuff? I was better off when me Dad was beating me every day..." He slid back down the bank ahead of the others and stood on the track, scowling at his boots.

"Sebastian," Lorna tried reasoning. "Listen to me. That man showed up not long after my Dad died. He creeped me out. I dunno, it was just something about him. It was my real Dad that gave me the Chronograph and I hid it away so that creep couldn't find it. I could've handed it over any time I wanted, but I didn't. Okay?" Sebastian looked away and was silent.

"I'm sorry, Lorna," Patrick said, "but I think your stepfather is the enemy I was warned about. He might call himself Latimer or whatever, but I'll bet he's the Keeper…" He stopped himself abruptly.

"Oh, he's the Keeper, is he?" Lorna sneered. "How many more are there in your little cast of characters? First, we had a Guardian, then a Maid and now there's a Keeper. You know something? I think you're making it up as you go."

Patrick was livid. "Think what you like. All I care about is getting that damn Chronograph back where it belongs, with or without you. Now are you coming or not?"

"Not." Lorna jutted her chin out defiantly. "Not until you tell us what's going on. Who are these Keepers and Guardians and what are they keeping and guarding? If they've caused a big mess, I don't see why we should be dragged into it."

"Jeez, you're a stubborn one!" Patrick looked as if he was making his mind up about something. "Okay, look. I was told not to tell you, but I can't see that it makes much difference, especially now. Where I'm from, we have different people who look after Time, make sure it runs as it should, that sort of thing. The Keeper was one of those people, but he turned bad. If he gets his hands on the Chronograph, it will be catastrophic. Maybe even the end of Time, I dunno. But he's willing to kill for the power it will give him. Now, feel any the wiser?"

Lorna shrugged. "Sounds like a load of crap to me, but I guess there's got to be some explanation for landing up in 1785."

"Very generous of you, I'm sure. Now, are we done, or does Sebastian have any objections he'd like to raise?"

The small boy shook his head. "I ain't got nowhere else to go, so I may as well come with you. But we're not following that creepy man, are we?"

"No, we're not following the creepy man. But we've got to get a move on. He's on a horse and we're on foot, and we've had two close calls already. I don't want him intercepting the Chronograph before we reach the Falls."

"He's not from this Time any more than we are," Lorna said. "Except Sebastian of course. He's probably just riding around guessing."

"I'm not so sure," Patrick replied. "That thing he had – I think it's the Dark Glass. It's some instrument of Time, it might be helping track us somehow. Not very well yet, because I don't think he's got it fully figured out, but I dread to think what it will do when he does. Now, which way?" They'd reached the crossroads.

"Not right," Lorna said. "That's the way the Keeper went. I say left so we stay as far away from him as possible."

"It doesn't look like it goes anywhere much," Patrick said. "Straight on looks like a better road and we might come to a town where we can ask."

"Might also be a town that's heard about Sebastian, and we get arrested."

"Great. Do you ever do anything without arguing?" Patrick glared at Lorna, who glared back.

"The river's that way," Sebastian said, pointing left.

"So now you know all of a sudden?" Patrick sounded thoroughly exasperated.

"Well, I'm going that way." Sebastian started off up the track to the left. Lorna looked at Patrick for a moment.

"Well, he's the local yokel, isn't he?" She ran to catch up with Sebastian.

"Hello," she said.

Sebastian looked at Lorna sideways from under his fringe and gave a lopsided grin. "What I said about you pretending to be my friend. Sorry."

"'S'all right," she grinned back at him. "Is the river really this way?"

"Think so," the boy said. "There's a stream running over the field there, see? It's got to be going somewhere." Lorna felt a grudging respect. The ten-year-old boy had more common sense than either she or Patrick. She looked over her shoulder. The young man was slouching along the track behind them, hands in his pockets and muttering to himself. Too bad. She took the Chronograph out of her pocket and looked at it. "I think it's going a bit faster," she said.

Sebastian shrugged. "Looks the same to me. Hey. Look over there!"

Lorna looked. Across the fields she could see a church spire rising above the trees. "Maybe we're getting close to Moorlands," Sebastian said.

"Let's cut across the fields," Lorna suggested, "It'll be quicker than following the track." She looked back at Patrick. He was staring in the direction of the spire. "Coming?"

He shrugged. "S'pose so. Can't leave you two kids on your own, can I?"

Lorna turned and stomped after Sebastian, cheeks burning. Sure, she and Patrick hadn't exactly hit it off, but sometimes she thought he looked at her like...well, like Simon looked at her right before he'd asked her out. Obviously, she was mistaken. Patrick probably had a girlfriend anyway. Maybe she was the one he was looking for, chasing across the centuries to save her from something. For a moment, Lorna felt a pang of jealousy. She couldn't imagine Simon chasing across the centuries for *her*. She glanced back and saw Patrick trailing behind. He was clutching at his head, almost as if he were trying to tear something out of his brain.

"You okay?" she shouted. He stared past her towards the spire, then nodded and broke into a jog to catch them up. Lorna shrugged. And people called her weird!

At the edge of the field, they crossed the stream where it gurgled through a shady copse and found themselves by the track again, opposite a few cottages that seemed to form the top end of a village. A woman came out of the front door of one of them, shook something and went back inside.

"I'm starving," Lorna said. "I wonder if she'd give us something to eat."

"More like she'll chase us off with a broom," Sebastian said. "That's what usually happens round these parts."

"Maybe she won't if I go," Lorna said. "I hate to say it, but she might be a bit more sympathetic, with me being a girl."

"Good luck, looking like that," Patrick said.

She glared. "Well, I know I'm a bit dirty, but…"

"No," Sebastian said. "He don't mean the dirt."

Lorna looked down at her jeans and Doc Martens. "Oh!" she said with sudden realisation.

"Leave it to me," Sebastian said.

"You mad? You already said they'll chase you off with a broom!"

"Who said anythin' about asking?" the small boy smiled slyly.

"You mean, nick it, don't you!" Lorna exclaimed. "What if you get caught?"

"Ain't bin caught before. Sometimes the only way I'd eat for days when I were hiding from me dad." He darted across the track. "You comin' or what?"

They followed to where a wall ran along the back of the first few cottages. Patrick gave Sebastian a leg up and he dropped down on the other side. After a while, they heard a huffing and scraping and the boy's face appeared like the Cheshire cat, grinning at them from the top of the wall. "See what I've got. Back door was open." He lowered down what turned out to be a woman's skirt with half a meat pie and several apples bundled inside.

"Thought the skirt might make you look a bit more normal," he grinned to Lorna.

"Thanks a lot!"

"Matthew!" a voice called from the cottage. "You taken that pie off the table, you greedy fat hog?"

"Let's get out of here," Patrick said. "Come on!"

They ran further along the backs of the cottages descending into the village, before coming to an abrupt halt by a high stone wall.

"Lift me up again," said Sebastian. "I'll have a look."

"OK," said Lorna. "Come on, Patrick, don't just stand there. What the hell is wrong with you?"

Patrick was leaning against the wall, drained of all colour, a dazed expression on his face again. "I can feel something," he said quietly. "I first felt it up on the track before we crossed the fields. Sort of magnetic, like something's pulling me."

"What's magnetic mean?" Sebastian asked.

"Not now, Sebastian." Lorna pulled the Chronograph out of her pocket. "Look," she whispered. The object was quivering in her hand of its own accord, the hands still progressing round the face in a steady march, but much too fast. Occasionally, the third hand, which she'd assumed marked seconds, swung slowly back a couple of steps, then swung wildly forward again to catch up with the others.

"Something's wrong," Lorna said. "The Chronograph's sensing it too."

"D'you want to know what's over this wall, or not?" Sebastian said.

"Oh yeah. Sorry. Here!" She re-pocketed the instrument and gave him a bunk up. "It's the churchyard!" called his voice from above her.

"Right then." Patrick seemed to shake himself awake. "Here, Sebastian, you go over first."

"Wait a minute!" Sebastian protested. "Hey!" Patrick gave him an almighty boost that sent him flying over the top before helping Lorna. Then he dropped down to join them.

Everything was quiet, the afternoon sun creating a dappled effect on the gravestones. Sebastian scowled. "I don't much like it here."

"It's quiet, that's all," Lorna said. "Come on, let's eat." She and Sebastian demolished the pie and most of the apples between them. Patrick was behaving oddly again, sitting as though in a trance a little apart from them, a half-eaten apple in his hand. Lorna shrugged and lay back in the shade of an oak tree by the wall. Let him be weird if he wanted, it meant nothing to her. Something tickled her under her nose, and she looked up to see Sebastian grinning down at her, a long piece of grass in his hand.

"Stop it," she laughed, lazily wafting it away. The boy lay down next to her and yawned. "Yeah," she said. "Forty winks sound like a good idea. All right with you, Patrick?"

The young man glanced at her briefly. "Do what you like." Then he resumed staring at the church as if he'd never seen such a building before.

They woke some time later, feeling chilled in the long shadows now cast by the gravestones as the sun moved across the sky. Patrick was still sitting where he had been earlier, unmoving like a stone angel.

"Come on," he said, without turning his head. "We're going in."

CHAPTER 9

The Woman in the Shroud

Reluctantly, Lorna and Sebastian hauled themselves to their feet and prepared to follow Patrick into the church, leaving the remaining warmth of the day behind them.

"Why are we doing this?" Sebastian asked Lorna in a cross whisper.

"Because Patrick wants to," she replied.

"I know that!" the boy grumbled. "But why do we have to do what he says? If he wants to go in, let him go on his own! I don't like churches."

Lorna looked at the small unhappy boy in front of her and felt a twinge of sympathy. "I don't get it either," she said, "but Patrick's been acting weird all afternoon. I think we should keep an eye on him." Sebastian looked unconvinced.

"Why don't you like churches?" she asked. "I thought a church would make you feel safer. Especially here, in your Time."

"Why in my Time?"

"Because people don't respect it much in mine," she replied. "But I thought they believed in it more in your day, like it had some special power or something."

Sebastian shrugged and wiped his nose on the back of his hand. "Don't know 'bout that. Didn't stop our Joseph dying. He was only three."

He followed Lorna grudgingly into the church, where Patrick was standing by a pew looking impatient. "Where have you been? We haven't got all day."

"What are we looking for?" asked Lorna, ignoring his tone.

"I don't know," he admitted. "I just *feel*, you know. Like there's something here I must find, or nothing will make sense."

"You're the one who's making no sense," she said. "Okay then. Where d'you want us to start?"

"Down there," Patrick replied quietly. He pointed to a small door in the corner, partially open, with a stone staircase descending into darkness beyond.

"The crypt?" whispered Lorna with a small shiver.

"No!" exclaimed Sebastian. "Not dead people. I'm not going anywhere near dead people!"

"Look, stupid," snapped Patrick in exasperation, "you just walked through a churchyard, didn't you?"

"That's different," stuttered Sebastian, "it's cold in here. It'll be dark and what if there's...ghosts?"

"You can be lookout," Lorna interjected. The boy was trembling, and she'd be damned if she let Patrick force him where he didn't want to go. She wasn't exactly keen herself.

"Don't leave me," Sebastian whimpered.

"Look, just hide if you want, and yell down the steps if you need us." Lorna gave what she hoped was a reassuring smile. "Here, have the Chronograph, so you can see how long we've been gone."

"You're not going to trust him with that are you?" exclaimed Patrick.

"Better with him, than me dropping it down there," she said. "Besides, he did make it."

Sebastian took the Chronograph from her outstretched palm and caressed it lovingly. Lorna watched enviously as he slid his thin body between the back of the last pew and the stone wall and settled back into this secret hiding place from which he could view the entryway and still scuttle along the back of the pew to the crypt unseen. Lorna gave him a small wave, then followed Patrick into the pitch black of the crypt.

The door threw a shaft of light down the first part of the stairway, after which it became treacherous, as the stone steps were uneven and worn from the previous centuries of passage. Soon they could see nothing but blackness before them. Lorna sat on her rear and bumped her way down, feeling the dampness of the cold stone through her jeans. Patrick did likewise for a few steps, then halted.

"This is ridiculous," he said. "Even if we get down there okay, we're not going to be able to see a damn thing. Maybe we should go back."

"You wanted to come," she said. "Ow!" She had bumped down on something hard.

"You okay?" asked Patrick.

"Yeah, I just sat on something."

Pulling her jacket out from underneath her, she scrabbled in the pocket and found a small hard object that had made its way through a hole in the lining.

"Look!" she said triumphantly. There was a click.

Patrick blinked in surprise as his face was suddenly illuminated by a flickering flame. "What the..?"

"It's Latimer's lighter!" she said proudly. "I forgot, I nicked it from him weeks ago!"

"What d'you do that for?"

"He kept smoking outside my room. It stank and I didn't like it, so I stole his lighter. And I knew it would drive him mad." She grinned to herself at the memory.

Patrick laughed. "You're something else!"

"Yeah, well…" she shrugged, glad of the darkness as a warm flush spread across her cheeks again. She cast the light around. "What's those?"

"Torches." They were in brackets, descending the length of the staircase. Patrick reached one down. "Here." They lit the torch and continued their descent. "You okay?"

"Uh huh," she nodded.

The bottom of the stairway opened into a narrow, low corridor, which in turn opened into a cavernous chamber under the church. Lorna shuddered. "It's a good thing Sebastian stayed behind," she said. "It's dead creepy down here. Whatever it is, Patrick, let's find it and get out of here."

They stood in the centre of the floor, the burning torch casting a pool of light around them. "This way," Patrick said, and set off slowly down a line of stone tombs in a narrow antechamber, pausing briefly at each one. Lorna followed him closely, not wanting to be outside the circle of light from the torch. Several times she bumped into him when he stopped abruptly to look at something. Eventually, he took her hand, and she was surprised at how pleasant it was to feel her small hand encased in his large, rough palm.

Suddenly he let go, dropping down on his knees beside a stone sarcophagus. The carved writing on the side was so worn, it was now illegible. The lid across the top of the sarcophagus was cracked, and part of it had fallen away leaving one corner open.

"This is it!" Patrick said excitedly. "This is it, Lorna! This is what I've been feeling!"

"How do you know?" she asked in a small voice.

"I don't *know*, Lorna, I *feel*, can't you understand that? I just know that this is it, it's what's been pulling me all along." He fixed the torch into a nearby bracket on the wall, then leaned over the broken corner and inserted his hands under the stone lid.

"For God's sake, Patrick, you're not going to open it!"

"What the hell do you think I'm going to do? Walk away? This is it I tell you!"

He heaved upwards. Nothing happened. He heaved again and a long grating sound emanated from the lid as it scraped against the stone tomb beneath.

"One more should do it!" he gasped, and putting all his strength into it, he gave one final heave and the lid fell back with a crash.

Inside was a froth of material, opaque and soft, and strangely iridescent, enveloping something underneath. As Lorna looked timidly over Patrick's shoulder, she could see that at one end, the material covered a face, a bit like a bridal veil. The material was a bright white and not at all yellowed with age. The flame from the torch cast shadows that played over the fabric, like ravens flying over a snowfield.

"Patrick, no!" she gasped as he reached out his hand and gently touched the soft folds of translucent fabric over the face and hair of the body beneath.

"Lorna, I have to," he said in a low voice, his eyes fixed on the shroud in his hand, and with one swift, smooth movement, he pulled the fabric back from over the face.

"Patrick!" Lorna screamed. The young man fell back, taut with shock against the wall of the narrow antechamber, his eyes wide and staring, his mouth open and gasping for air. For one moment, Lorna allowed her eyes to transfer from him to the face in the sarcophagus and then stared, transfixed.

It was the face of a woman, beautiful in its gentleness, with smooth porcelain skin bearing a hint of pink at the cheek bones. The eyes were closed, with long dark lashes; the lips were curved in a serene smile as if its owner were thinking warm and peaceful thoughts. It was a healthy face, like that of someone living, yet in a deep state of unconsciousness. Tiny diamonds sparkled on her cheeks which, when Lorna looked closer, proved to be the smallest of small snowflakes, sticking in a permanent frozen state to the skin. The hair was the most gorgeous of rich chestnuts, falling in lush waves from crown to chin. One tiny wisp had curled under the right eye, framing the socket and adding to the breath-taking tenderness of the features. The shroud that Patrick had pulled away now framed the face, stunning in its contrast with the darkness of the hair. This was a face you couldn't help loving.

"Patrick?" she said hesitantly. "Who is she?" His answer was the last thing she expected.

"She's my mother." He buried his face in his hands. Lorna stared. This was insane. "I don't understand," she said. "You're from the Future, beyond my time even. So, if this is your mother, how did she get here?"

"I don't know," exploded Patrick.

"But Patrick, think. This can't be your mother, it must be an ancestor, someone that looks like her from generations ago."

"You think I don't know my own mother?"

"Of course you do," said a deep voice. A familiar shudder ran down Lorna's spine and the tall dark figure of the Keeper stepped forth from the shadows of the crypt.

"Always think you know better, don't you, Lorna? And you," he said menacingly to Patrick. "Pleased with what you've found? She's been perfectly safe here. Until now."

"Safe!" Patrick exploded. "She's dead! And here in some Age of the Past, and I don't even know how she got here!"

"Dead?" laughed the man. "Oh no, Patrick, not dead. Suspended in Time maybe, but not dead. You remember when you last saw her, of course?"

"Yes," Patrick said, his voice tight. "I was…playing… in the astral meadow. I picked star flowers and put them in her hair. I ran to find more and when I turned back, she'd disappeared. I was ten years old." His voice cracked.

"I see you do remember," said the Keeper. "How I laughed, seeing you, the son of one of the great Guardians of the Ages, running around in circles crying for his Mummy. "Mummy, mummy, where are you, mummy? Mummy come back!" he mimicked. "And all the while, none of you great people of the Court knew that I had taken your precious Guardian of the Future and carried her back to the distant past to hold her in stasis for my keeping. To do with what I will." He leered at Patrick.

"You, bastard!" Patrick lunged forward, but Lorna grabbed his arm and pulled him back.

"Don't listen to him!" she said. "She looks peaceful lying there. If he'd even laid a finger on her, she'd be suspended in disgust!"

"Let's not forget, Lorna, that some women find men like me attractive," the man said. "Your own mother for one." Lorna felt Patrick's arm go round her as she clenched her fists, heat rising in her face.

"The trouble with you is that you're too damn clever for your own good," the Keeper continued. "So now, it's time for some co-operation. Or you'll meet the same fate as that scruffy little urchin that loved hanging around you so much."

"Sebastian!" gasped Lorna. "What have you done with him?"

"The same as you do with any dirty runt," spat the man. "Annoying little brat, snuffling about in rags. But don't worry, Lorna. He was a child of suffering, tired of life. He'll suffer no more."

Lorna swallowed hard, determined not to cry.

"Now," he said taking a step towards her. "Hand it over."

Lorna breathed an inward sigh of relief. The Keeper was lying. If he'd found Sebastian, he'd already have the Chronograph and wouldn't be asking her for it. The boy was safe. She stuck her chin out in defiance. "I don't know what you mean."

"Oh, I think you do." The Keeper paused a moment. "Come now. It's just an old watch."

"If it's just an old watch, then what's it to you? Get yourself a new one that actually works."

"Think you're so clever, don't you? Hand it over!" The man raised his fist as he towered over them. Lorna flinched and felt Patrick hold her even tighter.

"Leave her alone!" he said. "We don't have it."

"You expect me to believe that!" the man spat. "If you don't have it, where is it?"

"I don't know. Really, I don't!" The last of Lorna's bravado gave way. She'd seen her stepfather angry, but never like this. She began to fear for her life, and for Patrick's too. But then the man seemed to change his mind.

"Do you know what happens when you bring someone out of Suspended Time?" he said suddenly, crossing over to the sarcophagus. "No? Then let me tell you."

"You have to do it carefully," he continued conversationally, gazing down at Patrick's mother, "very slowly and carefully. Like thawing an object that has been frozen. If you were to hit it hard with a hammer while it's still in that frozen state, it will shatter. Quite easily." He fingered the folds of the organza veil. "So, it is with temporal suspension - if you do not bring the object out slowly, then the force of Time hitting it again is so powerful that it will be destroyed. Now...tell me where it is." He twisted his fingers in the veil, his eyes never leaving the face of the woman.

"I don't know," Lorna whispered. She looked up at Patrick, tears in her eyes. He swallowed hard and nodded. "Really, I don't know."

The man looked at her, his long face even darker in the shadows. "All right then," he said, and turned to leave. Lorna felt both bewildered and relieved. Was he really going to let them off that easily? She looked at Patrick, but he appeared just as confused. The Keeper had almost exited the antechamber when he suddenly turned. "You know," he said, as if something had just occurred to him. "I'll just leave you to think about this," and with a flick of his wrist, he revealed a strange crystal that he wore on his arm like a bracelet. Another flick and the crystal was off his arm and lying on the stone flags of the chamber.

"No!" yelled Patrick. But it was too late. The Keeper had already raised his foot and then stamped down heavily, shattering the crystal beneath it. At the same time, a sound of breaking glass came from the sarcophagus. Patrick's mother disappeared, and all that remained was a cloud of snow, falling like miniature diamonds into the place where she had been. While they stared in horror, the man turned and ran up the stairs, then they heard the echo of the door slamming and a key being turned in the lock, and they were left with the final glowing embers of the torchlight from the bracket above them.

Exhausted and drained of all emotion, the two of them slid down the wall and held each other on the floor. "I'm sorry," Lorna sobbed, "I'm so sorry."

"Don't," said Patrick. "Please don't. We couldn't tell him anything even if we'd wanted to. We don't know where the Chronograph is because we don't know where Sebastian is. But at least we know the bloody little idiot's safe." Lorna felt his chest heave and raised her hand gently to his cheek.

"Patrick," she whispered. "It's all right. Please, Patrick."

She raised her face nervously to his and kissed his cheek where the tears fell. Then she felt his mouth on hers as his lips pressed again and again, his arms now so tight around her, she felt she might break in two. The wall she'd built to shut out the world began to crumble. Everything she'd tried to feel with Simon, she felt now, even though she knew Patrick's kisses came from a crevasse of grief that she knew only too well from her own loss all those years ago. She knew that right now, in that moment, only she could save him, as the embers of the torch finally died, leaving them to find their solace in each other in the darkness.

CHAPTER 10

The Graveyard Encounter

Sebastian watched Lorna and Patrick disappear down the stairs, then turned his attention to the Chronograph in his hand. Gently and silently the hands ticked round the face. Sebastian set it down on the floor beside him and settled back against the wall. This was a good hiding place, he thought. From here, he could see the main entrance door of the church and all the way up to the altar. On the altar was a massive golden cross, and above it a stained-glass window with a picture of Christ surrounded by angels. Sebastian knew it was Christ because his mother had told him that day when Joseph had died and gone to live with Jesus, and they'd said prayers in church.

Sebastian blew out his cheeks and gave a big sigh. It already felt like Lorna and Patrick had been gone forever. He started counting the flagstones on the floor, then lost count and started chewing his thumbnail instead. Trust Patrick to lead them somewhere weird. Sebastian didn't like Patrick.

"Always looking down 'is nose at me," he muttered, drawing circles on the dusty floor. "Like he's some toff and I'm dirt." Lorna was different. She made him feel like he mattered, and he'd do anything for her. She'd understood about the crypt and trusted him with the

Chronograph, something Patrick would never do. "Just you wait," he muttered under his breath, "You'll see what I can do. Then you won't be Lord High and Mighty anymore. Just you…"

The echoing of footsteps made him look up. Someone was approaching, not from the main door, but from the vestry at the back, and coming up the nave. Sebastian crept quietly along the back of the pew. He was good at creeping. He'd had plenty of practice, having to sneak in and out of the house unnoticed when his father was around. The footsteps stopped, and he froze, hardly daring to breathe, but then they continued, going away from him. Sebastian cautiously poked his head above the pew, then fell back, his heart rattling hard against his chest. A tall, dark man was walking towards the crypt. Wretchedly, he watched the Keeper disappear through the door.

Sebastian flushed hot and cold. He'd let Lorna down. He was supposed to be lookout. He crept to the top of the steps and listened to the raised voices below. He heard Patrick yell, "You bastard!" then the voices continued, a little muffled so he could only hear snatches of the conversation. When he heard the man say, "Hand it over!" he backed away from the door, his thoughts whirling. What if they told the Keeper he had the Chronograph? The man would be back up the stairs in a flash, doing that pointing thing he'd done to Mr Hanson, and it would all be over.

Sebastian ran back along the pew, stuffing the Chronograph deep in his pocket, and made for the main door of the church. He hesitated for a moment, decided to avoid the lychgate at the front, and pelted through the gravestones across the churchyard towards the hedge at the back, hoping he could somehow squeeze his way through. In one corner he spotted a stile and leapt over, crashing headfirst into the chest of someone about to climb over in the opposite direction.

"Hoy!" exclaimed a deep voice, and before Sebastian could make a run for it, he found himself in a strong grasp, his arms pinned to his sides. Sebastian looked up into the face of a man wearing a black hat and a long black coat. It was the vicar.

"Where are you off to in such a hurry?" the vicar asked.

"Nowhere." Sebastian struggled in the man's grip. "Lemme go, I ain't done nothing."

The vicar peered at him. "I know most of the boys in the village, and you're not one of them. Who are you?" Sebastian shrugged.

"I see. Well, whoever you are, you'd better come with me. It's getting dark and I won't allow a child to spend the night out of doors. We'll lock the church first and then go back to the vicarage."

"No!" exclaimed Sebastian.

"No?" said the vicar. "You have somewhere else to go?"

"No, but..." Sebastian faltered. Telling this man about Patrick and Lorna with the enemy in the crypt didn't seem like a good idea. The vicar was a large man, but Sebastian doubted he'd be a match for the Keeper. He was so evil, you could almost smell it.

"It's locked already," he lied.

The vicar frowned. "It is? Maybe the organist called in earlier to practise and took care of it. All the same..."

"Think I'd be runnin' off somewhere else for the night if I could've got in?" Sebastian thanked heaven for the organist and faked a loud sneeze for good measure. As he did so, he noticed a tendril of black mist beginning to creep round the far corner of the church. Heart thumping, he looked at the vicar and sneezed again.

"God bless you!" said the vicar. "Well, I can always check later. Let's get you indoors." He put an arm round Sebastian, swathing him in his cloak and hurried him away from the stile towards the lane and the vicarage. Sneaking a look over his shoulder, Sebastian saw the mist hesitate for a moment by a far-off gravestone, then retreat and disappear. He gave a sigh of relief. Maybe the dark bad stuff didn't like vicars.

"We have a guest, Mrs Bradley," said the vicar handing his hat to a short, dumpy-looking woman as they entered. "This is ...?"

"Joseph," said Sebastian.

"Joseph. The coat of many colours." The vicar had an odd look in his eye. "I was on my way back from the Donaldson's – she's not doing at all well I'm afraid - and I gave Joseph quite a start by the churchyard."

"Indeed?" Mrs Bradley raised one eyebrow. "And will *Joseph* be joining you for supper, Reverend Cartwright?"

"He will," Reverend Cartwright replied. "Go with Mrs. Bradley now, Joseph. She'll take care of you." He disappeared into his study and shut the door. Sebastian felt a sinking feeling in his stomach. The housekeeper looked at him as if she had a nasty smell under her nose and he scowled back.

"Hurry yourself up then," she said. "Don't dawdle." Sebastian slouched after her to the kitchen at the end of the house. Mrs Bradley fetched a tin bath, which she placed before the fire and then started filling with pitcher after pitcher of water.

"In," she ordered.

Feeling he had no choice, Sebastian peeled off his clothes and did as he was told.

"Get that hair washed too!" Mrs Bradley snapped, throwing a bundle of rags on the fire.

"Hey!" Sebastian cried out. "You can't do that, them's me clothes!"

"Nonsense," she replied, "dropping to pieces they were. I have clothes for you here. The Reverend keeps some - for poor cases." She gave Sebastian a dark look and sniffed.

"But I need them!" he wailed, thinking about the Chronograph that he'd left in his pocket and was now going up in flames.

"Need them? What on earth for? Now stop being so silly and get yourself dried off. Reverend wants his supper and you're keeping him waiting."

They were interrupted by a jangling sound. "Now who on earth can that be!" Irritated, the housekeeper opened the kitchen door and bustled out of the kitchen. Sebastian followed as far as the doorway, then shrank back as a familiar dark voice floated down the passageway.

"Good evening, Madam. I'm looking for a small boy. Quite skinny, dressed in rags. It's most important I locate him."

"Who's asking?" Mrs Bradley asked suspiciously.

"Ah yes, I should have explained. I'm from St Mark's Bar. Doubtless you've heard about the murder of the clockmaker there. Harmless old man. The boy was his apprentice."

"A murderer!" Mrs Bradley exclaimed. "Well now, I probably shouldn't say, not without the Reverend here, but..."

"But I am here, Mrs Bradley." Sebastian held his breath as Reverend Cartwright's voice interrupted the others.

"Now, Sir," the Reverend continued. "What makes you think such a child would be all the way out here? St. Mark's Bar is a very long way, surely?"

"Ah, Reverend. Of course, you will believe the best of all God's creatures, but this one is devious and quite capable I'm afraid. And he stole a very valuable watch. I absolutely must have it back. Now I believe Mrs Bradley was about to say something."

"I...well now...," Mrs Bradley faltered. "We did have someone begging today. City child like you said, but I gave him some bread and sent him packing. I didn't mention it, Reverend, because you will always insist on taking them in, and I won't see you taken advantage of, not anymore!"

"You must stop fussing over me, Mrs Bradley," the Reverend replied. "I know you mean well, but...there you have it, Sir. I can assure you we have no murderers here."

The Keeper sighed. "You didn't see which way he went I suppose?"

"I did not," Mrs Bradley replied tartly. "Said he wanted money to get back to St Mark's Bar. I told him to try the stage down at the King's Head and see if he could work his way back, lazy little blighter. He ran off then. Didn't know he was a murderer though, and if he turns up here again..."

"You will let me know of course. Especially if you find the watch. Naturally, I am offering a substantial reward for its return..." The Keeper let the words hang in the air.

"We'll keep our wits about us," Reverend Cartwright said.

"Of course. I will try the inn. Maybe they will know something. Good evening."

Sebastian heard the front door close and breathed a sigh of relief. Mrs Bradley followed Reverend Cartwright back into his study and closed the door. Sebastian could hear the rise and fall of voices and crept forward to hear more. Suddenly the Reverend shouted "Enough!" and the door flew open. Sebastian shot back down the passageway as a tight-lipped Mrs Bradley emerged, smoothing her apron before stalking back into the kitchen. Sebastian was seated at the table as she entered, pretending he'd been there all along.

"The Reverend has asked if you will now join him," she said stiffly. "And I, apparently, am to go home." Sebastian watched as she gathered her things.

"I've told the Reverend that if he wishes to break the Commandments to protect scruffy little murderers and thieves that's up to him," she said, pausing by the back door. "But he needn't expect me to do it no more. You'd better be gone by morning!" She left, shutting the door with a bang. Swallowing hard, Sebastian made his way to the study and tapped on the door.

"Come in," the Reverend smiled, pulling out a chair at the table for him. Sebastian gave him a sideways look and sat with his hands in his lap. "Eat!" the man laughed. "You must be hungry, of that, I'm sure!"

Sebastian spooned egg slowly into his mouth and flicked a glance at the Reverend. He was drinking tea, watching Sebastian over the rim of the cup. Sebastian started on toast. The Reverend helped himself to more tea.

"Now, what can you tell me about this?" he said and placed the Chronograph on the table. Sebastian nearly brought his egg back up. Mrs Bradley must have found the Chronograph among his clothes and handed it over. Now there'd be trouble.

"I don't believe for one second that you murdered anyone," the Reverend continued. "But theft is another matter."

Sebastian said nothing. He looked down at his plate and wished Reverend Cartwright would disappear.

"The man that came here tonight. He did not seem a good sort of person," the Reverend said. "For a start, he seemed more concerned with this watch than the clockmaker who died. How did you come to be mixed up with him?"

Sebastian said nothing. Reverend Cartwright leaned forward. "You must trust me, Joseph. Otherwise, how can I help you?"

Sebastian looked up into the man's face. The eyes were kind. "I didn't kill no-one. And I didn't steal nothin' neither. My name's Sebastian. I'm sorry I lied." He dug his knuckles in his eyes. "So much strange stuff's bin happening. I don't understand. And you won't believe me."

"Let me decide what I will and will not believe," the Reverend said gently. "Tell me."

Sebastian felt the tension in him snap. In a great rush, he told Reverend Cartwright everything, about Hanson, the Chronograph, the murder, Lorna, Patrick, and the Keeper's appearance at the church. The Reverend didn't interrupt once, but sat back in his chair, his expression unfathomable. When Sebastian had finished, he miserably swung his legs and waited. Reverend Cartwright cleared his throat.

"For such a fanciful story, there are only two possibilities," he said. "Either you're an expert liar or you're telling the truth. But in my experience, a liar tends to tell a more plausible tale. Of course, you could be mad…but, for the present, we'll assume not. Where are the others now?"

"I don't know," Sebastian replied. "After he went down the crypt, I left sharpish. I'm not stupid."

"But your friends? They're still down there?"

"I didn't wait around to find out," Sebastian whispered. "What if he killed them?"

"And what if he didn't?" the Reverend said grimly. "But he may have hurt them. We must find out."

Sebastian followed as he strode out of the room to the kitchen. The Reverend rapidly filled three small bags with food, then handed a couple of heavy cloaks to Sebastian. "Here. Who knows what lies ahead. It's best we're prepared."

Then he retrieved a lamp from behind the door and, after locking the vicarage, they made their way quietly to the church. The night was warm, and the moon bright as they passed through the lychgate. The trees cast shadows that morphed from playful to menacing the deeper they walked into the churchyard, the gravestones lurking within them like shrouded ghouls crouched ready to pounce. Sebastian expected the Keeper to appear at any moment, and when an owl shrieked, he gasped and grabbed at Reverend Cartwright's coat in fright. The man tried the heavy church door, which opened.

"So, not locked after all," he said.

Sebastian blushed in the darkness. "I'm sorry."

"No matter. You acted for the best."

Cautiously, they entered, and when Reverend Cartwright was satisfied that nobody was lurking in the darkness, he took out a bunch of keys and locked the main door before they crossed the floor to the crypt. This time, the door was locked.

"The spare key usually hangs up there," he said, indicating an empty hook. "Our friend must have used it." He took another key from the bunch and turned it in the lock. "Now, Sebastian. Let us see what we shall see." Taking a deep breath, Sebastian followed the light of the lamp and descended into the darkness.

CHAPTER 11

Rescue

Something was digging Lorna in the ribs. For a moment she thought it was Simon, poking her with a ruler to get her attention in the lunch queue like he often did. In her dream she was telling him to get stuffed, she had someone else now. Simon looked like he couldn't believe he wasn't Mr Super-Stud anymore, then something nudged her again and a voice that wasn't Simon's said, "Wake up."

"What is it? Where are we?" she said drowsily.

"In that bloody awful crypt, remember? Your kind stepfather locked us in. We have to figure out a way out of here."

"Oh." She remembered now. The crypt. And Patrick. They'd been kissing, hadn't they? Sort of gentle and then ...well...It would have been pretty hot, if it wasn't for the fact that his mother had just been killed. That made it sort of desperate, like he thought he could kiss away the loss or something. Still, she didn't blame him. It had helped her too in a funny way, and it was years since her dad died. It probably wouldn't happen again.

"Any ideas then?" she said, sitting up. "It's pitch black in here. I can't see a damn thing."

"Do you still have that pocket-fire thing? We need to see if there's another way out of here."

Lorna found the lighter in her pocket and after a couple of clicks managed to conjure up a small flame. Casting the feeble light around, they found a torch above them on the wall and lit it.

"That's better," Patrick said. "Come on."

They poked about for a time without success and then sat down on the bottom step.

"We could jump on him," Lorna suggested. "When he comes back, I mean. Wait at the top of the stairs, chuck him down and run for it."

"It's worth a try," said Patrick, "or at least, I can try and hold him back while you get out of here. You could find Sebastian and Miller's Leap and all that…"

"You think I'd leave you to him. Don't be daft."

The sudden sound of the door above them grating across the stone floor made them jump. "Put it out," hissed Lorna, frantically blowing at the torch, "we don't want to make things easier for him."

"Oh my God, he's not alone," whispered Patrick. They froze as two sets of footsteps descended the stairs.

"I'll try and create some kind of diversion, and you make a run for it," Patrick whispered again.

"No way!"

"For once in your life, just do as you're told, will you?"

Before she could hiss back any retort, two shadowy figures appeared at the bottom of the steps. One was bigger than the other by far, the taller one bearing a lantern that cast barely enough light to see by.

"Quiet now," came a man's low voice. "And try not to trip on anything, it can be quite uneven down here."

"I'm all right," came a familiar whisper.

"Sebastian!" breathed Lorna in Patrick's ear.

"Wait," whispered Patrick. "Who's he with?"

The two figures advanced, then stopped. "Where now?" asked the boy.

"We'll start searching here," said the man. "Very slowly. Stay by my side."

It wasn't the Keeper, that much was clear.

"I think it's all right," Lorna whispered. "He doesn't sound scared." She called softly. "Sebastian!" The two shadows jumped simultaneously and turned.

"Lorna!" cried Sebastian, flinging his arms around her waist. Then he stepped back, embarrassed. She winked at him.

"Glad to see me then?"

He gave her a grin and nodded. "Where's Patrick?"

"Here." Patrick stepped into the light. "Who's your friend?"

"I am the Reverend Cartwright," The man held out his hand. "Young Sebastian fell into my care this evening. He told me of your circumstances, you might say."

"Really?" said Patrick suspiciously. "And just how much of our circumstances did he tell you, I wonder."

"You're unbelievable," Lorna said. "Sebastian brought help and that's all that matters. Now hadn't we better get out of here before the Keeper comes back?"

"My thoughts exactly," said Reverend Cartwright. "It's a fair way to the inn, but once he discovers that Sebastian did not leave on any coach to St Mark's Bar this evening, he's bound to start searching round here again…If you would follow me."

The Reverend led them back through the church and into the bottom of the bell tower. They stopped and looked at each other.

"What now?" Lorna said. "I don't suppose you know anything about a Maid of the Falls, Reverend Cartwright?

Seems like we're supposed to find her, but as far as I know there's no falls round here."

"Oh, but there are!" the Reverend exclaimed. "I don't know about a maid, but the falls are upstream at Miller's Leap, about five miles from here. Quite spectacular."

"Miller's Leap?" Lorna frowned, confused. "There's no waterfall there, just a bit of an outcrop, that's all."

Reverend Cartwright looked surprised. "Is that so? How sad that in your time, years from now, the Falls have disappeared." Lorna's mouth fell open. "Oh yes. Sebastian told me everything. I know exactly who you are. But do not worry."

He delved into his waistcoat and brought out the Chronograph. "I believe this is yours." He handed it to Lorna. "Guard it well. I don't understand its significance, I only feel that if this Keeper gets his hands on it, it will spell disaster. Whatever your mission is, you must succeed, for who knows what could be at stake?"

She pocketed the instrument carefully. "I understand. And thank you."

Reverend Cartwright nodded and unlocked the door. "You should be able to leave from here unnoticed. Cut across the fields, it will be quicker than following the river and safer than the road. Heed your instincts and be careful in whom you trust. Sebastian," he turned and shook the boy's hand. "A privilege to meet you. I do trust that you will visit me again - when times are better. In the meantime, I will pray for your safety. Now…"

He opened the door, then reeled back as an icy blast hit him. The others shivered. Beyond lay a carpet of snow, already several inches deep and growing deeper with the blizzard that now howled outside.

"Bloody hell," Patrick swore. "Sorry, Reverend. But what in the name of Time is going on? It's summer. We were sweltering only a few hours ago."

"The Chronograph!" Lorna was shaking. "Look, it's going crazy!" The hands were swinging wildly back and forth, then over each other, while the tiny silver wire snowflake was glowing so brightly, it looked as though it would burn its way through the glass covering the face of the instrument. "What does it mean?"

"I don't know," Patrick said, "But there's no way we can go through this. Maybe we can find somewhere else to hide until it blows over."

"It won't," Reverend Cartwright said. "Don't you see? First you fall through time, now the seasons are awry. I think the Chronograph is an indicator of how unstable things are becoming. Time appears to be falling apart and I fear that you have little of it left."

"He's right," Lorna said. "Besides, we can't stay. It's the snow or the Keeper, and I know which I prefer."

"All right," Patrick agreed. "But what about Sebastian? Maybe he should stay."

"What and leave me here for the Keeper!" Sebastian yelled, his small face red with anger. "Thanks a lot!"

"That's not what I meant; you know it isn't. I just thought…"

"Yeah, I know what you thought. Well, no such luck, mate. I'm coming."

"If I thought it would be safer, I'd insist that you stay," agreed Reverend Cartwright. "But I doubt I could protect you when the time came. Better you go on together - and I shall try to divert any unwanted attention."

Clutching their cloaks around them, they crossed to the far corner of the churchyard, bent against the bitter wind.

Reverend Cartwright helped them over the wall, before climbing over to join them.

"Go about a quarter of a mile till you reach a gate." He pointed up the lane. "Then cross the field beyond and keep going up the hill. Just over the other side there's a shepherd's hut, you can probably rest there for a while. But do not stay too long. And keep to the hedgerows where you can, they'll shelter you – and maybe hide you too. God be with you."

With a wave, he turned and trudged back down the narrow lane, disappearing quickly in the thick haze of snow. Lorna felt Sebastian's hand slip into hers.

"I wish he was coming with us," he said.

"Me too. But I guess we must do this alone. Come on now, Patrick's waiting."

~

Reverend Cartwright took the long way round the back of the churchyard and down several little lanes on his way back to the vicarage. With some relief, he saw the light that he had left in the front window, but then his heart sank as a tall dark figure crossed the path in front of him, standing between him and the gate.

"A bad night to be out, Reverend," said the Keeper.

"Indeed," the Reverend replied. "But sick parishioners can't wait. Now would you let me pass."

"Certainly." The Keeper gave a mock bow and stepped to one side. "I did not find the boy. I don't suppose he showed up. After my visit?"

"In Heaven's name!" exclaimed Reverend Cartwright. "Just look at the weather will you, man! A small child would freeze to death in this. Try looking in a few barns around here, he's probably in one of them trying to keep warm. Unless he managed to find his way to St Mark's Bar of course."

"There are two others with him," the Keeper persisted. "I don't suppose you'd know anything about them, would you?"

"No, I wouldn't," the Reverend snapped. "Now, I've had enough of these questions on my doorstep. I'm freezing cold and I've had a long day. Why don't you come back tomorrow if you want to continue this conversation?"

"No need, Reverend. But I must warn you that anyone found harbouring individuals wanted by the authorities will be in severe trouble."

The Reverend Cartwright stood his ground, "I don't see what that has to do with me."

"Then you have nothing to worry about," said the Keeper, in a tone that implied otherwise. He half raised his arm, then a thought seemed to sweep across his face, and he lowered it again. He nodded politely, before heading off in the direction of the village, his dark figure soon obscured by the worsening snowstorm.

"God willing that I will not see you again." The Reverend crossed himself and shivered, although not from the cold. "And I pray to Heaven the young people stay safe." With one last look after the Keeper, he hurried through the gate and into the warmth of his home.

CHAPTER 12

Winter's Journey

"This sucks!" Lorna said. No matter how tightly she wrapped her cloak round her, the cold penetrated as the snow whipped past, forming great drifts against the hedgerows. It was getting deeper, over the top of her Doc Martens now, soaking her jeans and making her legs feel like sticks of ice. She could just make out Patrick's figure ahead of her, doing his best to stomp out a trench for them while he walked.

"You okay?" she shouted to Sebastian behind her and waited for him to catch up.

"I'm all right," he said through chattering teeth. "But I think if I stop, I'll die." He ploughed on past her, a tiny hobgoblin hunched over against the wind with his cloak pulled over his head.

They'd found the gate easily. The snow had already piled up against it, forcing them to make a slippery climb over, before making their way round the edge of the field to the opposite side, sticking to the hedgerow as the Reverend had advised. Now another gate loomed in front of them, separating the field from the sweeping, open expanse of hill beyond.

"We'll have to climb over again." Patrick shoved at the gate unsuccessfully. "Then keep on straight up the hill. Think you can manage, Sebastian?"

"Course I can," Sebastian said obstinately. "Not the first time I seen snow, is it? Bet I'm more used to it than you are."

"Suit yourself, I only asked." Patrick began to climb the gate.

"For Chrissakes..." Lorna stopped. She wished the boys would stop sniping at each other. Things had been better when they were with Reverend Cartwright, but now the old tensions seemed to be growing again. It'll all end in tears, her gran used to say. Lorna remembered that now and shuddered.

"For Chrissakes what?" Patrick said. He was sitting astride the gate, looking down at them.

Next to her, Sebastian was almost up to his knees in snow. How the kid was going to manage if it got any deeper was anybody's guess.

"Nothing, I just wish it would stop snowing."

"I wouldn't be so sure," Patrick warned. "Snow's covered our tracks so far. Be careful what you wish for." He jumped down the other side, took a few paces and came back.

"What's up?" asked Lorna, jumping down next to him.

"It's getting really deep," Patrick whispered. They both looked at Sebastian who was peering through the bars of the gate at them.

"Wot yer whispering about?" he asked.

"Nothing," Lorna said. "Change of plan. Here, let me give you a hand."

Sebastian gave her a dirty look. "I can manage." He joined them in silence. "So, what's the problem?"

"Snow's too deep here," Patrick said shortly. "We'll have to find another way."

"I can walk in bloody snow!"

"Sure you can. It's up to your knees already. Anyway, it's not just about you, see? I reckon it'll be too much for any of us. We'll stick to the hedgerow on this side and keep going across rather than up. Maybe there'll be another path."

"What about the shepherd's hut?" said Lorna. "It can't be that much further."

"Maybe it is and maybe it isn't. Use your brain why don't you? The weather's getting worse, I can hardly see a damn thing in front of me. Without something like the hedge to guide us, we'll end up going round in circles. And I don't fancy being a frozen corpse on the hillside. We go this way."

They trailed along, the snow whirling thickly round them before settling with the silence of death. Lorna could feel the Chronograph ticking in her pocket, almost in time with their steps. It seemed daft, having this thing and not trying to use it. If it had landed her here, then maybe it could teleport them over to the Falls, or even to where it ultimately needed to be. Maybe Patrick could figure it out. It was something to do with his people after all.

His response to her suggestion was terse. "You crazy? Like things aren't fragile enough already." She was about to argue when Sebastian pointed ahead.

"Look!" The dark outline of a building rose out of the snow ahead of them.

"Bit big for a shepherd's hut, isn't it?" said Lorna. "D'you think it's safe?"

"It's shelter," Patrick replied. "We have to rest."

They increased their pace as best they could. The building turned out to be a barn set some way across the yard from a farmhouse. Everything lay in darkness.

"I don't like this," Lorna whispered. "What if someone comes out and finds us?"

"Don't be daft," Patrick said, pulling open the barn door. "They're all tucked in for the night. By the time they wake up, we'll be long gone. Can I have your pocket-fire thing again?"

"What on earth for? Don't you know there's straw in barns? That's all we need, you burning the place down."

"We have to see what's in here, don't we? Just hand it over, I'll be careful."

Patrick found a lamp on the wall and lit it. "Come on then. And close the door after you."

In the arc of the lamplight, they could see the place was empty except for two cows in the corner. One of them opened its eyes for a moment as the light hit its face, then closed them drowsily again. Something scurried next to Lorna's foot and she gave a little scream. "What the hell was that?"

"A rat most likely," Sebastian said. He didn't sound too bothered. Lorna shuddered. Patrick had set the lamp down away from the cows and was scratching around on the floor near the back wall. "What are you doing?" she said.

"Seeing if I can start a fire without burning the place down." He grinned up at her. "It's all dirt and stones here. And the wood's rotten over there. We can maybe pull some off and use it."

"Won't that leave a big hole?"

"You got a better idea? We've got to do something, or we'll freeze to death. Here, you can help, but watch for splinters."

The resulting fire was small, but as Patrick said, better than nothing. Lorna stripped off her wet jeans and huddled over the fire in one of the old sacks they found hanging on the wall next to the cows. Sebastian sat next to her, teeth chattering and trying to warm his hands over the flames. He grinned at her lopsidedly. "I'm feelin' warmer. I think. Ain't we going to eat?"

Patrick foraged in the bags. "Bread, cheese, ham…Thank you, Reverend Cartwright! We can have a feast!"

"D'you think we'd better save some of it?" Lorna said. "Just in case it's a while before we find food again?"

Patrick frowned. "S'pose so. Although this is a farm, isn't it? Bound to be food lying about somewhere. Maybe Sebastian can work his magic again."

"You mean send him thieving again. No way! It's too risky."

"All right, keep your hair on. Jeez. The kid can speak for himself, can't he?"

"I'll go if you want." Sebastian looked at Lorna, ignoring Patrick.

"No," she shook her head. "I don't much like it here. Let's not do anything else that might attract attention. We've already lit a fire and made a dirty great hole in the wall."

"I suppose you'd rather freeze," Patrick said snappishly.

"No. I'm just sayin'." She took the Chronograph out of her pocket. As she looked at it, it gave a strange little shudder, the big hand juddering around the number eleven before leaping forward ten minutes in one go. "See that? I don't think we should stay too long."

"We'll leave at first light," Patrick said. "Now eat something for heavens' sake. Then I'll keep first watch while you sleep for a bit."

~

A bright light woke Lorna next morning. Sebastian was fast asleep, half-buried in the straw next to her. Patrick was hunched next to the grey ash of the now-dead fire, eyes closed, chest moving in a deep, steady rhythm. So much for keeping watch. The daylight told her they'd slept longer than they should.

Lorna stood up, brushing the straw from her hair, and reached for her jeans. They were freezing damp, stiff as board. She gritted her teeth and began to put them on. She could hardly go about in the old sack. Just as she was doing up the zipper, she heard the clatter of hooves outside as a horse entered the yard, followed by the sound of voices, one male, one female. One sounded horribly familiar.

Quickly she shook Sebastian and then Patrick, putting a finger to her lips to hush them.

"Someone's out there in the yard," she whispered. "I think it's him!"

"What?!" Patrick scrambled to his feet. Sebastian had already scurried to the front of the barn, where he stood with his eye pressed against a crack in the boards.

"It is him," he hissed.

"Let me see," said Patrick. They all huddled against the boards and watched as a dumpy female slid down from the horse and held her hand up to the Keeper.

"It's Mrs Bradley!" Sebastian exclaimed. "The Reverend's housekeeper. What's she doing here?"

"Never mind that, we need to get out of here!" Lorna urged.

"In a minute," Patrick hushed her. "We need to know what he's up to. Not much point running out of here and bumping into him five minutes later."

The Keeper leaned forward on his horse towards the woman. "Thank you for your assistance, Madam."

"Not at all, Sir. It is fortunate that I met you on the road. If your runaway is making for Miller's Leap as you say, he will almost certainly have had to pass my brother-in-law's farm."

The Keeper dropped something in her upturned palm, and she grubbed at it greedily. "Thank you for your generosity, Sir. Most kind, I'm sure."

"He's only given her a few old acorns," Sebastian observed. "What's generous about that?"

"Fool's gold," Patrick said. "A rock in your Time, but it's a party trick in mine. Objects made to look like gold coin in the eyes of those with nothing but greed in their hearts. The Keeper certainly read her well."

"You mean, she really thinks she has a handful of gold?" Sebastian said. Patrick nodded. "Look!" Lorna hissed.

The Keeper had taken from his pocket the same small object he'd tried to use on the track. He looked at it closely, raising it almost to the end of his nose, shook it and peered again. A smile played upon his lips then he threw back his head and roared.

"Power from the darkness!" A spear of black mist shot from the object in his hand and began to curl across the ground towards the barn. Mrs Bradley appeared oblivious, still grubbing at the fool's gold in her hand.

"What's happening?" Sebastian looked up at Patrick.

Patrick pulled them back from the wall. "We've got to get out of here!"

"The hole in the back wall!" Lorna said. "I think we can squeeze through."

Patrick nodded, pale. "Main door's no good. We'd be seen. And anyway...look..."

Fine wisps of blackness were already curling under the barn door.

"Quick, Sebastian!" Lorna shoved at him through the hole. "What's the hold up?"

"I can't go nowhere!"

"What do you mean?" Lorna pulled him back and stuck her head through. A dense bank of black mist was already building a stone's throw from the back of the barn. "Can't we run through it?"

"You can try," Patrick said. "But if I'm right, it won't let you through. Look."

He chucked a stone at the mist advancing under the door. The stone bounced back at double the velocity, almost hitting him in the face.

"What the hell is it?"

"I don't know." Patrick sounded panicked. "Something to do with the Dark Glass... I think it's finally obeyed him."

A commotion came from outside. The mist hesitated. Patrick stepped towards it and flung out his hand, fingers splayed and started muttering under his breath.

"Nathan!" came Mrs Bradley's voice. "What do you think? A murderer is on the loose and making for Miller's Leap!"

"And what has that to do with me, Isobel?" came the reply.

"He must have passed by the farm. And he has accomplices!"

"I've seen no-one. Now be off with you. We don't need your nasty gossip here. Nor you bringing strangers here neither."

"This don't look good," Sebastian said, eye pressed to the crack again. Lorna joined him. The man, Nathan, had a gun levelled directly at the Keeper's chest, not noticing the black mist that was now rolling at knee height across the yard towards the barn.

"Nathan, I'm only helping this gentleman do his duty," Mrs Bradley said rather piously. "We don't want to be murdered in our beds, do we?"

"If I could just check your barn," the Keeper said. "The criminals may have sheltered there from last night's storm. Then I'll be on my way."

"You'll be on your way now, Sir, or I won't be responsible for my actions."

The Keeper raised his arm.

Sebastian leapt back from the wall. "He's doing that pointing thing! Oh, dear Lord, he'll be in here any minute now!"

"The Chronograph!" Lorna exclaimed, shaking it in desperation. "Patrick, if you've any idea how to use it, then for God's sake do it now!"

A shriek came from outside. "Nathan! What've you done to him? No, don't point at me like that, what…" Silence.

A cow wandered out of its stall, smacked into the bank of advancing black mist and tottered backwards, blinking in surprise. Patrick reached out both arms towards the mist now, straining every sinew, muttering what sounded to Lorna like gobbledegook.

"What are you doing?" Lorna flung her arm around Sebastian and pulled him close. "The Chronograph, Patrick. Patrick!"

The young man looked at her in despair. "I can't hold it, Lorna. I thought maybe I could, and somehow make a path through, but I can't."

"We must use the Chronograph! I don't care how fragile Time is. It's the only way!"

The instrument suddenly shuddered and trembled, glowing so brightly it was almost blinding. "Patrick, it's doing something! Hold on to me, for God's sake, or we'll be separated!"

The young man backed towards them, still staving off the advancing mist with all his strength. It seemed as though faces were starting to form in it now, great ugly smoke-filled faces with empty eye sockets and gaping mouths. With Sebastian holding her tightly round the waist, Lorna reached out and grabbed Patrick's arm, her other hand holding the Chronograph aloft as it burned brighter than any star in the sky.

One of the great smoky faces rose above them, then came rushing down, its mouth wide open in a hideous silent scream as if to swallow them whole. Lorna swore that she felt an icy coldness on her fingers as the mouth touched them, but then a dazzling white light seemed to shoot from the Chronograph blasting them backwards. They hit the ground with force and lay there panting, surrounded by whiteness.

CHAPTER 13

The Falls at Miller's Leap

Patrick was the first to stand up. "Where the hell are we?" Lorna joined him. Sebastian sat in the snow, rubbing his eyes.

"More to the point, *when* the hell are we?" Lorna said. "This is like last time. When I got pulled out of my bedroom."

"What did you do to the Chronograph?"

"Nothing. Last time, I dropped it, and that's what started it up again. This time, it just…sort of did stuff on its own. Maybe it didn't like that black mist either."

"What's it doing now?"

Lorna took the instrument out of her pocket. It lay in her hand, not moving. "I think it's stopped. Maybe whatever it did wore it out."

Sebastian stood up and brushed himself down. "It's snowing again." Great fat flakes were falling thickly around them once more. "Well, I ain't waitin' to freeze to death. Come on."

"You're going nowhere," Patrick said, blocking his way. "We could be anywhere or in any Time for all we know. Last thing we need is you wandering off and getting lost."

The boy glowered. "Why should I listen to you? First we goes in that creepy church 'cos you tells us to, and we gets caught. Then you stop us leavin' the barn, and that smoke stuff nearly gets us. Thought you was supposed to be on our side?"

Patrick stood stock still, his face a white mask of anger.

"Sebastian!" Lorna intervened. "Patrick did try to get us out of there. You know he did."

Sebastian shrugged. "All I'm sayin' is we could've bin miles away by now. And standin' round here won't get us nowhere will it? 'Cept caught by that Keeper bloke. I'm off. You do what you like." He shoved past Patrick, who made no attempt to stop him.

"Sebastian!" Lorna yelled. "Come back!" There was no response. The boy stumped on through the deepening snow, hunched over once more against the cold. She turned to Patrick. "We can't just let him go off on his own. Do something!"

"Like what? I haven't exactly got a handbook for petulant kids." Patrick ran his hand through his hair and looked at her helplessly. "All this is beyond me, Lorna. I don't understand any of it."

Lorna touched his arm sympathetically. "You're much nicer you know. When you don't know anything. Kind of... normal instead of pretending to be something else."

"Thanks a bunch." Patrick looked away, embarrassed. "Come on, we'd better catch him up. The kid's a pain in the arse, but we can't leave him."

"He's way over there, look. What on earth's he doing?" Sebastian was jumping up and down, waving his arms and yelling something. They raced after him, coming to an abrupt stop just before a sheer drop.

"Come away from there!" Patrick said angrily. "If the ground gives way, and you go over the edge, don't expect me to come down after you."

The boy scowled. "Why don't you hush your grumbling mouth a moment? You might hear something useful."

"Why you little…"

"No, listen, Patrick," Lorna interrupted him. "Sebastian's right. There is something." They stood in silence for a moment. A distant rumble seemed to be coming from far beneath them.

"The Falls!" Patrick exclaimed. "It has to be! We must be right over them."

"How do we get down?" Sebastian said.

"What about over there," Lorna suggested. "Looks like it slopes down there a bit through the trees. Maybe that'll take us further down."

They set off, following the natural curve of the land as it sloped and made a steep descent between a clutch of fir trees, before coming to a sudden stop.

"Wow!" Lorna breathed. "Just look at that!"

A magnificent waterfall plummeted from the ridge high above them, its edges frozen in long, sparkling ice-blue shards of different lengths and thicknesses, while the centre rumbled earthwards in full frothing flow. Their path had taken them right over the top of the great cascade, then along the edge of a steep gorge through which the river flowed far below. Unfortunately, the only visible route now took them even further along the gorge and away from their destination.

"Hell!" Patrick snapped. "All this bloody way, and we're stuck!"

"That's what I love about you, Patrick, you're always so positive." Lorna peered over the edge to the gorge below. "The Chronograph brought us here, didn't it? There's got to be a way down."

"For God's sake, be careful!" Patrick warned.

"Okay, stop fussing will you…" It was too late. As Lorna made to turn, she felt the ground soften beneath her. She flung a desperate look at Patrick before it gave way entirely, the boys shouting in desperation as she pedalled furiously in the air, hands grabbing for the edge of the cliff. The cliff face passed rapidly before her in a blur of brown and white, then she smacked into something solid beneath her, slid a way further and came to a halt. She sat winded for a moment, then started shaking with the relief that she was still alive. Looking up, it was clear that the initial fall was no further than dropping out of her bedroom window as she'd done many times at home, it was the slope that had taken her further down. She stood up gingerly and checked the Chronograph in her pocket.

"It's all right!" she shouted up to the others. "There's a sort of ledge down here. You can't see it from above."

"Thank God!" Patrick was lying on his stomach, looking over the edge at her, his face nearly as white as the snow from shock. Sebastian looked tentatively over his shoulder.

"How do we get her back up again?"

"I don't know. Lorna, is there any way you can climb back?"

"I can try, but the rock's all smooth, I don't think I can hold on."

"Don't risk it then. What about that ledge? Does it go anywhere?"

"It goes along here a bit. Hang on a minute." She walked on a few paces. The ledge rounded a bit of an outcrop, then continued, forming a pathway that jutted out from the cliff face. "You know what?" she called up to them. "I think it might go all the way behind the Falls!"

"Wait there!" Patrick shouted.

"Take your time, I'm not going anywhere." She sat down on a boulder as the boys' voices floated down to her.

"Come on, Sebastian, you go first."

"You barmy? I'm not getting meself killed. Go first yerself."

"Look you little twerp! You're not going to die. You just need to jump down to that platform-thing sticking out there, and then slide down to where Lorna is. I'll show you."

A moment later, Patrick appeared over the edge and slid about another ten feet to join her, giving her a shaky smile and a thumbs-up as he arrived. Sebastian stood tentatively on the edge, then, holding his nose like he was about to jump into deep water, took a large step into thin air and more by luck than judgement arrived safely next to them.

"Let's hope it really does go all the way round," Patrick said, "or we're stuffed. Lead on!"

They progressed slowly along the ledge, watching out for icy patches, until they eventually passed behind the curtain of water and stood facing the back of the Falls. A wave of disappointment hit them.

"Of all the…" Patrick smacked the solid wall of rock blocking any further progress. "You'd think there'd at least be a tunnel or something. Where the hell are you, Glenelven when we need you?" he yelled up at the sky. "Where's anyone?"

"What now?" asked Sebastian. "We can't go back."

"How the hell am I supposed to know? I'm sick of this. We just lurch from one bloody crisis to the next."

Patrick sagged against the rockface, drained of all energy. Sebastian sank down, head buried in his hands. The Falls roared behind them. Lorna turned and stared into the cascade of water pounding in a great sparkling sheet to the depths below. There was nothing useful to be said. The only saving grace was that the Keeper probably wouldn't find them here, but on the other hand, they couldn't stay forever. She wondered where on earth they could go now. They seemed beaten at every turn, every path a dead end, with the Keeper drawing closer all the time, breathing his evil down their necks.

"Lorna..." She turned round at the sound of Sebastian's voice, small and scared behind her.

"What is it? Where's Patrick?"

"I dunno. I just looked up, like, and ...he's gone."

"What d'you mean, gone? He can't just disappear into thin air."

"Maybe he magicked himself out of here. He's one of them Time people ain't he?"

"Don't be daft! He wouldn't do that. He wouldn't just leave us..." She could hear the doubt creeping into her voice. He'd had enough and if he had a way out... "Patrick!" she yelled. There was no answer.

"Think, Sebastian, what was he doing right before he vanished?"

"Dunno. He yelled a bit didn't he? Then he leaned against the rock there lookin' half dead."

"Hmmm." Lorna took the Chronograph out of her pocket. It shuddered a little, one of the hands swinging forward in a circle, then back on itself, then forward again. "Look at this. Forward and back but going nowhere. Like us. Maybe it's trying to tell us something." She felt along the rock face, deep in thought.

"It's solid," Sebastian said. "Ain't no way through there."

"I'm not so sure...look here." She pressed the rock where Patrick last stood. At first it felt solid to her touch, but with a gentle push, it seemed to soften and melt on the surface before turning solid again. The hand on the Chronograph made a final forward sweep in response, then stopped. She turned to Sebastian. "I think he got through here. Maybe it was something he said, or because he's one of them."

"Why didn't he say somethin' then? Reckon we can get through too?"

"Maybe. We've got the Chronograph, haven't we? That must count for something. Here, hold my hand and for heaven's sake don't let go."

Lorna pushed once more against the rockface. Gradually, it gave way in front of them, and they stepped into a gritty brown haze that felt damp and cloying on the skin. Suddenly, Lorna felt Sebastian being pulled forward by some unknown force, and his hand left hers with a jerk. "Sebastian!" she cried, but her voice came out sounding deep and muddy. The rock behind had solidified again, so there was no choice but to go on. She pushed forward, feeling the wall soften once more, then she was through. She found herself in a dark cavern, the only light coming from a small arc of silvery light, falling like a spotlight some way ahead of her. In it stood three shadowy figures. As Lorna approached, she could see that two of the figures were Patrick and Sebastian. The third was a woman with an ethereal beauty so arresting, it made Lorna stop in her tracks.

The woman had long golden hair that curled gently to her waist, crowned by a circlet of tiny pink rosebuds. It was impossible to guess her age, but her features reminded Lorna of Patrick's mother in the crypt, and she wondered if they might be related. Her dress, a pale blue shift with long sleeves, was reminiscent of pictures of mediaeval women in history books. A gold rope belt circled the woman's slim waist, at the end of which was an hourglass. The sand, Lorna noticed, was also pale blue in colour, and had nearly run through.

"Thank the Lord you're finally here!" the woman held out her hands to Lorna, sounding relieved. "I'm sorry I could not bring you further. I could only hope you would find the rest of the way and make it through the Veil in time, for this Age is nearly at its end."

Lorna looked at the boys. Sebastian stood with his mouth half open, while Patrick had the sort of look on his face that Simon had had when the new French language assistant at school turned out to be a young female with legs up to her armpits. Simon had followed her around for weeks like a besotted puppy, opening doors and carrying her bags, totally bewitched. Pathetic, Lorna said to herself.

"You brought us here?" she said aloud. "How?"

"I felt a great jolt of energy," the woman said. "It alerted me that you were close and in peril. I focused every ounce of strength I had to shield you, but the counter energy was so strong. The Chronograph must have aligned with my projection and pulled you out from wherever you were to safety."

Lorna's hand flew to her pocket, clenching protectively round the instrument that lay there.

"You do have it then?" the woman smiled.

Lorna looked at her defiantly. "Don't know what you mean."

"You need not fear me. I am the Maid of the Falls, Guardian of this Age of the Past. I have been expecting you. For it written in the Book that the Maker, Bearer, and Protector of the Chronograph, shall come to seek sanctuary and counsel."

"It was you what got us here then?" Sebastian said. "And the Chronograph? Not what Patrick done?"

"Patrick? What did Patrick do?" The Maid turned and looked at the young man for some moments, as if taking in every particle of Patrick's being. Lorna felt a pang in her chest.

"The Keeper." Patrick seemed to have woken up. "He summoned this kind of dark mist; I don't know how else to describe it. We were surrounded. I tried to hold it back, create a way for the others to get through…"

"You tried to create a borehole?" Patrick nodded. The woman reached out and touched his cheek. "Then it may have been that, clashing with the dark energy, that alerted me. A brave move in the face of such evil. Only an experienced Guardian may achieve such a thing, and even then, at great risk. You might have been killed."

"He has the Dark Glass," Lorna said suddenly. "Whatever that is."

"All the black stuff came out of it," Sebastian added. "It had all these spooky faces in it. They nearly swallowed us."

The Maid looked thoughtful. "So, he tried to summon the Armies. A step too far for our clever Keeper. Now it has failed, he may not use that method again."

"So, there'll be no more smoke?" Sebastian asked.

The Maid smiled at him. "No. No more smoke. And whatever visions he may have seen to track you will be greatly dulled. But be warned. He still holds an instrument that contains a deadly power. Let us hope that he does not use it…" She stood for a moment, seemingly lost in thought. "But come now. Enough of us standing in this darkness. Welcome to one of the Great Places outside Time. Welcome to my Garden."

With a sweep of her arm, the darkness faded to dawn then bright daylight, revealing an open parkland, teeming with roses. A secret garden behind the Falls.

CHAPTER 14

The Rose Garden

"Come." The Maid led the way down some steps hewn into the rock, then over a small stone bridge and along a broad path that wound to the horizon. Everywhere Lorna looked she could see and smell roses of every size, hue, and fragrance imaginable. Some stood tall and to attention, while others grew haphazardly round trees or wound round each other like great bridesmaids' posies on wiry stems that nodded and bowed in the breeze. From time to time, a haze of silver mist sprayed upwards from the ground, watering the blooms with gentle care. She wandered off the path and among the bushes, the assault of colour and perfume almost overwhelming her.

"Here." Patrick pressed something into her palm. It was a tiny red rose, devoid of thorns and perfectly formed. He smiled at her then, a strange smile she didn't quite understand. Was he mocking her? Or something else? She was suddenly aware of Sebastian, leaning against a tree, watching them.

"Thanks," she said gruffly, then winked at Sebastian and stuck her tongue out. Sebastian laughed.

"I love it here!" he shouted. "This is the best place I've ever bin!" He ran, whooping, up the path after the Maid.

Patrick gave a wry smile and stuck his hands in his pockets. "So long as he's happy I s'pose."

"He's a cool kid. You should get to know him instead of..."

"Instead of what?"

"Well, you haven't exactly made an effort have you?"

"For Chrissakes! Why're you giving me a goddam lecture about some grubby kid? What's he to you?"

"That grubby kid shouldn't be involved in all this!" Lorna said furiously. She looked down the path to where Sebastian was chatting animatedly with the Maid and felt a surge of protective warmth flood over her. "What the hell do your people think they're doing, Patrick, bringing a ten-year-old into a fight with some bastard like the Keeper? I just want to make sure Sebastian's okay. We can't all go wandering off when we like without saying anything." She watched as her last sentence hit home. Patrick whistled through his teeth.

"Jeez, Lorna, is your opinion of me so low that you think I'd abandon you and Sebastian?" Lorna's cheeks burned. She said nothing.

"Thanks for nothing." Patrick looked away, his mouth in a firm angry line. "For your information, the rock sucked me through before I even knew what was happening."

He glared at her for a moment, then turned and started to walk up the path away from her. "You coming or what?" he called over his shoulder. "Or are you waiting to accuse me of something else?"

Lorna's stomach churned with emotion. Why did she have to pick a fight with Patrick like that? It was stupid. The whole thing was stupid. Besides, it was nuts having feelings for someone who was such an arrogant pig and

so mean to Sebastian. Despite what happened in the crypt
— Lorna blushed at the memory — Patrick would never feel
anything real for her anyway. Look how ga-ga he was over
the Maid. She trailed her way behind Patrick until they
arrived at a lush green clearing surrounded by weeping
willows and bathed in soft light. Sebastian was already
lounging on the springy turf.

"Where you bin? This is great, like a big soft bed."

The Maid laughed. "I'm glad you approve. The Garden
has been a place of peace through the Ages, a sanctuary
where the weary can rest, safe from the troubles of the
world. The Spell of Sanctuary is what allowed you through
— only those in true peril may enter."

Lorna scowled. A hand slipped into hers. "Cheer up,"
Patrick's voice whispered in her ear. "I don't fancy her you
know. She's a stunner, but it feels like it wouldn't be right
somehow. Anyway," he looked down at her teasingly,
"she's out of my league. I prefer to play where there's a
safer bet."

"Get stuffed!" Lorna tossed her head and removed her
hand, wondering how he'd detected her thoughts about
him and the Maid. The young man looked at her, amused.

"Glad to be of service. Now stop sulking and come and
sit down. Look, I'll even sit next to Sebastian to make you
happy."

"Over here, Lorna," the Maid called. "You must be
hungry. Come and be fed." Lorna and Patrick sat either
side of Sebastian. The Maid began to walk around the
clearing, humming to herself. A gentle warm breeze began
to blow, bringing with it a sound like wind chimes, their
high and deep notes floating on the air. Before long, Lorna
heard a familiar whistling snore to her right. Sebastian was
asleep.

"Wake up," she hissed. "Don't you want anything to eat?" But Sebastian was gone to a land of deep dreams and unreachable. Looking over, Lorna saw Patrick slide down the tree he'd been leaning against and roll gently onto the turf, eyes closed. She wanted to feel panic, but the honeyed notes whispered in her ears, then cradled her mind before entering like a thick, rich chocolate, reverberating through the brain. The perfume from the roses grew stronger and the notes louder, like a great bath of sound. Lorna slid into unconsciousness and knew no more.

She woke to someone shaking her gently by the shoulder. It was Sebastian. Day had turned to dusk, the fragrance of the roses had faded, and the air was still. The peace of the garden had turned to silence - not at all the same thing, Lorna thought. The place seemed pregnant with apprehension. Patrick and the Maid were nowhere to be seen.

"Where's Patrick?" she whispered.

"Dunno," replied Sebastian in equally low tones. "He woke me up and said that the Maid seemed anxious about something. He went with her back to the entrance by the Falls."

"Without the rest of us?" said Lorna. "What's he playing at?"

"You still got the Chronograph?" Sebastian asked.

Lorna felt in her pocket. "Yes. It's still there."

"That's something then. At least she ain't nicked it." The small boy paused a moment. "You know what's weird? She said she'd feed us and all she done was put us to sleep. But I ain't hungry no more."

"Everything's weird," Lorna replied. They sat in the dusky gloom, hardly speaking. The light had turned a ghostly grey, and the blooms of the roses that had bobbed heavy with scented peace earlier in the day, now hung like phantom fists on spindly arms. Occasionally one moved, a shadow in the twilight, and made Sebastian jump. Lorna felt his hand slip into hers and she squeezed it in return, both growing more nervous by the second.

"Listen," whispered Sebastian. Footsteps were swishing through the grass towards the clearing. Patrick and the Maid had returned. She was wearing a dark green cloak, cowl-like around her head and shoulders, gathering it about her as if against a cold wind. Patrick looked grim. "Come on," he said, "we're going."

"Bit sudden, isn't it?" Lorna said, getting up. "What's going on?"

"Something's wrong," the Maid replied. "This stillness and the chill in the air, I've never felt it here, not in all the centuries that have passed. I had hoped you could rest longer, but I fear you must leave. Come." She turned and headed out of the clearing.

"What's the rush, Patrick?" Lorna hissed, as they sped along the path, Sebastian puffing behind. She feared they would lose sight of the Maid at times, she was moving so fast.

"I don't know," Patrick replied. "But she's worried all right. Something about this place being created so no evil could ever enter - a kind of bolt hole across the Ages for those in need. Now something doesn't feel right to her. She wants us out of here."

They could hear the drumming of the Falls in the distance as they grew closer. The Maid stopped abruptly. "This shouldn't be happening," she said, pointing.

The roses, which had been brimming with colour and fragrance, were curling, and shrivelling before their eyes.

It reminded Lorna of when she was seven years old and her late grandfather had mistakenly sprayed his prize blooms with weed killer instead of pesticide, just two weeks before the horticultural society annual show. After throwing a fit over his mistake, he'd torn the bushes up and paved the garden over, resorting from then on to geraniums in pots. He said they were less sentimental than roses. She recalled this now, looking at these poor crippled blooms. The sprays of silver mist that had nurtured them earlier, had now frozen like millions of glass pellets across petal and stem. The wind was blowing stronger and chillier, darkness spreading across the sky.

"Look at the Chronograph," the Maid urged.

Lorna took it from her pocket. "It's going crazy!" she exclaimed. The hands were sweeping backwards over and over, ever more rapidly. "What does it mean?"

"It means it's over," said the Maid in despair. "How I curse my foolish brother, commissioning this thing and thinking he could fix the world. He has only brought destruction upon us. The Past is unravelling before our very eyes. We must hurry."

"I'm not going any further," Lorna said heatedly. "Not till you tell us what's going on."

"For heaven's sake, Lorna, not now!" Patrick urged. "Why can't you ever..."

"...just do as I'm told? Well, get stuffed, Patrick! I'm not some stupid kid. Neither's Sebastian. We're all risking our lives for this Chronograph thing, and I think we deserve to know why." She folded her arms in defiance. Sebastian moved to her side in solidarity.

Patrick looked at the Maid in exasperation.

"Lorna's right," she said. "You've all faced the Keeper and the danger that comes with him. So, I will tell you. But we must keep moving. If we hurry, I can still send you on the next stage of your journey and there may yet be hope."

"All right," Lorna said. "Lead on then. We're listening."

"All my family are Guardians of Ages and Places Outside Time," the Maid continued. "The Chronograph was made at the behest of my brother, a Son of Time. He was saddened by all the evil that has befallen man in Past Ages, and thought that if he could unwind Time, then perhaps he could change some of those terrible events. He commissioned the Chronograph from Hanson, a trustworthy and excellent clockmaker - for if one is to create the instrument that will unwind Time, then it must be done with precision.

Your stepfather, Lorna, was a servant of Time. He served us well and rose to the middle rank as Keeper of the Hours, entrusted with the smooth running of small elements of Time. But none of us suspected that he was Dark. He wanted power. When he learned of my brother's project, he decided to seize the Chronograph for himself, to unwind Time for more nefarious purposes. He stole two instruments of power, the Dark Glass, and the Book of Infinity, and disappeared into the Dark Ages to study their secrets. Now he has returned, having grown in power and seeking the one thing that will make his power complete."

"You mean the Chronograph," Lorna said. "But if the Chronograph is needed to unwind Time, then why did you say that the Past is unravelling?"

"The Book of Infinity holds many secrets," replied the Maid, "secrets of Places Outside Time, of alternate outcomes and ways to manipulate years, but with less precision. All this must be done carefully and is dangerous in the wrong hands. It is written that when the balance of

Time is disrupted, then the Past shall unravel, the Present Age will be distorted, and the Age of the Future may not move into place as it should. And when that happens, this garden, this haven, shall come to an end."

"So where do we come in?" asked Patrick. "And what do you mean about Ages moving into place? That makes no sense at all. How could the Future not exist?"

"I don't get it either," Lorna said. "Look, we have the Chronograph. Why can't we use it to get us wherever we need to be? Then we can get rid of the thing and be done."

"Do not attempt to use it," the Maid warned. "Only in the direst moment, even worse than this may you try. The fabric of Time is growing weaker by the minute and will not stand much more of this amateur jumping around. And you know that the Chronograph must be returned to the hands of Time in the Future Age. But with the Guardian of the Age missing, the Future will not move to its rightful place in the sequence of Time, so Chronograph or no Chronograph, you can't just jump over to something that may not exist. However, there is another way."

By now, they'd reached the rock face through which they'd passed earlier. At the Maid's touch, it dissolved before them, revealing the sheet of water tumbling to the depths below. The Maid turned.

"Here we are. Now listen carefully. In one moment, I shall part the Veil and return you to Lorna's Age, in the Present. From there you must seek the Woman on the Hill. She can help you bring round the next Age using the Old Way, as when last our Guardians were under threat. You will find her at the Folly, a Place Outside Time, accessible only from the Present. There, with any luck, you will fulfil the Great Prophecy, and the Three will complete their journey from here at the Falls of the Past, through the Mists of the Present, to reach the Starlight of the Future and bring the Chronograph home. All of you, Maker, Bearer and Protector, must stand together at its return. And God willing, that will be the end of the matter."

"What about you?" asked Lorna. She felt a heave in her chest, like she was going to cry. It was as if they were witnessing a death, not just of a person, but of a whole part of humanity that would never exist again after this moment. "What about this place?"

"Come with us," Patrick added. "How are we to find this Folly? I'm sure we could use your help."

The Maid shook her head. "Alas no. This is your quest and yours alone. The answers are not mine to give. Except to say that as the Mists thicken, the Folly will arise from their obscurity. Remember that. Now come as I part the Veil."

"But what is there here for you?" the young man persisted. "All is in decay."

"Patrick, please…" The Maid turned to him, tears welling in her beautiful eyes. Their gaze connected for one intimate moment, then the young man bit his lip and looked away.

Lorna's face grew hot, and she felt Sebastian nudge her in the ribs. "So what?" she hissed.

The Maid cleared her throat. "Complete your quest, then stability will return and with it, this place. That is my hope."

"Then hope in vain," replied a deep voice. Chills coursed down Lorna's back as the Keeper appeared from the gloom. "You always were the hopeless romantic, Serena," he sneered. "Maid of the Falls, or should that be the Fallen Maid? Condemned by her father to tend a garden for eternity, for heroes that she can see... but not touch." He laughed lasciviously.

"Keeper!" exclaimed the Maid. "What is this evil? How did you enter this place?"

"Come now, Serena," he replied, strolling back and forth in front of the cascading water. "There was a time when you were glad to see me. Until your father made clear that he disapproved of your liaison with a mere servant."

"He knew your true character, Keeper," the Maid replied hotly. "Unlike I, fool that I was. He knew that you were only using me for access to something greater, for greater power that you would only abuse."

"Ah yes, but you wouldn't believe him," the man laughed again, toying with her. "All those nights, Serena, those long, long nights when you were with me and damned him to eternity for banning me from the house, poor misunderstood creature that I was. What happened to the child?" He fired the question like a bullet from a gun, and the Maid reeled.

"What child?"

"Oh, come now. You can't deceive me. The child you bore that I was not allowed to see. The child that was denied its heritage. The child you hid." He had moved closer and was at arm's length from her now.

"I don't even know if we had a son or a daughter," he wheedled. "Don't you owe me that at least, Serena? Don't you think I deserve to know?"

"Get the hell out!" Lorna shrieked. The Keeper stepped back in surprise. "Get out! This is a good place, it brings calm, and it heals! You have no right to be here!"

"Oh, but I do," smiled her stepfather. "You wonder how I came to enter? There are many things in the Book of Infinity, many useful things, among them the Spell of Sanctuary."

"Keeper!" The Maid looked frightened. "What have you done?"

"Yes, it should have kept me out," the man sighed, "but the Dark Glass showed me the means to reverse it, and now it's broken."

"What have you become, Keeper?" she shook her head sadly. "Why was Keeper of the Hours not enough for you? Look at all you are destroying with your thirst for power."

The man shrugged, unconcerned. "Why be Keeper of the Hours when I can be Keeper of All Time? My armies will rise, those from the Dark Ages of Time will join me and create a new world order. An order where things shall be played out at my behest, and my ultimate rule over all that exists, has existed and will exist, shall be undisputed."

"Then it is indeed over," said the Maid. "The Garden is no more."

"A regrettable, yet necessary sacrifice. Now just one thing remains." He turned to Lorna.

Lorna glanced at Sebastian. While the Keeper had been talking, they had a clear view of what was happening behind him. Huge, raven-like birds had been gathering. They started arriving singly, then by their tens, then by the hundred, wingbeats silent as they somehow soared in from above the cascade and settled on the rocks by the Falls. As the Keeper now advanced towards Lorna, the Maid flung back her head and raised her arms to the heavens. The ravens flew upwards and parted the waterfall like a curtain revealing not the landscape they had come from, but a veil of mist beyond.

"Now!" cried the Maid. Shoving Sebastian ahead of her, Lorna swerved to avoid the Keeper lunging towards them.

"Patrick!" she yelled as the young man turned, questioning, to the Maid. "Come on!"

"Fly!" the Maid cried. "You can do nothing here."

They pelted to the cliff's edge, then hesitated, seeing nothing but the mist ahead of them and a sheer drop below. Lorna looked back, panic-stricken towards the Maid who was trying to block the Keeper's way. He flung the woman to the ground and continued to advance towards them.

"Now," he said. "Hand it over."

The sky above was black with ravens circling, as if waiting for something. Lorna looked at the boys either side of her. Patrick nodded and took her hand. Sebastian gave a wan smile and took the other.

"Go to hell, Latimer," she said, and they stepped off into thin air.

Lorna felt the boys' hands ripped from hers as they fell like stones. Then a tornado of black feathers swooped down upon them, and Lorna felt hundreds of beaks pecking at her clothing and hair. The giant ravens had followed them, so many in number that they bore the weight of each of them. Lorna could hardly see for the black feathers surrounding her. The birds bore their cargo onwards, away from the Falls to the next Age awaiting them.

~

The Keeper, standing at the cliff edge beneath them, let out a mighty roar.

"You fool!" He turned towards the Maid, his face twisted with rage. The woman picked herself up and walked towards him.

"You bloody fool!" he repeated. "If you think that will save you and your precious Garden!"

"I think nothing of the sort, Keeper," she said, walking past him, unflinching.

With the ravens now departed, the Veil had returned to cascading water. A sudden realisation hit the man. "Serena, no!" he exclaimed.

"What, Keeper? Don't tell me you've suddenly found a heart?" With a final longing look at what used to be her paradise, she stepped back through the water with no birds to catch her on her journey down below.

The Falls stopped, leaving the Keeper alone on the ledge at the entrance to an empty cavern with a sheer drop beneath him. A memory from his past haunted the man for just a second, a flash of sweet laughter and golden hair. He swallowed hard and turned away from the edge. The Maid had gone and the Falls of the Past - the Falls at Miller's Leap - flowed no more.

PART II

THE MISTS OF THE PRESENT

CHAPTER 15

Uncle Kelvin

The black cloud of ravens flew onwards, bearing the travellers with them. It was impossible to keep track of time, and Lorna did not dare try taking the Chronograph from her pocket in case she dropped it into whatever lay far below. She could not see the others for the mass of feathers surrounding her or hear anything for the thrumming of the hundreds of wingbeats bearing her onwards. She had to trust that somehow the ravens would take them all to the same spot and they would be deposited at their destination together. Wherever that may be, Lorna thought.

After what seemed like hours, she had the sensation that she was gently falling. At first this scared her, then she realised that the birds must be making their descent. After placing her carefully on the ground, the birds ascended as if being of one body and whirled into the air above her, before disappearing as one enormous black feathery cloud into the distance.

"Where are we?" It was Patrick. He was sitting on a log looking extremely perplexed. "And where's Sebastian?"

"Here!" Sebastian rose languidly from the long grass, stretching and rubbing his eyes.

"You slept?" Patrick was incredulous.

"'Course I did. Wasn't much else to do was there? And it was so … soft!" Sebastian gave a satisfied grin, then scowled. "What's this place then?"

From the position of the sun, it was probably late afternoon. The birds had deposited them in an orchard, separated by a box hedge from an immaculately kept lawn on the other side. A strange silvery mist hung over the lawn, obscuring whatever lay beyond.

"Search me." Lorna took the Chronograph from her pocket. "Seems to be back to normal. At least, it's not doing that crazy stuff anymore like at the Falls."

She took a step towards the mist. "Well come on then. We're not going to find out much if we stay here, are we?" Together, a little cautiously, they advanced towards the mist that shimmered and shifted as they approached. Without warning, it suddenly dissipated, revealing the back of an ordinary brick house with a path winding across the lawn towards it. A mess of wildflowers grew in the beds, bending in the strong wind that had started to blow. The sky was growing darker, an occasional glimmer of sun forcing its way through the threat of rain. The Chronograph still ticked steadily in Lorna's hand.

"What does it say?" asked Sebastian.

"Dunno." She shrugged. "A quarter to spring, maybe…"

"Very funny." Patrick pulled back the branch of a young tree growing nearby and let it go with a twang.

"Don't," Lorna said. "Don't be such a …a child!" Patrick glared, then stuffed his hands in his pockets and looked away. Lorna didn't care. The place seemed peaceful enough, but not in a way you could call friendly. There was something more serious about it, almost telling you not to mess with it, or else.

"This is a strange place," Sebastian said, putting voice to her thoughts. "Look over there. Nature's got herself in a right muddle." He pointed to where a yellow and red patch of daffodils and poppies nestled together in the shadow of a tree which seemed to be making ready for winter, only a few coppery leaves remaining on its naked boughs.

A sudden noise made them turn. A man entered through a gap in an ancient stone wall they hadn't noticed till now and which seemed out of place in a modern-day garden. The man was tall, with rough-hewn good looks and windswept silver hair, his age hard to determine. He wore a strange dark tunic with leggings and high boots. A heavy cloak of midnight blue embroidered with gold moons and stars billowed around him in the wind. Lorna held her breath. The man leaned heavily on a tall staff, limping slightly, yet he exuded a strong, almost fearsome presence. She looked at the others and saw they were equally mesmerised by the figure moving purposefully towards them.

The man halted and looked them up and down with piercing blue eyes that settled on Lorna.

Then he smiled and a wave of recognition washed over her. "Uncle Kelvin!" she shrieked and flung her arms around him.

"Little Lorna," the man smiled affectionately. "Little Lorna, all grown up. And what are you doing in my garden?"

"*Your* garden? We didn't know it was yours. We didn't even know you were in the country. Mum said you were in South Africa somewhere and we'd lost touch."

"Yes, well." Uncle Kelvin frowned, then looked apologetic. "Time got away from me somehow."

"Know the feeling," Patrick muttered.

"For ten whole years? Never a call, never a letter? I thought you'd died," Lorna said reproachfully, her sudden delight evaporating.

"When your mother remarried, she made it clear that my presence was unwelcome," said Uncle Kelvin. "It was better I stayed away."

"Better for who?"

"Now, Lorna," he said, patting her head as he did when she was six. "You still haven't answered my question. How do you come to be in my garden?"

"Birds!" blurted Sebastian, then "Ow!" as Patrick kicked the back of his leg.

"Birds?" Uncle Kelvin arched one eyebrow.

"Odd ones." Sebastian scrambled to recover himself. "Never seen nothin' like 'em. I wanted to see what they were."

"Odd birds." The man looked sternly at the small boy, folding his arms. "And where are these odd birds now?"

"They flew away," Sebastian said lamely.

"Ah, well. I suppose birds do that, don't they?" Uncle Kelvin gave a loud laugh, ruffling Sebastian's hair in his amusement. Lorna laughed as well, her heart feeling light. Uncle Kelvin always made things feel better somehow.

"Well, come on!" the man said, rubbing his hands together. "All of you. Lorna and I have a lot to catch up on. Come on in and we'll make some tea. And I need to change out of these clothes."

"They're well weird," Lorna said. "You been to a fancy dress or something?"

"Oh, fantasy drama thing," Uncle Kelvin said vaguely. "Local theatre group. I like to get the feel of the part."

"Like players?" Sebastian asked. "We had some once. In St Mark's. They did a King Arthur story. You a wizard, like Merlin?"

"You have quite the imagination, Sebastian," the man replied, giving him a strange look.

"How d'you know my name?"

"Lorna called you Sebastian, so I assumed…"

"Oh…right." Sebastian shrugged. Lorna grinned and stuck her arm through Uncle Kelvin's as they strolled up to the house. For the first time in ages, she felt herself relax. It was almost as if the Falls had never happened.

~

Patrick hung back, looking thoughtfully after Uncle Kelvin. There was something about the way the man had looked at him, just for a fleeting second. As if he knew everything when they'd said nothing. A thought began to form in his brain, a vague familiarity, but the man's relationship with Lorna seemed to put paid to the one explanation that could have made sense.

"What's wrong with you?" Sebastian said, turning back. "Don't you want tea?"

"Wait a moment." Patrick grabbed the boy's arm. "Look Sebastian, don't mention the Chronograph."

"I'm not that daft," Sebastian replied, "can I go now?"

"I mean it. I don't trust him."

"I said I won't say nuffin' didn't I?" The boy pulled his arm away. "What's up with you, Patrick? The bloke *is* Lorna's uncle."

"An uncle whose garden grows things out of season, and wears clothes from outside his Time?"

"He told us," Sebastian said. "He's a wizard. Fantasy drama he said."

"This'll be a bloody drama if we don't watch out," Patrick replied hotly. "I'm telling you, something's not right. That cloak for a start."

"What about it?"

"It's shadow silk, made from silk thread spun by a special kind of spider. It only spins at twilight, that's why it's called shadow silk. Very expensive and rare. What's more, it was only discovered a hundred years ago."

"So what?" Sebastian was clearly getting bored, his mind on tea.

"Listen, dingbat!" Patrick said, exasperated. "A hundred years ago from *my* Time. So, what's a man doing in *this* Time wearing rare shadow silk that hasn't even been discovered yet?"

"Cor, I see what you mean!"

"And there's something else. Lorna didn't tell him your name. She didn't introduce either of us."

"So how come he knows I'm Sebastian?"

"Search me, but mark my words, he knows who we are. And I wonder how much else he knows…" Patrick looked down at Sebastian. The boy suddenly looked petrified. "You stick close to me," Patrick continued. "And don't look so worried. It's a dead giveaway that we suspect something's up."

"I thought we was all right for a bit, that's all. Do we tell Lorna?"

"No of course not! To her, Uncle Kelvin is some long-lost relative she loved as a kid. She won't believe us. Besides…"

"What?"

"I don't want to…to spoil her moment." Patrick stood for a second, watching Lorna enter the house, laughing, with her uncle. He felt a huge wave wash over him, knowing how much it would hurt her when the man turned out to be something other than she believed. "Let her be happy, at least for a little while."

Sebastian looked at him. "You in love with her?"

"Love?" Patrick gave a hollow laugh. "Lost cause, mate. She hates my guts. C'mon, thought you said you wanted tea."

~

Lorna felt elated. She slapped butter and ham onto thick slices of bread while her uncle filled the huge brown teapot she remembered from years ago and poured what looked like a large whisky for himself. When she was small, Lorna used to beg a taste, and her uncle would allow her a sip with a huge display of mock secrecy while her parents pretended not to see. Today, she did not ask, and the man did not offer. She wondered if he remembered. The slam of the back door disturbed her thoughts as Patrick came in with Sebastian, the two of them suddenly thick as thieves. Lorna shrugged to herself. It would make a change if they got along for once. For the moment, being with Uncle Kelvin was all that mattered.

"So," Uncle Kelvin enquired as they all sat down. "How's the family?"

Lorna scowled. She hadn't thought much about her mother and brother since the Chronograph tipped her out of house and Time and felt a mixture of annoyance tinged with guilt as Uncle Kelvin reminded her of them. "Okay I suppose."

"I see." Uncle Kelvin looked at her thoughtfully. "And your stepfather. What's he up to these days?"

"This and that," Lorna responded, catching the look Patrick was giving her across the table. "I don't really know what he does. We don't see him that much."

"Is that so?" Uncle Kelvin looked round the table. Lorna eyed the others wondering what they knew that she didn't. Sebastian, his cheeks bulging with bread and butter, turned bright red and fixed his gaze on the ceiling, while Patrick seemed fascinated with the ham on his plate, cutting it with the slow, careful precision of a surgeon. Uncle Kelvin took a deep breath and seemed about to say something. Then he got up to fill the kettle, whistling tunelessly.

"What the hell's wrong?" Lorna hissed at Patrick. "You two couldn't look more suspicious if you tried."

"He don't trust him," Sebastian whispered.

"Shut up, Sebastian!" Patrick snapped. They both looked at Lorna guiltily. She leaned forward, furious, casting a furtive look at Uncle Kelvin. The man had his back to them, whistling even louder above the noise of the boiling kettle.

"How dare you, Patrick! Uncle Kelvin's known me since I was a baby! He was my dad's best friend."

"He's not your real uncle then?"

"No, but…"

"Ha!" Patrick said triumphantly. Lorna treated him to the most withering look she could muster, but it seemed to have no effect.

"Look out!" Sebastian whispered loudly. Uncle Kelvin was now standing right at his shoulder with a fresh pot of tea. The man merely smiled and set the pot on the table.

"You could cut this atmosphere with a knife," he said. "So let's cut to the chase. Why don't you show me what you have in your pocket, Lorna?"

The girl's mouth fell open. "How did you know?" she said, entirely caught off guard.

"Shut up!" Patrick leaped out of his chair. "I don't care who you say he is, we're leaving. Now." He grabbed Lorna by the wrist and started to drag her out of her chair.

"Let go!" she screamed. "What the hell d'you think you're doing? You're hurting me."

"We're getting out of here," Patrick said fiercely. "The man's a con, Lorna, he's not who you think he is. Sebastian, get the door."

"Patrick, let go of me!" She tore her arm away. "This is my uncle for God's sake!"

"Don't you get it? Your so-called 'Uncle Kelvin' is of my world, not yours. There's only one thing he's interested in, and it certainly isn't you!"

"That's not true! Tell him!" Lorna felt a desperate anger rise within her. "Uncle Kelvin? Say something!"

The man leaned back in his chair, took a swig of his whisky, and looked at her steadily. "Say something!" she pleaded again. The tears rose and she felt Patrick's hand on her arm once more.

"He can't say anything, Lorna. Because it's true. Come on. We're going."

"Patrick." Sebastian's voice came small and scared from the doorway. "I don't think we can go anywhere. Look."

Outside, the strange silvery mist swirled upwards from the ground, obscuring their view. "What is this? What kind of stunt are you trying to pull?" Patrick turned angrily towards Uncle Kelvin who spoke at last.

"Stunt? Nothing to do with me, I assure you. It is the Mists of the Present. They will clear again in a moment, but each time they return, they return more thickly as the Age falls more into confusion."

"They've gone now," Lorna said. "I can see the orchard again. Who are you?" She turned accusingly to her uncle.

The man put down his glass. "I'm the same man I ever was, Lorna, and I assure you, you have nothing to fear from me. Now, are you going to show me what's in your pocket?"

Lorna looked at him feeling torn. Her father had trusted Kelvin. Maybe they should too. She drew out the Chronograph.

"I say no!" Patrick grabbed her wrist and looked at Uncle Kelvin defiantly. "You want it, come and get it!"

Uncle Kelvin gave a low whistle. "It seems I chose well, Protector. But now it's time to trust me. I've been waiting for your return."

There was a beat as Patrick's face seemed to register something. Lorna looked from one to the other feeling confused. She'd known Uncle Kelvin her whole life, but it suddenly seemed as if he and Patrick were sharing some kind of secret.

"Are you really from Patrick's world?" she asked miserably. "You've always just been Uncle Kelvin to me."

"And no matter what else changes, I always will be." The man looked at her fondly. Lorna scowled in return. He gave a sad smile. "All right then. Hold onto the Chronograph for now if that makes you feel better, but at least allow me to explain."

Lorna sat at the far end of the table, Sebastian next to her. Patrick slouched by the door, glowering at the man across the room.

"Patrick is right," Uncle Kelvin began. "I am not quite what you think. I am from this Time, but raised in Patrick's Time, born as the Ages moved through a half-cycle, as the world shifted through the darkness of World War Two, emerging in the light of new hope. A sort of temporal equinox if you will, where darkness was at its lowest point and light at its highest. Because of my very unique birth moment, the Court of Time allows me to move readily between this Time and Patrick's Time in the Future, as well as the Court itself. And for one very special moment, back to Sebastian's era. But that was only allowed once, with the very express permission of the Great Lord. Indiscriminate leaping about the centuries wreaks havoc with Time. As the Keeper has rather unfortunately proved."

Lorna slouched back in her chair, turning the Chronograph over in her palm. "So what?" She glowered from under her fringe. "What's all this got to do with the Chronograph?"

"I spent many years in the Future Age and at Court," the man continued, "studying all the great Lore. During that period, I met the man who became the Keeper of the Hours. I always felt there was something evil about him, but he could be very charming. He earned the trust of the Great Lord and the love of his daughter, Serena.

The Keeper also studied the Lore. Only a little, but enough to realise that with two of the Great Instruments of Time – the Book of Infinity, and the Dark Glass – he could find turning points in Time and thus travel between centuries. He also learned of the Son of Time's plans for a Chronograph, and knew that if he possessed all three, he could intersect with history with the greatest precision, turning events to achieve a different outcome. This would give him his greatest prize – the power to rule everything inside and outside of Time, bending ordinary people on earth to his will and bringing nothing but misery and chaos."

Lorna gave a grunt. "Sounds like Latimer. He certainly brought nothing but misery to me. What happened next?"

"He used his liaison with the Great Lord's daughter to access the Dark Glass and the Book of Infinity and rehearse his primitive travels through Time. When the Lord grew suspicious of the Keeper's sudden disappearances and reappearances, and discovered the affair with his daughter, the Keeper fled, taking the two great instruments with him. Some years passed. Then the Lord's son was murdered, having gone against his father to commission the Chronograph. The Lord knew the Keeper must be responsible and guessed what his final plan must be. The race was on across the Ages to find the last and most powerful instrument. What nobody knew was that the Chronograph had been lost in the mud at Ypres, only to resurface and be found by another soldier who presented it to his captain, who passed it down the line..."

"To my dad." Lorna looked up at her uncle, then away, blinking fiercely.

"Exactly," said Uncle Kelvin. "With a little deduction and historical reckoning, plus looking at reports of subtle 'out of Time' happenings, I worked out pretty closely where it might be. I also knew the Prophecy of the Three..." He cast a look round the room.

"So, I set out to locate the Chronograph and make sure it stayed in a safe place until the Three were in place to carry it back to its True Time, as must be done in accordance with the Prophecy, to fulfil its destiny. I befriended your father, hoping to discover whether he still had the object in his possession. One day, I was helping him clear out some old stuff in his home office – boxes, his desk, stuff like that. And he came across this old, battered watch. It didn't seem to work any longer and he was going to throw it away, but I persuaded him not to. I told him he should give it to you. That you might find it…well…amusing."

"Oh yeah, bloody hilarious!" Lorna said sarcastically. "He only listened to you because he thought you were his greatest friend. But you were only ever interested in the Chronograph!"

"Indeed not! Lorna, your father was a wonderful man and a very dear friend. It is my bitterest regret that I was the cause of his death."

"You? What do you mean?" Lorna wasn't sure how much more she could take.

"I grew complacent. I enjoyed your father's company and spending time with his family and half-forgot why I was here. I did not realise that the Keeper had learned of my travels and guessed what I must be seeking. He stopped trying to locate the Chronograph and turned his attention to tracking me instead. He noticed how much time I was spending with your father, and when I wasn't around, he killed him."

"But it was a car accident!"

"It was the Keeper. They never found another driver or car, did they? My guess is that he brought them out of the Past on that stretch of road, ensured the collision, and then took them back again. It could all be put down to careless driving, and no trace of who was really involved."

"But why not just break in and steal the Chronograph?"

151

"Because he didn't just want the Chronograph, Lorna." Uncle Kelvin paused. "He wanted you."

"Me?" Lorna looked at the others. Sebastian's eyes were like saucers. Patrick had joined them at the table, fascinated.

"Remember the Prophecy of the Three, the girl who must return to the point of the Chronograph's making, to walk with a boy of the Past and a youth of the Future to return it to its True Time and power. The Keeper knew this. He wheedled his way into your home in hopes of winning you over and discovering where the Chronograph was hidden. Maybe even thinking he could be your travelling companion, instead of Sebastian and Patrick here.

But you're too much your real father's daughter. The Keeper stood no chance." Uncle Kelvin smiled at her. "So that just about brings us up-to-date. At least mostly - apart from the story of your brother."

"David?" Lorna snorted. "Who cares about him?"

"You should. Very much so as it happens. But that will keep for now. You have enough to absorb."

Lorna sat in silence. Sebastian took her hand and squeezed it. She looked at him gratefully.

"Do you know anything about a Folly?" Patrick asked suddenly. "Somewhere near here, I'd think."

Uncle Kelvin thought for a moment. "I know of it as one of the Places Outside Time," he said. "But I can't say I've visited it myself or know how to access it."

"Maybe the Chronograph knows," Sebastian said. "It sometimes... jumps about, like. It might give us a sign."

"We can't just wander round waiting for the Chronograph to jump about," Patrick said witheringly.

Sebastian turned red and Lorna felt a surge of anger.

"I suppose you're full of suggestions," she snapped. "Go on then. Let's hear them!"

"I suggest bed," Uncle Kelvin said. "No arguments. Go on, Lorna, I assume you remember the way."

She flung Patrick a dark look and led Sebastian to the door. Patrick hung back. "You go on," he said, "I'll be up in a minute."

"But you heard what Uncle Kelvin said…"

"It's all right, Lorna." The man waved to shoo her and Sebastian away. "Do as he says. Just shout if you need anything."

He closed the door, leaving Lorna frustrated in the hallway, Sebastian yawning his head off beside her.

"Why does he get to have some cosy secret chit-chat with my uncle," she grumbled.

"Dunno," Sebastian yawned again loudly. "I'm tired."

"Come on then, or you'll be sleepwalking in a minute." She pushed Sebastian up the stairs and stomped up after him. She may have turned sixteen, but she had never felt more like a child.

CHAPTER 16

More Matters Explained

Patrick leaned against the sink, arms folded, and regarded the man in front of him. "Nice of you to show up, Glenelven," he said.

Glenelven smiled. "I wondered how long it would take you."

"It was the shadow silk that gave you away. And then when you mentioned the Chronograph and waiting for our return, I knew for sure."

"Ah yes, the shadow silk. You caught me just as I was returning from Court, I'm afraid."

"How is everyone?" Patrick said sarcastically. "Any more people that you've spirited to other Ages?"

"You know it was not the plan for you to travel alone," Glenelven said shortly. "But when the Chronograph was activated, something happened to pull me back to this Age where I am Guardian. I'm sorry you were left high and dry. As an Apprentice, by strictest definition you should not be travelling out of your Age at all, nor should I have tried to re-enter the Past without High Permission. We've acted illegally – but it is necessary." He paused. "Things at Court are bad. There are more and more Timequakes each day. Faramore and the Inner Circle are doing all they can to hold things together and find the Keeper, but he eludes them."

"You know he wants the Chronograph, and he knows it's with Lorna, so it stands to reason he'll be sniffing around her again soon," Patrick said. "It's hardly rocket science."

"Rocket science, you say. A quaint old expression." Glenelven smiled grimly. "Nonetheless, the Keeper has learned to conceal his footprint. He takes convoluted routes to reach his destination, hence we don't know exactly where he is until he pops up and then another rip occurs. But yes, we know what he wants. We must guard her carefully."

"He's using the Dark Glass somehow and he's getting better," Patrick said. "The Maid was shocked when he turned up at the Falls."

"He was at the Falls?" Glenelven looked up sharply. "Why didn't you say so before?"

"Not much chance while we were all playing happy families."

"This is serious. He is not supposed to enter the Places Outside Time." Glenelven poured himself another whisky and another glass, which he handed to Patrick.

"Well supposed to or not, he was there. He said something about managing to break the Spell of Sanctuary." The young man took a slug of his drink and grimaced. "How d'you drink this foul stuff? Do you think he'll be at the Folly?"

"Let's hope not, or the Future will be bleak indeed. However, one spell does not break all places, and the Woman on the Hill is stronger than her sister...and colder. What exactly happened at the Falls?"

Patrick recounted the details. "She sacrificed herself for us," he finished. "I saw her fall. I haven't told the others."

"Let's leave it that way," said Glenelven with a deep sigh. "At least for now."

"Who was the child?" Patrick asked.

"All in good time. I think we've talked enough for one evening."

"There is one more thing, Glenelven." Patrick hesitated. "I saw my mother."

The man gave a start. "You mean Celesta?"

"Who else would I mean? Yes, I saw her."

"Where was this? Our Guardian of the Future has been missing for the longest time."

"In the crypt of a church. She was…lying there. In a coffin." Patrick swallowed hard. "The Keeper found us there. He locked us in."

"And what were you doing there?" The older man spoke lightly, but his face was serious.

"I don't know really. I just had this feeling. It kind of…pulled me. The others didn't want to go, Sebastian especially. He ran away and got help when Lorna and I were captured."

"That was a very close call," Glenelven said. "I assume Sebastian had the Chronograph at the time?"

"Yes, he didn't want to go down in the crypt, so we left it with him."

"Listen to me," Glenelven said. "The Keeper needs Lorna and the Chronograph together. When she inherited the Instrument, she inherited its guardianship and must be there at its final return to hand it to its destiny. It is written that young people of the Past and the Future shall come together to protect the Present and what she carries, so the Present may in turn protect both her Sister Ages. You must guard Lorna at all costs."

"Why can't you do it?" Patrick suddenly felt hostile towards the man. "Why me? Why that kid, Sebastian?"

"Sebastian was at the making, besides, there are things about the child you do not yet know... And you? As Son of a Guardian, you are both useful and appropriate."

"Thanks a bunch. How did you know who I was? That night at the Tower?"

Glenelven shrugged. "I hadn't seen you since you were a small child, but an Apprentice who snoops among the Forbidden Books, researching the Great Disappearance as much as you did? It didn't take me too long to figure out. And it seems the Keeper has too, which is unfortunate. The Dark Glass can tell him many things."

"You mean he tricked me into going into that church?"

"I think he opened a channel between you and Celesta. That's what you felt, and naturally followed."

"You used me," Patrick said hotly. "You're no better than he is! Well, she's dead now, so there's no point in me continuing. Yes, dead, Glenelven. He'd held her in stasis and then smashed her phial and killed her. So now you can send me back to my own Time and find someone else to do your dirty work for you."

"Celesta is not dead," the man replied.

"Are you calling me a liar?"

"No but tell me exactly what you saw."

"I told you, he smashed her phial. It brought her out of stasis too quickly and she sort of...exploded and disappeared."

"Cheap conjurer's trick." Glenelven waved his hand dismissively.

"Why should I believe you?"

"Because if emotion weren't clouding your thinking, you'd remember that Guardians cannot be taken out of their assigned Ages, either willingly or by force. I am the only living example of a Guardian who can cross more than one Age- and even I was overstepping my bounds by attempting to enter the Past again without the Great Lord's permission."

"But the Keeper seems to hop across Time with no issues. Maybe he did remove her, despite what you're saying."

"He can only move where the Dark Glass leads him, and then Time is damaged whenever he appears." Glenelven shook his head. "No, I think what you saw was through a Time Lapse, a hole between Ages if you will. It allowed you to see and touch Celesta, then the Keeper broke the connection. In a very showy way, I'll grant you, but that's all he did. Celesta is still very much alive, in stasis surely, but safe in her own Age."

"Then why...?"

"...did he appear to kill her? To show you what he's capable of. Scare you into giving him what he wanted."

"Well, it didn't work, did it?" Patrick's old defiance was returning.

"No, but it will if you give up now."

"If my mother's in the Future, then that's where I need to be. How else am I to find her? Being dumped here with two kids doesn't help me at all."

"There are greater needs than your own," Glenelven said sharply. "Yes. I need you to accompany the Chronograph, but there is more. Because Celesta is missing, she cannot bring round her Age. The Keeper is counting on that so the Chronograph cannot be returned before he captures it. The Instrument must be returned through each of the Ages to its final destination in the Future, and if that Future is never brought into existence... well...everything is stuck."

"So where do I come in?"

"A Guardian's representative may act where a Guardian is not available to do so – you have to use the old methods, but you can bring the Age round, nevertheless. And in travelling with the Chronograph, I also hoped you might unearth some other clue to our Sister Guardian's whereabouts. As it is, you've done so more quickly than I expected. We know exactly where she is."

The young man looked at him, still not understanding. "You saw her in the crypt of a church," Glenelven said patiently. "A Time Lapse must connect the same spot between Ages."

"Like a parallel universe?" Patrick was growing interested again.

"Exactly."

"So, the spot where that church is in the Future, is where I'll find her!"

Glenelven nodded.

"Then I must go now!" Patrick felt a surge of excitement. "If you send me back, then I can release her. She's power on our side! She can bring round the next Age, and then I'll come back and finish things here!"

"Not possible."

"What do you mean?" Patrick looked at the man in desperation. "Look I know I sounded flaky a few minutes ago, but I promise I'll come back. My mother will help me."

"As I said, not possible. For one, as an Apprentice, nobody would allow you to make the journey back to the Present, and you cannot rely on another Timequake to deliver you safely. I broke many rules to get you here. And for another, your Age is not yet in place. It is not there for you to go back to."

Patrick exploded. "You mean, you sent me on a one-way ticket, knowing I couldn't return until I'd done what you wanted?"

The man gave a strange, twisted smile. "I make no apology, Patrick. You must complete your part. And that means finding the Folly on the Hill."

CHAPTER 17

A Close Encounter

Patrick drummed his fingers impatiently on the table. "Hadn't we better get going?" he said for the third time that morning. Lorna and Sebastian exchanged glances. Patrick and Uncle Kelvin had barely spoken during breakfast and, when they had, it had been with such forced politeness that Lorna would have preferred it if they'd thrown something at each other.

"I told you they'd been arguing," Sebastian whispered, his mouth full of toast. "I came down for some water and heard them."

"What was it about?" Lorna whispered back, a nervous eye on the other two.

"Dunno. Couldn't hear much through the door. But I think I heard Patrick say Glenelven."

"Glenelven?"

"Shh. They'll hear!" Now Sebastian looked nervous, but Uncle Kelvin carried on whistling at the kitchen sink, showing no sign of having heard anything. Patrick was leaning back in his chair, sullenly examining his fingernails.

"I said we should go," he repeated, without looking up.

"And what is your plan?" asked Uncle Kelvin, with a little too much jollity.

"Wander around. See if anyone's heard of this Folly."

"Until you bump into the Keeper?" said Uncle Kelvin.

"Do you think he's back?" Lorna asked.

"Most certainly," her uncle replied.

"All the more reason for us to get a move on," Patrick said, "instead of waiting for him to show up here."

"He won't do that," Uncle Kelvin said with certainty. "For one thing, he thinks I am elsewhere. And for another, I created a little illusion myself. This house stands in a small bubble outside Time where he cannot enter. For now, at least."

"So, we can stay here as long as we like!" said Sebastian.

Uncle Kelvin laughed. "Not quite. I can only hold the illusion for so long. A day or two at most. Patrick's right, you should leave soon. But you must be careful, for in this Age you are extremely vulnerable. The Keeper knows this is Lorna's environment and will know many of her usual paths and haunts. And, in all likelihood, he will know you are seeking the Folly. You must learn to be unpredictable."

"Maybe we can start at the library," Lorna said. "They have old maps there and stuff. And the library is a bit unpredictable as a hang out, at least for me."

"What's a library?" asked Sebastian.

"A building with lots of books and papers," Lorna explained. "Anyone can go in and look stuff up if they want."

"Bit public then, isn't it?" asked Patrick. "And won't the Keeper have the same thought? Especially if he thinks we're headed for the Folly. He'll want to find it so he can cut us off."

"You have any better ideas?"

Patrick shook his head.

"Well then. Let's go." Lorna reached for her shoes.

"Can't we leave the Chronograph here?" Sebastian asked.

Uncle Kelvin shook his head. "You'll need it with you if you find the Folly."

"I'll carry it," Patrick said. "Better keep you and it apart for the time being." Lorna looked at him in surprise, then at Uncle Kelvin. The man nodded and she handed it over reluctantly.

"I'll come with you at least as far as the library," Uncle Kelvin said, "but then I must leave you. I'm needed elsewhere."

The four of them set off in the direction of the town centre. The strange silvery mist was back, hanging round the front door as they left. "Wow," said Patrick, looking back over his shoulder. "A parallel world. That's clever!" Two small children were playing in front of the house, while their father tinkered under his car in the driveway. For all intents and purposes, another family was living where they'd just been.

"Thank you." Uncle Kelvin looked pleased with himself.

"I don't know this part of town at all," Lorna said, looking up and down the narrow-cobbled streets for a familiar landmark.

Uncle Kelvin tutted. "This is one of the most ancient parts of Middlebridge. It was first built in Roman times, then subsequent generations built on top of it for many Ages. It's incredibly old, and very sacred." Lorna rolled her eyes. "We'll come out onto the square," Uncle Kelvin said. "Right opposite the library. Just a few more turns."

"I don't like this mist," Patrick said.

"It often gets a bit foggy round here," Lorna replied. "The river's nearby. Odd for this time of year though."

"It's not that," Patrick said, "It's like that silvery mist back at the house. It made sense there, but not here..."

"Well observed," said Uncle Kelvin. "This is no ordinary mist."

"Is the Keeper making it?" Sebastian asked.

"No," Uncle Kelvin replied. "No Keeper or Guardian could make this kind of mist. It's being made by Time itself. The Mists of the Present. Maybe you were right, Patrick, we should have left sooner. And yet, maybe this will work to our advantage."

"You mean it makes us harder to spot," said Lorna.

"Exactly, but it also means that Time is short. The Keeper will know that too and it will make him more desperate. Hold on, it's lifting."

They were at the end of an alleyway that opened onto the town square. The library stood opposite, as Uncle Kelvin had said it would. But that was not all. In front of the library, a small number of policemen was trying to control the large crowd that had gathered there. Three fire engines stood in a half circle, the ladder of one running up the left side of the building where a firefighter could be seen clambering out of a top floor window with someone over his shoulder. From the ground, other firefighters trained gushing hoses on the roof in an attempt to quell the flames that licked at it like a great treat designed for their consumption.

"Wait here," Sebastian said. "I'll find out what's going on."

Before they could stop him, he scuttled along the covered arcade of shops on one side of the square, then darted across to the crowd. He skirted the edges for a moment, before disappearing into the throng of people.

"Little idiot!" said Patrick. "I hope he doesn't get caught!"

Lorna gave him one of her looks and he was silent. Five minutes later, Sebastian was back. "It's not as bad as it looks," he said. "Folks are saying it started on the second floor and it's only on that side of the building. I asked 'em, don't they keep a load of old maps in there, and this man said yes, but only in the basement, and the fire hadn't reached there. But they'll be closed for the rest of the day. Maybe longer."

The others groaned. "That's that then," Lorna said. "We'll have to think of something else."

"The Keeper certainly doesn't want us finding this Folly," said Patrick. "I assume he's behind this."

"Without a doubt," Uncle Kelvin replied. "The longer he can keep you here, the better, as far as he's concerned." He looked worried. "Wait here. I'm going to check on something."

Pulling his coat around him, he set off for the library, taking the same route as Sebastian. The others waited. Ten minutes passed, and still Uncle Kelvin did not return.

"Where on earth is he?" Lorna said. "Do you think we should go look?"

"He said to wait here," said Sebastian.

"Well, at least we could look in the shops while we're waiting," said Lorna. "Just along this side, we won't go far. Are you coming, Patrick?"

The young man shook his head. "What do I want to look in a load of old shops for?" He leaned back against the wall, whistling tunelessly, turning the Chronograph over in his pocket.

"I'll come," said Sebastian. "You can tell me what things are."

The two of them moved slowly along the shop fronts. Lorna left Sebastian mesmerized by a small steam engine puffing its way round the window of the toy shop, glanced briefly in the window of the antique print store, and moved on to the clothes shop next door. Those platform shoes were cool, she thought. Her mother would have fifty fits if she got those. She stopped suddenly. Something she'd seen briefly in the print store window had jogged her memory. She made her way back and peered again through the glass. There it was. A print of a tower, rising out of the trees below. Could that be the Folly? But where? She peered closer, shielding her eyes for a better view. The reflections in the window were really annoying, especially the one of that man...she froze.

"Hello, Lorna," the Keeper said. She turned slowly. He was wearing a black polo necked sweater and black jeans, dress of the present day.

"What do you want?" she said rudely. The man laughed.

"Oh, Lorna! Brazen as ever, trying to bluff your way out. You've some nerve, I'll give you that!"

She said nothing, but finally cracked under his piercing stare and looked away.

"Leave her alone!" It was Sebastian. Small as he was, he stood squarely facing the Keeper, looking him directly in the eye. The Keeper laughed again.

"The little runt from the Past! Time you returned. You have some charges to face." He raised his arm, fingers splaying. Seizing her chance, Lorna smashed down on the outstretched arm with her full strength, taking the Keeper by surprise.

"You little witch!" he yelled, grasping his arm in pain. Then, recovering himself, he started after them as they disappeared into the alley.

"Run!" yelled Lorna, taking Patrick by surprise.

"The Keeper!" screamed Sebastian.

Patrick finally woke up and stuck his foot out as the Keeper hurtled round the corner, sending him flying. Then he sprinted after the others.

They ran like the wind, Lorna taking the lead, with no clue where she was going, dodging in and out of alleyways, cutting across roads and squares and doubling back as they tried to evade the Keeper. He had now recovered from his fall and was in hot pursuit. Rain started to fall, making the cobbled alleyways treacherous in places. The strange silver mist had returned and began to waft across their path with varying degrees of thickness, meaning the boys had to pay full attention in case Lorna made a sudden turn ahead of them. The only saving grace was that these conditions also impeded the Keeper.

The old houses gave way to a row of small backstreet shops with signs indicating a bookbinder, a boot maker, and an apothecary. They swerved to avoid a man in a top hat and cloak emerging from one of them, then the mist swirled round them again and he was gone. Lorna made a sharp turn to the right and came to an abrupt halt. The moment she'd dreaded had happened. It was a dead end.

"Here!" Patrick ran wildly along the alley, pressing latches on doors to side passageways as he went, until he found one open. They darted through and into a passageway that ran between two of the houses, and then emerged in a long narrow yard at the back, enclosed by a high wall at one end. Not daring to stop, they pelted the length of the yard, Patrick now in the lead. Climbing on some dustbins at the end, he hauled the others after him, shoving them over the wall, which he then scaled himself and dropped down on the other side.

They emerged onto the high street, crowded with weekend shoppers all dashing to get out of the rain. Swept along by the crowd for a little way, they darted across the road, narrowly avoiding the cars that honked angrily at them, and dashed down the next side street. Lorna made a sharp left into an alley crammed with small cafés and boutiques.

"I think we lost him," she gasped. "In here." The three collapsed, panting, through the nearest doorway.

CHAPTER 18

Romans and Flapper Girls

They found themselves in a coffee shop, packed with it being Saturday and lunchtime.

"Here!" gasped Lorna, spying the last available table in the corner. The others slumped down, Patrick next to her and Sebastian opposite, breathing heavily.

"What now?" asked Patrick.

"What would you like?" A very bored, plump young woman had appeared to take their order.

"Ummm, can you give us a minute?" said Lorna.

The girl sighed, stuck her pencil behind her ear and plodded off to the back of the cafe where a raucous group of teenagers seemed to have taken up residence.

"I don't like it here," said Patrick, nodding towards the window. "We're too much on display."

"There's nowhere else to sit," Lorna replied, "and I'm not going out again."

"Fine," Patrick shrugged. "But we need to get out of the city. We've got to find this Folly on the Hill."

"There is no Folly I know of," said Lorna. "I told you. And dammit all, Patrick, which hill? There are so many around here. We can't just leave town and start climbing them all in case there might be an old folly on one of them. And not in this weather. Look at it."

They looked outside where people were fighting a losing battle with their umbrellas against the onslaught of hail and wind whipping around them.

"You can't just sit here and order nothing you know." The waitress was back, looking flustered. "If I don't take an order soon, Mrs McGinty will be over and then there'll be trouble." She nodded towards a stout woman with a grey French braid and half-moon glasses who was eyeing them suspiciously over a tower of Chelsea buns.

"Two coffees, a hot chocolate and three cheese and tomato sandwiches," gabbled Lorna. The waitress dutifully noted the order on her pad and stomped away. Mrs McGinty turned her attention to the teenagers in the corner, who had drained their drinks long since and were now flicking chips at each other across the table.

"I'm hungry," said Sebastian, "I hope this food's good.

"You'll like it," smiled Lorna, and turned her attention back to Patrick who was growing impatient. "Maybe we should look at the Chronograph again."

"Two coffees, one cocoa and three sandwiches," said the waitress, dumping everything on the table. "Pay at the door on your way out." She slapped down the bill and plodded off again.

Patrick organized the menus at the end of the table to shield them from view, then passed the Chronograph over to Lorna. The hands were ticking peacefully round its face. "No unusual behaviour to report," said Patrick. "We may as well eat."

Sebastian was very quiet, eyes seemingly fixed on some distant point beyond, chewing his sandwich thoughtfully.

"You all right?" Lorna asked. The boy turned red and blinked hard.

"Yeah. It's just them flowers." He indicated an enormous pot of fake yellow broom by the door. "Just reminded me of me mam, that's all. She always had it in the house when she could. Made her...happy."

"I'm sorry, Sebastian. You must really miss her."

The boy shook himself. "Nah. Not so much really. She was me mam but didn't feel like me mam. I know that sounds weird. Anyway, she's one less of us to feed now ain't she. She'll be all right." He polished off his sandwich and started picking at the crumbs on his plate.

"Here," Lorna said, giving him her remaining half. "I'm not as hungry as you."

"Cor, thanks!" Sebastian beamed. Patrick scowled.

"What's up with you?" Lorna asked, irritated. "You can order something else if you're still hungry."

Patrick shook his head. "It's not that. Look."

Lorna turned and looked out the window. The hail had stopped, and the ground was now saturated and muddy. A woman in a big crinoline skirt walked past, accompanied by a man in a heavy cloak and top hat, who was guiding her around the puddles. "Oh that! Probably just a couple of people advertising the local theatre production. They're doing 'Jane Eyre' or something." She turned back unperturbed.

"I don't think so," Patrick said. His tone made her turn again. The weather had changed once more. The strange mist was back, and the number of people in crinolines and top hats seemed to have increased, walking incongruously alongside the people in raincoats and trousers.

"Big production is it?" said Patrick sarcastically. A horse and carriage had somehow made its way down the far too narrow alley. Three women in flapper dresses and cloche hats now hurried by, laughing light-heartedly and seemingly not noticing the rest of the crowd.

"Look," croaked Lorna, her voice cracking. She held out the Chronograph in the palm of her hand. The hands were now swinging back and forth between the nine and three, like a pendulum. "Lorna," said Sebastian nervously. She raised her head. People in all states of attire surrounded them, eating and drinking all manner of things and seemingly oblivious to each other. Three Mrs McGintys were bustling about behind the counter, one in a long dress and apron, up to her elbows in flour, one in a black twenties style dress and wearing pearls, and the third being the Mrs McGinty that Lorna knew from her present time. Each of them seemed unconcerned by the presence of the others. The mist outside was now thick fog.

"This is beyond weird," said Patrick, as a regiment of Roman soldiers appeared through the mist and marched through the walls of the coffee shop as if it did not exist. Sebastian was slumped down in his chair behind the table, as if for protection, his eyes wide with disbelief. Lorna looked alternately at the Chronograph in her hand and the happenings around her, wondering what to do next.

"Strange, isn't it?" said a deep voice above them. The three of them had been so occupied with the bizarre nature of the situation that they had not noticed the arrival of the Keeper. Lorna's hand closed over the Chronograph, and she stuffed it back into her pocket. The man gave a deep laugh. "See what happens when you meddle with things you don't understand? If you would only give it to me..."

"Never!" Sebastian, erupting like a small volcano, sprang out of his chair and kicked the Keeper hard, aiming high. The man yelled and doubled over. Patrick grabbed his chair and smashed it down on him for good measure. The Keeper dropped to the floor and did not move. Lorna stared.

"Have you killed him?" she whispered.

"I don't think so," said Patrick, "But I'm not waiting to find out. Come on!"

They darted out of the coffee shop and down the alley, leaving the man still slumped unnoticed on the floor.

"Stop!" Lorna cried, before they had gone too far, and the two shadows running beside her halted.

"I can hardly see you," came Patrick's voice from the mist.

"I know," she said, "Here, hold my hand or we'll lose each other. Sebastian?"

"Here," said the boy, and she felt his hand slip into hers on one side while she held Patrick's on the other.

"I don't know where we are," she said nervously. "I've lived here all my life and I recognise nothing. This mist is too thick."

"I'm not sure it would matter," said Patrick, "seeing as we don't know where to go anyway."

As a three-person chain, they now advanced through the thickening fog, no longer surprised by the shadowy figures that swirled around them from the Ages that had passed before.

"I really don't like this." Sebastian's voice sounded hollow in the gloom.

"I think we should try to get back to the house," Patrick said. "Glenelven – I mean Uncle Kelvin - will probably have gone back there to wait for us."

"That's all very well," said Lorna, "but I told you, I don't know which way is back."

"You don't recognise anything?"

She shook her head. "Things seem familiar one minute, and the next, they don't."

They emerged onto the High Street. "End of season sale!" screamed the windows of the boutique in front of them. "50% off summer stock!" As they stared through the great plate glass windows at the people within, the whole picture began to fade in and out. A boy in hipster jeans merged with another in leggings and a jerkin, while a girl with a pierced navel melded disconcertingly with a nun.

"See what I mean?" Lorna said.

Further along the road, some shop fronts seemed to be ghosts of themselves, their predecessors drifting in and out, sometimes disappearing altogether where no shops had previously been. Most disturbing was the ground beneath their feet, paved one minute, then turning into muddy slop the next. Side alleys that they may have run down earlier had given way to fields. Then the whole present-day picture would suddenly rush back in again with all its modern noise and bustle and look as solid as ever, before the fog swirled round to confuse things once more.

They stood deliberating their next move. "What's that?" Sebastian said suddenly.

A light seemed to hang in the sky, piercing the fog for a moment. "I'm not sure," Lorna said slowly.

The fog drifted round them again and the light reappeared. This time, they could just make out a tall shadow reaching up to the sky. Lorna frowned, as if trying to recall something. Then she took the Chronograph out of her pocket.

"Look!" she cried. One hand on the instrument was ticking forwards, while the other was ticking slowly backwards.

"How odd," said Patrick. "It's as if it's trying to be in two Ages at once."

"Of course!" Lorna looked excited. "We need to follow the light!"

"Hey, wait for us!" Sebastian shouted as she headed quickly into the mist.

"This is madness," Patrick said, swerving to avoid a butcher carrying a pig's carcass into a shop on the left. "One minute you're saying you don't know which way to go, and the next you're rushing off towards some bizarre light."

"The Watch Tower!" Lorna replied. "I knew I recognised it! In that print in the antique shop."

"Watch Tower?"

"They had them in olden times. To watch out for the enemy and stuff."

"So, we're heading to an old watch tower?" said Patrick.

"Yes, but listen." She could hardly speak for excitement. "Middlebridge never had one, then this mad bloke called Josiah Edgington decided to build one on a hill outside town. Mid- eighteen-hundreds, I think. The town's grown up around it now, so you don't even realise it's on a hill anymore."

"And your point?" Patrick said.

"Well, it was just some wacky idea, wasn't it? It wasn't like the town needed one at that point. They called it Josiah's Folly!" She looked at him triumphantly.

"You're kidding!"

"No, really. It doesn't even go by that name anymore, it's just this weird building in the middle of all these crappy

Victorian houses. We did it in local history at school ages ago. It was dead interesting." She stopped abruptly. "Well, if you like that sort of thing I suppose."

Patrick snickered.

"Oh, shut up." She tossed her hair and started walking again.

"I hope you're right," said Sebastian, "and it's not the Keeper with some sort of trap."

"I think I am," said Lorna. "Remember what the Maid said. 'When the Mists thicken, the Folly will arise...' And see how we seem to be walking uphill?"

"Look behind us," said Patrick, "there's nothing there."

He was right. Even the shadows of the shops on the High Street had disappeared. "The Chronograph's still ticking in opposite directions," Lorna said, checking it, "only faster now. This has to be right."

"The fog's clearing." Sebastian pointed. "Look!"

A hazy curtain hung before them, permeated by sunlight beyond. Then the mist and shadows of Middlebridge disappeared, giving way to green slopes dotted with trees. The ground rose steeply before them, and there, crowning the incline some way ahead, stood a tower, the sunlight blazing through the open arches at the top.

"That's it," Lorna said softly. "The Folly on the Hill. We've found it."

CHAPTER 19

The Folly on the Hill

The climb reminded Lorna of the time she'd tried to walk up a downwards moving escalator. What had looked easy proved otherwise and the Folly remained elusive and out of reach, never seeming to get any closer. The path had become rocky and pitted with holes, the air thick and still. Lorna's hair and clothes stuck to her unpleasantly with the heat, and sweat dripped off the end of her nose and fingers. Behind her, she could hear Sebastian panting with the strain of the climb, his feet skidding occasionally on the loose stones. Only Patrick seemed unaffected by the unpleasantness of the dust and the burning sun as he strode up the hill ahead of them, eager to reach the stone building at the summit.

She stopped for a moment, fanning herself, and waited for Sebastian. "You okay?"

"Yeah." The boy grinned up at her. He took a huge step forward into air and Lorna only just stopped him from falling.

"Sebastian, for heaven's sake!"

"Sorry. The ground went all funny again."

"Patrick!" Lorna yelled up the slope. "Hang on a minute. I think Sebastian's got heat stroke or something."

"What? Oh, for heaven's sakes!" Patrick retraced his steps back down the hill towards them. "He looks all right to me. Just fan him off a bit and let's get on. We're nearly there."

"Like hell we are. We've been walking for hours. The kid's done in and I don't feel so good either. Let's get him to that big rock over there where there's some shade."

Patrick sighed. "Here. I'll carry him."

Out of the heat of the sun, Sebastian seemed to perk up. "I ain't half thirsty."

"We didn't think to bring anything," Lorna said, worried.

"There might be water up at the Folly," Patrick said. "Why don't you and I go on up there? We can do whatever we need to do, get some water and collect Sebastian on the way down."

"We can't just leave him!"

"We're losing time!" Patrick turned away, frustrated. "We should've left him at the house this morning. He was only ever going to slow us down."

"You mean bastard! You know it must be the three of us together. Uncle Kelvin said so!"

"Stop talkin' like I ain't here," Sebastian said. "Ain't my fault I ain't feelin' well."

Patrick glared. "Nothing ever *is* your fault, is it?"

"I'm staying here." Lorna slumped down next to Sebastian. "I need some rest too, even if you don't. You do what you like."

Patrick glared at her for a moment. "Have it your way. You usually do." He sat down in the shadows a little away from them. Lorna stole a look at him. The young man was propped against the rock, eyes closed, jacket rolled into a ball behind his head as an impromptu pillow. He'd undone the top three buttons of his shirt and Lorna felt tempted to reach out and gently touch the bare skin underneath. She shook herself.

Patrick created such a mix of emotions in her. He could be arrogant and mean, especially the way he treated Sebastian, yet at other times he only had to look at her and her heart felt like it would burst through her chest. It was so confusing and wasn't helped by how he seemed to treat her like a kid one minute and something more the next.

"Oh dammit, like I care," she muttered. Sebastian had fallen asleep, his head on her lap. Maybe she'd take a short nap too.

She didn't wake until much later, chilled by the sudden drop in temperature caused by the setting sun. She shook Sebastian gently to waken him, then poked Patrick in the ribs. "Come on. Let's move."

The hill, which had been challenging enough by day, now seemed downright foreboding. The sun seemed to fade more quickly than usual, and they stumbled along in the half-light. Lorna felt cold and dirty, which was no improvement on feeling hot and dirty earlier in the day. The hill seemed to be tricking them, casting long shadows that disguised potholes and made their progress even slower, while the Folly still did not seem to be getting any nearer. Gradually the stars came out, one by one, and a full moon rose, casting a weak, silvery light. Suddenly, the ground seemed to flatten. "We're there!" Patrick cried ahead of them, and with two more steps, Lorna and Sebastian joined him on the summit.

The crumbling Folly looked mournful in the pale moonlight, fissures and ivy running over the stonework like scars on some battle-weary face. As they drew closer to the blackness of the entrance, even Patrick seemed to slow his step.

"I don't like it," Lorna said. "It feels…unfriendly."

"You do talk crap," Patrick scoffed. "It's just an old building and I want some proper sleep, preferably with a bit of shelter, even if it is a crumbling heap of stone. Let's go in."

"Come on, Lorna," said Sebastian, following him. "The Maid of the Falls told us to come here. She wouldn't have sent us if it wasn't safe."

"Maybe it just used to be safe," said Lorna. "Before what happened at the Falls. Maybe it's all changed."

"Oh, for God's sake! Wait here," Patrick said impatiently and strode into the Folly. A couple of minutes passed before he reappeared.

"There's nothing in there," he said. "It's just a stone floor with a few twigs and a crumbling old staircase in the corner. Come on. We might be able to make a fire."

"I still don't like it," Lorna said. "It feels like a trap."

"Quite right, Lorna," said a voice to her right. Lorna swung round with a sharp cry. The silhouette of a female figure stood black against the night sky. Sebastian hid his face, and even Patrick looked as if his insides were turning to water with the shock of realising they were not alone.

"Who the hell are you?" he said, the quiver in his voice undermining any attempt to sound brave.

"I?" said the voice. "I am the Woman on the Hill."

The figure walked closer until it was standing directly in front of them, and they could make out a pale and rather haughty face framed by long, sleek black hair. The Woman on the Hill was tall, even taller than Patrick, slender and dressed in dark floating garments. Above all, she was breathtakingly, though coldly beautiful, her features as though carved from marble. Lorna felt a sense of mistrust and looked at the boys. Sebastian looked apprehensive. Patrick was entranced.

"You do well to be cautious," the Woman said. "What you carry is sought after by many and danger wears many faces. However, my sister was right to tell you to come here."

"Your sister?" said Sebastian, sounding doubtful. "She didn't look much like you."

"Yes, my sister," said the Woman. "She who you call the Maid of the Falls, also the Guardian of the Past."

"What is this place?" Lorna shuddered. "It feels sort of...cold. Not at all friendly."

"It isn't," said the Woman. "It is neither friendly nor fearful, neither welcoming nor foreboding, it just is. This is the neutral place. A Place outside Time."

"Outside Time?" said Patrick, suddenly coming back to life.

"Yes," said the Woman. "The Hill can only appear to those who can pass between the Ages. It is one of the Two Places of Passage, the other being the Garden Behind the Falls, which you know. The Folly may appear to crumble with age yet stands immovable. It is here that Time stands still, waiting for the next Age and I am its Watchguard. Come inside." The boys followed her, Lorna lagging behind.

"Sit down." As the Woman moved around the room, the only one in the Folly, a pale light followed her, and chairs seemed to emerge from the darkness.

"I thought you said there was nothing in here except a few old sticks," whispered Lorna to Patrick.

"There wasn't," he said. "Or maybe there was, and I just didn't see with being so tired. Or maybe it was just a trick of the light. I don't know." He shrugged.

They sat down and waited for the Woman to speak. "What do you know of your task here?" she asked.

"We're supposed to bring round the Future," Patrick said. "My mother's missing, but Glenelven said something about old methods ..."

"Glenelven? Ah yes. Such a friend to us. And you are my sister's boy."

"Celesta is your sister too?" Patrick was startled. The Woman looked at him curiously.

"I see there is much you don't know," she said. "But things shall be revealed at their proper Times. For now, we must focus on the task in hand."

"What does Patrick mean about bringing round the Future?" Sebastian asked. "Lorna and me, we're in this as well. It ain't right if he knows more than us."

The Woman laughed, waving Patrick to be quiet as he started to protest. "Well spoken, small one. I can see that what you lack in stature, you make up for in courage." She glanced up through the open roof of the Folly at the moon. "We still have a little Time. I will tell you what I can. The Chronograph you carry, enables you to traverse between the Ages. You may call them Past, Present and Future, but they are all Ages which, in essence, have already been created. All flow from one to the other, yet intertwine, existing both sequentially and simultaneously, a complex web of seconds, minutes, and hours that, for now, run freely, according to Man's will.

Yet someone wants control," she continued. "Someone who does not want Man's will to control his own destiny. Someone who wants to pull the threads of time, unravel them, and reknit them to his own desires."

"My stepfather," said Lorna.

"Yes," said the Woman. "The Keeper of the Hours. He grew jealous of the Guardians of the Ages, those who see that the Past, Present and Future flow as they should, never touching visibly to Man, whose mind would fall in and descend to madness if he were exposed to the true nature of Time. The Keeper of the Hours desires control and he is growing stronger, but his powers are still limited. The Chronograph will give him the ultimate power over Time, to skip back and forth to the most precise of Dark Moments, and then…"

"What will happen if he gets it?" Patrick asked.

"The collapse of Time itself," the Woman said. "He will pull apart the threads of the Ages and reweave them into a new tapestry of chaos that will change the nature of Time and the universe and lead to its eventual end."

"Why would he do that?" said Patrick. "If Time ends, then he doesn't only destroy humanity, he destroys himself as well, doesn't he? It doesn't make sense."

"Self-destruction is never a fear of the insane," said the Woman. "And his newfound knowledge shows him only how he may profit, not what he may lose. But in any case, there are the places that stand outside Time."

"The Folly," said Lorna. "Where we are now. And the Falls."

"The Falls are no more," said the Woman. "But I do not believe he meant their destruction and will have learned from his error. If he can come here, to the Folly, at the moment Time collapses and ends, then he can create a new set of Ages over which he can have total control and cause the misery and desolation he so desires."

"But aren't you the Watchguard here?" said Sebastian. "Couldn't you stop him?"

"Alas," said the Woman. "I cannot. I cannot halt the actions of others; I can only advise." Her voice hardened. "I oversee, but I do not own. My father saw to that. The price for defending my sister, Serena."

She turned her back on them, fiddling with something above the fireplace. "The cup of golden liquid," she continued, "is the old way of bringing round the next Age. It is many Ages since its last use, when the Old Guardians fought and died in many dark battles, and other brave souls had to act in their stead. It must be drunk at the right moment and outside of Time."

With this last statement, she turned to face them, and the pale light that had seemed to follow her now emanated from within and illuminated something she held raised in her hands. As they looked, they saw a goblet, carved from something which Lorna realised in horror, was bone. The Woman lowered the goblet, and in the shimmering light that now surrounded her, they could see its contents, a thick gold liquid that seemed to shudder as they looked at it.

"The blood of the Great Dragon," said the Woman. "He who sits at the pinnacle of Time and will swallow the world when the Ages must truly end - as decided by the Great Guardian of All Time and NOT as decided by another. One of you must drink it, as an entrusted servant in lieu of the Guardian." She set the goblet down on a raised tablet of stone that none of them had noticed before. "But remember, not too soon."

"Or what?" said Patrick suddenly. "Look, I've heard enough. Glenelven told me that my Age isn't yet in place and you're supposed to help us fix that. But all you've done is tell us some crap about Dragons and co-existing Ages. I don't believe one word you've said."

"You had better, Future Boy," said the Woman, looking at him stonily. "Or you will have no Future to return to."

"What do you mean?" Lorna sounded nervous.

"In the absence of a Guardian, the cup of golden liquid can give birth to the next Age. It brings it out of parallel existence and sets it in its rightful place in the sequence of Time. If that does not happen, then the Present cannot move to the Past, and the Past cannot move to the Far Past and into more distant history. Events cannot unfold. Your Age of the Future cannot move forward, you cannot move forward. Things stagnate and decay as they have no place to go. Your Age will simply cease to exist."

"But I came from the Future," said Patrick. "So how can it not exist, when it co-exists and then moves forward - when I've moved backwards to begin with," he ended lamely.

"It's like a chess board," said Lorna suddenly. "All the squares are in front of you and behind you, but they are on either side too. So, you can move either side, but also forward and backward because all possibilities exist at once. But eventually you must move forward, because otherwise you never get anywhere. Is that right?" she said to the Woman.

"Something like that," smiled the Woman. Lorna looked smugly at Patrick, who rolled his eyes in response.

"Each set of Ages co-exist for a while," the Woman continued. "They gestate as it were, then when ripe, must fall into the linear chain to fulfil their potential. The golden liquid sets the next movement in motion. But it must be drunk at the right time, and only by someone designated, or nothing will move as it should, and may even be unstable."

"Terrific," Patrick said sarcastically. "And exactly how do we know when to drink this...this... slop?" He wrinkled his nose disdainfully.

"The moment is close," the Woman said, ignoring him. "As to its precise arrival, that is your judgement and yours alone. Use what you have available to guide you." She walked towards the door. "It's a beautiful Moon," she said.

Then the darkness enveloped her, and she was gone.

There was a long silence. "She was a bit creepy," said Sebastian. "When d'you think we should drink this stuff?"

"How the hell should I know!" Patrick snapped. Sebastian glared at him.

"Look!" Lorna interrupted. "The Chronograph. It's going berserk. The hands will fly off if it doesn't stop."

Patrick and Sebastian looked at the small instrument in her palm. The hands had taken on a life of their own and, rather than moving methodically around the face, they were whirring round it so fast that they were almost a blur. Not only that, they were moving backwards.

"I don't like the look of that," said Patrick. "Has it ever done anything like that before?"

Lorna shook her head. "I think we should go outside. There was something the Woman said about it being a beautiful moon. It was like she meant us to go look at it."

"Dunno about that," said Patrick. "She seemed a bit nuts to me.

"I don't care. I'm going to take a look."

"Have it your way." Patrick got to his feet. "You bring the liquid," he ordered Sebastian.

Outside, the moon seemed fuller and brighter, casting a pool of surprisingly strong light across the hill.

"Look," said Lorna, "the Chronograph's slowing down." The hands had stopped their maniacal travels around the face of the instrument and were now proceeding more sedately, although still backwards. As they watched, they moved ever more slowly, from a second between movements to two or three.

"Look at the moon," said Sebastian in a quivering voice. The moon had grown still larger and was now hanging lower in the sky. With every movement of the Chronograph's hands, it moved still lower, looking as though it would crash into the Earth at one point, but then started to disappear behind the Hill.

"It's time," said Patrick suddenly.

"What do you mean?" Lorna said.

"To bring the next Age into its rightful place. It's obvious now, isn't it?" he continued airily. "Use what we have to guide us, she said. The Chronograph. As the hands slow, the moon is falling lower. At some point, it's going to disappear entirely."

Lorna hated to admit it, but Patrick was right. With every tick of the hands round the face of the Chronograph backwards towards twelve, the moon moved in slow, deliberate steps, lower in the sky and further behind the Hill. Only a quarter of it was now showing. It was evident that when the hands finally reached twelve and, in all likelihood, stopped, it would coincide with the moon's final disappearance behind the Hill.

"It's at that point we have to drink it," said Patrick. "Time is slowing down as one Age ends and when it stops, the new one moves into its rightful place. As the final second ticks by, we drink it. Just as Time seems to stop, we start it again."

Lorna looked at him. Patrick merely glanced back, his air of superiority creating even more distance between them. It was obvious he thought himself above her, above

Sebastian, probably above the Woman and Glenelven as well. Something in Lorna snapped.

"So, *we* have to drink it, do we? You're the one who's supposed to be the Son of the Guardian. Or is it so beneath you to drink this disgusting looking slop, that some other mere mortal has to do it for you?" Her eyes flashed.

"If he won't do it, I will," said a quiet voice. It was Sebastian.

"No!" Lorna panicked. This wasn't meant to happen. She'd only meant to cut Patrick down to size. "You can't, Sebastian. It's not your job. What if we've got it wrong? Besides – it's too dangerous."

"We haven't got it wrong," said Patrick, "and it's my mother who should be doing this. I'm supposed to act for her."

"Oh yes?" Sebastian suddenly exploded with resentment. "You'd love that, being Mr Big Hero, like the rest of us ain't done nothing. It was Lorna what said about the moon. And me what helped build the Chronograph. Besides," he continued rashly, "who's got the cup? Oh look, it's me. Anyway, the moon's just about gone."

"Bloody hell!" cried Patrick. "Come on Sebastian, hand it over."

"Wait!" exclaimed Lorna. "The Chronograph! We have to be sure the hands won't move again!" As if in response, the hands made one more click, both stopping just before twelve. Then nothing. The three of them stood and waited, but although the hands seemed to have stopped, the moon now continued to fall behind the hill.

"It has one more second to go," said Lorna. "We can't get this wrong or it won't work! Then what will happen?"

"We can't wait any longer." Patrick retorted. "The Chronograph isn't moving, and the moon's almost gone! Maybe we don't wait for the last second to pass, maybe it's *on* the last second that we start the new Age, so Time doesn't stop altogether! Yes, that's it!" He looked at Lorna full of superiority again. "We mustn't wait for Time to stop altogether." He held his hand out to Sebastian, who still clutched the goblet close to his chest.

Patrick gave a nasty laugh. "My goodness, runt. You are determined, aren't you? Very commendable, I'm sure. I'll have to make sure your bravery is mentioned in dispatches. Now hand it over."

Sebastian set his teeth.

"Don't call me runt. I'm every bit as good as you."

"Go on then," Patrick folded his arms and looked mockingly at the small boy. "The Woman only said it had to be someone designated. As chosen representative of the Guardians, I designate you."

"Patrick, stop it!" Lorna urged. "You know this isn't right. Besides, I still think it's too soon and...Sebastian, no!"

"For Chrissakes, Sebastian, I didn't mean it!" Patrick lunged forward, but it was too late. With one look of pure hate in Patrick's direction, Sebastian raised the cup and chugged back the whole heaving mass within.

"No!" screamed Lorna. The Chronograph shuddered in her hand as it clicked the last second to twelve. Then the glass cracked, the pieces fell on the floor and the hands whizzed round the face again, clockwise this time, and stopped at one second to twelve.

There was a stillness. Then the wind started to blow.

"Well, I suppose you've done it," Patrick said grudgingly. "Here comes the next Age. Here comes the Future!"

Sebastian wiped his mouth on his sleeve. "Tasted bloody 'orrible. Now mebbe you'll..." He doubled over suddenly, gasping for breath and fell to the ground.

"Sebastian!" Lorna cried.

"Pack it in, Sebastian," said Patrick. "So, you did it, no need for drama. You're scaring Lorna."

The wind suddenly blew stronger and large clouds started to gather above them in the moonless sky. The boy on the ground started choking violently.

"Patrick, he's not mucking about!" Lorna ran over and fell to her knees beside the small boy, shaking him in desperation. "Patrick, help me!" she cried.

Rain started to fall, heavier and heavier, a rumbling sound could be heard in the distance, and then the rushing sound of water. The Hill, which had been so high when they climbed it earlier, was now rapidly becoming smaller as the water swirled around it, rising dangerously higher with every second.

"Get into the Folly!" Patrick pushed her roughly out of the way. "Go on! We need to climb to the top, away from the water. I'll bring Sebastian." He bent to lift the boy, then stopped.

"What are you doing?" Lorna shrieked against the now raging wind.

"I can't lift him. It's like he's-he's stuck or something."

"What!"

The two of them, now soaked to the skin, tried again, but the boy remained pinned to the ground by some invisible force. His eyes stared, bigger and bigger as he choked and gagged. Then suddenly he lapsed into unconsciousness. The water was now lapping the very edges of the summit.

"We'll have to leave him."

"No!" Lorna cried. "We can't. He'll drown!"

"So will we if we don't move! What good will it do if we all die?"

She was crying hysterically as he dragged her away, into the Folly and up the crumbling stone steps to the top where they stood and watched the scene unfold below. The water was now a raging torrent all around the Hill. The summit finally succumbed as the water surged over the last of the ground and reached Sebastian. The boy's body, now seemingly weightless, floated on top of the water, and then in a split second was carried away.

Then, as suddenly as it had come upon them, the water started to retire. The raging torrent became a flowing stream, the flowing stream became a receding lake. The summit re-emerged like a small island, gradually growing bigger, and then the water completely disappeared.

The two descended the stairway and walked out of the Folly as if in a trance. The ground was firm and dry. The clouds had cleared, and the stars were out. The moon had disappeared to who knows where. And Sebastian had gone.

"No!" Lorna screamed and fell to the ground as the depth of the excruciating loss hit home. She felt Patrick's arms go around her as he helped her to her feet, then held her tightly against him, stroking her hair.

"Bring him back," she heaved, her words barely discernible.

"I wish I could," he whispered. "God knows I wish I could. I'm sorry, I'm so sorry for everything. There's nothing I can do."

She shook herself free and stepped away from him, the rising fire of hate running through her veins.

"You bastard," she said. "You could never be nice to him, could you? The last thing you did was...was mock him. He only drank that stuff to prove he was worth something. But he always was worth something, to me anyway. You as good as killed him, Patrick, and that makes you nothing but a bloody, bastard murderer!"

Patrick looked at her evenly for a moment, then turned and walked wordlessly into the Folly, leaving her alone with her grief in the darkness.

CHAPTER 20

Truth

Uncle Kelvin was tying up sunflowers in the back garden when Lorna and Patrick returned. They had spent the night in silence in the Folly, Lorna finally joining Patrick inside when the chill wind became too much for her. She'd ignored Patrick, sitting hunched up in the shadows that prowled along the opposite wall to where he was seated. Neither had slept well.

Stepping out from the Folly at daybreak, they found themselves back in the Present Age on a warm day and on what Lorna said was "the wrong side of town." This was her only comment during the long walk back to the house, and she did not even look at Patrick when she spoke.

Patrick didn't need further conversation to understand what she meant. The Folly was surrounded by old, terraced houses, dark with dirt from the industrial era, spreading like grimy fingers down the hill until they reached the river that separated them from the better part of town.

Children ran about in the street, untamed and as grimy as the homes they came from. A broken bicycle kept company with the litter on the pavement and a few net curtains twitched at upstairs windows as unseen eyes watched the two strangers walk down the hill. The thick fog from the previous day had disappeared.

It was a good thing the fog had obscured all this before, Patrick thought. He was glad they were leaving the place rather than walking into it as they would have been yesterday. Then he remembered that perhaps none of it had been there at all, what with the time-shifting, and then of course they had stepped out of Time themselves when they made the final climb to the Folly.

As he and Lorna reached the bottom of the road and crossed the bridge over the river, he also thought how lucky it was that they had somehow crossed it in the mist and not walked straight off the bank into the depths below. He almost mentioned all this to Lorna, but one look at her face told him to keep his counsel. Now here they were with Uncle Kelvin tying up flowers as if nothing had happened. It felt surreal.

"There you are!" Uncle Kelvin looked relieved. "I'm sorry. I was gone much longer than I'd intended, and you'd all disappeared. I hoped you'd come straight back here though."

He tied the last sunflower in place and wiped his hands. "They're springing up from nowhere," he said. "Time playing havoc with Mother Nature. Anyway, we should plan our next move." He looked at them. "You're both very quiet. Where's Sebastian?"

"He's dead," Lorna said flatly.

"Dead?" Uncle Kelvin looked shellshocked. "But how?"

"He drank the cup - at the Folly. It did something to him. Then the flood came and washed him away."

"You found the Folly?" said Uncle Kelvin, perplexed.

"We found it all right," said Patrick, "after being chased all over town by the Keeper and then walking for hours in thick fog and then in searing heat up a great big hill. Didn't you wonder where we were?"

Uncle Kelvin shook his head. "I'm afraid not. I've only been back an hour at most."

"But we spent a day climbing the hill and a whole night at the Folly!"

"Remember the Folly is outside Time. Things flow differently there. But none of this matters. What happened to Sebastian?"

Lorna flung an evil look at Patrick and recounted the events at the Folly. "Sebastian drank the liquid?" Uncle Kelvin exclaimed. "But why? No wonder he collapsed. It was too powerful for a small boy of his age."

"It was my fault." Patrick looked at his boots. "I goaded him. I don't know what got into me."

"Your malice and arrogance have cost us dear," Uncle Kelvin said grimly. "This is not good news, Patrick. Your Age is still stuck."

"You mean after all that, we've failed?"

Uncle Kelvin nodded. "Had you succeeded, we would not be standing here in the Present. You would have stepped off the Hill into your own Time. The Chronograph would be in its rightful Age where it could be returned to the Great Lord to decide its destiny, and the Guardian of the Future – your mother – would be free.

We'd have returned Lorna and Sebastian to their own Ages by other means, and although the Keeper would still have had some minimal power, he would have been caught fairly easily. Of that, I'm sure. We've been dealt a severe blow."

"And we've lost Sebastian," said Lorna. She turned fiercely to Patrick. "I told you," she shouted. "I told you it was too soon. The hands weren't exactly on twelve. And all you did was make fun of him, so he drank that dumb stuff!" Patrick turned scarlet.

"Enough!" interrupted Uncle Kelvin. "If anything, I blame myself. I shouldn't have left you. I was too anxious to see the Keeper's handiwork at the library."

"Did you learn anything?" Patrick asked bitterly.

"Only that one of the curators in the archives had noticed a dark-haired man disappearing with an old volume of local history," Uncle Kelvin replied, "but before he could raise the alarm, the fire started. Then the book showed up in a litter bin, unharmed except for one page that had been torn out."

"A picture of the Folly?" asked Patrick.

"One would assume." Uncle Kelvin sighed and rubbed his hand over his eyes.

"Will he be able to get to the Folly then?" said Lorna. "And drink the Dragon's blood and take control himself?" Uncle Kelvin shook his head.

"I don't understand why he didn't get there first if he'd figured it out," said Patrick.

"Because you had the one thing he needed to pass into that place," said Uncle Kelvin. "If he'd captured the Chronograph and Lorna with it, he could have passed through very easily and set things in motion exactly as he wanted."

"We're out of our depth here, Glenelven." Patrick slumped against the wall. "Don't you think we should admit defeat and take this back to the Court of Time?"

Uncle Kelvin shook his head. "The Prophecy has been set in motion. The Chronograph has been brought through two Ages; it must complete its journey through the third in order to meet its final destiny."

"But what happens if we just cut to the chase and bypass the Future Age?" Patrick persisted. "It's only some dumb old prophecy in an old book. It probably doesn't count anymore."

"Enough!" Uncle Kelvin looked furious. "The Prophecies were written by those greater than I, greater than the Great Lord, and certainly greater than you! This was set in motion from the moment the son of the Great Lord conceived of his wretched Chronograph. Now the path must be walked as the only firm thread through chaos, the only guidance to resolve the matter. To deviate would put us on the wrong side, against Time as it were, and give the Keeper an advantage, maybe even one where he wins. So no, we must make the best of it.'"

"What do we do now?" Lorna asked. "Was the Folly the only way?"

Uncle Kelvin ran his hands through his hair. "The only way I know. The Guardian of the Future must go to the Folly outside of Time to bring round her Age. It is constructed precisely this way as protection against any insurrection at the Court of Time – which did happen several Ages ago. It was near disaster. As Celesta is missing, Patrick was the next best thing, as a relative. I told you this. No-one else is permitted to bring round the Age that she nurtured and was chosen by the Court of Time. Why on earth you thought it was a good idea for Sebastian to take your place is beyond me."

"I didn't!" Patrick exploded. "I didn't think he'd drink it, not really. He was being a pain, I just wanted…I just wanted…"

"To put him in his place? Well, you did that all right, didn't you?" Uncle Kelvin sank onto the garden bench, head in his hands. Patrick stuck his hands in his pockets and said nothing.

Lorna broke the silence. "So, what happens now? If there's literally no Future, what is there?"

Uncle Kelvin shrugged. "For now, nothing. If we try to go forward from here, probably only barrenness, a Time of dust where nothing real exists. Until some other Future is chosen. But I dread to think what that might be, especially if the Keeper gains greater power. Even without the Chronograph he may find means via the Book and the Dark Glass to stage some sort of coup at the Court of Time. Then heaven knows what will happen."

"What do you mean, 'until some other Future is chosen?'" Lorna asked.

"The Court chooses from a set of possibilities. There are several, all exist in parallel, bred from the circumstances of the Present Age, and not all of them good. This is why the Court presides over the Ages and why there is a Guardian of the Future. It is insurance that there will always be some sort of future hope for the human race."

"You mean, the Guardian and the Court manipulate the Future?" Lorna asked, astonished.

"Manipulate is a little strong," Uncle Kelvin mused. "We simply pick the best of the Future possibilities that flow naturally from mankind's actions in the Present. Sometimes none of the options are very good, but in this case, the Future that Celesta had managed to mould from the Present circumstances was excellent, which is why it was chosen."

"I could go back," Patrick said hesitantly. "To the Court, I mean. I don't care if I'm blasted into a Time Vault or whatever. I could at least tell them where we saw Celesta and that must be some sort of clue. They could find her and bring her back."

"They'd hardly listen to a mere Apprentice who's broken the Law," Uncle Kelvin said disparagingly. "In any case, although we know Celesta can't be taken out of the Future Age altogether, the Keeper could have placed her in any one of the possible Futures available to him. One thing's for sure — he will have used the Dark Glass to assess them and place her where there is the greatest evil and despair. It could cost many months and many lives to find her. And we don't have that kind of time."

Patrick flushed deep red and looked murderous. Lorna bit her lip. Uncle Kelvin was clearly angry, and she could hardly blame him, but it wasn't helping matters with Patrick. She twizzled her nose stud nervously.

"If the mere Apprentice is allowed to speak, I do have another thought." Patrick stood with his arms folded, his face an angry mask.

Uncle Kelvin looked at him. "Go on."

"If the Keeper opened a channel to my mother, couldn't we do the same? And somehow wake her?"

The older man thought for a moment. "It's a long shot, but...maybe you have something there."

"But we don't know which Future she's in," said Lorna.

"We know where you were connected in the Past though." Uncle Kelvin looked at Patrick.

"You mean go back to the crypt?"

"That's exactly what I mean. You said you felt a strong pull there. What you saw was an illusion, but it's one that may have left its energy on the place. If we can tap into that, it's possible that a connection could be made. I'm not sure if we can bring her out of stasis though, not across that kind of temporal distance."

"We can try though, surely," said Lorna. "Oh…" her face fell as she realised something. "We can't go back there! We don't have Sebastian, and you said that the three of us can only travel together."

"That is correct," Uncle Kelvin said. "But we don't need to go back to the Past."

"But that's where we saw her!"

"I get it," Patrick said. "The channel can only be opened in the same spot across the Ages. And since you said the Keeper can't transport a Guardian out of her own designated Age, that crypt must still exist in the Future, which means…"

"It's still here in the Present!" Lorna finished.

"Exactly!" Uncle Kelvin nodded. "All we need do, is find the church. Do you remember where it was?"

"It was some village around here," Lorna said. "Near somewhere called Moorlands in the Past. It might not even exist anymore. Even the village Sebastian was from disappeared a long time ago. I'll bet he could have figured it out though. I wish we could ask him!" She gave a deep sigh.

Uncle Kelvin looked thoughtful. "Tell me again. Exactly what happened when he drank the liquid?"

"He sort of choked," Lorna said, fiercely blinking back tears. "Then the water came, and we tried to lift him, but we couldn't. He was so heavy, like he was stuck to the ground. Then the water washed him away. I wish he was here."

"Maybe he is," Uncle Kelvin said.

"What do you mean?"

"I think it's time I told you something about Sebastian, Lorna. Have you never realised who he is? Why you feel so devastated by his loss?"

"No…he was just this sweet kid. I felt a bit protective of him in a weird way. He shouldn't have had to die."

Uncle Kelvin took a deep breath. "Sebastian is a time changeling." Patrick gave a low whistle. Lorna looked at him, puzzled. Uncle Kelvin continued.

"A time changeling is switched at birth with someone in another Age. Sebastian was switched from the Present Age and carried into the Past where he could never be found until the time was right. He belongs in this Age, not the Past. It's David who is the cuckoo in the nest. He was raised as your brother but does not belong here. Sebastian is your real flesh and blood."

Lorna was flabbergasted. "How do you know all this?" she said eventually.

"Because it was I who made the switch," said Uncle Kelvin. "After your father was killed, and your brother was born, the baby had to be hidden. I knew that a child of your father, who had been entrusted with the Chronograph, would be the one to unlock its powers. The Book of Infinity had said that the child was a girl, but I believed your brother could be insurance, just in case."

"Thanks a lot!" said Lorna. "So, if Sebastian was time-switched, then who was he switched with? Just who is the boy I've been calling my brother?"

"Ah," said Uncle Kelvin. "You met Serena, the Maid of the Falls. It is true that she bore a child, a son, who was fathered by the Keeper of the Hours."

"Wait a minute! You don't mean that David is my stepfather's son? That's insane!"

"Indeed, I do. Where better to hide the Keeper's child than under his very nose? He does not know that I was entrusted with Serena's secret. As far as he's concerned, his child is somewhere in the Past and he would never think of looking in his own house, especially while his obsession has been with you and the Chronograph. Mind you, we should probably look to move David soon, especially if the Keeper has seen Serena again recently. We can't risk the Keeper recognising him for who he is."

Lorna was silent. Suddenly, there was a sound of slow clapping. It was Patrick, brimming with sarcasm. "Wonderful, Glenelven! Quite the mess you've created. Pulling people out of their own Times seems to be a habit with you. As you know so much, perhaps you'd like to tell me *my* family history, seeing as people at Court look away at any mention of my father. You pulled me out of my own Age and can't get me back, maybe you did the same for him."

Uncle Kelvin looked at him angrily. "Does your lack of maturity know no bounds? Well, I suppose you must know the full truth about your parentage sooner or later, so it might as well be now. The woman you have been seeking, who you call mother, is not."

Patrick laughed. "Try again, Glenelven! She's always been there, way back as far as I can remember. Until that day…" He looked grim.

"I'm sorry," said Uncle Kelvin, shaking his head. "She was indeed a mother to you in every way possible, but not biologically. What did she tell you about your father?"

"My father," Patrick said haughtily, "was a great man. He was killed in a time quake when he was on a dangerous mission, I was just a baby. When he died, Celesta was heartbroken. I don't know for certain who he was, but I know she was a favourite of the Son of Time…" He let these words linger.

"Is that who you think you are?" Uncle Kelvin asked. "The child of the Son of Time?"

"She told me," Patrick persisted. "A great man who died in a time quake. I know they were cousins, but she was very close to him. My governess told me so, after my mother disappeared."

"Your mother and your governess certainly created a wonderful past for you," remarked Uncle Kelvin.

"And what exactly does that mean?" said Patrick hotly. "If you've got something to say then either say it or shut up!"

"Very well." Uncle Kelvin took a deep breath. "Your adoptive mother, Celesta, was indeed close to the Great Lord's son, the Son of Time, but not in the way you think. She was a very intelligent woman, very learned in the ways of Old Time and an authority on the Book of Infinity – beyond him in intellect and maturity if the truth be known. There was certainly a great fondness between them, and she was devastated when he was killed. But he was not your father." The man hesitated before continuing. "The Maid of the Falls did not just have one son. She had two. Non-identical twins. One was time-switched with Sebastian as you heard. The other…" He looked at Patrick who stared back in disbelief.

"No!" he shouted. "How the hell can that be? I'm not even the same age as David, he's far younger, he's…"

"I know," Uncle Kelvin said more gently. "It's very hard to understand. Hiding one child was enough of a problem, but two… Celesta agreed with her uncle, the Great Lord, to raise you as her own, in the Future Age. She built her own legend, disappeared from Court for a while and then appeared sometime later, speaking only of an affair with a man who was then killed before they could marry to legitimize the child. Everyone assumed that the man was the Son of Time and that she was keeping quiet to protect him. And nobody was inclined to ask questions. We both knew that the Keeper of the Hours could never return to Court and given that you don't favour him the slightest in looks, it seemed like a foolproof plan."

Patrick was white and Lorna allowed herself to feel sorry for him. It was a big enough shock for her, finding out that Sebastian was her own brother, but at least she hadn't just been told she was the child of their enemy.

"What went wrong?" she asked.

"The Keeper had been silent for several years and I'm afraid we allowed our guard to drop," Uncle Kelvin said. "He's evil but he's not stupid and would have his ways of learning at least some of what was happening at Court. It was inevitable that he would learn of Serena's disappearance eventually and put two and two together. Celesta became an obvious target for information. He waited till she and Patrick were at the Astral Meadow and struck. At first, we feared he may have killed her, but the Keeper always did have an eye for beauty, so he's been holding her hostage. It's certain she confirmed no more than he had already guessed, or he would have known who Patrick and David were."

"I can't get my head around this," Lorna said, bewildered. "How can Patrick be David's twin? There are years between them! And then Sebastian made the Chronograph when they were just babies... I don't get it."

"The Past is unravelling," said Uncle Kelvin. "And the Future, that is, Patrick's Future Age, has been speeding up. Time is falling in on itself and the parallel Ages, instead of running at the same pace, are in chaos. This has been happening since the creation of the Chronograph. The Son of Time was a damn fool, he didn't know what he was doing. The Ages are in crisis, and the Keeper isn't helping matters."

There was silence. "My father has been long dead to me," Patrick said finally, "so in that respect, nothing's changed. I think you were saying something about Sebastian, Glenelven. Before all this time-changeling stuff I mean."

"All may not be lost," Uncle Kelvin said, brightening. "The flood that washed Sebastian away at the Folly was simply the Waters of Time in action as they tried to wash in the next Age."

"So what?" Lorna said. "We still don't know where he is. Or even if he's alive."

"The Waters of Time are very powerful. If someone is caught in them, they tend to be taken *back to where they belong*." Uncle Kelvin paused to let his words sink in.

"You mean... because Sebastian is a child of the Present, he's here!" Patrick said, incredulous.

"If the Waters are working the way they should, then yes."

Lorna felt her spirits lift for the first time since the Folly. "We need to find him! He could be wandering anywhere, totally lost." A horrible thought hit her. "Or maybe he's just washed up somewhere round here and he's still...dead."

"I don't know for sure," Uncle Kelvin said. "There is only one other case I know of where someone was caught out of Time in the same way."

"What happened?"

"She was a child of the Future. And unfortunately, the Waters placed her back in a parallel Future that did not move into place. We couldn't get her back." His eyes grew a little distant for a moment, and a fleeting look of what seemed like grief swept his face. He shook himself. "This time it's different, I'm sure. The Present is solidly in place, so there can be no such mistake with Sebastian. Mind you, what...er...state we may find him in is unclear."

"Come on then," said Patrick, impatiently. "Where do we start?"

"The Folly," Lorna said. "That's where we last saw him."

"It's as good a place to start as any," said Uncle Kelvin. "You stay here with the Chronograph, Patrick, I don't want to take it with us. But be on your guard. Ready, Lorna? Then let's go."

CHAPTER 21

Gain and Loss

The angler pulled his waterproof around him against the mizzling rain and sighed.

"Bloody waste of time this is," he said to his companion. "I'm off." He began to pack up his things.

"No staying power, that's your problem." His friend lit a cigarette. "At least we ain't got that fog no more. Right peculiar that were, never seen it so thick."

"Suit yourself, Johnno, but I think you're barmy. All you've caught today's that old bicycle wheel."

"Ah well, Fred." Johnno took a long draw on his cigarette and cast a look at the rows of terraced houses straggling up the hill to the watchtower behind them. "Come here often enough, I'll soon have enough to build a whole bike!"

"Yeah well, be seeing you...hang on a minute." Fred pointed to the middle of the river. "What's that out there?"

"What, that old log?"

Fred nodded. "I swear there's something on it. Looks like a body."

Johnno strained his eyes. The log seemed to have jammed against a mudbank in the middle of the river and was swaying to and fro as the current swirled gently around it. "You sure? I can't quite see it from here."

"Oh, I'm sure all right. The old boatman around today?"

"He'll be along the bank down there somewhere," Johnno said. "He's usually tinkering with something. Hang on, I'll come with you."

The boatman was in his shed, feet up, smoking his pipe and reading the paper. When Fred explained, he at once proposed launching one of his boats to investigate.

"Matter for the police innit?" Johnno looked nervous. "If it's a body, I mean."

"What you scared of?" Fred said, stepping aboard. "Get along home if you don't want to know. Come on, Boatman."

Taking an oar a-piece, the two men rowed towards the log. "Don't you run 'er aground," the Boatman said through gritted teeth as they pulled alongside.

"It *is* a body!" Fred said excitedly, then, "Oh dear Lord! It's a child." The child lay face down on the log, one hand trailing in the water. His clothes were indistinguishable from the mud, his hair was matted and stuck against his skull. "We should get someone."

"No time," the Boatman replied. "Look at him, it's a wonder he hasn't fallen in already. If we leave him, he could drop in and drown before we get back."

"Assuming he's still alive."

"Well, there is that. Here, I'll get us in a bit closer, then you pull the end of the log and try and get it alongside."

Gently, the two men manoeuvred the boat and the log, then awkwardly scooped the boy from his perilous position into the bottom of the boat. He lay there, unmoving.

"Poor little devil," Fred said. "I think he's still breathing though." He took off his waterproof and laid it over the child. "Let's get him back to shore."

A small knot of people had gathered on the riverbank, where Johnno was delivering a running commentary on the proceedings.

"Good thing I spotted it!" he was saying as the two men moored the boat. "Floating on a log like that. Who knows how long it's been there!"

"Shut your yammering and give us a hand," Fred said, lifting the boy onto the bank. "Now then. Anyone know who he belongs to?"

People shook their heads. "Bit hard to tell, state he's in," one woman said. "But I never seen 'im. Not from round here I reckon."

"Could have floated downriver a long way," another said. "Better call the police I reckon."

"Can't we look after him?" Johnno suggested. "Till he comes round, like? We don't need no coppers nosing round 'ere."

"Worried they might ask about all of them crates of cheap booze in your garage, Johnno?" called a tall man from the back of the crowd. "What lorry did they fall off this time?" The crowd laughed.

"Regular comedian you are, ain't you?" Johnno glowered.

"Shutup, Johnno for Chrissakes," Fred said. "Thing is, what are we going to do with 'im?"

"Stand aside," came an authoritative voice from the back of the crowd. "Stand aside I say!" A dark, bearded man made his way through and knelt by the boy. "Thank goodness! You've found him," he said. "My son! He fell in the river back there and I thought I'd lost him. How can I ever thank you?"

"There you are then, problem solved," beamed Johnno. "Boy's father come to claim him. I love happy endings!

Let 'im through now!" The man lifted the boy in his arms and turned to leave.

"Not so fast!" Fred said. "Something ain't right here. How do we know you're his dad?"

The man turned on him savagely. "How dare you!" he snarled. "I have suffered the utmost torment and you question my rights to the boy?"

"That's exactly what I'm doing." Fred stood firm. "That boy's never just fallen in the river. Look at the state of 'im! Caked in mud he is, looks like he's been there for days. Your story don't stack up."

"Yeah," the tall man added. "He's right! Who the hell are you anyway?"

The boy opened his eyes and whispered. "He's not my Pa."

The dark man laughed nervously. "Boy doesn't know what he's saying!"

"Is that so?" Fred's eyes narrowed with suspicion.

"Of course he doesn't!" the dark man retorted. "Must have banged his head!"

"No, I didn't!" Sebastian was now struggling in the Keeper's grip. "He's not my Pa, I'm telling you, he's evil. Don't let him take me!"

"Don't you worry, son," Fred reassured him. He looked at the Keeper. "Now what's really your interest in the boy?"

"He's a bloody perv!" one of the crowd suddenly shouted. "Trying to take the boy! We know what to do with the likes of 'im, don't we lads?"

"You're making a grave error!" the Keeper growled, momentarily losing his grip on Sebastian as the men advanced. Taking his chance, Sebastian wriggled free and fled.

Looking back as he ran, he saw Fred sock the Keeper hard on the jaw, before two others picked him up and threw him in the river. Not looking where he was going, Sebastian pelted headlong into two people coming in the opposite direction, knocking the breath out of him.

"Look out!" said the man, then the girl cried, "Sebastian!" and threw her arms around him.

"Almost didn't recognise you," grinned Uncle Kelvin. "That's quite a disguise you're wearing!"

Lorna wrinkled her nose. "Bit of a smelly one too!" She gave a trembling kind of laugh, then wiped something from her cheek. "Something in my eye," she said gruffly.

"You'd be smelly if you'd been fished out of the river," Sebastian said.

"So you were down there!" Lorna exclaimed. "We guessed you might be. What happened?"

Sebastian shrugged. "Dunno really. Last thing I remember is drinking that goo. Next thing I know, I'm lying all wet on the riverbank with a load of people, and the Keeper tried to take me."

"The Keeper! He's here?' Lorna looked alarmed.

"Yeah, it's all right though. Some blokes chucked 'im in the river." Sebastian laughed.

Uncle Kelvin looked concerned. "Where was this?"

Sebastian pointed. The crowd had begun to break up. The rain was coming on again, harder than before, and soon only three men remained, pointing anxiously at the water.

"Excuse me one moment," said Uncle Kelvin, and strode off towards the men. Lorna and Sebastian exchanged glances and followed.

Johnno, Fred, and the Boatman were in deep conversation with Uncle Kelvin as they approached.

"Didn't come up," Fred was saying. "Only meant to teach him a lesson."

"That was some punch you gave him," said Johnno accusingly. "Might have dazed him a bit like."

"Wasn't me what threw 'im in!" Fred retorted. He suddenly spotted Sebastian. "You back again, sonny?"

"Er...yeah. I wanted to thank you," said Sebastian.

"You all right now then? Know these people, do you?"

"Yes," Sebastian said, avoiding Fred's eye. "Um...this is my real Pa, and this is my um...sister."

"Yes, that's right," said Uncle Kelvin. "Thank you for rescuing my...son."

"Listen, Mister," Johnno lowered his voice. "Do we have to involve the rozzers? I mean - if that bloke was a you-know-what, he got what he deserved, didn't he?"

"It's not up to us," Uncle Kelvin said sharply. "That's why the law is there to decide. However... in this case, I'm pretty sure the ...er...rozzers would be wasting their time. So, let's say no more, shall we?"

"Thanks," Fred said gruffly. Johnno gave a shaky thumbs up. The Boatman crossed himself, muttering something.

"Don't worry," Uncle Kelvin said, putting his hand on the old man's shoulder. "I won't cause you any trouble and your conscience may rest easy about the man in the river. He sounds a slippery type, and a good riddance to me."

The Boatman looked doubtful.

"We must go," said Uncle Kelvin. "Come on you two, let's get Sebastian home."

Halfway up the bank, Sebastian glanced back and saw the three men looking after them. "D'you think they believed us?" he said.

Uncle Kelvin shrugged. "Maybe they did or maybe they didn't. I don't really care. Hurry up now. We need to get back to Patrick."

"Where is he?" Sebastian asked, scampering along to keep warm.

"At the house," said Lorna. "Looking after the Chronograph. D'you think the Keeper really drowned?"

Uncle Kelvin shook his head. "I doubt it. Things happened fast, but a time-jump could be done in a split second to land him somewhere safer – and he is becoming increasingly accomplished." He looked more serious than they had ever seen him. "We shall have to be careful," he said. "Very careful indeed."

~

Patrick was still reeling from the earlier revelations. All of them at Court, they'd played him for a fool. Glenelven was the worst as far as Patrick was concerned, an audacious and wily man who'd taken a huge gamble with Time Changelings and tricked Patrick into undertaking a dangerous journey with no means of return. If anything, Glenelven's interference made him responsible for Sebastian's death, at least indirectly. Not that Lorna would see it that way. It was obvious she could hardly bring herself to look at Patrick, and now she knew that Sebastian was her real brother, she'd never forgive him.

Deep down, Patrick was disgusted with himself, knowing he'd taken his anger and frustration with events out on Sebastian, just because the kid was an easy target. He pushed down the guilt welling up inside and allowed anger to rise again in its place. Even his mother wasn't who he thought she was. Everything was going wrong.

He'd been so proud of his double life, a foot in each camp as both a Child of the Future, and as an Apprentice and Son of a Guardian at the Court of Time. To learn he was the illegitimate child of a traitor...it was humiliating.

Suddenly Patrick felt six years old again. He wanted to talk to Celesta, tell her that mother or not, he loved her so much and did she feel the same? He should be out there, looking for her, not stuck here with that damn Chronograph. He flung himself into a chair in the corner, hurling Lorna's jacket, dumped on the seat, out of his way and across the room. Something shiny flew out of the pocket, landing under the small sofa opposite. Patrick sat for a moment, breathing hard. He supposed he'd better retrieve whatever it was, probably that pocket-fire thing. He got up with a sigh and fumbled under the sofa. It wasn't the lighter after all, just some lipstick in a fancy case. Something else was under there too. Curiosity burning, he pulled it out to see what it was.

It was a small book of old maps. That crafty devil, Glenelven, must have found it in the library after all, but why hadn't he said anything?

Light suddenly dawned on Patrick. All this business about needing Sebastian to remember the village was a bluff. Glenelven already knew, he'd figured it out! But he knew that Patrick would have insisted on going to the crypt first and looking for Sebastian later, so he'd pretended not to know.

Now his anger doubled. All this time being wasted instead of going to connect with Celesta, to wake her maybe, so that she could play her role as Guardian and sort this mess out. The Great Moment at the Folly may have passed, but she'd come up with something else, he knew she would. A thought entered his mind. What if

Glenelven didn't want her found? What if he wanted to solve this whole thing and take all the credit? Become Guardian of the Future himself maybe? After all, he'd been taking care of the Present for so long, and the opportunity to craft the Future must be very tempting. Well, Patrick wouldn't allow that to happen.

If he could find the crypt and wake Celesta himself, then everything could be sorted out before the others even returned, and he could return to Court a hero! Lorna would have to start speaking to him then - if he could be bothered to acknowledge her. And Glenelven would be shown up for what he was – a fool who'd wasted time running round after a Time Changeling who'd died in a flood.

Patrick flipped the book open, searching for something to jog his memory. A red ink circle caught his eye. Glenelven had circled a wood, which Patrick realised must be where he'd touched down in the Past. With his finger, he traced the markings of an old track headed towards the Moorlands estate and then a river flowing north to south down the page, passing several villages. But which one was it?

A name caught his eye, underlined in red. Elmwood-by-the-Water. That must be it! The first village south of Moorlands and there was a symbol for a church. He felt a shiver of excitement run down his spine, then frowned. The only problem was how to locate it now, in this Time, when the town had grown up in a massive urban sprawl covering all the land between. He studied the map again. He was on the far edge of Middlebridge now, next to the oldest part of town. That meant he had to go about five miles southeast. What he needed now was a present-day map and transportation. He'd find both if he went back into town.

For a moment, Patrick hesitated. He ought to wait for the others and see if they'd found Sebastian. Then a ticking sound broke into his thoughts. The Chronograph. It had been silent for a while, maybe it was starting up again. He picked the timepiece up and looked at it. The third hand had stuck on the miniature flowers by the number three. The other two were swinging wildly in opposite directions, crossing at twelve and six. It was almost as though it couldn't make up its mind which way to go.

Like Time itself, Patrick thought. It doesn't know what it's doing, as the Future hasn't been cut free. This was proof, if nothing else, that further delay was not an option. He stuffed the instrument into his pocket, thinking it might be useful in opening the channel with Celesta, then tore the page out of the old map book and strode out of the house towards town.

The walk was shorter than he remembered, and he soon found himself at the square by the library. The fire engine had gone, a charred upper window and some foam blowing along the ground being the only evidence of the drama earlier that day. There was a tiny tourist information centre next door and Patrick went in.

A young woman, about his age, was slouched behind the counter, chewing gum. She looked up disinterestedly when the bell above the door rang, but seeing Patrick, she straightened herself and smiled.

"How can I help you?" she asked.

"I need a map," Patrick said. "Please."

"Certainly," she said. "There's a very good map of the local area here for two pounds, or I can give you a free one of the town centre."

Patrick inwardly kicked himself. He had no money, at least none that would be accepted here.

The young woman noticed his hesitation. "Do you know where you want to go?" she asked. "That might help you decide."

Patrick took a deep breath. He hadn't wanted to tell anyone where he was headed, but he'd have to risk it.

"Elmwood-by-the-Water," he said. The girl pulled at her ponytail and frowned. "Elmwood-by-the-Water? You mean the Elmwood estate way over the other side of town?"

"That must be it!" Patrick said. "It was a village once, by a stream, and it has an old church there, hundreds of years old now, with a crypt."

The young woman looked doubtful. "Don't know about any of that. Hang on a minute though, my Auntie grew up round here, she might know. Auntie Fran!" she yelled. "Elmwood. Know anything about it?"

Patrick shuddered. A couple of tourists who'd entered after him looked up from the postcard rack. Why don't you yell a bit louder? he thought, then maybe everyone'll know where I'm going.

"What about Elmwood?" A stout woman in her sixties appeared from the back of the shop.

"D'you know it? This young man wants to go there." The girl flicked her ponytail, then batted her eyelashes at Patrick and simpered.

"Course I know it," the older woman snorted. "Grew up there didn't I, you stupid girl!"

The girl blushed. "Well, I didn't know." She slunk back behind the counter. Patrick almost felt sorry for her.

"Lived there till I was twelve," the woman continued, "then my dad got a job the other side of Middlebridge so we moved."

"No recent knowledge then," the girl said slyly.

"You mind your manners!" her aunt snapped. "What d'you want to go there for?" she asked Patrick.

"I'm looking for my mother," he said. "We were...separated when I was a kid, and I heard she might be there."

The girl gasped. "Oh, how sad. He's trying to find his mum!"

Her aunt ignored her. "Any idea where? Elmwood's a big place and changed a lot since my day. I get lost whenever I visit friends there."

"Somewhere near the church I think," said Patrick. "There's a stream nearby."

"Don't know about that," the woman thought for a moment. "I did hear of old Bert, years ago, digging foundations for a new extension and finding he had a small river running under his house. All the building must've sent it underground at some point. None too pleased he was, I can tell you. Maybe that was your stream, but how you'd know about that, I'm sure I don't know. None of us even knew it was there. The church though, that's easier."

"That's great!" Patrick leaned forward encouragingly. "Where can I find it?"

"Oh, it doesn't exist anymore," the woman said. "Hit by one of them doodlebugs during the War. Flattened it and killed the vicar while he was polishing the brasses or something." Patrick's face fell.

"Yes," she continued, "only thing that's left of it now is a bit of a graveyard and the crypt."

Patrick looked up, hopes beginning to rise. "And where is that?"

"That's easy," the woman said. "Old Church Lane. Sounds idyllic don't it, but it's anything but. Lots of run-down shops now with crappy flats over them. What's left of the graveyard is over the back of them. Not a nice area. You don't want to go there, luvvie."

"I have to," Patrick said. "My mother. I have to find her."

The woman shrugged. "Suit yourself, but don't say I didn't warn you. Number 6 bus will take you there, should be another one in about ten minutes. Catch it over the other side of the square, four pounds return. Assuming you *do* return…" she added darkly and turned to go.

"One more thing," said Patrick. "The crypt. Can you still…er…go down it?"

"Go down it? What d'you want to go down it for? I thought you were looking for your mum – unless you think she's down there of course!" The woman laughed hysterically at her own joke and Patrick gave a nervous smile. Her niece didn't laugh. She observed Patrick closely.

"Doesn't matter," he said hurriedly.

"All covered with iron grating and locked now, luvvie," the older woman recovered herself. "Keep out the nut jobs. Don't need people down there defiling what's left of the dead. Good luck!" She waved over her shoulder and disappeared. Patrick turned to leave.

"Wait a minute," the young girl said to Patrick, then called to the tourists. "You decided what you want? We're closing soon."

After final deliberation, the female of the pair decided that she didn't want any postcards after all, the mail wouldn't deliver them before they arrived home, and it was a bit old-fashioned these days anyway, wasn't it? Her husband smiled apologetically and the two of them left.

"Idiots," the girl said, and turned the sign to "Closed" behind them. Then she turned to Patrick.

"Your mum," she said. "You think she was murdered, don't you?" Patrick looked surprised. "Come on," the girl continued. "You don't fool me. Why else d'you want to go looking down an old crypt?"

"I didn't actually say…" Patrick began to protest.

"You didn't have to. It was written all over your face. You don't have any money either do you?" Patrick shook his head. "I suppose it's no good telling you to leave it to the police? No, I thought not. Here." She shoved an area map and ten pounds across the counter to him.

Patrick looked at her astounded. "I can't! What about your aunt?"

"What about her? The tenner's my money and I'll put the cash in the till for the map." She pushed the items at Patrick. "Go on. Take them, or you'll miss the bus. You can pay me back when you find your mum."

"Thank you," Patrick said gratefully and left.

~

The girl waved Patrick across the square and watched him board the Number 6 bus, then checked her watch. If she closed up now, she'd just about have time to get ready before meeting that sexy fireman who'd been in earlier. She made to close the door but was stopped by a foot in the doorway.

"We're closed," she said, without looking up.

"I'll only take five minutes of your time," said the dark stranger. "I just want a map for Elmwood."

~

"We found him!" Lorna burst into the kitchen, dragging a grinning Sebastian behind her. "Patrick, we found Sebastian, and he's alive!"

She looked round the empty kitchen and shrugged. "He must be upstairs. Shall I put the kettle on while Sebastian has a bath?"

"By all means," Uncle Kelvin said, folding his coat and propping his boots by the door.

"I'm going to have one of them shower things," said Sebastian, "and find Patrick. He'll die of fright when he sees me!" He ran whooping down the hallway and thundered up the stairs. They heard a door slam, and then the sound of running water which stopped after only a few minutes.

"I don't know how clean he's going to be," remarked Uncle Kelvin. "Just a moment. What's this?" His eyes fell on the torn map book on the table and his face grew dark.

"What is it?" asked Lorna.

"I hope this doesn't mean what I think it means," Uncle Kelvin replied, holding up the book.

Sebastian reappeared, towelling his hair. "He's not there." He looked at their faces. "What's wrong?"

"Uncle Kelvin," Lorna said in a small voice. "I left the Chronograph on the counter, and it's gone."

"Has the Keeper got them?" Sebastian asked anxiously.

"No," Uncle Kelvin looked grim. "No. There is no way the Keeper could have entered without leaving some sign. I'm afraid Patrick has gone in search of Celesta and taken the Chronograph with him. Stupid, stupid!" He beat his fist on his forehead.

"Patrick wouldn't do that would he?" said Lorna. "Are you sure it's not the Keeper? He's broken through in other places."

"I think I still have just enough power left to keep the Keeper at bay," the man snapped. "Besides, I would feel it if he'd been here. No, Patrick has gone and it's my fault."

"How so?" Sebastian asked, sounding a little scared.

"I knew how desperate he was to find Celesta. I should have watched him more closely. He was bound to take matters into his own hands sooner or later."

"He's always been so - so bloody arrogant!" Lorna said furiously. "I can't believe he'd just go off like that. He doesn't even know where to start."

"He found this." Uncle Kelvin picked up the old map book. "It's the one the Keeper threw in the litter bin, but he was hasty in what he ripped out. I intended to show you the way to the Folly when you came home. I also realised that Elmwood-by-the-Water was where you'd found Celesta, although had you succeeded at the Folly, it would hardly have been relevant. But when you and Patrick returned there seemed to be greater priorities than old maps. Retrieving Sebastian was uppermost in my mind."

"Thanks," said Sebastian with a grateful smile. "But what do we do about Patrick?"

"We have to find him," said Lorna, "It'll be dark soon, and we can't leave him wandering around all night with the Chronograph. Stupid ass, we're wasting so much time!"

The three of them headed back into town, Uncle Kelvin striding anxiously ahead.

"We can get the bus to Elmwood over there, Uncle Kelvin," Lorna said as they entered the square.

"I know," he replied. "But I want to see if I can get a little more information first." He ran over to a young woman who was locking up the Tourist Information office.

"Excuse me," he said. "I know it's late, but do you know anything about an old church in Elmwood-by-the-Water?"

The girl rolled her eyes. "Not you too! What is it about Elmwood? You're the third person that's asked today."

"Who else has been here?" Uncle Kelvin asked.

She eyed him suspiciously. "What's it to you?"

"Listen. Was one of them a young man, about seventeen, bright blond hair?"

"It's important," Lorna pleaded. The girl looked at her. "You his girlfriend?"

Lorna blushed. "Don't be daft."

"Wouldn't blame you. Quite fancied him myself. Yes, he was here. And then some other bloke just after him, dark hair, bit creepy."

Sebastian groaned and Lorna looked at Uncle Kelvin in horror.

"He in danger then?" The girl looked worried. "Look, I only tried to help. I gave him some money for the bus. Sounded like he wanted the crypt. Old Church Lane."

"Thank you!" Uncle Kelvin took some money out of his pocket and hurriedly pressed it into her hand. "Whatever you gave him, I hope that covers it. Come on you two!"

They ran on, leaving the girl looking astounded at the fifty-pound note in her hand. "Hey!" she shouted after them. "Hey! You've made a mistake! I only gave him a tenner!" But the three were already more than halfway across the square.

"The bus is the other way!" Lorna panted.

"We're taking a taxi," Uncle Kelvin said, rounding the corner to the taxi rank. "No time for buses!"

He flung open the door of the nearest cab and bundled them inside. "Old Church Lane, Elmwood, please!"

"You sure, mate?" the cabbie asked. "That's not a great part of town after dark you know!"

"I'm well aware," Uncle Kelvin said. "And yes, I'm sure. Now, step on it!"

The cabbie shook his head and stepped on it.

CHAPTER 22

Greater Loss

Patrick was the only one left on the bus when it stopped at the top of Old Church Lane. When he first boarded it was packed and he'd stood a good part of the way, trying to avert his face from the armpit of a man with a personal hygiene problem standing next to him. Between the BO, a youth picking his nose, and a drink-sodden girl who fell onto the bus and promptly threw up, it had been a very unpleasant journey. Patrick was more than glad when he got off, carefully stepping round the pool of vomit on the floor. How could anyone be that drunk so early in the evening?

"You sure you'll be all right?" the bus driver had asked. Patrick nodded. "Suit yourself then," the driver said, putting the bus into gear. The doors closed, leaving Patrick alone on the wrong side of town. He took a deep breath and strode off down the street, trying to look as though he knew where he was going.

Old Church Lane was as dark and depressing as Auntie Fran had promised. Although it was technically summer, the evening had drawn in early, and the shops already had their steel shutters drawn down over their windows for the night. A loud argument could be heard issuing from one of the flats above, while music blared from another.

Patrick made his way down the dimly lit street to where a gaggle of girls was hanging around outside the chip shop.

One of them whistled as he approached.

"What've we got here then?"

Patrick ignored her.

"Got any money?" asked another.

He shook his head.

"You don't get somethin' for nothin', you gotta earn it!" admonished her friend, a brunette with way too much makeup, whose bra was showing through her half-open shirt. She grabbed Patrick's hand and clutched it to her chest. "I can start your evenin' right for a tenner."

"You gone soft, Kaz?" said one of the other girls. "You're normally double!"

"Nah," Kaz said, "I just like the look of 'im. Call it an early bird discount!" The gaggle shrieked again.

"Thanks," Patrick said, removing his hand, "but I'm looking for something else."

"Oh yeah?" she winked to the others. "And what would that be then?"

"Do you know where I can find the crypt? I was told it was back here somewhere."

"The crypt? You've got weird taste ain't you? It'll cost you twenty to get me back there, bloody creepy place."

"Maybe he's a vampire," one of the others suggested. More laughter.

"Look," Patrick said impatiently, "I don't want anything you...er...offer. I just need to find that crypt."

"You pushin' something?" The girls suddenly looked serious. "You wanna watch out you don't run into Mikey," one of them warned. "He does business back there. He'll slit your throat if 'e thinks you're musclin' in on his patch."

"It's nothing like that," Patrick said. The girls looked at each other uncertainly.

"Come on," Kaz took his hand. "I'll show you." She led him further down the street to the loud jeers of the others. "They'll be laughin' the other side of their faces once I've made enough to get out of this dump," she said. "I've already got two grand stashed at me gran's. Another couple an' I'll be gone."

"That's a lot of twenties," said Patrick absently.

Kaz laughed softly. "You're funny! Wish they was all as nice as you."

She led him down a narrow alleyway which was sealed at the other end by a wrought iron gate. Beyond was a patch of empty space. "You'll 'ave to climb over," she said. "It's easy. Everyone does it. That old crypt is over to your right by a big tree. You can't miss it. Watch out for Mikey though."

"I will," said Patrick. "Thanks."

Kaz ran her finger down his chest and leaned in towards him. "You sure you're not interested?"

Patrick shook his head.

"Shame. I don't suppose... a kiss. Just one?"

He looked into her eyes, big blue pools, searching his own hopefully. It wasn't a kiss she wanted, he realised, it was just one moment of tenderness in her rough and lonely life. "All right then."

Her lips grazed his for one moment, then he bent his head and gently returned the gesture. The girl sighed.

"Thank you. That was... nice." She stepped away, wiping something from her eye. "S'pose you think I'm daft." He shook his head.

"Here now, just look at me." She laughed. "Oh well, back to business! You watch yourself in there."

"I will. And you."

He watched her shimmy her way back down the alley, a girl who felt she had no choice but to sell herself so she could improve her life. It was a bitter irony. She couldn't be much older than Lorna. Maybe that's why he needed to grant Kaz her request. There was a vulnerability about her that reminded him of the other girl, wrenching his soul while making him glad that, for all the present danger, at least Lorna didn't have Kaz's life. Not that he cared about Lorna of course. Patrick pushed these thoughts aside and turned his attention to the gate.

Kaz had been right. The gate was easy to climb, and Patrick dropped down lightly on the other side. The open space was unlit, but luckily there was still a little twilight left. Patrick made his way carefully through the old churchyard towards the tree that Kaz had described. Some of the old gravestones had fallen over, while others lurched drunkenly in the ground, their faded inscriptions obscured by graffiti in places. "Bev 4 Jon" one of them announced, next to "Baz 'n Jen woz ere." Something shifted and rustled behind the gravestone, followed by a low moan. Patrick grimaced. Maybe Baz and Jen were still there.

Finally, he reached what he had been looking for, a low grating covering the ground, under which Patrick could just make out a large, flat stone. Long grass grew over the edges and a few needles glinted dangerously in the half-light. It was a mournful place.

Now he was here, Patrick no longer felt angry, but very foolish. Just what had he hoped to achieve by himself? He should have waited. Another couple of hours would have made no difference. With a sinking feeling, he realised that he had again jeopardised their mission. He should just go back and apologise. He turned to go.

"Good evening." A steely voice cut through the dwindling twilight. Patrick shuddered as the Keeper stepped from the shadows. "I believe you have something of mine."

"I have nothing of yours," Patrick said calmly. "You're mistaken."

"I think not," the Keeper grinned through bared teeth. "I knew you would come here, and I knew what you would bring. Now hand it over."

"I don't know what you mean."

"Resistance is pointless," the Keeper said. "There is no-one here to protect you. It's just you and me."

"Not quite." Glenelven emerged from between the gravestones, with Lorna and Sebastian on either side. "Patrick, come here."

"Nobody's going anywhere," came a new voice, and Patrick suddenly felt cold metal against his throat.

"Now," said the voice from behind him. "Nobody does business on my patch except me. So, give." It was Mikey.

"I don't have anything," Patrick choked.

"Oh yeah? Then what does this geezer want then? I heard 'im tell you to hand it over."

"It's not drugs."

"Release him," the Keeper said. "And go. This is none of your business."

"Like hell it ain't. You're on my turf."

"It would be best if you do as he suggests," Glenelven urged. "There's no drugs being traded here."

"We'll see about that." Mikey started feeling in Patrick's pockets. "Don't move or I'll slit your throat. Now, what do we have here?" He gave a low whistle as he held up the

Chronograph, which glowed faintly in the gloomy evening light.

"Give that to me," the Keeper demanded.

"Oh, I don't think so." His knife still at Patrick's throat, Mikey swung the instrument to and fro on its chain, eyeing it greedily. "Nice little trinket like this? What's it worth to you?"

"Hand it over you impertinent youth!"

"At least release the boy," Glenelven said.

Mikey hesitated, then lowered the knife and gave Patrick a shove. He stumbled towards the others and fell at Sebastian's feet.

"Now the way I see it is this," Mikey continued, still swinging the Chronograph to and fro. "Both of youse wants this little bauble I reckon. But it's me what has it. So that makes things interesting, don't it?"

"Don't give it to him!" Sebastian cried. "He'll use it for evil!"

"Oh no! He'll use it for evil!' Mikey mocked. "I suppose I should just give it to you then? Well, I ain't that stupid. Highest bidder gets it. Starting price two hundred I reckon. Not a penny less. Now what do you say?"

"Enough!" the Keeper shouted, splaying his fingers. Mikey flew into the air, slammed into the tree, and then fell in a crumpled heap on the ground.

The Chronograph soared high into the sky, and it was Sebastian who had the presence of mind to catch it as it fell to earth. Small and agile, he snatched it from under the Keeper's nose and fled into the darkness. The Keeper, mad with rage, grabbed Mikey's knife which lay beside him and with one leap, swept the unsuspecting Lorna up in his arms before landing on top of the grating that covered the crypt.

"Let her go," Glenelven said, stepping towards them.

"Back," said the Keeper, pointing the knife at Lorna's side. "I mean it, Glenelven. One false move and I'll slide this knife straight up between her ribs." Lorna gave a low cry.

"Now here's what's going to happen," the Keeper continued. "You are going to find that little runt and get the Chronograph, and then you will bring it to me. If you do not do this, I will kill her."

"You need her alive," Glenelven said. "You know the prophecy as well as I do – that it is the girl who must carry the instrument to its destiny. Without both together, you can accomplish nothing."

The Keeper hesitated, then flung his head back in arrogance, teeth bared. "What care I for prophecies, Glenelven," he spat. "I have already accomplished much. I have stopped the chosen Future moving into place and, when I leave with this girl, the Present Age shall end and *my* Future, the one *I* have created, is the one that all shall know!"

"You have created no Future," said Glenelven. "If the chosen Future is not cut free, then there will be nothing when this Age ends. You will move only into barrenness. Release the girl. Let us take her and that infernal Chronograph to the Court where it can be given to the Great Lord. I will persuade him to at least reset the Past to give you another chance."

"Never!" the Keeper shouted. "Just who do you think you are, Glenelven? Making out that the Great Lord is in your pocket, when we both know that he alone shall decide what the Past, Present and Future can hold."

"I did not seduce the Lord's daughter or kidnap one of his Guardians," Glenelven replied. "Therefore, I do think he will be a little more disposed to my point of view than yours."

"I will have the Chronograph!" the Keeper yelled, his eyes wide with the madness of rage. "I will have it, and the Lord will be sorry he threw me out and did not listen to my ideas for a New World of Ages."

"A cruel New World of Ages, Keeper."

"The Great Lord will decide!" the Keeper cried. "I will take him the Chronograph and he will decide. In the meantime, he will see the Future that I, a mere Keeper have created, for this Present Age ends now!"

His arm still firmly round Lorna, he yanked a small dark object from his pocket and threw it on the ground, where it shattered. Almost at once, there was a loud crack across the sky, and a great fork of lightning split the tree by the crypt in two. The wind blew strongly, then became a gale, whipping the Keeper's cloak around him, binding Lorna ever more closely to his side.

"You fool, Keeper!" Glenelven yelled, barely making himself heard over the wind. "You damn fool! You've broken the Dark Glass!"

"Break in case of emergency!" laughed the Keeper maniacally. "Break when all in an Age has been seen and must be brought to an end. Now my Future will begin!"

"The ending of an Age is not for you to decide! Never has the Dark Glass been used thus! Your Future is no Future. The only way to save it is…" Glenelven stopped, suddenly understanding. "This was your plan," he said. "This was your plan all along."

"Who's the fool now, Glenelven," sneered the Keeper. "Yes, the only way to save any of it now is to reset Time. And that means you will bring me the Chronograph. That, or face battle!"

With a final roar of glee, the Keeper threw the knife, point down, through the grating into the stone covering the crypt. With an almighty crack, the crypt opened beneath his feet, and Lorna and the Keeper plummeted to the depths below.

"No!" yelled Patrick, rushing forward.

Glenelven held him back. "There is nothing you can do," he said.

"But he has Lorna. She could be lying injured down there!"

"Have you learned nothing!" the man roared. "They are not there! He has taken Lorna to his lair, to his so-called Future time, which is actually a Time outside Time and no Future at all."

Patrick sank to the ground in anguish. "It's all my fault," he choked. "It's my fault he's taken her! I know, okay? I let my anger get the better of me, and I've made everything worse."

"Yes," Glenelven said simply. Patrick raised his wet eyes, expecting to see fury in the man's face, but only finding sadness there. He felt even worse.

The wind had now dropped and the sun was coming up, night having seemingly been forgotten. Glenelven walked over to where Mikey's body lay lifeless at the foot of the damaged tree. He nudged the corpse gently with his foot, then gave a deep sigh.

"What are you going to do about him?" Patrick asked.

"Nothing. People will think he was killed by another drug dealer. Get up now, Patrick. Let's go."

Patrick stumbled to his feet and wiped his hand tiredly over his face. "Where to?"

"To find Sebastian. He has the Chronograph. Then we must all get some rest while Time allows."

"What about Lorna? What if he kills her?"

"He won't. For all his bluster, he knows the prophecy all too well. Then again, if he gets desperate…" Glenelven paused. "As fast as this Age is now ending, we still have a few hours to rest, and you will need all your strength for the Time Outside Time."

They exited the graveyard onto Old Church Lane, Patrick still bowed with remorse. "Forgive me," he said. "I won't disappoint you again."

"We were all young once," Glenelven said abruptly. "Now, what have we here?" He kicked at a small foot poking out from behind a dustbin. "You'd be better hiding *in* the dustbin, Sebastian if you don't want to be seen!"

The boy's face popped into view. "I've still got it," he grinned, swinging the Chronograph from its chain.

"So you have. Well done. Now put it out of sight."

Sebastian obligingly stuffed the Chronograph down the front of his trousers and grinned at them again.

"Where's Lorna?" he said.

CHAPTER 23

Time Shadows

"So, the Keeper's got her?" Sebastian threw a black look in Patrick's direction. "We've got to get her back!"

"Indeed," said Glenelven. "At least we have one advantage. We still have the Chronograph. She will be safe for a while I think."

They'd caught the bus back into town, Patrick sitting on his own while Glenelven brought Sebastian up to date with what had happened in the graveyard. They were now walking down the high street in the direction of the square on their way to the house.

Sebastian spoke first after a long silence. "Won't he be expecting us to rescue her?"

"And hoping that we fail so that he can get his hands on the Chronograph too," added Patrick.

"Correct on both counts" replied Glenelven. "But we have little choice..." He stopped suddenly and looked heavenward, as a deep throaty sound filled their ears. The other two followed his gaze.

"What is it?" whispered Sebastian.

"Aeroplane," said Patrick. "No, whole squadron, look!" As they watched, a bomber came into view, followed by another and still another.

"I've seen those in books," said Patrick. "They're really old. Couple of centuries at least."

"Lancasters," Glenelven noted. "World War II. But there's only a couple left that can still fly in this present time. Yet there's a whole squadron up there."

"What's that?" said Sebastian, pointing.

Glenelven looked worried. "Barrage balloon," he said. They looked up at the sky filled with the oval silk objects and aircraft flying above. Nobody else on the high street seemed to notice. Two teenage girls flirted with a young man in the doorway of Top Shop and a woman battled through the crowds with her pushchair, remonstrating with a little boy who was none too happy that he'd dropped his ice cream. All of them were oblivious to what was happening above their heads.

"What's going on?" asked Sebastian.

"We've seen this before," Patrick said. "Remember the coffee shop?"

"Time shadows," said Glenelven. "The fabric of time is weakening."

"But that stuff went away on its own before," said Sebastian, "so won't it just stop again?"

"Unlikely," the man replied. "It was weak before, now I think it is truly fraying since the breaking of the Dark Glass. Unless we find Lorna, we stand little chance of reweaving the threads that the Keeper of the Hours has pulled apart in his recklessness. Come."

"Where are we going? I thought you said we needed to get some rest?"

"That was before. I don't think we can delay. I want to go to that coffee shop – that's where this first started."

They hurried along the narrow streets, sometimes sidestepping a cart, sometimes a car, stopping to allow a crinolined lady to pass one moment, narrowly avoiding a skateboarding youth the next. After a while, they ceased to be amazed.

"Why can't everybody else see this?" Sebastian panted.

"Because they are not Children of Time," said Glenelven shortly.

"So, aren't we Time Shadows too?"

"No. You can interact with anything in any Age. For you, these Shadows are reality."

"But I drowned," said Sebastian, "in that flood by the Tower, remember? So doesn't that make me a Shadow at least?"

Glenelven stopped and looked exasperated. "That happened in a Place Outside Time," he said. "And you weren't dead, you were merely suspended. You would have stayed in stasis, like Patrick's mother, unless something happened to bring you back. Now please stop talking and save your breath. We have little Time."

They were now nearing the coffee shop. The crowds seemed to be thinning, the shops were emptier, and it grew quieter with every corner they turned.

"Something's wrong," said Patrick.

It was not just quiet, but eerily silent. There was now no sign of life. The streets grew dustier and the buildings more dilapidated. When they turned into what should have been Coffee Lane, an horrendous sight met their eyes. The bustling alleyway of centuries-old shops was laid waste. The city beyond was flattened and black. When they looked behind them, from where they had come was a surreal mix of buildings and bustle, overlaid with desolate blackness and ash, like two movies recorded on the same piece of film. Cruel, craggy rocks rose up about them. The floor of a valley opened out in front of them, rising to black cliffs in the distance. At the top of one stood a castle, nearly in ruins save one tower that rose from the rubble beneath.

"What is this?" said Patrick.

"Don't you know?" said Glenelven.

"It reminds me of the Valley of Seasons back home, with the Castle of the Keepers on the hill over there. But this is all wrong, it doesn't look like this. What's going on?"

"More Time Shadows," said Glenelven.

"Then we must go back. We must go back and think of something else."

"No. These are Time Shadows of the Future."

"Not my Future!"

Glenelven looked at him calmly. "No, the Keeper saw to that," he said. "This is barrenness and decay. The Keeper of the Hours may not yet control all Ages, but his meddling has still created this Time outside Time, poised to move when all else ends."

"Doesn't look very shadowy," remarked Sebastian. "These rocks and things look solid to me."

"This Future is not quite upon us," said Glenelven. "There is still time to set things back the way they should be. But not much. I'm afraid this is now Near Reality. I'd hoped that the second prophecy in the Book of Infinity would remain secret and that the day would never come, but it seems I hoped in vain."

"What second prophecy?" urged Patrick.

"The Great Battle for the Salvation of Time," Glenelven replied. "Prepare yourself, Patrick, for if I'm correct, you're the one who must fight it."

PART III

THE STARLIGHT OF THE FUTURE

CHAPTER 24

The Hall of Glass

Lorna groaned and opened her eyes. Velvet blackness surrounded her, so black that for one panic-stricken moment, she thought she had gone blind. She blinked hard and wondered where she was. She was lying on something smooth, hard and cool with her face seemingly pressed against a window. In the distance, she could make out a square of gloomy twilight where a dark shadow flickered from time to time. Her body felt numb, as if it had gone to sleep although her brain was now wide awake. She must have been lying in one spot for too long. Lorna tried to sit up, but to her horror she was bound by some kind of paralysis and literally could not move. Her heart began to race. Stay calm, she said to herself, over and over.

Try to remember. Think.

The events of the graveyard began to return, and she wished she could forget them again. She felt the point of the steely blade the Keeper had pressed against her ribs and saw Patrick's horrified face disappearing above her as she and the Keeper fell down into the earth. Her stepfather yelled some ugly sound and a great gale of wind swept them up and away. Lorna screamed as he pinned her to his side with an iron grip, and everything rushed past in a blur of blue, sandstone and dust. Then the rushing stopped, and they were in a dark room.

She remembered her stepfather looking at her, his steely eyes boring into her skull. He'd said nothing, which scared her more than if he'd flown into the kind of madness she'd seen in the graveyard. Her knees began to shake as he raised his arm and pointed.

"Please," she stammered. "Don't!"

Something invisible slammed against the side of her head and she remembered no more, until waking up now in the darkness. Lorna began to tremble inside. Try as she might, she could not stop her thoughts turning to what might lay in store, her mind playing host to phantom shadows with great toothless mouths rising out of the darkness to swallow her.

The square of twilight in the distance began to grow bigger and Lorna realised that somehow, she was being moved towards it. When she reached the square, the dark shadow she'd seen within it stepped forth. It was the Keeper. He crouched down and peered at her, then gave a cruel smile.

"Hello, Lorna," he said. "We're going to have a little chat." Great dark pictures began to enter her mind.

~

It was a long trek across the arid valley and an even longer climb up to the Castle of the Keepers on the far side. When Patrick, Glenelven and Sebastian arrived, they had no trouble entering. The great gates hung twisted from crumbling gate posts and as the three of them crossed the cracked, moss-covered paving of the courtyard, nobody greeted or challenged them. The only sound came from the central fountain, the tinkling of which sounded false and harsh against the blanket of unnatural silence.

Patrick looked at Glenelven, eyebrows raised in query.

"Where is everyone?"

"Remember the Castle sits outside the Court and borders the Future Age," Glenelven replied. "Hopefully the Court recalled them for their own protection when the Dark Glass was broken. If there was time…"

Patrick swallowed hard.

"Cheer up." Glenelven gave a hollow laugh. "Most of the central part's still standing and it's not in bad shape. That's good news."

"It is?"

"Oh yes. If we'd found it full of shadows and dust like the valley beyond these walls, there would be very little chance for us at all. Time would almost certainly have fallen in on itself completely. Then who knows what dreadful Future may have been forced into place – if one at all."

They crossed the courtyard to where the Tower rose, dark and foreboding on the far side. Dark-green ivy crawled around the slits that served as windows, up the walls and out of sight.

"Bit creepy, innit," Sebastian whispered to Patrick.

"I'll say," Patrick looked down at him, still wracked with guilt over his role in the catastrophic turn of events. "Sebastian, I…well, look, stay close, okay? Don't go wandering off anywhere."

"No fear. I'm not that daft." The boy grinned.

"Pay attention now," Glenelven said in a low voice. "In this place beats the heart of Time. It is here that the seams of the Past are stitched together with those of the Present and the Future - metaphorically of course. Good rests alongside evil, and truth and falsehood cohabit. We must be careful."

The heavy oak door creaked on its hinges as they entered. After a moment's hesitation, Glenelven beckoned, and they followed him up the stone staircase that wound its way up inside the Tower. At the top, they turned right and progressed down a long corridor until they reached two heavy doors carved from ebony and set with mother-of-pearl. The doors were covered with shapes of strange mythical beasts and peculiar swirling letters, intertwined with images of clocks, muses and planets.

Interspersed were yet more carvings, of ships and trains and rockets, and images of men and women, some of whom Patrick recognised from books. There were buildings and ruins, images of creation and destruction. The whole piece both disturbed and pacified, instilled both pain and ecstasy in one instant. On the one hand, it seemed as though the craftsmen had thrown together whatever images had come into their heads as a fancy; yet the whole work ebbed and flowed across the doors in a way that made perfect and logical sense.

Travelling from left to right across these incredible portals, the images became fewer, until on the far right the panels were blank.

"I don't like it," whispered Sebastian. "What is it?"

"It's the Story of Time," said Patrick. "And the blank panels are the Future, where nothing yet exists." He looked at Glenelven, who nodded.

"Yes. And as you are of the Age that is yet to be written, only you can pass through these doors to see what lies beyond."

"Let me go with him!" Sebastian begged.

"You may not." Glenelven shook his head. "The workings of Time are very delicately wired, Sebastian. I have a feeling that only Patrick will be able to open these doors and if either you or I should try to accompany him, we would be blasted out of Time before we had hardly crossed the threshold."

"I can't just do nothing!" Sebastian threw himself at the doors, but he had barely reached them when there was an almighty cracking sound, and he flew backwards, landing in a heap about ten feet away.

Patrick helped him to his feet. "Leave it," he said. "You've already acted for me once, Sebastian, and paid the price. It's up to me now."

Taking a deep breath, he reached out, fingers merely grazing the ebony, and the doors swung silently and magnificently inwards. Patrick gasped at what lay beyond. The doors opened onto a cavernous hall made of glass, with soaring transparent columns and walls etched with more mysterious writing. The floor was chequered in black and white like an enormous chess board. Way off, at the end of this long hall, something that looked like a huge crystal was hanging from the ceiling on a single thread, surrounded by several objects that looked like chandeliers. There was no light in the room, yet the crystal seemed to emit its own light, a kind of grey twilight hue that extended the length of the room.

"Cor! Look at that!" Sebastian peeked under his arm. "It's like a... like a palace or something. I wish I could come!"

"You're the bravest kid I know," Patrick smiled. "You've nothing to prove, Sebastian, least of all to me." The boy stared at him. "I mean it. Now stay here with Glenelven and look after the Chronograph. I'll be back."

He gave Sebastian what he hoped was a reassuring wink and stepped across the threshold. The doors swung shut silently behind him and he was alone.

Patrick took a few hesitant paces forward, his footsteps echoing against the glass floor. Either side of him stretched the walls of glass, neither transparent like windows, nor reflecting like mirrors, just smooth, smooth blackness like a deep, bottomless lagoon.

Gaining confidence, he strode forward more quickly, then reeled back, cupping his hands to his face as he smacked into something. Stepping forward more carefully now, his hands stretched out before him, he discovered what had brought him to a sudden halt. Another wall of glass stretched the breadth of the room, completely transparent and rising from floor to ceiling. Patrick felt his way along the wall, first to the left, then to the right. Just when he was about to lose hope, he felt something. It was a small narrow opening which, if he turned sideways, he found he could pass through.

Patrick moved on, but soon found his way similarly barred, not only ahead this time, but also to the left. A few paces to the right, he found another opening and was about to step through when he stopped himself and looked back to where he had come from. He realised that he could no longer discern the gap through the wall behind him.

"I'm in a maze," he said to himself. "A maze of glass. If I get lost in here, I'll never find my way out." Suddenly feeling tired, he slumped against the wall and sat down, his hands in his pockets. His fingers curled around something, and he slowly drew it out. It was Lorna's lipstick that he'd retrieved from under the sofa at the house, when he'd found the map book and made the fateful decision to go to the graveyard. He must have pocketed it without thinking. Patrick stared thoughtfully at the lipstick in the palm of his hand. It was such a small thing, but maybe...

He got up and walked back the way he had come, and after a while, located the first gap that he had passed through. To the right of it, he drew a reasonable sized X on the wall, not massive, but big enough to be a marker. He stepped back and looked. The deep red of the lipstick stood out fairly well on the clean, transparent glass. Not perfect, but it would do.

Slowly he made progress through three more walls, marking his pathway in a similar fashion. But the lipstick soon broke and after two more pathways were marked, he was back to where he was before - quite literally, for he realised to his horror that he had made a complete circle.

There was no sense of Time in the Hall of Glass, and Patrick had no idea how long he had been in there. He felt along the walls again for other gaps he may have missed, but there were none.

Glenelven might have some ideas, he thought. I know he can't come in, but I can still go out and ask him. He made his way back to the first lipstick cross that marked his entrance to the maze, but to his surprise, could not find a way through. At first, he thought he must have made the mark in error and felt along the wall back and forth until he realised the grim truth of the matter. The gap had sealed itself. He was stuck in the Maze of Glass with no way back and seemingly no way forward either.

At this discovery, Patrick finally cracked. Howling with rage, he flung himself against the walls, beating and kicking them, but they held firm. "Enough!" he yelled, dealing great blows with his fists. "You hear me? Enough! You think this is some joke?" Silence. He flung himself at the wall again before collapsing against it, chest heaving in anguish. "For Chrissakes," he sobbed, "Just help me find her. Please!"

As he spoke, the light in the room seemed to change and as it did, Patrick noticed a face in the glass wall ahead. He stepped towards it. "It's only you," he said to himself. "Your own reflection. Idiot!" Except it wasn't because the young man in the glass was smiling and he wasn't. And then the reflection seemed to blur and morph and became more female-looking. As she came more into focus, he saw the cloud of dark hair surrounding her face and knew who it was.

"Lorna!" he exclaimed and stepped forward. The girl turned, with a teasing look over her shoulder and ran off to the right. A gap in the wall ahead opened and Patrick stepped through. The girl came back, and looked at him through the wall and then, laughing at him once more, ran in the opposite direction. Another gap opened in the wall. Patrick was about to step through again when Glenelven's words suddenly rang through his brain.

"Here truth and falsehood cohabit." Was the girl really Lorna, or some figment of his imagination? Would the real Lorna have laughed in his face and run teasingly from him?

"I don't believe in you," he said. "You're imaginary. A mirage."

The girl came back and looked at him crossly through the wall, tossing her curls. "You're a falsehood," Patrick continued. The girl's lip curled, and then she disappeared as quickly as she had come, leaving a shaft of dust spinning in the place she had been standing a few seconds before.

"Once more, enough!" Patrick raised his voice again. "Show me what really is. Show me the Truth."

Something at the end of the Hall began to glow, faintly at first and then more brightly, an iridescent silver light sending its beams through the glass walls of the Maze. It came from the large crystal that Patrick had seen from the doorway, hanging from the ceiling at the end of the Hall.

As he stepped towards the beam of light, the glass seemed to melt before him, and he passed like a ghost through the solid wall. So it continued, as he followed the beam of light, until he had passed through the final wall and with a tinkling sound the whole Maze fell in a pile of shards behind him, then melted into the floor.

Patrick looked about him. There were now more reflections in the glass walls, and he wondered where they must be coming from. As he looked closer, he could make out figures, and then he realised that the figures were *in* the walls, encased in glass. Not just single figures either, but columns and columns, seemingly going back into the walls like stacked reflections. Some were cloaked in black, sinister and harsh; others in white, peaceful and serene. None of them moved, but stood stock still, eyes closed as if waiting for something.

Above his head hung the enormous chandeliers, comprised of thousands of crystals and as he looked closer, he saw that each was a phial like the one that the Keeper had had in the crypt. Each phial contained a sparkling powder like silver snow, a powder that Patrick knew to be stardust.

What on earth was this place? Something slowly awoke in his memory. A theory mooted in one of the forbidden books he had stolen glances at as a young Apprentice. It had spoken of taking people out of Time and keeping them until they could serve a greater purpose than in their own Age. But to keep them in such a way meant removing what composed them as people, the good and the evil that formed their souls, and keeping it until such time as they needed to be reawakened. Patrick finally understood the shocking truth that the people behind the glass were being kept in stasis and that the stardust in each phial was the dust to restore their souls.

"Greetings," said a steely voice. Patrick started as the Keeper of the Hours descended some glass steps at the end of the Hall and crossed the floor towards him. He was oddly dressed in a dark suit of armour and carrying a plumed helmet. Behind him was a boy, a few years younger than Patrick, yet almost as tall as him, smirking as he followed the Keeper down the steps. The boy was dressed in jeans and a football shirt that said, 'Wolverhampton Wanderers.' Patrick thought he could have been at a fancy-dress party, had the situation not been so serious, they made such an incongruous pair.

"I wondered when you would get here," said the man. "Now our circle is complete. Me and both my sons, ready to receive the inheritance that I have worked so hard for."

"I'm no son of yours," growled Patrick.

"Come now," the Keeper said lightly, "I know that Glenelven, the interfering old fool, has told you about the Time Changelings. Granted, I was surprised when Lorna told me the details and I learned of not one son but two – then again, it's amazing how a little pain can loosen tongues."

Patrick took a half step forward in anger, then checked himself. "I am nothing to do with you," he said, raising his chin in defiance. "I was raised by the woman I called Mother and the people of my Age. I owe no fealty to you."

"Indeed," said the Keeper, surprised. He looked at Patrick thoughtfully. "You have my confidence and surety of spirit. And I sense great power from you as a Keeper of Time." Patrick flinched. "Oh, you're not comfortable with the concept? But a Keeper you are, my son. A Keeper-in-Waiting certainly, but a Keeper nonetheless." Patrick said nothing while his father paced back and forth.

The boy, who Patrick knew must be Lorna's changeling brother and his own twin, David, sat on the glass steps, holding the plumed helmet. Patrick observed him, trying to feel some sort of connection with this boy who was of his blood, maybe from some faint memory somehow implanted a long time ago. Yet he sensed nothing but a blank emptiness between strangers.

As he watched the boy in silence, the plume on the helmet waved from side to side of its own accord and from time to time gave a gentle hiss. Patrick stared more intently and realised the Keeper had not chosen feathers to adorn his headgear, but dozens of small black snakes who swayed in synchronized movement as if under the spell of an invisible charmer. He stared at this in horrid fascination. The other boy seemed unfazed.

"You know," the Keeper continued. "You puzzle me, Patrick, you really do. You had the Chronograph in your hands, you even ran away with it. You felt its power. I can unlock that power, share it with you and your brother here. Together we can rule Time, rewrite the Ages, and control man to deliver us opulence beyond all imagining. And yet you set yourself against me. Why?"

"I am not you," said the young man, determined. "I do not want what you want. You want only to use human beings for your own entertainment and cast them away when you are done. I cannot cause them that pain. In my soul, I cannot carry that burden."

"How touching," the dark man sneered, then suddenly became fierce. "You will join me for we are the New Three, cut from the cloth of Time itself. You will not undermine what I have laboured for all these years. You will join me or die."

"Then kill me now," said Patrick. "For Death would be preferable to the sort of Future you're proposing." The Keeper stared at him in disbelief, watching this passage from boyhood to man in front of his very eyes. He raised his fist and Patrick closed his eyes, waiting for him to strike.

"Stop!" It was Glenelven, with Sebastian by his side.

"How did you get here?" yelled the Keeper furiously. "You should have been blasted out of Time!"

"When the Maze fell, the doors opened," Glenelven replied. "I knew it would be safe to pass. We've been here for some time."

"Come no closer," spat the other man. "You know that you may not interfere."

"As you may not," Glenelven replied. "There will be no killing here, not in the Hall of Glass. You know that the Higher Law forbids it."

"To hell with the Higher Law!" the Keeper said roughly.

"You know that if blood is shed here, it is to no end," Glenelven said. "It is written very plainly. Death is not possible in any of the places outside Time. That is why the boy, Sebastian, could not drown in the flood at the Folly on the Hill."

The Keeper paused for a moment, then spoke. "You know how this must be settled. The Armies must be raised one way or another. And I shall be victorious in this Battle, for there are great powers in the Army of the Dark."

"As there are in the Army of the Light," said Glenelven. "Come now. Would you really risk Time in such a way?"

"There is no risk," the Keeper said savagely. "The Army of the Dark will win, and we will rewrite the Ages. Our cloak of shadow will cover all Time, we will ride great ships across the oceans of blood and gorge ourselves on the meat of our slain enemies."

He licked his lips and the snakes hissed loudly. "We will feast for eternity on the lust and gluttony that has befallen man across the centuries. And Time can be turned back again and again so we can reap and create more, and our well will never run dry."

"You are wrong," said Glenelven. "The Ages will not be rewritten. They are already falling apart. Time shadows are crossing between the centuries, you will not sail smoothly across them as you believe, you will fall down the crevasse in between. For the more you disrupt the flow of Time, the more it falls in on itself until the final implosion. Then nothing will be left."

"Not if I have the Chronograph," said the Keeper, triumphantly.

"Ah yes," Glenelven rubbed his nose. "Well, I'm afraid that isn't possible."

"And why not?"

The Keeper took one menacing step towards Sebastian, but Glenelven pointed to the wall. Behind the glass was the instrument, its hands ticking a few seconds forwards, then a few seconds back.

"We placed it there," he said. "Or at least, Sebastian did. As the one who was at the making, only he had the power to do so."

The Keeper stared at him. "Are you mad? You know what this means?"

"Of course. Only the Victor can take it out again. But as you are crazy enough to awaken the Armies anyway, the final Battle was always going to be inevitable."

"And you!" cried the Keeper, turning back to Patrick. "Do you still side with this … this dithering fool and this dirty little runt of a boy? Will you risk being on their side in the bloody death that will rage in moments in the Valley of Shadows when the Armies are unleashed? Or will you now join me and your brother, on the side that will have certain victory?"

"I will never join you," said Patrick shortly.

"Not even," said the man, leering, "for this?"

He pointed upwards to the huge glass crystal hanging above their heads, the crystal whose silvery light had brought Patrick safely through the Maze. Once he had stepped through the final wall, the light had faded, and the glass had turned to cloudy blackness. Now, at the command of the Keeper, it grew light again, then transparent, and Patrick looked at it aghast.

Inside the crystal, pressed against its wall, hung Lorna. At first, Patrick thought she was suspended, like the people in the walls, in unknowingness just waiting to be wakened. But as he looked, he realised that although she was frozen in movement, she was perfectly conscious, her eyes wide and fearful, looking at him pleadingly.

"You bastard!" He would have flung himself at the Keeper but for Glenelven restraining him. "They're supposed to be kept in stasis!"

"Conscious suspension," Glenelven said, appalled. "Most cruel. Most cruel indeed."

"So, we have an interesting turn of events," sneered the Keeper. "Join me, we can win the Battle, take the

Chronograph and you can have her. Or fight against me, lose, and watch me kill her first before you die."

"You're sick," choked Patrick. He looked at Glenelven.

"I know what you're thinking," Glenelven said. "But you cannot feign it, Patrick. If you join your father, then with the three of you at the head of the Army of the Dark, the Battle will be much bloodier, much harder, for the Army of the Light will be missing its key player. There can be no pretence, no tricks in hope of a rescue from behind the lines. You must decide, in Truth, and stand by it."

Patrick gazed up at the girl encased in the glass above his head and a lump came to his throat.

He looked at the floor, then at the Keeper.

"I will not join you," he said quietly. "God forgive me, I hope this comes right somehow. But I must do what is right. You're on your own."

"Fool!" spat the Keeper and drew his sword. With a deft sweep, he cut across the phials of glass hanging from the closest chandelier. The heavy object swayed, hitting the next and the next, and like a domino effect the chandeliers began to shatter and, as each phial broke, the stardust swept up into a cloud and then shot towards the glass walls.

The walls began to disintegrate and the beings behind them to stir as the Keeper finally released the Armies he had tried to summon through the Dark Glass before.

"To war!" cried the Keeper, sweeping out of the room, and with a mighty roar the dark figures from behind the glass swarmed round them, writhing with great toothless mouths open as if to swallow them before shooting through the massive doors that had swung open in the rear wall. A similar swarm of white whirled in the opposite direction and through the portals at the other end. David remained in the room.

"Are you staying?" said Glenelven kindly. The boy only looked at them malevolently.

"You're mad," he said, "we're going to win. And then I'm going to have everything I want. My father said so." Then he turned and ran.

"Look!" said Sebastian. In wreaking destruction on the chandeliers, the Keeper had been careless. In the middle of the floor lay Lorna, scrunched up in a ball, the shards of her glass prison surrounding her. She stared up at them, eyes wide. Sebastian crouched down beside her. "You all right?"

"Help me," she whispered. "I can't move." Tears welled in her eyes, and she tried to blink them away.

"She can't still be in conscious suspension, can she?" Patrick said fearfully to Glenelven.

The man shook his head and laughed grimly. "No. That pleasant little charm was broken along with the crystal when the Armies were released. It'll take some time for her to get the feeling back in her arms and legs though. Let's bring her over to the steps."

Patrick picked Lorna up and carried her. They sat on the steps for a while, Lorna lying with her head on Sebastian's lap. Glenelven crossed to a narrow window and seemed preoccupied with the courtyard below. Eventually, and with some difficulty, Lorna sat up.

"I couldn't help it," she said in a low voice, not looking at them.

"Couldn't help what?" Patrick asked.

"Telling him. About you... and David. He...he put pictures in my head. Horrible pictures. Those dark phantom things with their huge mouths, swallowing you, swallowing Sebastian and blood... blood pouring...and...I'm so sorry!" Her voice broke and she began to sob quietly.

"Hush." Patrick held her awkwardly while Sebastian clung to her hand on the other side. The heat of rage rose in his face as he looked at Glenelven. "What did that... what's he done to her?"

Glenelven looked grim. "Torture of the mind. All while kept in conscious suspension. She had no control at all, over her body or her thoughts."

"Will she be okay?"

"In time. At least she's talking about it. That's a good sign." Glenelven looked out of the window again. "The mist is rising. We need to leave."

"Can you walk, Lorna?" Patrick asked. She nodded, some of her old defiance beginning to return.

"'Course I can. I'll be ok." She stood up, leaning on Sebastian a little for support.

"The Army of the Dark has its leader. The Army of the Light awaits theirs," Glenelven said. "Ready, Patrick?"

The young man nodded. "Now or never, Glenelven. Let's go."

CHAPTER 25

The Valley of Shadows

The Valley of Shadows lay beneath the same thick, shimmering mist that had wound its way deceivingly through the Present. Patrick pointed it out as they descended the mountain from above.

"Look at that lot! Don't tell me the valley's down there?"

Glenelven nodded in reply. "We'll need to pass though. Keep your wits about you and focus on getting down to the Valley floor. Remember how deceptive this mist can be."

"It's hypnotic," Lorna said as they reached it. Up close, the mist looked like layers of gauze, studded with something to make it sparkle. A dreamy feeling came over her, then she shuddered. "That's weird. One moment it's all shimmering and calling me, then it feels all damp and like spiders crawling down my back."

Patrick agreed. "It's kind of tempting you in but then there's this lack of sound that's sort of pressing on my ears. Are you sure it's safe, Glenelven?"

"I never said anything about safe," Glenelven replied. "But we have no choice. Look, the path narrows here, but we can still manage two by two. Here, hold my hand, Sebastian. It could get quite thick in there and we mustn't get separated."

The mist rapidly enclosed them as they entered, pressing on their ears and lungs, making it hard to breathe at first. Shadows seemed to whirl from nowhere, breathing both taunts and temptations in their ears. Lorna thought she saw her own mother looking wildly for her and would have stepped straight off the side of the mountain if Patrick hadn't pulled her back.

"It's an illusion," he said. "Ignore it." Then a wraith-like figure taunted him with his failures during the mission, and he felt the anger rise in him. Maybe these figures in the mist weren't so easy to ignore after all.

Meanwhile, Sebastian was saying something to Glenelven, when he looked up and saw the face of his old master, Hanson, where the other man's should have been.

"Clear off," he said, and the face left. "I saw Mr Hanson," he explained, "but it was a trick of the mist."

"Indeed," Glenelven replied. "The mist reflects what has most been at the back of your mind – people, places, feelings of guilt. It is hard not to be waylaid by them. I'm hearing taunts of my own."

After what seemed like hours, they left the mist behind and stood looking down on the Valley that lay barren and dusty, bathed in grey half-light below.

"I hope we don't have to go through that again," said Patrick.

"You only pass through once," Glenelven assured them. "The mist makes you face your greatest doubts and fears, so once you've passed through, you're worthy of being here."

"Maybe the Keeper and David won't have made it," Lorna said hopefully.

Glenelven shook his head. "I wouldn't have wanted their journey down for sure - goodness knows what must be in their heads and reflected in the mist - but they'll be here. And the Armies didn't have to pass through."

"Why not?"

"They've been in stasis for hundreds of years. They've no thoughts left to reflect. Now, that must be camp." Glenelven pointed to where a fire was blazing under the shelter of a craggy outcrop.

"You sure that's our lot?" asked Sebastian.

"Look over there," Patrick replied. Across the Valley was something trying to behave like a fire, but instead of vibrant flames, it billowed thick, black smoke that rose in a tall pillar from the Valley floor.

"Oh," Sebastian said. "Come on then. Hope there's food. I'm starving!" He bounded off down the path again.

"At least someone's not letting this get to him," Patrick said lightly. Lorna squeezed his hand. He might be trying to act as though none of this bothered him, but his face was looking strained. He didn't say anything, but after a few moments she felt the warm pressure of his fingers round hers as he held her hand more tightly for an instant before letting go altogether as they entered the camp.

Everything was strangely quiet. Lorna's impression of battles came from films, where camps were hives of activity with people bustling in and out of tents, carrying and responding to orders, discussing battle plans, or practising swordplay.

This camp was very different. Aside from the crackling of the fire, there was no other sound. A single, stark white tent stood in the middle, a white charger standing patiently alongside.

Soldiers in shimmering armour moved noiselessly into ranks, or mounted horses, then remained quite still. There was no cooking, no sharpening of weapons, no bellowing of orders. The whole atmosphere was one of waiting for something to happen.

"Is there any food?" whispered Sebastian. Glenelven nodded towards the fire. Some kind of roasted meat was hanging on a spit, with some bread on the ground nearby. Sebastian and Lorna pulled some meat off the great haunch, blowing on their fingers as it was still hot from the fire.

"I know it's for us," Lorna said in a low voice, looking over her shoulder, "but I can't help feeling guilty."

"S'pose so," Sebastian shrugged, his cheeks already bulging. "Isn't Patrick eating?"

"He's gone in there with Uncle Kelvin." Lorna indicated the lone white tent. "He said he didn't want anything. Can't say I blame him. If I was in his shoes, I'd want to throw up."

A sound rattling across the Valley interrupted them and they ran to investigate, pushing their way through the silent bodies that already stood waiting in the rows and columns of an army ready to move.

"Oh my God!" Lorna whispered.

Across the Valley of Shadows, they could see a single black tent next to the column of smoke. Like a swarm of giant ants, black figures were moving across the Valley, seemingly all emerging from the tent, to form rows facing them, their black pennants flying in the warm breeze that had suddenly started to blow.

"There's really going to be a battle, isn't there?" Sebastian said. Lorna nodded. She looked at the ground, swallowing hard. "He'll be all right," Sebastian reassured her. "He won't have to fight."

"Oh, won't he?" The flap of the white tent had just opened and Glenelven emerged, followed by Patrick. The young man had never looked as strikingly handsome as he did now, nor so evidently more adult than boy. He was wearing a pure white suit of armour, a silver sword hanging at his side, and he carried a helmet tipped with a great, white plume. His pale skin and stark blond hair radiated light, whether from inside himself or reflected from the armour, was hard to tell. Sebastian's mouth fell open like a startled goldfish.

"Cor blimey," he said.

Lorna stood for a moment, taking in this transformation and her heart plummeted to the pit of her stomach. She felt so small. Patrick, on the other hand, looked like some sort of archangel, transported to another plane, far beyond her reach.

Then she felt his hand under her chin, tipping her face up to look into his.

"I have to do this," he said. "As his son, I must be the one to oppose him in battle. You do understand?"

She nodded, barely recognising the face looking down at her, its arrogance replaced by courage, its haughtiness by wisdom. Patrick had shed the last of his adolescence and put on adulthood with his armour. The realisation that he might die hit her all of a sudden, and only now did she feel how much that mattered to her. She bit her lip.

He smiled. "Don't be scared. I'll return. One way or another."

She watched while he took the reins of the white charger and had one last word with Glenelven.

"Remember all I have told you," the older man was saying. "It is the Valley of Shadows for a reason. The souls of all who have died in battle still lurk here, and although they can no longer fight, they can still cast their feelings of hope or despair upon you. The Keeper may use that to his advantage by calling on them. Do not try that yourself. Remember their poor souls should be left in peace, and he who calls on them may unleash something he least expects. The shield you carry is the Shield of Virtue and will protect you. The Silver Sword, you will use as you must. Now go."

Patrick nodded, mounted the charger, and took his helmet from Glenelven. Then he wheeled the horse around, and without a backwards glance, rode to the front of the army. The front of *his* army, Lorna thought.

"Will he die?" she asked.

"It will be as it must be," the older man replied. He started back up the slope behind them to watch events unfold.

"This is all my fault," Lorna whispered.

"How d'you make that out?" Sebastian was at her elbow. "You heard what he said. He's the Keeper's son, it has to be him. This ain't our fight."

"If I hadn't talked...if I hadn't told the Keeper who Patrick was...don't you see, Sebastian?"

"No, I don't," the boy said stubbornly. "'T'wouldn't have made any difference. That Book they talk about, and the prophecy. It would've happened anyway."

"How d'you know?" She dug the heels of her hands in her eyes. "I feel so...so bloody powerless!" Patrick was riding up and down the front line, inspecting his troops. It wouldn't be long now. There must be something...

"It ain't our fight, Lorna," Sebastian repeated. He looked at her levelly. She felt an overwhelming rush of emotion and pulled the boy close to her, ruffling his hair and kissing the top of his head.

"'Ere, gerroff!" Sebastian struggled free, then grinned.

Lorna gave a watery smile in return. "All right, little brother. Look, sorry I shouted, okay? You go join Uncle

Kelvin. I'm going to hang out here for a bit, and I'll see you…afterwards."

"Okay. Just don't do nuffin' crazy, that's all. He'll be okay."

The boy jogged away and up the slope. "Sorry, Sebastian," Lorna whispered, and walked into the white tent.

CHAPTER 26

The Battle

Sebastian joined Glenelven as Patrick was addressing his troops. The young man rose high in his saddle, his voice clear and unwavering.

"Today is a day of great reckoning! A great evil has entered this Land of all Times. An evil that aims to conquer all Ages and devour them with the letting of blood and the satiating of lust, until all peoples of all Pasts, all Presents, and all Futures, shall crumble to be reborn in agony and despair.

A thousand years your souls have waited for this great reckoning, and now your Hour has come. We will not allow a return to the Dark Ages. The Light will bring liberty where there is repression, unity where there is division, and a healing of all grievances across all Times. The Light will vanquish. The Light will conquer. The Light will triumph again!"

The thick silence that had been present since their arrival shattered as the approving army beat their swords on their shields. "Cor!" breathed Sebastian. "He's something, ain't he?"

Patrick placed the great, white-plumed helmet on his head and wheeled his horse round to face the opposing army. As he did so, four great white horses bearing riders bigger than any of the other soldiers advanced from the ranks to flank him. Slowly, the horses started to trot forward, the rest of the cavalry and troops behind them, gradually gathering speed. Then the Silver Sword flashed high in the air, and with a cry of "Charge!" Patrick and his army swept down the Valley to meet the Army of the Dark rushing their way.

Sebastian swallowed hard. He didn't blame Lorna for not wanting to watch and waiting it out below. He should go and see if she was all right. He started back down the slope. The flap of the white tent was wide open, and Sebastian could see it housed an armoury. Swords and other nasty-looking weapons were strewn across the floor as if someone had been looking for something in a hurry. There was no sign of Lorna. Sebastian's mouth ran dry. He pelted back to Glenelven.

"What is it?" The man looked down at him impatiently.

"Lorna. She's gone. I think she's ..." Sebastian pointed down the Valley where the white and the black of the two armies seemed to clash, then rise up and interweave like two great banks of smoke.

"What?" Glenelven turned white. "The stupid, stupid little fool! This isn't a game!"

"She thinks it's her fault. That if she hadn't talked, Patrick wouldn't have had to fight."

Glenelven looked grim. "It was foreseen," he said. "And I cannot stop what is in motion."

Sebastian watched the thrashing armies in the distance, a lead weight in his stomach. No sound travelled up the Valley, but sometimes, little puffs of black or white would rise up from the battlefield, then pop and dissipate.

"Where do they go?" he asked.

"They return to the Great Lord of Time," Glenelven replied. "He returns them to the Ages from which they were taken. They cannot die, so to speak."

"But what about Patrick?" the boy asked. "And Lorna?"

"They were not souls held in stasis," was the short response.

~

When Lorna found the remaining weaponry in the tent, it took all of two seconds to decide what to do. As Patrick began his speech, she'd already squeezed into a row of silent foot soldiers, sword and shield in hand. When he yelled, "Charge!" she felt a sudden leap of fear mixed with exhilaration in her veins. The troops began to run, and she felt herself picked up and carried along by the sheer volume of bodies around her.

As the Armies met, a great dark cloud rose above them, and she raised her shield above her head as it descended rapidly from the sky. Then swords were clashing and shields clattering on all sides, except the troops themselves made no sound. The spectre of a Dark soldier loomed over her, green fire flashing in his eyes, mouth open in a black cavern with smoky fangs. Lorna shrieked, stuck out her sword and hoped.

The Dark soldier simply disintegrated, and the particles swept upwards, something she had not been expecting. It was quite disconcerting. Another bore down on her, knocking her to the ground and her sword out of her hand. As she shrunk in fear, one of her own side stabbed the Dark body, which dissipated as before. "Thanks," Lorna croaked. The soldier of the Light turned and grinned down at her, then gave a sudden look of surprise before whirling white particles took his place and streamed up and away to some destination unknown.

What would happen if someone stuck a sword in me? Lorna wondered, then blocked the thought hastily from her mind.

"Regroup," she heard a voice yell. Patrick! He was just visible on his horse above the checkerboard of bodies fighting around him. Lorna struggled to her feet, swords swishing frenetically above her head. The soldiers on neither side seemed to notice her now, she was so much smaller than they and she squirmed her way around the bodies towards Patrick. She could see he was under attack from two Dark soldiers, one of whom was pulling hard on his shield arm to unseat him. Patrick slashed his sword through him, but not before tumbling to the ground where the other soldier bore down, raising his sword in triumph.

"No!" Lorna yelled, and she charged forward, running the Dark soldier through on her own blade. She saw him twist for a moment towards her, the malevolent grin turning to a silent scream of anger, then a small tornado of dark particles swept into the air.

Patrick gaped up at her, as one of his four great horsemen arrived, sword raised and ready to strike. "No, she's with me!" he said, getting to his feet. The horseman gave a look of surprise, then rode off again, fire flashing like blue ice from his eyes as he hacked through the enemy. Lorna felt glad he was on their side.

"What the hell do you think you're doing?" Patrick turned on her.

"I just saved your life!" she retorted.

Patrick lunged past her in reply, and another shower of black rose above them. "Yeah, and now we're quits!" He pulled her back against the flank of his horse standing rock-like behind them.

"I had to do this!" she shouted. "If I hadn't told the Keeper who you are…"

"That's why you're here?" Patrick slashed at an advancing dark soldier. "You idiot. This was always going to happen."

"I can still help, can't I?" She stuck her sword into another dark spectre looming over Patrick's shoulder.

"By getting yourself killed?" Patrick felled two more soldiers and particles flew in the air like funereal confetti. Suddenly he seemed to weaken, total despair etched across his features. "This is hopeless!"

"What?"

"I said it's hopeless. We'll never win. The Dark may wane, but it will never really be defeated. What's the point?"

Lorna felt a great sense of wretchedness welling up inside. A Dark Wraith suddenly rose up and bore down with its coal black sword slicing towards Patrick's arm. "Patrick!" she yelled, and he raised his shield in the nick of time. The sword bounced off, and with his own Silver Sword, he finished the wraith.

"It's the souls," Lorna said suddenly. "The souls of all those killed in battle. Don't you remember what Uncle Kelvin said? That the Keeper might try using their despair against us."

The souls of the war dead were calling loudly now, sometimes in great agony, sometimes accusingly. Even the soldiers of the Light started to be affected by them, a gush of white particles shooting into the air as the voices took their toll. One of the four great horsemen galloped over, looking concerned.

"I think you're right, Lorna," Patrick said and turned to the horseman. "We mustn't listen. It's just Shadows. The enemy is trying to trick us." The horseman nodded, and somehow in his wordless language, communicated this to the troops.

Patrick raised his shield. "You are not needed," he announced to the souls. "We did not call you from rest. Your labours are done. Return to your sleep."

The Shield of Virtue flashed brightly as he spoke, radiating light in all directions. The souls began to find peace, and the feelings of despair to abate. As a new sense of hope swept over them, the Army of the Light gave another surge and the Army of the Dark fell back further, then rushed backward in retreat. The Army of the Light began to surge after them.

"We've won!" Lorna cried, but her jubilation vanished when she looked at Patrick.

"Something's not right," he said, then yelled, "Halt! Regroup!" His army did as it was commanded.

The Army of the Dark had gone, but an eerie silence remained. Mist began to rise once more from the ground.

"I don't like this," Patrick said. "Look, you need to get out of here."

"I'm staying with you," Lorna said obstinately. "I can fight. You know I can."

"For God's sake, grow up and stop being so bloody selfish!" Patrick was angry.

"Selfish?"

"Don't pretend that coming here was some great selfless act because it wasn't. It's all about you, Lorna, and this…this need to prove something all the time! Did you ever think about the consequences? What if we're both killed? What happens to the Chronograph if you're not there to return it? And what about Sebastian? He's your kid brother for God's sake! If you don't care about anything else, at least care about him!"

Lorna flushed. "I was only trying…"

"Shut up!" he said roughly. "I need to think. Look, I want you to take a message to Glenelven. We need more help. This mist is getting thicker, and I don't like it. The Keeper's up to something."

"You just want me out of the way."

"I can't send one of this lot can I? They can't talk. It has to be you. Besides, being the messenger is dangerous. The enemy could still be out there. Should suit you down to the ground." Lorna looked glumly at her feet. One of the great horsemen came forward with another member of the cavalry, who dismounted and handed over the reins to Patrick.

"Here," he said to Lorna. "Get on."

"I can't ride!"

"You'll have to." Then, as Lorna blinked away her tears, she suddenly felt his lips press against hers. "Jeez, Lorna," he said, then shook himself. "Here, I'll give you a bunk up. Now just lean forward and hold on."

"Patrick…" she started to say, but he gave the horse a solid smack across the rump, and it shot forward, carrying her back up the Valley.

~

Patrick watched Lorna go, knowing he had lied. As she disappeared from view, the mist began to lift, and darkness began to materialize once more. He'd got her out in the nick of time. Then he glimpsed something out of the corner of his eye and his pale face drained of all colour.

"My God," he whispered. "Oh my dear God!" Another army was advancing on their right, but this one was not of the same making as the armies of the Dark and the Light. It was human. Another human army was advancing on the left, and a third from behind. The Army of the Dark had regrouped in front and began to advance once more.

Patrick looked at his four great lieutenants. "What the hell is going on?"

~

Lorna clung to the horse's mane as it broke out of the fog and charged up the valley, praying she wouldn't fall off. Casting a look over her shoulder she thought she saw something dark start after her, then fall back to join a blot of darkness growing like an inky smudge in the mist behind. The wind in her face made her cheeks flame and her hair streamed back with such force she thought it would be ripped out of her head, the horse was so fast. They finally reached the end of the valley, where her steed tipped her off and galloped back to join the action.

"Don't say anything," she gasped, scrambling up the slope towards Glenelven and Sebastian. "I know you're angry. But it's just as well I went."

Glenelven raised his eyebrows. "Indeed?"

Sebastian gave her a sorrowful look. "You left me," he said. "I didn't think you'd do that. Ever." He turned away. All the exhilaration Lorna had felt from the battle and Patrick's kiss, the pride in being his messenger and doing something that mattered, drained out through the soles of her feet.

"Sebastian, I'm sorry. I…I just didn't think."

"You don't say."

"All right hate me then, but we don't have time for this. Uncle Kelvin, those souls you told Patrick about. The Keeper tried to use them like you said. Only we realised what was going on. Then it looked like we'd won. Only the mist came, and Patrick sent me back with a message."

"Which is?"

"To send more help. He didn't seem to think it was over."

A scream broke from Sebastian's lips. "No!!!" He pointed down the Valley. The mist had lifted. Four armies were now approaching the Army of the Light on all sides.

"By the Great Lord of Time!" cried Glenelven. "This cannot be! It is against all Laws!"

"What's happening?" stammered Lorna.

"The Keeper has brought armies out of the Past," he replied, "great armies taken out of their Time. It is strictly forbidden!"

Squinting a little, Lorna could make out the troops of Genghis Khan, the army of the Third Reich, and a marauding band of Norsemen advancing on the Army of the Light from three sides, while the Army of the Dark boxed them in on the fourth.

"Do something!" she cried.

"What exactly would you have me do? Patrick has everything he needs. He must use it."

"But the message!" Lorna shouted. "He said to tell you to send help."

"There is no help to send," the man said. "Patrick knew that."

"You mean…?" Lorna's heart squeezed. Patrick had sent her on a false mission to get her out of danger. She turned on Glenelven. "You don't care, do you? You pulled him out of his Time, you stopped him finding his mother, and now you've thrown him into a battle he can't possibly win! You're just using him."

Glenelven looked away. "We're all pawns, Lorna."

She couldn't believe her ears. "Is that it? Patrick, Sebastian, me? Just pawns in some stupid game you play in your stupid Court of Time? You've known me since I was a baby! You were my father's best friend. Did it never mean anything?"

"You meant everything," he said quietly. "You still do. But I did what I had to do. The three of you had to be protected and then brought together at the right time. What's at stake is more important than any of us."

Lorna glared. Glenelven sighed and turned back to the battle. "You may not trust me, Lorna, but have a little more faith in Patrick. It's not over yet."

~

Patrick had organised his troops in a square with each side facing outwards towards each of the approaching enemies. The four lieutenants stood around him in the middle of the army, one on each side, in front and behind him, also facing outwards. He'd told them to go lead the troops, but they'd refused to move. They also refused to let him through to speak to his men. All Patrick could do was flash the Silver Sword and try and shout directions over their heads.

The enemy moved in co-ordinated attack, each side advancing at the same moment, putting equal pressure on all sides of the square. Patrick watched helplessly as one by one, the rows of white disappeared in their puffs of smoke, until only his four lieutenants and three rows of foot soldiers stood between him and annihilation. Suddenly the enemy stopped advancing.

"You see?" The Keeper, still clad in his black armour, rode through his troops, his black charger snorting dark smoke from its nostrils. "I told you to join me, but you refused. Now you must watch while I take all you love and make it mine. Finish them," he said to his men, "but take this foolish young man alive!"

"Never!" Patrick yelled. "The Dark shall be vanquished!" and he thrust the Shield of Virtue in the air. Shafts of light blasted from it in all directions, blinding the enemy on all sides.

"Never!" came an echo. "Never shall we be defeated! We Souls of the War Dead did not sacrifice in vain."

His four great lieutenants finally spoke. "Never!" they shouted, and they reared up on their horses and charged, followed on all sides by a great swirl of khaki and blue and red, as the Souls of the War Dead rose up to destroy the army of the one who had awakened them. They cut through the enemy like a scythe, screams ringing through the air as the armies fell back into their own Times. Then finally, the Souls of the War Dead swarmed into the air and, led by the four lieutenants and the remaining soldiers of the Light, they fell back into the earth to find final rest and never be disturbed again. It was over. The young man on the white charger was alone.

Patrick wiped his brow, then turned his horse up the Valley to meet the others running towards him. Nobody was sure what to say as he dismounted. He and Lorna looked awkwardly at each other, while Glenelven stared intently into the distance.

"What is it?" Sebastian asked.

"Someone approaches."

It was a black horse and rider. The Keeper. "Felicitations," he smiled, with a mock bow towards Patrick. "I suppose you think you've won?"

"We did win," Patrick said tiredly. "There's no 'suppose' about it."

"You cannot win through trickery," said the Keeper.

"Trickery!" Patrick was livid. "You raised the Souls of the War Dead from their eternal rest! You brought human armies out of their own Times! Even I can see that you must have broken the Laws."

"Speaking of breaking the Laws," the Keeper said, stroking his beard, "I assume it was you, Glenelven, that made sure four great military men were encased in the Hall of Glass. Wellington was one of them if I'm not mistaken, King Arthur another. General Wolfe, and Ulysses S Grant? Yes, I thought so. Without their expertise, the boy would have failed."

"The *man* did very well on his own," Glenelven retorted. "The four were bound by honour not to speak and only to protect. It was Patrick who raised the Shield of Virtue and inspired the Souls of the War Dead – the souls *you* awakened – to seek their final victory."

"Nonetheless," the Keeper smirked, "I think you will find that the Great Lord, if asked, would rule a draw. You may claim victory, Glenelven, but if you try to remove the Chronograph from its place of safety, you'll find it stuck there. As will I."

"Better frozen forever than in your hands," Glenelven replied.

"So, you do admit breaking the Laws! I see your game now, Glenelven. You hoped I would slink off into the shadows with my tail between my legs, while you made your plea to the Great Lord to release the Chronograph and destroy it."

"Say it isn't true," Patrick said wearily. "Face me, Glenelven, and say it isn't true!"

"I couldn't take the risk." Glenelven looked away. "I knew the Army of the Dark and whatever tricks it used could be defeated if the Four were involved. Without them… it would have been harder, I'll admit. And yes, I had hoped he'd surrender, and the Lord would quietly destroy the Chronograph somehow." He turned to face the Keeper. "That was centuries ago, when I did not know you as well as I know you today. If I had to prepare again for this moment, I doubt I would make the same choices."

"You know what this stalemate means?" said the Keeper. Glenelven nodded.

"I'll give you a fighting chance," the Keeper continued. "Your champion against me. Unless you'd rather it was the two of us of course…old man."

"I will do it," Patrick said. "Do not try to stop me, Glenelven. Nothing would give me greater pleasure."

"Beware, Patrick," Glenelven warned. "He knows you better than you think. Why else did he suggest fighting my champion, but for knowing you would volunteer? You know what this means?"

"Do we really have a choice? You can hardly fight him yourself. He has to be stopped."

The Keeper threw back his head and laughed. "Such hate," he said. "Such arrogance! You really are my son! I could almost be proud of you."

"I will serve Glenelven and protect all Time with my dying breath," Patrick said. "Whether it is against you or anyone else. I do not call that arrogance." He paused for a moment. "I wish with all my heart that I could have known my father. It isn't too late. Surrender. Please. Accept the punishment you deserve. And maybe…"

A dark look crossed the Keeper's face. "My punishment? How dare you presume to judge! Fight if you must, even though you know it means your certain death. I take back what I said - no son of mine could be such a fool. We meet back here once the shadows have lengthened to meet that rock across the Valley."

"That will hardly be good light," Glenelven protested.

"I've already allowed you to hide behind your champion," said the Keeper. "Now I call the shots."

"You would really kill your own son? Your child and Serena's?"

"I have another," said the Keeper and rode away.

CHAPTER 27

Duel

"What now?" said Lorna, once the Keeper was just a dot on the horizon.

"I need to rest," said Patrick, dropping onto a large boulder. "I don't think he was in the battle, at least not until the end. He's in a better state than me."

"I have food," said Sebastian, ignoring Lorna and pulling some bread and meat out of his pockets. "And water. I took them from the tent."

"Thanks, mate," Patrick said wearily, reaching for the water bottle. "And good thinking, seeing as the camp's disappeared."

It was true. As both armies had gone, so their camps had dissolved with them.

Lorna sat down next to Patrick, hugging her knees to her chest. His face seemed even older after the battle, hardened and bearing a great sadness.

"D'you really think you'll have to kill him?" she said. He didn't look at her, tracing patterns in the dust with the point of his sword.

"This is what I feared," Glenelven said. "That he will play to your sense of decency when he has none! If only I were younger..."

"Well you're not," Patrick said matter-of-factly. "And I will do whatever proves necessary. The man is only my father in name. Beyond that, he is nothing. Lorna's known him far longer. He's her stepfather. She has more right to protest than I."

"He killed my Dad," she said and shivered. It was still hard to think of Stephen Latimer her stepfather and the evil Keeper as one and the same person. She'd certainly despised him, but the real possibility of seeing him killed, and by Patrick, was beyond surreal.

"Look!" Sebastian pointed. "It can't be time already!" The shadows had lengthened rapidly and reached the rock the Keeper had indicated only minutes earlier. A black horse was approaching, its armour-clad rider seated upon it, a vicious black sword at his side.

"The Keeper knew what he was doing," muttered Patrick. "Black armour and dark shadows. This won't be easy." He walked out to meet his rival.

The rider was sitting bolt upright, already wearing his helmet, the visor down. From where Lorna stood, he seemed quite small, but maybe that was because the black charger was so big. Or maybe a trick of the light. It was hard to tell in the rapidly gathering darkness.

"Ho there," Patrick called. "Dismount and make yourself ready!"

The rider merely levelled his sword at Patrick and spurred his horse to charge. Lorna shrieked as Patrick ducked just in time.

"Dishonour!" Glenelven yelled. "Dismount and meet your opponent!"

The rider paid no heed but swung his horse round and readied for another charge. Patrick looked round wildly for his own mount, but the white charger, like the army and the camp, had long disappeared. The black horse sped forward, and its rider slashed again, Patrick dodging successfully once more.

"Not very good is he," Sebastian observed. "The Keeper I mean. I thought he'd be much better."

"Something's not right," Glenelven muttered. "This is too easy."

The horse turned again, but this time the rider rushed his mount too soon. The horse stumbled on a rock, the rider's arm flailed uselessly, and Patrick was able to yank him from his seat.

Patrick offered his hand to his opponent to help him up, a sure sign of fair play, but the rider only swished his sword wildly in reply. Patrick dodged neatly and raised his own sword in response. Lorna held her breath and the pathetic skirmish finished quickly. The rider, still on his back, refused to be helped to his feet or surrender, and thrust his sword upwards at Patrick. Patrick thrust downwards in defence. The Silver Sword cut straight through the dark armour, like a hot knife through butter, and into his opponent's chest. There was a blood-curdling shriek, then silence. Patrick picked up the vicious black sword, which melted at his touch, his own sword flashing red in the final rays of the setting sun.

"Has he won?" It seemed to Lorna that the whole thing was over almost before it had started.

"It is done," Glenelven said shortly. "Wait here."

"No way." Lorna couldn't control herself. "Come on, Sebastian."

Patrick, when they reached him, was in a high state of distress. "I tried to help him up," he kept saying. "I tried to play fair, but he wouldn't. He just kept… slashing at me. I only meant to injure his arm, but he rolled at the wrong moment. And this sword – it went straight through the armour like it wasn't there! I think he's dead."

Glenelven put his hand on Patrick's shoulder. "If you hadn't defended yourself, he would have killed you for sure," he said.

Patrick removed his helmet and ran his hand through his hair. "Something's not right," he said. "I thought so when he rode in, but I assumed it was the shadows playing tricks, and then he charged at me, and I had no time to think. Look at him down there. He's too small to be the Keeper."

Glenelven nodded in agreement. "I had the same thought," he said. "I wanted to stop it, but things happened too quickly, there was no chance."

"I hope to God it's not what I think." Patrick avoided Lorna's gaze.

"What?" she said. "What are you not telling me?" Patrick made no reply but continued to stare at the body of the fallen knight at his feet.

"You gave him every opportunity," said Glenelven. "Now, we should remove his helmet and then give him a proper burial. Enemy or not, it's the respectful thing to do."

Patrick nodded and bent down to open the visor of the fallen knight's helmet. As he did so, the figure gave a low moan. "He's still alive!" the young man whispered.

"Open his visor," Glenelven urged, "give him some air."

Patrick did as he was asked. "Dear God!" He turned away, rubbing his hand over his face. "It's as I feared! Dear God in Heaven, what have I done?"

"Stay back, Lorna," Glenelven said, bending over the dying knight. "This you must not see."

"I don't need protecting," she said defiantly and pushed her way forward. Then she wished she hadn't been so adamant. Lorna found herself looking into the frightened eyes of her changeling brother and Patrick's blood twin. The knight that the Keeper of the Hours had allowed to fight in his stead, was David.

Gone was the arrogance, the twisted smirk of a smile. The pale face that stared up at her bore a mixture of incomprehension and pain. "Lorna?" he croaked.

Lorna swallowed down the vomit rising in her throat and nodded. "Yes," she said.

"I'm sorry," David replied.

She shook her head, suddenly filled with overwhelming compassion and sorrow for the boy that had taunted her back in their Present Age and had been turned by his father towards all that was corrupt and evil.

"There's nothing to be sorry for," she said gently, taking his hand.

"Don't let go," pleaded David, still looking up at her. He gave a hideous cough. "Jeez. It hurts."

"Help me take off his helmet."

Glenelven helped her, then she took the rolled-up cloak Sebastian offered, and placed it under David's head, trying to make him as comfortable as possible.

"Evil and a coward," Glenelven muttered under his breath. "Setting his sons against each other. And one a child. What kind of sick mind...?" He turned away, his face dark.

Patrick hovered on the sidelines, his face a picture of inner turmoil. Then he knelt beside his brother and laid a hand on his head.

"I will get him for this," he said. "He will pay. That I promise you."

David smiled weakly, then gave a small shudder of pain. "I knew you weren't bad," he whispered. "I shouldn't have listened to him." He coughed again and then spasmed. "There are things... things you should know."

"It doesn't matter," said Lorna, "just rest."

The boy looked at them, suddenly seeming many years older. "I'm dying. You must listen. There's a book. Some weird book. I tried reading it but he got mad. I hid it...in the Tower."

He grimaced again, his breath now coming in deep rasps. "A Wheel. I think it said a Wheel. Hold it back. Only you can."

"What wheel?" asked Patrick gently.

But David was fading. "Get the bastard," he whispered, looking at Patrick. "Promise me."

"I promise you," Patrick said. "On my life." He bent closer to his brother, and as their foreheads touched in those final moments, he felt the flash of recognition, a connection remembered from all those years ago.

With one last effort, the boy kissed Patrick's cheek, then smiled and closed his eyes. "I did something good," he whispered. Then he spoke no more. Lorna remained kneeling beside David's body, tears streaming silently down her face. Patrick bit his lip hard, blinking fiercely. Sebastian shifted his feet and stared at the ground.

"He could be such a pain," Lorna whispered. "But he was just being a kid, wasn't he? He didn't deserve this."

"I blame myself," said Glenelven. "Hiding you both seemed such a good idea at the time but look at the outcome."

"So, you could have kept us together," Patrick said, "and let the Keeper find out about us much sooner than he did. Can you imagine what he could have done? With the Son of Time dead, he'd have used us, the grandsons of the Great Lord to leverage a claim to the Court of Time itself. And with us as tiny babies, he'd have assumed full rule of course. With that power and the power of the Chronograph, there'd be no stopping him. You acted for the greater good, Glenelven. And all David did was fall under his spell, same as our mother did. But he came good at the end. And he knew that. I believe he knew…"

"What did he mean?" asked Sebastian. "About the Wheel?"

"In a moment," said Glenelven. "But first we have to…" He stopped suddenly. A small object buzzed around his head, followed by another. Then both descended upon the boy on the ground.

"Wait!" said Sebastian urgently, as Lorna made to swat them away. "They're little birds!"

He looked curiously at the small birds whose wings were beating so fast they were only a blur.

"What are they?" he asked.

Lorna knew. "Hummingbirds," she said. She sat back on her haunches and watched. They all remained perfectly still as the hummingbirds circled round the dead boy's head. One then descended and perched on his nose.

"What's it doing?" whispered Sebastian, as the bird tipped its head forward and appeared to kiss David on the lips with its long thin beak.

The bird remained there for about half a minute, unmoving, while the other continued to circle above. Then, without warning, it suddenly flew up in the air, something in its beak. Lorna gave a little cry of alarm, but Glenelven put his hand on her arm. "Watch," he said.

The bird rose, holding what appeared to be the end of a silver thread. As it flew higher, the thread grew longer and they could see that along its length it was adorned with shimmering stars, so quivering and vibrant they almost seemed alive. Both the thread and the stars were emerging from David's mouth.

When the bird was high above them, the other stopped circling and dropped like a stone, plucking the other end of the thread from David's lips, and then rising into the sky to join its companion. The two hummingbirds continued to ascend till they were out of sight and their buzzing could no longer be heard. The stars drifted upwards for a while, then hung suspended in the sky, unmoving, and shining brightly even though it was day and not night.

Glenelven gave a low whistle. "Well! I heard tell of such a thing in legend, but to think I should see it." He shook his head.

"Look," said Patrick. They had been so distracted by the birds carrying the stars that for a few moments they had not been looking at David on the ground. Now they all turned towards the spot where he had lain. The suit of armour lay empty. The boy had gone.

"The ascent of the spirit," said Glenelven. "Well, well, well."

"What does it mean?" asked Lorna nervously.

"It means," Glenelven replied, "that in the end, David's goodness outshone all that he might otherwise have been. A young boy who knew good from evil in his heart. And good always outshines evil. To the point, in his case, where his goodness will now shine in the sky forever. A new constellation." They looked at the new stars for a few minutes in silence.

"Now the Wheel," said Glenelven. "There must be no more delay."

"But we don't know nothing about a Wheel," said Sebastian. "Except in some book."

"What David saw must be the Book of Infinity," said Patrick. "The Keeper stole it years ago. Thing is, I can't imagine him leaving something so powerful behind."

"David said he hid it," Lorna replied. "And the Keeper lost no time getting out of here after his army was defeated. It's probably still in the Tower somewhere." She looked anxiously at Glenelven. "What's the matter, Uncle Kelvin?"

The Guardian was looking into the distance, brow furrowed in consternation. There was no breeze, yet his cloak mysteriously billowed round him, as if in a great wind.

"I must go," he said. "I feel another Timequake is on its way, and I must be there when it strikes, to hold what's left of the Ages together."

"But you can't just leave us!" Lorna was shocked. Sebastian didn't look so happy either. Maybe it was the prospect of Patrick being in charge again. Although, to be fair, he wasn't the same person anymore, not as he was at the Folly or in the graveyard. None of them were. She looked over at Patrick, but he was carefully avoiding eye contact.

"I leave you in Patrick's care," said Glenelven, as if reading their minds.

"You can't just say that and walk away, Glenelven," the young man protested. "What happens after the Tower, assuming we find the Book? What then?"

"I have no idea," the man replied. "Find the Wheel is as much as I know. The Book had not written itself beyond that moment when I studied it. I know no more than you. You are more than capable without me. You solved the Maze. You refused to join with your father. You fought the Battle and were prepared to face him and possibly die in the Duel. You are no longer an Apprentice, Patrick and have been through more than many in ranks higher than you. I now appoint you Junior Guardian. The Court will agree."

Patrick held his head high. "Thank you, Sir. I will not disappoint you."

"Of that I am sure." Glenelven turned to the others. "Put the mistakes of the past behind you. You have all proven yourselves, one way or another. Remember this is no time for petty bickering or individual heroics. Stay together, for the danger is now even greater than before and will grow the closer you come to the Wheel."

His cloak billowed again, tugging at him in the way Patrick had seen before. The man looked at him gravely. "Look within you for the answers," he said. "They will come."

They watched as he strode across the Valley. The dust kicked up behind him, soon obscuring him from view. Patrick turned to the others.

"You heard the man," he said. "Let's go."

CHAPTER 28

The Room in the Tower

It was a hard ascent from the Valley of Shadows, and not just physically. Patrick climbed far ahead in his own silent world of guilt and grief. Lorna, shut out by Patrick's refusal to talk, now found herself thrown back into self-doubt and confusion.

"You'd think he'd talk to me of all people," she complained to Sebastian, "As far as I knew, David was *my* brother for all those years. We lived in the same house. And my real dad was killed by my stepdad! Can you imagine how that feels?"

Sebastian shrugged. "I felt sick when Mr Hanson was killed, he was like a real Dad to me. But look, Lorna. You and me – we've lost people, but we've found each other ain't we? Real family. Patrick lost his as soon as he found 'em. His real Ma, his brother, and he don't even know where his other mother is. And as for his Pa...who wants the Keeper for a father? He's got nobody."

"He's got me."

"Not the same though, is it? And besides..." Sebastian hesitated.

"What?"

"You didn't just kill your own flesh and blood, did you?"

Lorna stared after Sebastian as he scrambled up the path. Since when did he get so wise? He was right, of course. Patrick needed time, yet that didn't stop her wanting to feel his arms around her, for all this to be over. But what about when it *was* all over? Would he still want her, or would it be back to her old life and the humiliation of being Simon Shawcross's ex-girlfriend?

And what about Sebastian? He was a great kid. Would they be allowed to stay together or be like Patrick, destined to find their family, only to lose it again? She wiped dust and tears from her eyes. There had to be more to it than that. The Tower suddenly rose up before her. They'd arrived.

All was much as they had left it, save for the courtyard fountain which had fallen silent. The moon now rose rapidly in the sky, and the three crept across the flagstones to the entrance at the bottom of the Tower.

"D'you think he's here?" Lorna whispered.

Patrick shook his head. "No. He's long gone. As loser of the Battle, he can't return here."

"How do you know?" Sebastian asked.

"I just do," Patrick shrugged. "It's…something I can't explain. Sort of like a sixth sense. I've had it ever since…"

"Since David," Lorna said.

He nodded. "Come on. Let's go in."

It was dark inside, but the moonlight streaming through the window lit their way, until they reached the stairs. At this point, there were no more windows to let in any light and they stood at the foot, staring up into the pitch black above. "No point trying tonight," Patrick said. "We'll only end up breaking our necks. We'll wait till morning."

"Do you think there's time?" Lorna said anxiously.

"The way Time's behaving, morning will be here before we know it," Patrick replied. "Where's Sebastian?"

"Here!" a voice called. "I've found the kitchen!"

The kitchen turned out to be a disappointment, revealing the remains of some ham and bread, and a few apples in the pantry. Patrick located a pump over the sink and splashed out three mugfuls of water.

"Tastes all right," he said, passing one to Sebastian. "Here."

They ate in silence, then went back through the Tower in the moonlight, finding a small ante room that seemed to be a dumping ground for odds and ends of sofas and rugs.

"This'll do," Patrick said. "Try and get some sleep."

Lorna curled up on a sofa, pulling a rug around her. Sebastian's familiar whistling snore soon reached through the darkness from where he slept in an armchair nearby. She pulled the rug tighter and shivered. "Patrick?"

"What?"

"I'm cold."

"Find another rug then."

She scrabbled about for a while unsuccessfully, then sank back into a miserable heap, trying to keep warm. Patrick's shadowy form crossed over to her.

"Budge up then."

She made room, and felt his arms go around her as he lay down by her side. "I'm sorry," he whispered. "It's just…"

"It's all right," she whispered in return. "I know."

She laid her head on his chest, snuggling into his warmth as his arms grew tight around her and he buried his face in her hair. Lorna didn't move as she felt his chest heave with the final release of tears. Only when his breath finally became deep and even, did she herself fall asleep.

She woke to a loud crash. "What the…!"

"Morning!" Sebastian grinned. The grey fingers of dawn were already prising through the windows. He bent down to pick up whatever he'd sent clattering to the floor. "Candlestick!"

"Might be handy for looking around upstairs," Patrick said. "If we can find candles."

They started searching through the mess of boxes stacked haphazardly around the room, while Sebastian disappeared to the kitchen in search of breakfast. He returned disappointed.

"Nothing, we ate it all last night. I got some apples off the tree outside though."

"I hope this quest is over soon," Patrick grumbled, "before we starve to death."

"Tada!" Lorna emerged triumphant from one of the boxes. "Candles!"

"Great, that's something at least. You still got that whatchamacallit you used in the crypt?"

"Lighter? I think so?" She felt in the pocket of her jeans. "Yep. Here we go!"

"Good, we're ready then. Let's go."

Steadily, they began to climb the spiral staircase until they reached the top and the long corridor that Patrick and Sebastian had walked down with Glenelven to the Hall of Glass. Lorna gave an involuntary shudder. Sebastian squeezed her hand. "Still feel it, don't you?"

She nodded.

"You okay?" Patrick said. "I didn't think. You can wait for us downstairs if you like."

"No fear!" She tossed her head. "Where you go, I go. So there!"

He looked down at her with a strange look she couldn't quite fathom. "I see that," he said quietly.

"Look at the doors!" said Sebastian.

"You mean, what *were* the doors," Patrick replied.

The great doors to the Hall of Glass hung forlornly, half off their hinges. A huge crack ran across the one on the left, almost rendering it in two. Another ran across the door on the right, stopping just above a final set of blank panels.

"It's still cracking," Lorna said, pointing to where the fissure was still making very slow but steady progress down the length of the door. "What does it mean?"

"The doors are the Story of Time," said Patrick. "Which means that a line has been struck through everything that has ever happened to date, and if we don't hurry, it will be struck through all possibility of a Future too."

"You mean...nothing exists anymore? And won't exist?" Lorna turned pale.

"That's pretty much it. Time's been played with too much. Glenelven said it was fraying round the edges. It can't be pushed much further, it will just collapse."

"The Chronograph's still here," Sebastian interrupted. "I can hear it ticking."

"So can I," said Lorna.

They stepped tentatively into the Hall. The great chequered floor was now a misty grey. The glass walls had melted to nothing after releasing their armies, and the thousands of phials that had hung overhead now lay shattered under their feet. One lone segment of mirrored wall remained, and within it lay the Chronograph, exactly where Sebastian had placed it.

Encased by the glass, it looked larger than they remembered, and although they could hear it ticking, its hands did not move, save for the occasional jump of the second hand at irregular intervals. Time within the glass wall was almost standing still. Lorna reached out her hand, then stopped as her fingers hit the hard glass.

"It has to be you, Sebastian," Patrick said. "Remember, you were the one that put it there. If anyone's allowed to take it now, it'll be you."

Sebastian pushed his hand gently against the mirrored wall, then gave a small gasp as his fingers pressed into it, as if pressing into butter. "Now," Patrick urged. "Don't hang about!"

Sebastian's hand closed around the instrument, and he drew it slowly out of the wall, tugging hard at the end. "Blimey!" he said. "I thought my hand was going to get stuck in there."

"If you'd taken much longer, it might have done," Patrick replied. "Now, let's see if we can find the Book."

"Just a minute." Sebastian held out the Chronograph to Lorna and, with a little bow, placed it ceremoniously in her hand. "Now we can go."

Lorna smiled at him with affection and ran her fingers fondly over the instrument before placing it in her pocket. "Sometimes you're a lot older than your years, Sebastian," she said. The small boy blushed with pleasure.

"Come on," Patrick said impatiently. "We don't have much time."

As if on cue, a shudder ran up the Tower, and the Hall lurched a little to the left. "Earthquake?" queried Lorna.

"Timequake," Patrick said. "I've a feeling there's going to be more of them from now on."

"Where to?" asked Sebastian as they exited the Hall.

"Why don't we start at that end and work our way back?" Lorna suggested, pointing to one end of the long landing.

"It might be quicker if we split up," Sebastian said. "You and I can try the rooms along here, and Patrick start at the other end." But Patrick wouldn't hear of it.

"I want us together," he said as the Tower gave another lurch. "Things are becoming more unstable. I don't want any of us getting whisked off somewhere with no warning."

Each room was different, some ornate with lavish furnishings and bedecked with gold and silver; others quite grim and austere, with ebony trim round their fireplaces and windows. They tapped on walls for secret panels, opened drawers and checked in cupboards, but none of the rooms seemed to contain any books or papers.

"Still nothing," Patrick said, kicking the wall in frustration. "We're nearly at the last one. Come on now, we must hurry."

~

Lorna fell further behind the others as they progressed along the corridor. She felt suddenly tired. The return to the Hall had had a strange effect on her and she felt as if she were moving in a bubble, almost as if looking through the walls of the glass phial again, unable to get out.

The Chronograph, which at first, she had been delighted to have back in her possession, was now weighing heavily in her pocket, almost dragging her down as if it did not wish to leave this place. She took it out and looked at it.

While the Chronograph had been in the wall, ticking but not moving, it was as though Time had been standing still. Now, it was behaving oddly, giving frequent little shudders as its hands almost jumped round the dial, moving five minutes in a single bound, instead of making steady progress by minutes and seconds. Each time it completed an erratic circle, the Tower gave another shudder. Lorna guessed that they didn't have long left.

She stopped and gave a heavy sigh, looking about her for inspiration. The grey stone walls stretched in front and behind, punctured here and there by the doors they had already opened and looked behind.

A huge ancient tapestry hung on the wall next to her, and she ran her eyes idly over the detail. In the distance was some sort of hunting scene, while in the foreground a young man and woman were flirting, a stag watching them from behind the trees. A path ran off to the right and up a hill to a castle with a tall tower. The tower presided over a small courtyard with a fountain and trees.

"I reckon that's this tower!" Lorna said to herself. "Yes, I'm sure it is. Hang on a minute..." Squinting a little, she peered closely at the tapestry.

"There's another floor!" she whispered. She looked up at the sound of running footsteps.

"What the hell are you doing?" Patrick was angry in his relief at having found her. "I told you to stay close."

"Look," she said, ignoring him and pointing to the tapestry. "Look at the tower."

Someone was waving from a window at the very top of the tower in the tapestry. The window was right up in the turret, cut like a small bay in the roof.

"It's above us," she said, "There's another floor."

"You really think it's *this* Tower?" Patrick sounded doubtful. "Even if it is, I don't see how it helps. We've tried every door on this floor and there's no other stairway to be found. This is the top floor."

"I think she's right," Sebastian said, taking a closer look. "It's got a fountain in a courtyard and trees and stuff, like here."

"I know I'm right," Lorna said. "The Chronograph's acting weird so there's got to be something powerful nearby."

"It's always acting weird," Patrick replied. "And it's not surprising with all these Timequakes going on. If anything, it just convinces me that we're running out of time, maybe even faster than we'd thought."

The Tower gave another, more violent lurch. Lorna made a grab for the tapestry to steady herself but ended up pulling it half off the wall as she fell to the ground. Patrick was first to recover as the Tower stopped rocking.

"My God. You're right!" The tapestry, now barely clinging to the wall, had given up its secret. Behind it, painted to match the stone wall, was the faintly discernible outline of a door.

"Is it real?" Sebastian asked. "Not just painted to look like one?"

Patrick felt the wall and located a latch. "Nope. It's real all right." He pressed downwards and the door opened easily. "This has been used recently," he said. "We're going to need those candles."

Inside was another, much narrower staircase, twisting up into the roof. Patrick went first with the candlestick, the flames casting long shadows on the walls as they climbed. The top opened out into a wide circular room. Patrick set the candlestick down on a small desk and they looked around. In the shadows, they could just about make out an assortment of cogs and springs that had been thrown onto a table, while a bunch of dark objects huddled against the wall.

"Shouldn't there be a window somewhere?" Lorna said. "Like in the tapestry?"

Patrick picked up the candlestick and cast the light around the room. "There!"

He crossed the floor and they heard him undoing a latch. Then he threw open the shutters and grey light poured in, making them all blink.

"Blimey!" Sebastian exclaimed.

The room was a treasure trove. The pile of dark objects proved to be old clocks whose innards had been removed and scattered into various boxes labelled "good," "no good," and "possible." A stack of books teetered precariously on a chest, some of them so old their leather binding was cracked and peeling. Scrolls of parchment spilled out of a basket on the floor, so ancient that their edges crumbled to the touch.

"Careful," Patrick warned as Sebastian tried to open one of them. "It'll disintegrate." He ran his finger down the spine of the books, reading the titles. "'Time After Time – a History of the Ages.' 'Keepers and Protectors,' 'Passing Time – the Management of Hours, Minutes and Seconds.' None of these is what we're looking for."

"What on earth is all this?" Lorna wondered aloud.

"I think I know," Sebastian said in a small voice. He was leaning over an unrolled piece of parchment, weighted down on a table among various cogs and springs.

"What is it?" asked Patrick.

"It's the design for the Chronograph," Sebastian replied.

"What! Are you sure?"

"'Course I'm bleedin' sure! I worked on it, didn't I? I stared at these plans every day for weeks. I'd know 'em anywhere."

Patrick gave a low whistle. "Jeez. He must have thought he could build another!"

"How did he get them?" Sebastian flashed in anger. "We locked 'em away. We were careful."

"It would have been better if you'd destroyed them," said Patrick. "Locked doors don't keep out someone like the Keeper."

"We would've but we never got the chance," Sebastian said. "The Keeper saw to that."

"Do you think he succeeded?" Lorna asked.

"Built another Chronograph?" Patrick replied. "Nah. This stuff's been here a while. If he'd succeeded, he wouldn't have needed to keep hunting the real thing."

"These plans are dangerous," said Sebastian. "We should get rid of them."

Patrick laid a hand on his arm. "Not so fast. The Great Lord might be interested to see what his son accomplished. I think we should take them with us."

"You're barmy," Sebastian protested. "What if they fall into the wrong hands and this happens all over again?"

"It's exactly because we *don't* want this to happen again that we need to take them to the Great Lord so he can come up with a counter plan."

"Sure you don't want them for yourself?" Sebastian grew hot with anger. "Always fancied yourself as the son of the Son of Time didn't you?"

"How dare you! These plans are the property of the Court of Time, and as Guardian…"

"*Junior* Guardian. Didn't take you long, did it? All high and mighty with your new bleedin' title!"

"Why you little runt!"

"Stop it, please, both of you!" Lorna begged.

Sebastian flew at Patrick, knocking the table and sending its contents flying. The parchment rolled up with a snap and disappeared in a cloud of dust.

"Look what you've done!" cried Patrick. "That was the property of the Court! I can have you arrested for that!"

"Oh yeah?" The boy flew at Patrick again, catching him off balance and knocking him to the ground.

"Stop!" Lorna screamed, but Sebastian and Patrick rolled over and over across the floor, sending the boxes and their contents flying, and an old grandfather clock crashing to the ground. "Stop!" she yelled again.

Sebastian was sitting astride his adversary, slapping and punching him, while Patrick put his arms up in self-defence. Much bigger than Sebastian, he could have easily overcome him, but suddenly he began to laugh.

"What...are...you...laughing...at?" Sebastian huffed with each punch.

"You...ow, stop it...ow...you look ridiculous!"

Sebastian paused for a moment, then rolled off Patrick and lay on the floor next to him, laughing till the tears ran down his cheeks.

"What the hell has got into you both?" Lorna shouted. The outburst had scared her, reminding her of the time leading up to the flood at the Folly when Sebastian disappeared.

"Dunno," Patrick frowned.

"You called me a runt," said Sebastian, suddenly looking serious. "Don't do it again."

"Yeah. I know. Sorry. Bang out of order." Patrick gave a lopsided grin and sat up.

"That was horrible," Lorna said. "Sebastian, I've never seen you like that, and Patrick, you looked so..."

"So what?"

"Like you were when we first met you. All full of yourself like a great, fat know-it-all."

"Thanks a bunch!"

"I mean it. I thought you'd changed." Her voice cracked.

"I have." Patrick stood up and helped Sebastian to his feet. "Believe me, Lorna. I don't know what happened."

"It's this room," said Sebastian. "You can feel *him* in it. I think we should go."

"Yeah, you're right. There's nothing here anyway. I know David said he'd hidden the Book here, but maybe he was confused. Or maybe the Keeper found it and took it with him after all."

"If David said it's here, then it's here," Lorna said. "And the Chronograph knows it's here." She laid it on the table where it shivered so much, it buzzed against the surface.

"Cor!" Sebastian said. "I've never seen it do that."

Patrick looked around. "Let's tidy up a bit," he said to Sebastian. "While we think what to do next."

"It was a mess when we got here," Sebastian complained.

"Yeah, and we've made it worse. Come on." Patrick went over to the grandfather clock and started to lift it back into position.

"Its face is all smashed," he said as Sebastian came to help him. "Watch you don't cut yourself." The two of them heaved. "Dammit!" Patrick said through gritted teeth. "Something's jamming it at the back. Have a look will you, Lorna?"

"Hang on." She squinted behind the clock. A door had popped open in its back. She pushed on it, but something was stopping it from closing. She tugged and whatever it was came away in her hand, allowing her to push the small door back into position. "Okay."

"Jeez," Patrick wiped the sweat off his hands. "You took your time…"

Lorna wasn't listening. In her hand was a small volume, bound in maroon leather, its spine embossed with strange gold script, covers held together by a silver clasp in the shape of a dragon. A lump rose in her throat.

"David said it was here," she said quietly. "It was in the back of the clock."

The look Patrick gave her confirmed it. She'd found the Book of Infinity.

CHAPTER 29

The Waters and the Wheel

"Are you going to open it?" Sebastian said eventually. Lorna shook her head and held the Book out to Patrick. He placed it reverently on the table and undid the clasp. The Book fell open with a snap. The three of them gathered round to see what was in it.

The Book was written in beautifully illuminated text, in a language Lorna did not recognise. Deft up-and-down strokes and flamboyant scrolling letters covered the pages, which almost seemed to quiver with power.

"What does it mean?" she asked in a hushed voice. Sebastian shrugged and turned away, bored. He couldn't read anyway and, beyond finding it, the book held no real interest for him.

Patrick looked up from the ancient text. "The Book of Infinity is the Story of Time," he said.

"Wasn't that on the doors of the Hall of Glass?" Sebastian said. "Why look for the Book if that's all it is. We already know it."

"The Doors depicted actual events," Patrick explained. "Things that had actually happened and were solid. Remember there were empty panels too..."

"...for things yet to come," Lorna interrupted.

"Exactly. The Book though, that's something else. It's not just the story of what took place, but every other possibility too. So, every possible version of what would have happened in the Past if a different Age had fallen into place, the different versions of the Present, and all the possible Futures. Remember that the Court chooses which Age should move into place after each has been carefully crafted. Some Guardians are not so generous in what they want to give the human race to work with..."

"So, this is the Story of all Parallel Times?"

"Not only that, but prophecies. See here," Patrick smiled, "this bit is about you."

"Really?" Lorna felt momentarily flattered. "Me? In a book?"

"Am I in there?" Sebastian was suddenly interested again. Patrick laughed. "Of course you are. Look, this is about you as a fellow traveller."

"Is that all?" Sebastian sounded disappointed.

"There's not much about any of us," Patrick said. "Just three travelling companions from the Past, Present and Future, in a quest to return an instrument of Time. That's it really."

"Oh." Sebastian leaned on his elbows across the table. "Anything else?"

"This bit looks scary." Lorna said. "It's so thick and black and heavy. It's hardly illuminated at all."

"That's the story of the Dark Ages," said Patrick. "Frightening times but swathed in mystery too. Look, things get better here – the Golden Age of Good Queen Bess." The pages he indicated were sumptuous, written in a light, feathery text and so lavishly illuminated they seemed to glow.

"What about this Wheel?" asked Lorna.

"Hang on a bit... First World War... Swinging Sixties... terrorists... Pope Francis... the Silver Cloudburst..."

"The Silver what?" said Lorna.

"After your Time, before mine – parallel Age. Seems like some nutter tried to fix the weather..." He turned yet more pages, frowning harder.

"I wish I'd paid more attention in 'Lore and Language of Time' class...hang on, here we are. Mechanics of Time. Keepers and Guardians...Instruments...the Waters and the Wheel!"

He narrowed his eyes and read intently, moving his finger slowly under the words as he tried to interpret them. The others waited in silence, letting him concentrate.

The next pages were written in the same heavy black text as earlier in the Book. At this point, Patrick looked up in dismay. "So that's his game," he said.

"What now?" Lorna asked.

"Can't be worse than what he's done already," Sebastian added.

Patrick sighed heavily. "I wouldn't bet on it." He flipped back several pages. "This bit is about the Waters and the Wheel. The Waters are the Waters of Time. They connect the Ages and the Places Outside Time."

"Like the Folly on the Hill?"

"Right, Sebastian, like the Folly on the Hill. But the Waters also flow through many great rivers like the Euphrates, the Ganges, the Amazon. Even rivers like the Thames. They flow in and out of the centuries, neutral but powerful, powerful enough to eradicate people and even places if they are allowed to get out of control and flood.

The flow of the Waters and therefore of Time, is regulated by a Wheel. If the Wheel slows down, then Time stabilizes for a while, like in the Golden Ages of the Great Kings and Queens. The Wheel speeds up, and the world seems more rushed and chaotic."

"Don't tell me," said Sebastian. "The Keeper wants to speed up the Wheel."

"I'm afraid it's worse than that." Patrick paused for a moment. "I said earlier that, if not controlled, the Waters will eradicate people and places. But if they're allowed to go truly wild, they'll also eradicate happenings. Remember, the Keeper wanted the Chronograph so he could change events to outcomes of pure evil and darkness that he could wallow in across the centuries. But he lost the Chronograph and, with it, the ability to fulfil his scheme."

"So where does the Wheel come in?" asked Lorna.

"If he can't manipulate Time, he'll do the next best thing," Patrick replied. "He'll eradicate it."

"What?!!" Lorna and Sebastian stood horrified.

"Can he really do that?" Lorna said. "Just wipe everything out?"

Patrick nodded. "I'm afraid so. Not only that, he'll destroy the Court of Time if he can make the Waters rise enough and grab the Future Age for himself. Not the one that was intended, but one of its evil parallels. He might have lost many centuries of possible evil from Past and Present, but a new Dark Age of violence and ignorance wouldn't be a bad second."

The others were silent. "At least we won't know about it," Sebastian said finally. "Not if he wipes out history. He'll take us with it."

"Sebastian!" Lorna exploded. "How could you? We can't just let him do what he wants. Didn't you say the Book contains parallels, Patrick? So, this can't be the only outcome?"

"Right," Patrick said. "The prophecy says that the Keeper will use the Wheel to speed up the Waters of Time, but there is another outcome."

"What then? Don't keep us in suspense!"

Patrick hesitated. "It says there'll be a bright star, a star that will appear in the daytime. Misty portals will turn to glass, and Time will start anew."

Sebastian snorted. "Sounds like hogwash if you ask me."

"I don't know what it means," Patrick admitted. "You know, maybe this is too big for us now. We've got the Chronograph and now we've got the Book of Infinity. We should try to find our way back to the Court. Let the real Guardians take over."

"Like they've done such a great job up till now," Lorna said sarcastically. "Come on, Patrick. The whole Court was in denial over the Keeper, only Uncle Kelvin believed what he could do. And they treated the Book of Infinity like it was Grimm's Fairytales or something. Do you really think they'll listen?"

"They might now. With Time so disturbed and fraying."

"What does the Book say?" Sebastian asked. "Does it mention us again?"

"Let me try again." Patrick squinted at the pages. "This is hard. Very few people study the language of the Book of Infinity. I was only just learning. There're big chunks I don't understand. David must've had a real gift to even understand the bit about the Wheel."

He read for a few minutes, then looked up. "I don't know. I'm positive I'm right about the Waters and the Keeper's intent, and later I see the words 'travellers' and 'chronograph,' but I don't understand any more. It's like the language is evolving as I look at it. I don't know if the rest has anything to do with us and the Wheel or not."

"I do," said Sebastian. "We have to stop him. 'Course it has to be us. It has been all along, why wouldn't it be now?"

Patrick looked at him for a moment. The boy was radiating a new confidence. "You're right," Patrick said. "It has to be us." He looked at Lorna.

"Let's get on with it then," she said.

They descended the Tower, then crossed the courtyard and went out of the gates, following the walls around until they were standing on the banks of a small river flowing by the eastern side, exactly as Lorna had remembered seeing in the tapestry. They debated which way to go, finally deciding on upstream.

"It makes logical sense that the Wheel will be there," said Patrick, "assuming logic still applies of course." The journey was uninspiring. The dusty landscape looked greyer than ever, and the river was a stream of darkness, now flowing quite quickly.

"I hope he hasn't sped it up already," said Sebastian. Nobody answered him, but everyone quickened their pace. They seemed to walk for miles yet getting nowhere. The landscape stretched on forever, every rock looked the same, and the strange light cast no shadows. The faster they walked, the quicker the river seemed to flow.

"It's like we're treading water," Lorna commented. "Let's stop a minute."

She and Patrick paused, while Sebastian ran about, jumping from rock to rock. Lorna took the Chronograph out of her pocket. The instrument was quivering more than ever, its hands stuck shuddering at noon.

"Maybe we should have gone the other way after all," she said.

"Let's see," said Sebastian, leaping off a nearby boulder. He mistimed his jump badly, crashing into Lorna and sending her flying backwards. She stood up, rubbing her rear end. "Sorry," he said. "You all right?"

"I'm fine," she said. "But I dropped the Chronograph. It seemed to sort of jump out of my hand. I think it rolled somewhere over there."

They walked along the edge of what had now become a sheer cliff face rising above them, eyes to the ground. "Over there!" Sebastian pointed to where something was glinting. "It has to be the Chronograph, nothing else would shine in this rotten light."

He was right. The Chronograph had rolled into a wide fissure in the rock face. He picked it up, then looked at the others with a puzzled expression.

"What is it?" called Patrick.

"I dunno. Come over here." The others joined him. "Listen."

They listened. A strange booming sound seemed to be coming through the rock.

Sebastian wriggled into the crack in the cliff face. "I can see light," he said.

"D'you think this goes all the way through?" asked Lorna.

"Worth a try," Patrick said. "Hey, Sebastian, don't get stuck!"

"It gets wider," the boy's voice came back. "Come on!"

They squeezed themselves in and edged along, having to turn sideways much of the way as the crack narrowed again.

"The Chronograph thinks we're right," Lorna said at one point. "Look!" The little instrument now glowed as it shivered, the hands jumping quirkily forward and back. "It knows," she said. "It knows we're bringing it home."

"Look!" Sebastian said suddenly. They had reached the end of the narrow passage. The scene in front of them looked remarkably familiar, the cliff rising up on the opposite side, a sheer drop at the end of the valley, and a river running through the middle.

"It's the Falls at Miller's Leap!" Patrick exclaimed. "Only without the Falls."

"We must have cut off a whole bend of the river," Lorna said.

"Or we've just walked through a crack in Time," said Patrick. "Maybe the Chronograph did know after all."

"I'll say it did," said Sebastian, "Look!" Below them and off to the right was a massive wheel, and next to the wheel was the familiar dark figure of the Keeper.

"What's he doing?" Lorna whispered.

"Don't know," Patrick replied. "We need to get closer. Come on. Careful now." They crept from the safety of the fissure and slowly behind the rocks that ran along the riverbank until they could observe the Keeper. The man stood facing the Wheel, arm outstretched and rotating his hand. Sometimes he went quickly, sometimes slowly, as if proving to himself that he really did have the power to make Time flow at any speed for his own amusement.

Finally, he seemed to grow bored of his little game, and rotated his hand faster. The Wheel turned in response, churning the water passing underneath into a boiling froth before it rushed onwards.

"Blimey!" gasped Sebastian. "Look at it, it's rising!" He was right. Another few minutes and the river would break its banks.

"Can't you do something?" Lorna turned to Patrick. "Don't you know any words or spells to make him stop?"

Patrick shook his head. "Only Full Guardians know, and only the Senior Guardians know the most powerful. How he knows any is beyond me. I can do nothing."

"Maybe we can jam it with something," Sebastian suggested.

"Like what?"

"Dunno."

Patrick glared. "Any more useful ideas?"

"I wonder..." Lorna was staring thoughtfully at the Chronograph in the palm of her hand.

"Lorna," Patrick's voice carried a warning, but she ignored him.

"This little knob, Sebastian. If I pull it out, can I make the hands turn?" The boy nodded.

"Lorna, don't," Patrick pleaded. "Glenelven warned against trying to use it."

"Since when did you care what Uncle Kelvin says," she retorted. "Anyway, he isn't here is he, and he never will be again if we don't stop the Keeper."

"Let her try, Patrick," Sebastian said. "Worst that can happen is that she blasts us into some other Time."

"Go on then." Patrick gave Lorna a wan smile. "Like I could stop you anyway..."

Slowly, Lorna pulled out the small knob on the side of the Chronograph and began to turn it, as if adjusting the hands on an ordinary watch. At first, she turned the hands slowly clockwise. She couldn't be sure, but she thought the Wheel may have slowed down just a little. The Keeper evidently thought so too, for he looked at his hand, then spun it so fast it might fly off his wrist. The Wheel didn't slow down, but it didn't go any faster either. Lorna gave a strange smile and started to turn the hands backwards. The Waters slowed and the level began to drop.

"You've done it," breathed Patrick.

"'Course she has." Sebastian beamed in admiration.

"Look out, he's at it again!" Patrick warned.

The Keeper yelled something at the Wheel, then turned his hand again. The Wheel responded.

Lorna turned back the hands on the Chronograph once more. The Wheel ground to a halt, then reversed. The Keeper looked wildly about him.

"He knows something's up," said Patrick. "We need to get him away, and then maybe we can find a way to disable the Wheel."

"Leave it to me," said Sebastian.

The small boy scampered the length of the rocks, then took aim with a stone and hit the Keeper squarely on the back of the neck. Then he ran further along and threw another.

"Who's there?" yelled the Keeper. "If that's you, Lorna, I'll kill you!"

A volley of stones came in response. Then after a few short minutes, Sebastian suddenly appeared on top of one of the rocks much further along the river.

"You!" the Keeper shrieked. "You dirty little runt! How did you get here?"

Sebastian stuck his tongue out in reply and ran off along the rocks. The Keeper hesitated a moment, then left the Wheel and gave chase.

"Now!" said Patrick.

"I hope Sebastian'll be okay," Lorna said, worried. "What about that pointing thing the Keeper does?"

"He's small and fast, he'll dodge him. For God's sake, come on!"

The two of them sprinted over to the Wheel, Lorna turning the hands of the Chronograph backwards as she ran. The Waters continued to slow to a more reasonable flow. Unfortunately, the instant she stopped, the Wheel resumed its rapid pace, and the Waters began to flow more quickly and rise again.

"Can you do anything?" she asked Patrick, who was inspecting the Wheel. "I can't keep turning the hands like this forever."

"You might just have to," he said shortly. "Hang on, maybe I can jam a rock in here, that might do something."

"Step away," came the Keeper's chilling voice. He carried a struggling Sebastian under one arm. "Step away, or I'll throw him in, and he'll be lost forever."

"I'm sorry," Sebastian spluttered. "I fell."

"Do you really think you can outwit *me*?" the Keeper sneered. "I set the Wheel in motion, and only I can stop it."

"But I can slow it down," Lorna said.

"With the Chronograph? Of course! An instrument of Time with the power over Time. Things couldn't be better. Not only will I wash away the previous Ages and bring in the New Darkness, I will be able to reset the particularly enjoyable pieces again and again. Now hand it over."

There was a pause. Then Lorna spoke.

"Let Sebastian go first."

Patrick looked at her aghast. "Lorna! What are you doing?"

"Let Sebastian go," she repeated.

"A trade?" the Keeper smiled.

"If you like."

"I'm not sure why, it won't change anything. Soon none of your lives will be worth living. Nevertheless." He set Sebastian down. "Now hand it over."

"Not yet. He comes to me first."

The Keeper sighed. "How tiresome you are. Very well, I'll play along. You." He nodded to Sebastian. "Go halfway. But don't try anything or I'll blast you out of Time." Sebastian walked forward then stopped where he was told.

"Now you," the Keeper called to Lorna. "Come forward and bring the instrument to me. That's it. No, don't go too close to the boy."

Lorna passed Sebastian and looked at him meaningfully. "Don't fall over next time," she said. The boy nodded.

"No talking," the Keeper commanded. "Just keep walking. Good. Just a few more steps." He held his hand out greedily for the Chronograph. As he did, Lorna turned and lobbed the instrument as hard as she could in Sebastian's direction.

"Run," she yelled.

Patrick, now understanding the plan, also began to run. "Here!" he yelled. Sebastian threw the Chronograph to him.

"Fools!" shouted the Keeper, flinging his arm out towards Patrick.

"Patrick, look out!" Lorna screamed, but it was too late. The young man rose in the air, twisted and fell to earth, but not before flinging the Chronograph to the still fleeing Sebastian. His aim was bad and Sebastian not quick enough. The instrument fell to earth with a smash.

"It's broken!" Sebastian cried in despair.

"The Wheel!" shouted Lorna, for the Wheel was turning strongly again, gathering momentum, the Waters frothing and rising once more. She ran towards it, and the Keeper made no attempt to stop her. He threw his head back and laughed. Patrick struggled to his feet and limped to join her.

"We've got to stop it!" She looked at him desperately, willing him to come up with something.

"Lean against it," Patrick gasped, and the two of them put their backs against the mighty Wheel, but it flung them off almost immediately.

"No, Lorna!" Patrick pulled her back as she made to try again. "It's too heavy, it'll drag you under."

"What about jamming it? You said we could jam it!" She started picking up rocks and handing them to him, almost flinging them in her desperation.

"Even if that happens and we break it, the Waters are flowing too fast now. If we could have done it when they were slow, then maybe...It won't make any difference now."

"Then it's over?" Her eyes were large and pleading. She looked from him to Sebastian who had come over to join them. The young man and the boy looked at each other, then Sebastian looked at his feet.

"I'm sorry," Patrick said.

CHAPTER 30

The Guardian of All Time

"I can't believe it," Lorna said. "I can't believe he's won."

Patrick said nothing. They watched the mighty wheel turning ever more rapidly, the Waters of Time tumbling and frothing with each giant rotation, while the Keeper capered on the bank cackling maniacally. Sebastian sat on the ground, his head hanging between his knees, scarcely daring to watch. The shattered Chronograph lay pathetically at his side.

On the horizon, storm clouds gathered, black and threatening. They gathered quickly and then approached rapidly, shrouding the earth in gloom. The water rushed over the banks and covered stones and small bushes before descending with a roar down into the valley below to wash away all sense of what had gone before.

By the mighty Wheel, on one of the few remaining patches of dry ground, the three watched helplessly.

Lorna bent down, picked up the broken Chronograph and shook it.

"What's the point?" said Patrick, his voice cracking with tiredness and emotion.

"I don't know," she said mournfully and closed both hands over the shattered instrument, cupping it in the palms of her hands.

"You must accept that things are changed," said the Keeper. "It is as it should be, as was prophesied in the Book of Infinity."

"I don't believe this is it," said Sebastian in a small voice, now standing and facing the Keeper. "The prophecy spoke about glass doors and starlight and stuff, and time beginning again."

"Yes, yes," said the Keeper irritably. "And indeed, Time is starting over, only now it is I that have the power, I have the control, I can command Time to do whatever I wish. For it is all mine, and now the instrument is broken beyond repair, Time shall always be under my reign. The kingdoms of the world shall do my bidding and worship me as their Overlord on pain of an excruciating eternity in the black dungeons I shall build under the old Towers. All shall know me..." he broke off suddenly. Lorna was looking up at him, a strange smile on her lips.

"You, madam, shall be the first to know my wrath," he snarled.

"I don't think so," she said, and held up the Chronograph on its chain. The others gaped in astonishment. For while the Keeper had been giving his speech, Lorna had felt the Chronograph shudder in her hands, like a small bird, almost as if it had started breathing, and then she felt a steady pulse in her palms. The instrument now shone like a diamond where she held it, its glass face unscarred, the hands sweeping backwards. Above them, a star broke through the black and thunderous clouds, and streamed brilliant rays down to the earth, while a red sun began to illuminate the eastern sky.

"How?" said Patrick, baffled.

"I am the Guardian of the Great Instrument of Time." Lorna spoke in a trance, her voice strange and deep. "My destiny passed down from generation to generation. With me the instrument rests peacefully and heals before starting again to advance the New Age." She shook herself and grinned, back to her normal self again.

"What the devil...?" came a voice they recognised, and Glenelven stepped from the shadow of the great Wheel.

"Where did you spring from?" said Sebastian.

"Hard to say," the man said, scratching his head. "I was with many others of the Court, desperately trying to hold the Present Age together. The sky was falling in and a great deluge of Time shadows was rushing in on us. Then I felt something pulling me out of the Age and I landed here. Do I understand rightly that the Chronograph has been remade?" He nodded to the instrument in Lorna's palm.

"I'm not sure," she replied. "It's sort of...mended itself."

"Give that here!" The Keeper had been skulking in the shadows since Glenelven's reappearance. Now he lurched forward, making a grab for the Chronograph in Lorna's hand and lobbed it into the rushing torrent beside them.

"Noooooo!" she screamed.

"Did you seriously think you could beat me?" laughed the Keeper.

"Bastard!" Patrick rushed at him, and the two of them hit the ground, struggling in the dust. The Keeper soon gained the upper hand, pinning Patrick to the ground by the throat and grabbing a rock to smash his skull, but the young man brought his knee up smartly between the Keeper's legs. The Keeper fell back, and Patrick stumbled to his feet, but his enemy recovered and lunged again, grabbing him in a headlock and edging him closer to the water. Lorna threw herself onto the Keeper's back, trying to pull him off Patrick, and Sebastian grabbed at his legs, but the Keeper had the strength of ten men and flung them off easily.

"Don't just stand there!" Lorna turned on Glenelven. The man was watching with a strange smile.

"Patience," he said.

"Patience! For God's sake, he's going to kill him!"

"Patience," he repeated, and nodded towards the raging river. The water was still a foaming cauldron, but the level was dropping.

"Look!" Sebastian cried. The Keeper stopped struggling with Patrick, letting him fall to the ground and stared at the river with his mouth open. Not only had the level dropped, the water was now flowing backwards, pushing the great Wheel in reverse, and then up the hill away from them, leaving an empty riverbed, dry and hardened as if the water had never been there.

"What in the name of...?" The Keeper turned savagely towards Glenelven. "You! You have done this!"

"No, no," said the man, shaking his head. "It is not I, but you who have brought about this turn of events."

Patrick had stepped down into the dry riverbed where the Chronograph was lying untouched. "I think this is yours," he said, handing it to Lorna. She brushed off a little dust and looked at it.

"It's ticking," she said, "but the hands aren't moving at all now. Strange."

"The Chronograph is the most powerful instrument of Time," said Glenelven. "It knows not good nor evil, only the flow of Time itself. When it was thrown into the Waters, how was it behaving?"

"The hands were moving," said Lorna slowly. "Moving backwards." She looked up, suddenly understanding. The Keeper let out a wail and tore at his hair as he too understood in an instant what he had done.

"The Chronograph rules the other Instruments of Time," Glenelven continued. "They cannot go against it. The Chronograph was moving backwards when it went into the water - backwards indicating the unravelling of Time itself. The waters were moving in the opposite direction, forwards to herald a new Age - one of Darkness had the Keeper succeeded - but they had to reverse once the Chronograph entered them, to synchronize with its flow. Hence the waters flowed backward, disabling the entrance of the new Age, and continuing to unravel Time in harmony with the great instrument that rules them all. Evil will always fall in on itself, given the opportunity," he finished under his breath.

"What now?" said Lorna. "It's ticking but not moving."

"It's waiting for the next Age to arrive," said Patrick.

"Indeed," Glenelven agreed, "and I feel that our wait shall not be long."

"What about him?" said Sebastian pointing at the Keeper. The man was standing with arms raised to the heavens, yelling something to the sky above.

Suddenly he turned and flung his arms towards them, face twisting as a dark language they could not understand spewed forth from his lips. Lorna held Sebastian close to her and pressed herself against Patrick as the three of them braced for the onslaught of something evil. Nothing happened. The Keeper turned white as a sheet, then wheeled round and started pacing the bank of the dried-up river, muttering under his breath.

"Quite the performance," Glenelven remarked. "Interesting." It was getting lighter as the rising sun cast a rosy hue across the dusty landscape and started to paint fingers of red and gold across a craggy mountain ridge in the distance that they had not noticed before.

"It's beautiful," breathed Lorna. Patrick put his arm round her, and she leaned wearily against him. "I'm glad this is all over," she said.

"It's not though is it," he said a little tensely, and gripped her shoulder more tightly. Sebastian kept his gaze fixed on the mountains in the distance, watching them intently.

"What is it?" Patrick asked.

"I'm not sure." The boy scratched his head. "I think... I think I saw them move." He looked enquiringly at Patrick, who smiled down at him.

"You have good instincts," Patrick said, "so if you say the mountains moved, then they probably did."

"Well, this is all very cosy," came a sarcastic voice from behind them. The Keeper seemed to have reconciled himself to the fact that his powers had disappeared, and now stood only a few feet away. "I really have no intention of staying here with you pathetic beings," he continued, "so if you'll just hand over what's mine, I'll be going."

"And where do you think you'll go?" Glenelven asked. "Look around you. The earth is but dust and stones. Nothing else exists. It is yet to come."

The other man was silent. "Just give me what's mine," he said eventually, holding out his hand. Lorna looked at him. He was no longer a powerful and scary force, but a shell of a man, defeated and shabby. She almost felt sorry for him.

"The Chronograph is not yours," said Glenelven. "And it is no longer ours. It will soon be returned."

"They *are* moving, look!" interrupted Sebastian.

The mountains were slowly shifting, the two highest peaks at one end growing in height. The whole range was now bathed in fiery red and gold - though not from the sun. As they watched, the mountains made a lumbering turn towards them and then a wisp of smoke seemed to emanate from one end. The truth slowly began to dawn on them, and when the smoke was followed by a great belch of fire, their suspicions were confirmed. The mountains slowly rose off the ground at one end, the whole range seemed to stretch and shake itself, and they knew that what was heading towards them was a great, golden dragon.

As the Dragon made its progress, Lorna thought she had never seen anything that could be so beautiful and yet so terrifying at the same time. With every step, the creature turned its head this way and that, exhaling great torrents of flame that scorched the earth wherever it walked. A great wind came from the east, rushing across the ground, accelerating the spread of the flames and sending ash soaring into the air. The group stood watching this fire and dust storm advancing towards them in horrid fascination.

"They know what this is about," said Lorna suddenly, as both the Keeper and Glenelven took a step forward. The Keeper's dark cloak billowed behind him as he stood, hands on hips, teeth bared in a cruel and twisted smile. Glenelven folded his arms and watched the onslaught with his jaw set firm, looking the oncoming Dragon in the eye.

"The Keeper looks way too pleased with himself," Patrick said. "I don't like it."

The wind grew stronger and the fire hotter. Lorna tried hiding her face in her sleeve, but it was poor protection from the heat and ash. Finally, the mighty Dragon came to a halt in front of them, then opened its great jaws and spoke.

"Who woke me?" asked the Dragon. Its voice was low and rich yet held the hint of a threat. "Who released the Waters of Time?"

"Oh, Mighty Guardian," came the confident voice of the Keeper, "it was I. It was I who released the great waters."

"Indeed?" The Dragon turned to him. "Then you must have good reason. For you know that I must only be awakened at the great unwinding of Time, when the world is reset for an altogether new millennia of Ages."

"Oh yes," the Keeper continued earnestly. "The world has fallen into disarray, oh Mighty Guardian. Men are at each other's throats, the world is on the point of collapse. The human race is drowning in its own greed. It is time for Time itself to start anew, with a new power over all beings, to replace the rule of chaos and weakness with that of discipline and strength."

"Really?" The Dragon gave a huge yawn. "And who shall wield this new power. Who shall exert the discipline and strength of which you speak?"

"I, my Lord."

"Don't let him!"

The Dragon turned to see who had spoken.

"To speak out in this manner marks you as either courageous or stupid, small one," it said to Sebastian. "We will see which it is. Continue."

"He's evil! He'll have wars all the time, and...and murders and worse things. He lies. Don't let him have the power."

"Neither evil nor goodness concern me," said the Dragon. "Simply the release and reset of Time."

"Why does he call you Guardian then?" Sebastian persisted. "Don't sound like you're guarding much to me."

"The mighty Dragon is the Guardian of All Time, Sebastian," Glenelven said, looking grim. "And the Guardian of All Time does not take sides. Not of good, not of evil; not of darkness, not of light. He is like Time itself, he simply exists. The great Masters of Time needed an independent Guardian who would not try to bend the will of Time for his own purposes, but simply safeguard Time, resetting it only when humans were so hell-bent on their own destruction that Time must be restarted to save them from themselves. And to preserve even the existence of Time itself."

"So, he should restart it for good stuff then," said Sebastian. "Not evil, like him!"

"The Guardian is only interested in order," said the Dragon. "What care I if order is kept by the joy of peaceful rule or the fear of maniacal power? Both can keep the human race from self-destruction and prevent the spread of chaos."

"You're a rotten Guardian then," Sebastian said. "We've got a Guardian too, and she's heaps better than you!"

"Sebastian!" Lorna hoped he hadn't overstepped the mark. A look at Patrick told her that he was thinking the same thing. The Dragon turned towards her with interest.

"Tell me," it said languidly, "of what are you the Guardian?"

"Well," Lorna said, putting her hand in her pocket, "just this really." She held out her hand. The Dragon breathed heavily sending a cloud of steam over the group.

"The Chronograph," it hissed. "The one instrument to rule Time, its passing, and the bringing round of New Ages."

"It was stolen, my Lord," interrupted the Keeper. "And ended up in the hands of this girl. They have all impeded me in my quest to retrieve it... and return it to you as its rightful owner."

"My Lord, you know he lies!" Patrick exclaimed.

The Dragon raised one eyebrow. "Do I?"

"If anyone was trying to steal it, it was my father."

"Your father? Ah, of course. Now I see. But perhaps the son has inherited the father's economy with the truth. Maybe you also lie."

The colour rose in Patrick's cheeks.

"The Chronograph was made at the behest of the Great Lord's son, a Son of Time," Glenelven interrupted. "He hoped to use it to undo specific moments of evil across the Ages without returning to the beginning of Time and resetting it all over again. Well-meaning, but naïve."

"Releasing the Waters of Time would have achieved as much," said the Dragon.

"Yes, but while the Waters eradicate the happenings of the Ages, they are indiscriminate. The Chronograph allows a return to more specific points in time - for more surgical management between events and Ages if you will. The Son of Time did not crave the power and responsibility that comes with the release of the Waters - for the Waters also place the power to rebuild the Ages in their entirety in the hands of he that releases them. They do not reset them for independent reconstruction, with good and evil being free choices, as you do, my Lord."

"The Waters were released," said the Dragon thoughtfully. "But then they were turned back. It was the turning back that awoke me. Who turned them?"

"That was also I, my Lord," said the Keeper.

"You didn't mean too, you coward!" Patrick exploded. "You just wanted to get rid of the Chronograph when it started again, so you chucked it in the river. You didn't know what you were doing!"

The Dragon raised its great head. "Another lie?" It turned to the Keeper. "Or does the son speak the truth?"

"No," replied the Keeper flinging a look of pure hate at Patrick. "I wanted to reset Time."

"But why? You had released the Waters. You have told me that you want to be given custody over the new Ages to instil order by dark means. You did not need to wake me to rule by pure evil, the Waters were already washing away centuries' worth of events. You did not need me to put a stop to all Time and rebuild it again from nothing."

The Keeper looked disconcerted.

"No one person can rule Time when I reset it," said the Dragon.

"But you said you didn't care! You said you didn't care whether order was kept by fair means or foul, that only the order of Time was important."

"That is true," said the Dragon. "But the fair means or foul must be decided by the human world, with equal opportunity on both sides - not by one power-greedy underling who thinks he can manipulate all rules and instruments for his own purposes.

I am the Guardian of All Time, given custody over the workings of Time itself by the great Masters. And I will not be played for a fool by a mere Keeper of the Hours!"

The Dragon raised up on its haunches, spreading its wings and towering above them. For one moment, Lorna thought it would crash down upon all of them, but it gave a mighty inhale and then billowed a great jet of fire in the direction of the Keeper, incinerating him on the spot. Lorna thought she would faint and held onto Sebastian who was doubled over, vomiting on the ground. Even Glenelven looked pale. Patrick was the only one who seemed unperturbed. He walked over to the pile of ash where the Keeper had been and kicked it to the wind.

"That," he said, "was for David."

CHAPTER 31

Return to Court

The Dragon turned to the four who remained. "Well?" it said. "What more do you want from me? You must hurry. Time is starting over and there is much to be done."

Patrick stepped forward and gave a low bow. "My Lord. My companions and I have travelled for many days fraught with danger, and more recently with little to eat or drink. I beg of you, some time to rest." He looked at the others.

Lorna nodded. "I could sleep for a month." The Chronograph ticked happily in her hand, a few steps forward and a few steps back, waiting for Time to settle so it could march forward. She caressed it, lost in thought for a moment, then looked up as she felt the Dragon watching her.

"I guess I should hand this over," she said.

"You would rather keep it perhaps?" The Dragon's voice held a note of warning.

"No. It's not mine to keep, is it? It's just…"

"What is it, child? Speak."

"It reminds me of my dad," she whispered, fiercely brushing away the tear that rolled down her cheek.

"The girl's father gave her the instrument," Glenelven explained. "It had been in the family for generations, passed over for safekeeping by the Son of Time before he was murdered. Lorna's father never understood what he had, but he kept it safe, nonetheless. He was a great friend to me and a friend to Time, and he paid for it with his life."

"The Keeper?" queried the Dragon. Glenelven nodded.

"Here," Lorna said, placing the Chronograph at the Dragon's feet. "It's a relief really. Handing it over to you I mean."

"Indeed?" The Dragon raised one eyebrow. "I thank you," it said.

"As for your request," the Dragon turned to Patrick, "it is granted. You will all go to Court for a short period of recovery. But not for too long. The mists shall soon rise one last time, and you must all return from whence you came before it is too late."

"I thought you were resetting Time!" Sebastian cried. "How can we go back?"

"Things will be reset to how they were when you left them," the Dragon said, "allowing you to pick up where you left off, so to speak. With a few minor differences of course – you no longer have a stepfather." It nodded to Lorna. "As for the Future, the Guardian shall bring it round as planned."

"You mean my mother's back?" Patrick said.

"The spell that kept her in stasis died along with the Keeper. Celesta is an intelligent woman. I have no doubt she will find her way back from the parallel Future in which she was imprisoned."

"But I don't want to go back!" Sebastian yelled. "I had a rotten life. My Pa beat me, and he hit me Mam."

"Don't you miss your mother?"

The boy shrugged. "She was nice, but she wasn't my real ma, was she?"

"Then you would rather return to your original Time, which is the Present Age, with your sister?"

"Are you going back there?" Sebastian looked at Lorna.

"I don't know." She looked at Patrick and turned red. He turned away, equally embarrassed.

"If I might make a suggestion, my Lord," Glenelven said.

"Very well, Glenelven," the Dragon said. "But I warn you, be quick about it. The mist is already rising." As it spoke, a fine silver mist was indeed beginning to curl in fine wisps from the ground.

"We owe these young people so much," Glenelven said. "Surely they should be allowed to choose their own destinies?"

"Go on," the Dragon said.

"I propose the following. A return to their own Ages, or a fresh start here in the new Future Age as it moves into place. They are intelligent young people. Allow them to decide."

The Dragon thought for a moment. "Very well. You have until the mists have fully risen and begun to turn. But choose wisely. There will be no Chronographs to help you if you make the wrong decision. Or Guardians," it concluded, looking at Glenelven.

"To Court, I think," Glenelven said hurriedly. "We've delayed long enough. And thank you." He gave a low bow to the Dragon, then strode away, followed by Sebastian and Patrick. Lorna, however, remained.

"Well?" A low growl rumbled in the Dragon's throat.

Lorna felt her knees shaking but ploughed on. "How do I know? What's right I mean? My mother…well she's on her own now, and it doesn't feel right somehow. She wasn't always so…so hard, y'know. It was when Dad died. Maybe now Latimer's no longer around she'll be more her old self…" She trailed off and looked miserably after Patrick walking into the distance.

"You wish I had just returned you to the Present Age and given you no choice?"

"It might have been easier."

"And the young man?"

Lorna sighed. "You mean Patrick. Yeah well… he's kind of cool I suppose. And then there's Sebastian, my real brother. I think he'd be really happy staying here, I can't make him give that up…Oh jeez, I don't know what to do. Can't you tell me?"

The Dragon regarded her for a long moment. "Child," it said gently. "Nobody can decide your Future but you. All I will tell you is that whatever choice you make, it will be the right one. Now you should go."

"Thank you," Lorna whispered and, reaching up, kissed the Dragon on the cheek. Then she ran before she could lose sight of the others.

The Dragon, surprised by her sudden and fearless show of affection, looked after her for a while, then touched the Chronograph thoughtfully with its claw.

~

"Where were you?" Sebastian asked. Since catching them up, Lorna hadn't spoken a word, but had tramped along in the dust a short way behind them as if in a world of her own.

She shrugged. "Just talking."

"What about?"

"Nothing really. Look, we're here."

A trumpet sounded as they walked through the great gates to the Court. "Just in time," Glenelven remarked.

"Five more minutes and we'd have been locked out for the night."

"Glenelven!" A tall, good-looking man was running across the courtyard towards them. "Glenelven, you're back!"

"Indeed, I am, Faramore!" The two men embraced.

"And who are these?" asked Faramore.

"These are the Three," Glenelven replied. "We owe them everything."

"The Three! Then I am honoured!" Faramore gave a small bow. "So, it's over?"

"It's over. The Great Guardian has reset time and taken possession of the instrument that caused so much trouble."

"And the Keeper of the Hours?"

Glenelven drew his finger across his throat and smiled grimly.

"Dead?" Faramore said. "The Great Lord won't be happy about that. He was hoping for some showy trial."

"The Great Lord should be grateful he still has Time to rule over. I have no problem with our Lord Guardian's actions."

"Of course. Now, introductions," Faramore said enthusiastically. "I can't keep calling you 'The Three.'"

"This is Sebastian," Glenelven said, "child of the Past. His sister, Lorna, daughter of the Present. And you already know Patrick, our former Apprentice, now Junior Guardian."

"Junior Guardian?" Faramore raised his eyebrows. "Well earned, no doubt. Forgive me, Patrick, you are much changed. I did not recognise you."

"Who's that?" Sebastian hissed to Lorna, indicating the figure watching them from across the courtyard. As he spoke, the figure moved smoothly towards them, its long white robe and blue cloak shimmering as it walked. It came within a few feet of them and stopped, pushing back its hood to reveal a face that Lorna recognised immediately. Patrick gave a cry, and flung himself towards the woman, wrapping his arms tightly around her and stooping to bury his face in her hair. It was Celesta.

"My son," was all she said.

The young man raised his head. "I know," he said. "I know everything."

She looked at Glenelven, who nodded. "Can you forgive me?" she asked Patrick.

"There is nothing to forgive," the young man replied.

"Go," said Glenelven. "I do not think the mists will turn till morning. Tell Celesta all that has happened."

Patrick did not need telling twice. The others watched as he and Celesta crossed the courtyard arm-in-arm and disappeared through a narrow archway in one corner.

"And now," Glenelven said, "what about something to eat?"

CHAPTER 32

Misty Portals Turn to Glass

"That was good!" Sebastian leaned back in his chair and burped loudly. "I tell you, my decision's made. I'm staying 'ere. This apple pie's the best!" He grinned at Lorna, who smiled wanly.

On hearing of their return, the Great Lord himself had already been to find them and seemed particularly taken with Sebastian. The boy's sheer enthusiasm for everything at Court endeared him to the man, who had already declared him Apprentice material by the end of their lengthy conversation. Sebastian was still beaming with the memory, and Lorna felt happy for him. Nobody in his previous life had made him feel important or clever, except maybe Hanson for a short while. The pride she felt in her newfound brother was tinged with sadness though, as a tough decision became even harder.

She looked round the dining hall. There was no sign of Patrick, he must still be with Celesta. Glenelven was speaking with Faramore over near the door and seemed ready to leave. He'd spent the past couple of hours addressing the Inner Circle and looked shattered. Suddenly, all Lorna wanted was a hug from the man she knew as her uncle.

"Lorna?" Sebastian interrupted her thoughts. "You all right?"

"Huh? Yeah, I'm ok. Just tired. Think I'll go to bed. Enjoy your pie!" She smiled weakly and left Sebastian shoving pie into his bulging cheeks as fast as he could. The doors closed behind her, abruptly cutting off the sound from the hall. The corridor was empty and silent. Glenelven had disappeared.

She leaned against the wall and closed her eyes. She felt exhausted but knew she wouldn't sleep with her mind so full and spinning. Footsteps approached and she opened her lids slightly, then brightened. It was Patrick.

"Hello," he said.

"Hello."

"How was dinner?"

"OK. Didn't eat much. Sebastian's having pie."

There was an awkward silence. Patrick stuck his hands in his pockets and looked away. Lorna shifted awkwardly against the wall.

"How's Celesta?"

"Oh, great! Just…a ton to catch up on, y'know."

Lorna looked up at him, wanting him to say something more. Everything suddenly felt like a big anti-climax. Now the adventure was over, they seemed to have nothing to say to each other. A big lump seemed to form in her throat, preventing her from speaking. She took a small, hesitant step forward, wanting to just lean against his warmth for a while, but he continued to avoid her gaze.

"I've missed her. Celesta. A lot, Lorna. I…"

"I get it. Really." She bit her lip and blinked hard. She was damned if she'd cry in front of him. There was another pause. "You know Sebastian's staying? At least I think he is…"

There was a gale of laughter as the doors of the dining hall flew open. A huddle of girls came past. "Hi Patrick!" they said in chorus, and tittered. Patrick grinned.

"They're throwing a Welcome Back Party in the Great Hall," one of them said, ignoring Lorna and flashing her dark eyes at Patrick. "You coming? Celebrate your return and all that."

Patrick shook his head. "Maybe later."

"Oh." The girl looked disappointed. She cast a look in Lorna's direction. "Well never mind. If you feel you have to stay…There'll be plenty of other times…" She left with her gang, long chestnut hair swinging down her back.

Lorna scowled. Just like the Populars at school.

"Who was that then?"

"Her? Oh, that's Alaina. Faramore's daughter. She's a real pain." He grinned, eyes following the girl down the corridor until she turned the corner. "So, Sebastian's staying then?"

"I guess. The pie's very tempting." Lorna gave a hollow laugh.

"And you?…I mean, you must miss your mum…"

She shrugged. "Maybe. Patrick…" She reached up and touched his cheek.

"I have to go," he said abruptly, brushing her hand away. "I'll see you tomorrow." He strode off down the corridor. Lorna walked aimlessly through the cloister, drowning in misery. Laughter tumbled from the windows above her.

This was a time of celebration for people here, but for her and Patrick it was only a countdown to the desolation of permanent separation. He couldn't leave Celesta. That's what he'd been trying to tell her. And he didn't expect her to give up on her mum either, just for him. Who knew if it would work out anyway, with girls like Alaina around, and then what would she have? Sebastian?

Her thoughts turned to her brother and her heart gave another squeeze. He was loving it here already. The Court had far more to offer him than anything back in the Present Age. Maybe she should stay for him, if not for Patrick. On the other hand, there was her mum. Her mum had no-one now. Sebastian would bounce back and be okay anywhere, Lorna or no Lorna. She wandered across the courtyard, her confusion growing thicker with the rising mist.

"Oh, bloody hell!" She threw back her head and roared. "Oh, bloody hell! What about ME?"

"Are you all right?" It was Faramore, on his way home.

"I...I don't know..." she stammered, on the verge of tears.

"Where to go?" the man spoke gently. "Glenelven told me he'd asked the Great Guardian to allow you the choice."

"Where is he? I ...I need to talk to someone..."

"In conference with the Great Lord, at least till morning. I'm about to join them myself, but I can spare a few minutes. Do you want to talk to me?"

She shook her head. "No. I'll be okay. I just wish I knew..."

Faramore looked thoughtful. "I probably shouldn't tell you this, but ... the mists are thin in places. If you can find such a place and concentrate on it, you may learn something to your advantage."

"You mean, see different Ages?"

He smiled. "I'm saying no more. Just be careful not to fall through, that's all. The ground here is solid, through the mists it's softer, that's how to tell. Now I must go."

Lorna watched him go. He was right, the mist was patchy in places. She crept along, testing the ground under her feet, trying to find where the mist was thinnest. Eventually, she settled on a spot under a huge oak tree and stood and concentrated.

For a while, she only saw the hazy figures of other people of the Court scurrying home. She was almost ready to give up, when another figure emerged, not going anywhere, but appearing to be seated. As she stared harder, the mist began to clear right on the spot she was looking at.

It was her mother. She was seated at the kitchen table at home, drinking coffee and doing the crossword as she often did. There was no sound as Lorna watched herself enter the kitchen and have a conversation with her mother. Her mother suddenly threw her head back and laughed and a hand came out of nowhere and laid itself on her mother's shoulder. The Lorna in the kitchen didn't seem to mind this and smiled at the owner of the hand.

The mist blew across thickly. Then it seemed to lift slightly, and the scene changed. This time, she saw a room in a different house. An older Lorna was curled up on the couch, her head on someone's chest. It was Patrick. As she watched, he bent over and kissed her, and the older Lorna's hand crept round his back. Lorna in the courtyard turned away, embarrassed to be witnessing this moment of intimacy with her older self. When she looked back, the mist had returned. So far, she had two possibilities: a happy-looking future with her mother or perhaps some kind of future with Patrick. The Dragon was right – no choice was bad. But something was missing from each. So much for Faramore saying this might help, she felt more conflicted than ever. She needed something to help her decide.

As if in response to this thought, the mist swirled tightly round her again and another gap opened. Her mother reappeared, seated in the kitchen as before, but this time she was crying. She looked more vulnerable than Lorna could ever remember, so unhappy. Lorna felt her heart constrict. This must be her mother's future if Lorna didn't go back. As she watched, her mother rose suddenly from the table and walked off somewhere to the right, still wiping her eyes and with a strange look on her face.

We could start again, Lorna thought. Maybe we'll move, or… She hesitated. Once, she'd have given anything to escape her life, but things had changed. There'd always be the Populars and the Simon Shawcrosses of the world, wherever she went. And Latimer and David were never coming back. If she stayed, she would have Patrick and Sebastian and Celesta, but her mother would have no-one. And she is my mother, Lorna thought, wiping away a tear. Patrick has Celesta now and there's tons of girls that'll want to date him. And Sebastian has a great future here. Much better than if he came with me.

She knew she should wait till morning and talk to the others. On the other hand, she needed to act now before anyone could change her mind. She stepped forward through the mist and onto the street where her home was in the Present Age.

~

"Have you seen Lorna?" Patrick flew into the dining hall next morning, highly agitated.

Sebastian looked up from his toast and shook his head. "She must still be asleep. You all right? You look like you bin run over by a cart."

"Thanks a lot. So, you haven't seen her?"

"I said, didn't I? Not since last night. She looked pretty bad."

"I know. I saw her." Patrick ran his hand through his hair. He hadn't been to bed. Why had he walked off like that? They needed to talk, and he'd been a coward trying to avoid it.

"You're barmy you know." Sebastian heaped marmalade on his toast and took another bite. "If you love her, you should tell her. 'Stead of mopin' about like some old tom cat off his game."

"Aren't you a bit young to be saying things like that?" Patrick rubbed his eyes irritably. "It's not as simple as that. I can't leave here, and she's got her mum. And you of course."

Sebastian looked thoughtful. "Can't Celesta switch with Glenelven and be Guardian of the Present? Then we can go live with Lorna at her mum's and Celesta can visit when she wants."

Patrick looked at him. "Nice try, but the Guardians don't work like that. They're kind of born to the Age that they can be assigned to. And there's no cheating that old Dragon. Apparently, the Great Lord's furious he granted us a choice in the first place."

"There's your mum and Glenelven. Maybe they can do something." Sebastian waved and the two Guardians hurried over.

"Have you seen Lorna?" Celesta looked worried. "I checked her room, and her bed hasn't been slept in."

"No, I've been looking for her too." Patrick rose to his feet. "Has anyone checked round the cloisters? Maybe she went for a walk."

"Don't go out alone," warned Glenelven. "The mist is so thick now you could easily get lost, even in the courtyard, with unintended consequences."

"Like what?" asked Sebastian.

"The mist is a veil between the Ages," Celesta explained. "It is thickening as Time renews. It would be all too easy to walk through a hole in Time and not be able to get back before all is sealed."

"What if that's happened to Lorna?" Sebastian turned pale.

"For God's sake!" Patrick exploded. He raced out into the courtyard, where he found the mist swathing the Court and its surroundings in a thick, silver shroud. In places it would drift apart momentarily, giving a glimpse of something beyond.

"Patrick, wait!" Glenelven shouted. "Have a care! We must be certain that what we see is the here and now, before we pass through it."

"Hey!" called a voice. It was Faramore. "Oh, it's you," he said. "The Great Lord has declared an emergency. Until the mist has fully turned, no-one is to go anywhere. Except the Three – time is short now and we must have their decisions."

"The problem, Faramore, is that we only have Two of the Three," Glenelven said sharply. "Lorna appears to be missing. Have you seen her?"

"I saw her last night," Faramore said, then hesitated.

"What is it Faramore?" Glenelven's voice grew hard.

Faramore stroked his chin nervously. "She was confused. She didn't seem to know what to do so I... well, I'm sure she didn't take me seriously..."

"What have you done?" Patrick flew at Faramore and would have had his hands round the man's throat if Glenelven hadn't pulled him back.

"For God's sake, boy, do you think this helps? Faramore, what happened?"

Faramore looked at his feet. "I told her to look into the mist. To find the weakest places."

"Why would she do that?" asked Sebastian.

"So she could see her alternative futures." Glenelven spoke grimly. "You fool, Faramore! Nobody is supposed to know their Future, or the impact their decisions may have on it. What gives you the right to think you can show her that power?"

"The same right that led you to send her and two others on a dangerous quest for a stolen Instrument of Time!" Faramore replied angrily. "Anyway, she is still a mortal. She may not have seen anything."

"She is a mortal who carried the Chronograph," said Glenelven. "The problem is not what she may have seen, but how she may have interpreted it. If she acted on something she saw..."

"The mists are turning, Glenelven," Celesta said. "Look!" She pushed against a pocket of mist, which dissolved at her touch. A crowd of people moved beyond, running to and fro while something burned in the background.

"The Great Fire of London," said Glenelven. He reached out his hand, but it met with something clear and solid. "That part of the Past is reset. Only the Guardian of the Age may pass through now." Patrick felt a sickness rising in his stomach.

They were interrupted by a sudden commotion on the other side of the courtyard. "It's the Watchers of the Tower," said Celesta. "The Great Lord dispatched them to the Future Age below. The people were afraid of the mist and starting to panic."

"Surely they're not bringing them here!" Glenelven exclaimed. "Once the mists have fully turned, the Future Age will finally be cut loose, and they'll be marooned!"

A small knot of people made its way carefully across the courtyard, following the Watchers of the Tower who were swinging their lamps in front of them as they slowly picked their way through the mist.

"Lorna's not with them," said Faramore, craning his neck. "I recognise most of them. Foolish Apprentices who didn't heed the warnings and thought they'd eke out a few last moments in the new Age. And a Future girl. I believe she's engaged to one of them. I hope she knows what she's doing." Patrick glared at him.

"There are two more," Celesta said, "only I don't recognise them. They do not look as if they are of this place."

The mist swirled and parted for a moment, giving a clearer glimpse of a man and a woman bringing up the rear of the group.

"Good Lord!" Glenelven was dumbfounded. "What are they doing here?"

"Who?" The others looked at him, but he wasn't listening.

"We have to get Lorna back," he said. "Wherever she is, we need to find her now before the mists have fully turned."

Patrick looked helplessly at Celesta. "I should have told her, Celesta. I should have told you how I felt. We all should have talked, spoken to the Great Lord, worked it out somehow..."

"I don't understand," Sebastian said. "All this talk about the mists turning - what does it mean?"

Patrick gave him a look of despair. "Remember the prophecy..."

"The misty portals turning to glass..." Sebastian suddenly saw. "You mean..."

"The mists turn to glass and time restarts. Meaning," Patrick swallowed hard. "... the borders between the Ages are solid once more, as they should be."

"So, Lorna will be stuck?" The boy's eyes grew wide with fright.

"Once the mists have turned," Glenelven said, "Lorna will have to stay wherever she is. And nobody, not even I, can ever bring her back."

CHAPTER 33

Time Starts Anew

Lorna's footsteps echoed along the deserted street. Not a living thing moved. No birds sang. The neighbour's cat wasn't sunning himself on the wall like he normally did. The buildings and trees seemed to shimmer and the footpath underneath her feet felt tacky, a bit like that day David had spilt lemonade on the kitchen floor. It was as though things weren't quite solid. Lorna reached the gate and pushed it open, then pulled her hand back sharply. It was almost as if it had bitten her. She went round the side of the house and wrapped her hand in her sleeve before turning the handle on the back door, which swung noiselessly open.

"Mum?" There was no answer. She entered the kitchen. "Mum? It's me!"

No answer. The eerie silence from the street also penetrated the house and made her feel uncomfortable. She was used to noise and bustle. David yelling about something, the radio talking to itself, the clatter of dishes in the sink. She'd never hear David's voice again, she reflected. Even the reset of Time couldn't change that. David was dead and would never be coming back. She felt a lump rising in her throat. "Mum?" she called again.

She opened the biscuit tin that was standing in its usual place on the counter. Nothing in it. Too bad. She'd eaten hardly anything at dinner and was hungry. She checked the fridge and cupboards. All were equally empty. By now, Lorna was starting to feel a little scared. Mum always had food in the house. Where was she? Where was anyone, come to that?

She crept up the stairs and opened the door of what she knew to be her bedroom, and went in. Her bed, the dresser, the posters on her wall, were all as they should be, except for an iridescent shimmering. She ran her fingers down one of the posters, then wiped them on her jeans. It felt damp, like the ink on it was still wet.

Slowly it dawned on Lorna what was going on. The Age was being reset but was not yet done.

Hence, no food in the kitchen, the damp poster on the wall, and – significantly – the absence of any people. Her mum wasn't there because she had never been there in the first place. Not yet. "I guess I'll just wait," Lorna said to herself. "Once it's all been reset, she'll come." Yet the knot in her stomach grew more painful and twisted.

She sat and contemplated the mirror on the dresser. It seemed to have a sort of film over it, distorting her reflection. She tried rubbing it, but her hand seemed to scoop it. The mirror was still soft and being formed by Time. This was where she'd first seen the others, the day she'd been swept out of her room with the Chronograph. She began to regret not telling them she was leaving. That was pretty hurtful, selfish of her even. Maybe they would have chosen to come too, but she hadn't even given them the opportunity.

Lorna bit her lip and was about to turn away when something caught her eye. Shadows seemed to be moving inside the mirror. As she peered closer, the shadows suddenly grew solid, and Lorna realised she was looking back at the Court of Time. Glenelven was there with Patrick and Sebastian. Patrick looked deeply distressed and Sebastian was yelling something. Celesta was there too, talking urgently to a woman who had her back to Lorna. Faramore was talking to a stranger in the shadows, probably some other man of the Court.

The woman with Celesta suddenly turned around, and Lorna gave a small cry. It was her mother. What was she doing at the Court of Time? Tears were pouring down her mother's cheeks, and she was clearly trying to go somewhere, but Celesta and Glenelven were holding her back.

Lorna began to panic. She'd made a big mistake. "I'm coming," she yelled to the mirror, banging on it as if she could attract their attention by doing so. Then she looked at her hand. She shouldn't have been able to bang on the glass like that. She poked her finger at the mirror. It was solid.

"No!" she screamed, realising what it meant. She tore down the stairs, out of the house and up the street, her heart pounding. A bird started singing in one of the trees, and the cat suddenly materialized on the wall. The Age was nearly set. Still no people yet, she might just make it. She reached the end of the road and made for the spot in the still lingering wisps of mist where she had come through, then reeled back. She'd hit something hard. Solid glass.

"No! Oh no, no, no, no, no!" Through it she could see the Court and the people she'd left behind but could not reach. She ran further along the wall of rapidly dissipating mist, trying to find a way through, her hand meeting the solid glass of the boundary between the Ages every time. Then she saw Sebastian turn and spot her, yelling to the others to do something.

Patrick reached the boundary first. He was right there within arm's reach yet could not touch her. She pressed herself against the glass, splaying her fingers against it. He responded, mirroring her movements, then pressing his face against the glass. One last glimpse, one last kiss, and he would be gone. Behind her, someone was whistling in the street. The figures on the other side began to grow less defined.

"No!" she screamed. "Don't go!"

Suddenly Patrick tore himself away from the other side of the glass and she could just make out a smaller figure, presumably Sebastian, pointing at something. Lorna followed the line of sight. A patch of mist, a small one, still hung thickly under the great oak tree a little further along the street, where the enormous branches kept the ground cooler. Her last chance! Lorna pelted as fast as her legs could carry her. As she drew closer, a shadow seemed to form in the middle of it, and a pair of strong arms thrust through the mist and pulled her in.

"Help me!" she heard Patrick's voice yelling. "She's sticking! The Present's trying to pull her back!" Lorna felt another pair of hands upon her and suddenly the mist seemed to give way and she fell through, landing on top of Patrick and Sebastian in a heap on the ground. The next thing she knew, her mother's arms lifted her up and enfolded her.

"You cut it fine," Glenelven said, tapping where the mist had been.

"I know." She shook in her mother's arms. "How did you get here?"

"Later." Her mother's voice cracked. "My God, I thought… I thought…" A crowd was gathering about them.

"Get back," a male voice shouted. "Give them some air."

Lorna gave a start. The voice tugged at something in her memory. Then her gaze landed on the stranger who had been speaking with Faramore in the shadows in her mirror. Only he was no stranger at all.

"Dad," she said. The world danced before her eyes, and then she knew no more.

CHAPTER 34

New Beginnings

"Come here," Patrick said, pulling Lorna towards him and kissing her for the thousandth time. They were sprawled on the riverbank beneath the Tower of Watchers and Keepers. It looked a lot different to when they had last been there. The banks were lush, and the river flowed along lazily.

Lorna didn't mind complying. Simon Shawcross couldn't have kissed like this in a million years. She wondered who he was dating now.

"What are you thinking?" Patrick asked.

"Nothing." She smiled up at him. "Just thinking about how...unbelievable this all is."

"I know." He held her tight. "I wanted to tell you, you know. I wanted to tell you I didn't want you to leave, but I didn't think it was fair to pressure you. And then I nearly lost you..."

"Well, you didn't, did you, so stop going on about it." She squeezed his hand and looked over to where her mum sat talking to Celesta while her dad helped Sebastian bait the hook on his fishing rod. The peace of the day felt good after the emotion of yesterday's reunion. As if that weren't enough, the Great Lord had summoned them all to his private chambers for dinner last night in search of answers.

"You can ask all you want, but you won't hear anything different," Lorna's mother had said.

You had to hand it to her, Lorna thought, she wasn't letting the Lord intimidate her at all. "I came home to find Stephen leaving with David and some wild story about David being his son and I'd better not try stopping him. He was totally demented, and I was terrified he'd done something to Lorna. I hadn't seen her for days. Then I was having a damn good cry in the kitchen and this mist started creeping under the door. I looked outside and instead of the garden there was a valley and this castle on top of the hill." She paused. "Next thing I know, I'm standing at the bottom of the hill, and Adam's walking towards me. I thought I must have died!"

"I can't explain things either," Lorna's father said. "One minute I was driving home, the next there was this kind of flash. Then I'm walking up the hill and there's Jennifer."

"Maybe a time lapse?" Glenelven queried, looking at the Lord.

"In two separate places at two separate points in time, Glenelven?" The Lord arched his eyebrows doubtfully. Lorna's parents looked confused, which wasn't surprising.

"Sorry," Glenelven apologised. "It's just that you're supposed to be dead, Adam."

Adam choked on his wine. "Sorry to disappoint you, Kelvin."

"What about David?" Lorna's mother demanded suddenly. "And Stephen? That man should be arrested."

"I'll leave that one to you, Glenelven," the Lord said, and rose from the table leaving them to it.

Lorna sighed. Her poor mother. She'd been inconsolable learning of David's death and when she heard about the Time Changelings, she went ballistic.

"What in hell were you thinking, Kelvin!" she yelled, nearly smothering Sebastian as she clasped him to her. "This poor boy…"

The 'poor boy' seemed to take it all in his stride, Lorna thought. He was already calling Jennifer and Adam 'mum and dad' and it was his idea for everyone to come fishing this morning. Uncle Kelvin had not joined them.

"Think she'll ever speak to him again?" Patrick said, reading her thoughts. "Feisty, isn't she, your mum? I can see where you get it from."

"Shut up!" Lorna thumped him. "She will in time. In about a million years maybe." She laughed. Everything felt good. The Great Lord had finally agreed that none of them could exactly help being where they were and that he would find homes for them at Court. Sebastian would start his Apprenticeship soon and Lorna would be working with the Keepers of the Records, learning to look for anomalies in the flow of Time. Patrick would work under Celesta for a while until he became a full Guardian.

"You coming fishing, or are you going to sit 'ere all day." Sebastian appeared, flicking water over them.

"Be right there," Patrick said. He gave Lorna one more kiss while Sebastian made a gagging noise. Lorna giggled.

"Come on then," Patrick said. "Race you!"

Lorna watched them run down the hill towards the river. She had journeyed so far with these two boys, learned to love them fearlessly through danger and loss, and survived.

"Come on, Lorna!" her father shouted. Her mother and Celesta waved. "Hurry up!"

"I have it all," Lorna breathed. "I have them all."

She ran down the hill to join them, hair streaming in the wind. She was the luckiest person in the whole of Time. And there'd be Patrick and fishing again tomorrow.

EPILOGUE

Glenelven sat on a rock and watched the sunset. The valley was bathed in hues of gentle red and rose gold, making it warm and inviting, a contrast from only two days ago. The river flowed gently below, and the last remaining workers were returning to Court after dismantling the Wheel on the Great Lord's orders. Time would flow naturally from now on, not regulated by a man-made mechanism, open to corruption.

The Book of Infinity was now back in the Tower under lock and key. It had already updated itself to reflect recent events, and a new set of prophecies and alternatives had begun to appear in its pages. Glenelven could not resist taking a quick look. Lorna and Patrick's children would go on to be Guardians of one of the most peaceful Ages of all Time, one that would last so long, the Book itself was not written beyond that point. Sebastian, it seemed, was destined for true greatness.

A small black spot appeared on one of the pages halfway through this new chapter but went away when Glenelven rubbed it. No Future ever ran completely smoothly, he reflected. He ran his hand over his eyes and sighed tiredly. Most likely, it was nothing.

Closing the Book, he'd descended the Tower. Too many questions remained that even the Book had not answered for him. So now, he sat on the rock as the sun set over the valley and asked the one source he knew could answer them.

"You used it, didn't you?" he said.

The Dragon looked at him lazily. "I knew you would come," it said. "I've stayed awake for you."

"Answer my question."

The Dragon gave him a long look, then lifted one of its great paws. The Chronograph, still intact, lay underneath. "It was the girl," the Dragon said. "She was being torn apart by love. It was too much to ask her to choose."

"It was not your place to interfere," Glenelven protested. "You are the Great Guardian of All Time."

"Do not lecture me, Glenelven. You who walked into Ages where you had no business to be, carrying Time Changelings with you!"

"That was...different."

The Dragon laughed smokily. "And they say *dragons* have no heart. Don't tell me things haven't worked out for the best."

Glenelven was silent for a moment. "I know you brought Jennifer in through a Time Lapse," he said. "That's one thing. But Adam. You brought Adam back from the dead."

"You told me he had been a great friend to Time!"

"But what about the others?" Glenelven exclaimed. "What about Hanson and David? Or Serena? Or the Son of Time himself? Why not restore them too?"

"Because I could not," the Dragon replied. "None of them died through a trick of Time. They died at the hands of the Keeper during the natural course of events. But you should not worry about them. Hanson and the Son of Time are peacefully tinkering with their clocks in the Caverns of the Deep Past where they can do no harm. And Serena – well, did you not realise that hers was the star that rose at the renewal of Time once the Keeper had been defeated? Look where it sits in the sky."

Glenelven looked. The bright new star rested close to the constellation he had seen born through the ascent of

David's spirit. As he looked, the bright star and the constellation seemed to move even closer together. He rubbed his eyes and blinked hard. This wretched dragon had him imagining all kinds of things.

"Tell me about Adam," he said firmly.

"The Keeper created a Time Lapse," said the Dragon. "He delayed a car travelling along the road earlier on and made it run straight into Adam before returning it to its previous position in Time. Thus, no other car or driver could be found."

"What happened to the other car?"

"The driver felt a massive bump and veered off the road into a ditch. They got him out with a broken leg. Other than thinking he'd suffered a blackout, he was fine."

"So, you used the Chronograph to pinpoint when the car ploughed through Adam?"

"Exactly. Then I lifted him out a nanosecond before he was hit. The car went off the road without him in it. Then I held him in stasis until Time intersected with Jennifer's arrival. Quite simple really." The Dragon looked pleased with itself.

"You still interfered," said Glenelven.

The Dragon sighed. "Indeed. This little toy is such a temptation. We should get rid of it."

It breathed hotly on the Chronograph, which began to melt immediately, finally seeping entirely into the ground. "There," it said. "Gone forever. And now I must return to sleep. I don't think I've been quite so busy in over ten thousand years."

The Great Guardian closed its eyes and a gentle whistling soon emanated from its nostrils. Glenelven stood up. "Thank you," he said. "Thank you for using that infernal thing to do some good."

The Dragon opened one eye. "Good?" it said sleepily. "I am on the side of neither good nor evil, Glenelven. I am neutral, you know that." The eye closed again.

"Oh yes," Glenelven laughed softly. "I'd forgotten. You're neutral. Yes. Most definitely...neutral."

He turned and walked back up the hill in the lengthening shadows to the Court, where a brand-new Future awaited him.

THE END

ABOUT THE AUTHOR

Harriet Innes began writing her debut novel, *The Chronograph*, while living in Silicon Valley, California.

Before finding her calling as an author, Harriet pursued a career in the high-tech industry which took her around the world. At the same time, she never forgot her creative passions, training as an actress, singer, and voiceover artist, and playing piano and flute before finding her bliss in writing. *The Chronograph* emerged from a poem she originally wrote as a creative challenge, which ignited the desire to write a "good old-fashioned adventure story" of good versus evil.

Harriet now lives in the U.K. and writes from her home in North Lincolnshire.